MANNAHATTA

A SEQUEL

Happy Reading!

Shelly V. Ostroff

BY

SHERRY V. OSTROFF

THE LUCKY ONE
CALEDONIA

MANNAHATTA

SHERRY V. OSTROFF

Bushrod Press

For Arne

In memory of my mother, Elaine Vernick
A wise woman who had a saying for every occasion

More and more too, the old name absorbs into me. Mannahatta, 'the place encircled by many swift tides and sparkling waters.' How fit a name for America's great democratic island city! The word itself, beautiful! how aboriginal! how it seems to rise with tall spires, glistening in sunshine, with such New World atmosphere, vista and action!

Walt Whitman

Island of many hills – Lenni Lenape

PART ONE

CHAPTER ONE
PUNTO ESCOSÉS
2008

"ALEC! WE FOUND IT."

"Huh?" Alec rubbed his eyes and mumbled, "Wait! What?"

My declaration brought Alec into a sitting position, almost toppling him out of the hammock that dangled two feet off the dirt floor. He grabbed the center tent pole to check his balance. The fragile shelter wobbled, cascading rivulets of rainwater down the nylon roof into mud puddles.

This tent and three more made up our campsite adjacent to Darien Bay. The largest served as an all-purpose room for dining, instruction, and meetings. This one and another were designated as sleeping quarters for the archaeological team. The smallest tent sheltered the tools of our trade: storage for artifacts, camera equipment, chemicals, logbooks, and buckets filled with assorted trowels and shovels. Each tent had walls made of fine mesh allowing the cool ocean breeze to enter, but did not entirely deter, mosquitoes, no-see-ums, and other Dracula-like insects.

"Oh, sorry to wake you. Go back to sleep."

Dr. Alec Grant, history professor and my fiancé had every right to be tired. He had traveled from Scotland to join me on a dig in Darien National Park not far from the Panamanian and Colombian border. The first leg of his journey, a sixteen-hour flight to Panama City, was the easy part. What should have been a short trek across the isthmus to our campsite was not. The contrariness of the Kuna tribe and the remoteness of *Punto Escocés*, once called Caledonia by 17th century Scottish colonists, made the trip unpredictable, chaotic, and dreadful. The next part of Alec's journey included a stop in Muluputu, a tiny island off the eastern coast of Panama. Although it was a one-hour boat ride away from Caledonia, a guide with a motorized *cayuco* had to be hired. But first, shrewd negotiations along with enough cash to grease the palm of the local chieftain were necessary.

1

Since Alec arrived in Muluputu late in the day, the tribal chief postponed Alec's request until the next morning, forcing him to shell out more cash than was necessary for a plate of fried fish, rice, and a can of beer. Alec also paid an exorbitant fee for a dirty cot in the back room of a noisy makeshift cantina.

"No. Stay. It's fine. It's time I was up," Alec said. He slapped his bare arm and then his neck. "I thought I left the midges at home."

I tossed a small bottle of insect spray into his lap. "Use this liberally, button up, and roll your sleeves down. The bugs are worse at sunrise and sunset. And keep your shoes on. You don't want bullet ants making a meal of your toes."

One of Alec's eyebrow perked up. I adored that look of his, a mixture of surprise, playfulness, and flirtation. It reminded me how much I'd missed him since we parted back in Scotland. And how much I loved him.

"Bullet ants? Sounds delightful." Alec swung himself out of the hammock; his head, almost grazing the roof of the tent. The smell of unwashed male and days-old clothes filled the tent, but jungle existence eliminated the luxury of hot showers and clean dry clothes. Alec buttoned his shirt at the neck and then the cuffs. "So, what's all the excitement about?"

"I told you there were two other digs here, a while back. One in the seventies and the other in 2003. The BBC did a documentary on the last one. I watched it many times, to see where Anna had lived." Alec placed his hand on my knee, and then inched his way up my thigh. Before we were both distracted, I brought him back. "Don't you remember? I suggested another dig. Max...er...Dr. Jones wasn't so keen about the idea. He said there was nothing left to find in Caledonia. But he changed his mind after reading Anna's journal and learning about the knife. And now, I think we may have found it. Filib's knife."

Anna Rachel Isaac MacArthur was my many-times great-grandmother. When I tell anyone how I learned of her existence, they are shocked to hear that it was a result of my father's death at the World Trade Center on 9/11. Their response is always the same: How could 9/11 have anything to do with an ancient ancestor living on another continent?

The answer is: I inherited a three-hundred-year-old key that opened a safe deposit box in Edinburgh. That's where I found artifacts that

2

uncovered Anna's story: a silver candlestick, a ring, a lock of hair, and, most importantly, her journal.

"So, the real reason for the dig wasn't to search for the remains of the Scottish colonists?"

"That was for public consumption, a plea to open checkbooks."

"But you know, returning with even one bone would make headlines. *The Scotsman* would crown you a national heroine."

"Yeah, true. I'd be famous like, um…Carter discovering King Tut's tomb." I chuckled as I remembered checking out every book at the local library on the famous 1922 find. By the time I was fourteen, I planned to be an archaeologist. My friends scoffed at the notion. Grams worried I'd get lost in the Egyptian desert and never come home. But not Dad. He fueled my passion with a visit to an exhibition on the boy-king in Washington, DC.

"With only a few days left, I'd just about given up hope. Max has insisted on our working from dawn to dusk."

Alec's forehead sprouted furrows, and his eyes turned dark. This was his usual reaction whenever I mentioned Max: my professor and mentor. Then, as if to reclaim what Max could never have, Alec encircled me with his arms and brought me tight against his damp shirt, pressing his lips on mine. I didn't flinch at the sheen of moisture on his scruffy beard. Although we were alone at the campsite, I wished more than anything for the privacy of a tent meant for two.

Alec stepped away from our damp embrace, but I pulled him back. "I'm glad you're safe. I worried when you didn't arrive on schedule. I feared the Chief had other plans for you." I chuckled as I straightened my shirt. "A trussed-up Alec for dinner."

He smiled but then turned the conversation back to his nemesis. "Your Dr. Jones sounds like a slave-driver."

"He's not 'my' Dr. Jones." I edged closer and stared into his eyes. "But you are 'my' Dr. Grant. And don't forget it. Besides, work keeps our minds occupied living in such unbearable conditions. I've never experienced such suffocating humidity. I'll never complain about summers in Philadelphia again."

Alec was right about one thing. I talked a lot about Dr. Maximilian Jones. He was the first instructor I met at the University of Aberdeen. Like Alec, he was a gifted teacher, and I signed on to do several independent studies with him. When Max received the grant for a dig in Caledonia, I jumped at the chance, hoping to take a leadership role since I was close to earning my Ph.D.

Dr. Jones hinted at the possibility of my teaching at Aberdeen. That didn't thrill Alec. But my going back to college had been his idea, and with a job offer, I was assured of remaining in Scotland and becoming a citizen. Dr. Hanna Duncan. Dad and maybe even Grams would be proud. The thought of them unleashed an often-suppressed sadness that wrapped itself tighter, suffocating me, until Alec unknowingly brought me back to the present.

"You know, we should have married in Philadelphia when we went to your friend Jess' wedding. I'm a hungry man, Mistress Hanna." He said my pet name and raised his eyebrow again. "There's only so long I will wait. You promised to marry me three years ago."

"I have to finish my degree first. You do remember how much work is involved. I promise as soon as I'm done."

Talk of marriage reminded me of Alec's unusual proposal sent in a letter. It was New Year's Eve, and I was at the bedside of my dying grandmother in a Philadelphia hospital. Alec was 3,000 miles away, celebrating Hogmanay with his family. His words are seared into my memory.

> *I know this is probably not the way you dreamed it would happen. Maybe I should've waited until you returned. But the events of the last few days, have made me realise that we shouldn't waste another moment apart. Mistress Hanna, I am on bended knee, asking for your hand in marriage. I want to spend the rest of my days by your side. Allow me to be your lover, your friend, and your husband.*

A year later, when my best friend Jess was planning her wedding at a vineyard in Brandywine, she begged me to have a double ceremony. We could've shared the costs, and her father offered to walk me down the aisle.

But life got in the way.

I remembered insisting, "We should wait until after we find a new flat." Our old place, Alec's rental, was a five-minute walk from the University of St. Andrew. But it had been broken into. The thief had stolen Anna's ring. I didn't feel comfortable living there after that.

4

And then there was my doctoral work.

"Let me get through my first year and get used to a school routine again."

The third excuse came from Alec.

His father had fibrodysplasia, the clinical term for Stoneman's Disease. His muscles were calcifying, and the illness was progressing at a much faster pace than the doctors expected. As Alec's future wife I was included in family discussions, but I was hardly welcome. The issue was my religion, or lack of one, and now it seemed my ancient ancestor, Anna, was Jewish.

Alec's mother, Mora, was polite, said the right words, but was distant. Iain, his brother, a fierce Nationalist, wanted nothing more than a return to the old ways which didn't include me. Iain once said I would never be accepted into the family.

Two weeks ago, my schoolmates and I had flown here on a prop-plane from Panama City. When the pilot realized we were an archaeological team headed for Caledonia, he announced we would fly over *Punta Escosés*, the Scottish Point. From the air, the point looked like a giant's left thumb jutting into the Caribbean. As a defensive position, it was a perfect location for the Scots to set up a colony in the New World in 1698. A crude fort was built on a promontory to protect the fledgling settlement meant to control the overland trade between the two oceans. Had the scheme worked, Scotland would be independent today. But it failed, and the only way out of massive debt was for Scotland to unite with England in 1707.

Dr. Jones reminded us that the Scots had been unwelcome by the Spanish, the English, and the Natives. Add into the mix the constant rain, extreme temperatures, poor soil, lack of food, yellow-fever, malaria, and inept governance; the colony was doomed. In six months, the first expedition limped back to Scotland with only one-fourth of those who began the adventure.

The flight attendant, a middle-aged woman, offered an impromptu tour. We peered out the small windows straining to hear her words over the roar of the twin engines. "The Pan-American Highway runs right through the jungle below. It's part of a 19,000-mile-long road that connects the two Americas from Alaska to Chile."

"You mean I could drive from LA to Darien?" asked one member of our team – a cute blonde who looked like she belonged in high school.

"Unfortunately, no. Fifty-five miles in the Darien Gap are still unpaved. The jungle, the hilly terrain, the gangs, the weather, and the indigenous tribes prevented the job from getting done. But that doesn't stop the flow of drug smugglers and human traffickers swindling immigrants on their way north."

The flight attendant's comments were disconcerting and that was in addition to the pictures of gigantic spiders and poisonous frogs I had seen in an old *National Geographic.* I must have looked concerned because the next thing I knew, Max reached over the aisle and squeezed my hand. I smiled politely but found his forwardness uncomfortable.

But now I could put aside those unpleasant memories. Alec was here, ready to start his research for a book he was planning about the Caledonia colony. Although that was his announced purpose for coming, I suspected Alec wanted to ensure I didn't get kidnapped either by the notorious gangs or by Dr. Maximilian Jones.

CHAPTER TWO

SEEDS OF DOUBT

EARLIER THAT MORNING, the metal detector's pinging had been unexpected. Not believing what I heard, I hovered the machine inches over the same spot. There it was again. Perhaps what was buried under my feet was the treasure I'd hoped for.

An all-call went out. Every team member, regardless of what they were working on, came running to the site. Each slipped effortlessly into their pre-assigned roles and like firefighters who've rehearsed for a catastrophic event, they were cool and capable.

Hadrian, the team photographer, was assigned to capture every detail before, during, and after the dig. Even the area around the site had to be photographed to restore it properly. The pretty blonde's job was to record the data: timing, measurements, GPS coordinates, and findings. Sketches, completed by another student, would serve as back-up in case of camera malfunction.

Before excavating began, a known area that contained nothing of value had to be chosen as a dumpsite. Once Hadrian completed his initial shots, three undergrads hauled away fallen branches and cut off exposed roots and ropey vines, unleashing a smell of something rotten. A swarm of flies flew around our heads, undeterred by flailing hands.

As I watched the students ready the area, I realized Alec had not made an appearance. Perhaps he'd returned to his hammock. Couldn't blame him. It was still early.

The pounding of mallets, forcing pegs into the packed earth, momentarily erased my thoughts of him. The pegs marked off one square meter around the spot identified by the metal detector. Dr. Jones explained each step of the process, including the Pythagorean Theorem, to ensure a perfect square. Additional pegs were placed outside the square, and bright colored twine was attached to each, creating a stringline. Thus, one square meter of the 2,236 square miles of Darien National Park was marked off.

I glanced at my watch and did a quick scan of the group. Forty-five minutes. Still no Alec. He had been with me from the beginning and deserved to witness the unearthing of what lay beneath the surface.

"Hold up a minute," I said. "Let me get Alec."

I turned to go, but Dr. Jones grabbed my wrist. His clenched jaw was an unwelcome surprise. I twisted out of his grasp, stepped back, and just as quickly, he looked away like a little boy who'd been caught with his hand in the candy jar. Resuming a proper distance between student and teacher, he gestured toward the metal detector leaning innocently against a tree. "We need to get started."

I ignored his effort to save face. "Has anyone seen Alec?"

A few students shrugged. The rest pretended to concentrate on their tasks rather than acknowledge the embarrassing confrontation.

Max cleared a throat that didn't need it and resumed a professional voice. "The area must be double-checked, so there's no mistaking this is where we dig." He snapped the metal detector by the handle, stepped inside the stringline, and swept the machine an inch above the ground. When the sweet spot sang again, no one said a word.

※

One student scooped out a layer of matted root. The jungle turf was placed on a large tarpaulin, and the exposed area was troweled and leveled. Measurements and photos were taken.
Dr. Jones glanced furtively at the students and flicked his wrist for the time. Was there some phantom schedule none of us were aware of? Lunch was the only item on the agenda, but with a possible break through, we were flexible about our next meal. However, I could easily diagnose his anxiety. The symptoms included his untoward advances, grabbing me moments ago, and his rising irritation. It all started the moment Alec had arrived.

A shovel was thrust in my hands. "Let's not keep everyone waiting. If your boyfriend misses out, he can always look at Hadrian's photos. That's if he's interested."

"No. Not without Alec." My loud refusal silenced the chatter of birds, but not Hadrian's muffled laughter. I thrust the shovel into the earth; the wooden handle stuck out like an exclamation point.

Just then, Alec appeared. His timing was perfect. He stepped from behind the jungle curtain, walked directly to the front of the group, and stood by my side.

"Sorry, Hanna. Dr. Jones. I apologize for my delay. I did not mean to keep everyone waiting. But my reason," he said as he turned and faced his audience, "is rather simple." For emphasis, he paused a moment, ensuring maximum advantage for the punch line. "I forgot the location of the latrine. In the jungle, every tree and bush look the same. I was desperate…to release the monster." He chuckled. "That's my excuse. Poor though it is, I'm sticking with it."

Hadrian doubled over and turned away. A few others brought their hands to their mouths.

Alec looked at me. One eyebrow shot up. I knew he had heard everything.

My legs wobbled and my hands felt sweaty. Whether they needed it or not, I wiped them on the side of my pants. Alec's hand pressed against the small of my back to calm me, while I unfolded a sheet of paper, a copy of a page from Anna's journal. My plan was to set the scene and provide context for what I hoped lay beneath the soil. I took a deep breath and began.

Caledonia - June 22, 1699

> *Today our ship sailed from Caledonia. The colony is lost. We are doubly aggrieved because in our haste to get on board, six were left behind. It was too late when we realised that one of the stranded was our dear friend & kinsman, Filib. Captain Drummond refused to turn back. His order was to sail with the tide. Alain readied himself to jump overboard, to save Filib, even if it meant leaving me & the child. But in the end, it did not matter. We watched helplessly as the Little Scot raised his dirk & drove it into himself. The Indians approached, found Filib dead, & left him on the beach.*

> *Perhaps Filib took his life in fear the Natives might torture him. I prefer to believe that Filib gave us a gift. He*

sacrificed himself for us. For me. So, I wouldn't be left alone.

I paused long enough for Anna's words to resonate in a world she once occupied; her voice, loud and clear, returning in the body of her descendant.

"You all know the reason for our coming to Caledonia," I said. "To locate artifacts not realized by earlier teams. Not because they were sloppy or inefficient. Because they lacked Anna's insights." I looked intently into the eyes of each team member, willing them to understand the importance of this moment. "The prize is Filib's knife. The Little Scot dropped it over 300 years ago, and if we find it, that will verify Anna MacArthur's story, and provide a new perspective on the Darien Scheme."

I tucked the paper back into my shirt pocket and picked up the shovel, ready to scoop the next layer. I was surprised that Anna's words left me feeling a sense of dread, or even terror, rather than accomplishment. I couldn't help but wonder, what if there was nothing here, and the journal was a fraud, a hoax? A tiny seed of doubt began to grow.

Three years ago, when I began work on my doctorate, I introduced Dr. Jones to Anna's story. I vividly remember the first time I walked into his office. My initial thought was that for an older guy he was attractive and distinguished looking. Clean-shaven with a bit of salt and pepper going on in his hair.

Like most professors, his office was a smallish affair loaded with books. His desk was strewn with papers, the latest edition of *Archaeology* magazine, and a stack of multi-colored undergrad research folders. It appeared he was about to start grading, but he pushed them aside when I placed the journal in front of him. Dr. Jones was an eminent archaeologist, known throughout the profession for his successful digs and the many books he authored. I was flattered he would pay any attention to me, but it was the first time I worried someone would doubt the journal's authenticity.

His reaction was the opposite.

Dr. Jones offered me a seat after informing the department secretary that he was not to be disturbed. He shut his office door, and instead of returning to his desk, he chose a chair across from mine.

"I'm impressed, Hanna." He learned forward releasing his woodsy-smelling cologne. He carefully turned the pages of the journal, nodding and looking up every so often; his soft russet eyes latched onto mine. As he read snatches of Anna's story, he managed to inch closer; his cologne stronger - filled the shrinking gap. Like reading Braille, his fingertips gently inspected the cover. I couldn't help but notice his nails were perfectly manicured. Unusual for one who poked around in the dirt. "This journal is exceptional. Where did you find it?"

I repeated the tale that I had told many times before. "Do you believe the journal's authentic? Dr. Ira Mason, at St. Andrew, thinks it's—"

"Ira? We've worked on several projects. The man's a genius. I trust his expertise." In the excitement of his exclamation, it appeared he was about to place his hand on mine when he stopped midway. "Do you mind if I keep the journal for a week or two? I'd love to read it...more thoroughly. The Darien colony is a special interest of mine. I can call you when I'm done so we can talk further."

I bit my lip. I had no problem with Alec and Ira Mason handling the journal. But Dr. Jones' request made me uncomfortable. I rationalized this was silly and my hesitation was due to an emotional attachment I had for Anna. I surprised myself when I answered, "Sure. But when you're done, there's something I want to ask you."

Not two weeks but two days later, Dr. Jones called and asked me to return in the late afternoon. The secretary was gone; the halls were empty. No need to shut the door, but he did anyway. When he took my jacket and hung it on a metal hook, his hand brushed the nape of my neck and shoulders. I chose the chair closest to the door. While Dr. Jones began talking about Anna's writing, he made excuses to move his seat closer to mine.

"This is an amazing document. There were only a few women in Caledonia. This is a rare glimpse of the female perspective. I'm honored

11

you brought it to my attention." The woodsy smell intensified. "I have some ideas I'd like to talk about." His voice, breathless, almost a whisper. "More in-depth. Perhaps, we could—"

I grabbed the journal, hugged it against my chest, a wall between us. "There was something I had hoped to ask you." I had to turn the conversation around. "Anna's description. Filib's suicide. What did you think of it?"

He scratched his head and chuckled. "Gripping. A warrior to the end."

I lowered the journal when he retreated to the far side of his desk. "There may be more to uncover in Caledonia," I suggested.

"I doubt it. After two digs, the area's finished, nothing more to exhume."

Now I became the aggressor, edging closer, hugging the journal tighter. "But no one knows about Anna's journal. And Filib's dirk. It could still be there. Anna never mentioned that the Indians took the weapon. They just walked away from his lifeless body."

"Hmm. Hard to believe that warriors would leave such a weapon. But if it's still there, that would be the find of the century and would corroborate the journal, guaranteeing its accuracy." He stopped for a moment, deep in thought, and brought his fingers to his chin. "Let me think about it. I'll have to secure resources from the university to fund an expedition. Or find a rich donor who can be persuaded once I show them the journal."

I was stuck on *guaranteeing its accuracy*. This opened the frightening possibility that the authenticity of the journal was in question.

That was the moment a seed of doubt first sprouted.

Dr. Jones ended the conversation with an invitation. If funding were available, would I join him on the dig? He hinted that such a discovery could lead to a teaching position at the university, or any university for that matter: Harvard, Cambridge, Oxford. I almost forgot my earlier concern regarding his uncomfortable forwardness and instead, dreamt of my illustrious future. But I had no illusions. Not about a priceless artifact boosting both of our reputations, nor Professor Jones' intentions.

It was a short time after that conversation when Dr. Jones suggested I call him Max. But only when other students and faculty weren't in earshot. I promised myself I would never be alone with him again.

Dr. Jones explained the excavation process while I continued shoveling through layers of earth and another student worked the screen.

"Hanna is removing the soil, one-inch at a time. Every shovelful dumped onto the screen is given a wash to reveal any hidden treasures. The small, gauged mesh ensures we won't miss a musket ball or a button. If the soil is dry, forget the wash. A few rough shakes of the screen will do. Anything found is placed in a tray or bucket." He reached over to one of the trays from the fifth scoop. "Look. Here's a bird feather, a claw, and two small shells. Nothing is overlooked. Take the shells. They may look ordinary to some, but the colonists or the Natives may have used them as a tool or some adornment. We'll continue using the shovel until we hit something. When we do, Hanna will revert to a trowel, a brush, or her gloved hand."

Four more inches of soil were displaced. Every clump of soil raised expectations, but I knew time and the oxidation process had probably halved the original dirk and camouflaged the remaining metal with dirt and rust. The dampness and saltwater would have deteriorated the wooden handle.

The slow process allowed another seed of doubt to germinate.

Maybe Ira, Max, and Alec were mistaken about the journal. It wouldn't be the first-time academics were fooled. My father told me about the Capone incident in the mid-1980's. The entire country, glued to their television sets, waited for the opening of the gangster's safe. Instead of the vault filled with millions in cash, it contained nothing.

I started to doubt this whole dig. Maybe the metal detector's pinging was the result of a thirsty guerrilla tossing a beer can. Or a piece of cheap jewelry left by a hostage hoping to leave a trail for her rescuers. What if Anna's story was a desperate attempt to garner the sympathies of the Scots back home? I couldn't blame her. The reception for the few returning colonists was pitiful. They were branded as cowards; their families disowned them. Even if the journal were a true document from the late 17th century, no expert could say for sure whether her experience was genuine. Only the discovery of the knife would do so.

The seeds of doubt were growing into a forest.

After I removed an additional four inches, Dr. Jones turned on the detector and held it over the pyramid of dirt to be sure the blade hadn't escaped detection. Then he scanned the eight-inch crater. The pings assured us the trail hadn't changed.

While shoveling through layer nine, I hit something. It was firm, solid, and it made a recognizable metal-on-metal clunk. I immediately picked up a small trowel and the same sound was heard again. Dr. Jones nodded for me to continue. I scooped the dirt out on the one side of the object. My gloved hand helped to speed up the process. The tape measure was placed on the revealed side. Four inches. Hadrian and the blonde moved in to do their jobs.

Then I continued clearing the object. It had a right angle which led to another four-inch side, and then another. What I uncovered was not a knife, but a square metal box about two inches deep. Before it was unearthed from its grave, more pictures were taken, drawings were made, and data noted.

I placed the box on a tray and wiped as much of the dirt as I could with my hand and a brush. The blonde noted a latch was missing.

Alec peered at the relic. He whispered, "Don't feel bad, lass. This could still be a great find."

"Let's get on with it," said Dr. Jones. "Alec, if you would kindly move aside."

Without waiting for a response, Dr. Jones stepped in front. "Hanna. Pull gently on the lid. You may have to tug at it. Easy. Easy now."

"It's not budging."

He moved in even closer. The heat from his body snaked its way down my spine. "Here. Let me try." In the groove where the lid met the box, he inserted a dull flat blade and worked on the debris which, over time, had glued the lid shut. "Ah, there we go." The lid opened and the box appeared to be filled with dirt.

Hadrian jumped in and snapped. The blonde barely looked at her notebook as she scribbled.

"Screen, please." Dr. Jones brushed out the dirt in the lid and in the box. Whatever was interred started to take shape; brown pieces of something that clung to one another.

Alec said, "I think you've hit the jackpot."

"Let's not jump to any conclusions," said Dr. Jones.

Alec ignored the reprimand. "Coins. Looks like you've found a treasure."

The irregular-shaped coins were bunched like grapes still attached to their stem. As they were cleaned, several dropped on the screen. The metal began to twinkle.

Alec picked up one silver piece and turned it over in his palm. He rubbed his thumb on one side. "Looks Spanish to me."

Dr. Jones inspected another. "Could be part of the Spanish Silver Train."

"What Silver Train?" the blonde asked.

"It was a trail the Spaniards used to move their silver from Peru to Panama City and then across the isthmus to Portobello, near where Colon is today. Once it reached the coast, the silver was loaded onto ships for the voyage to Spain. The Train was heavily guarded across the ocean because of French, English, and Dutch privateers, but the Spaniards weren't always successful."

Hadrian stopped shooting. "Maybe a sailor stole some coins and buried them here hoping to come back some day."

I turned to Alec. "I'm afraid this isn't going to help with your research. About Caledonia."

"Well, who knows what else you may find," said Alec. "You never—"

"Let's get back to work," Dr. Jones cut in. "Maybe the latch is still in the trench."

Alec stepped back as I picked up the metal detector. Hadrian moved in to photograph the trench but stopped. The camera's fall was saved by the strap around his neck.

The blonde dropped her pen and let out a muffled scream.

Alec's eyes widened.

I turned to follow his gaze. There, at the edge of the jungle were six men. Their guns aimed in our direction.

CHAPTER THREE

THE LION

THE ACHE IN my shoulders spread slowly up my neck, and then, following the laws of gravity, it continued down the middle of my back. Pins and needles played viciously with my raised fingers until the tingling lessened and they went numb. But this was the least of my worries. The barrel of a gun was pointed directly at my head.

From the moment the gunmen showed themselves, they fanned out to discourage any attempt of escape while simultaneously screaming orders in a foreign language and shoving two frightened students who didn't move quickly enough. One student begged not to be hurt. But the intruders did not understand the young man's plea. They waved their guns wildly, barely missing his head.

It was the first time I understood the meaning of a fear so great it could be smelled. A raw animal scent, a mixture of sweat and urine was only slightly noticeable, at first, perhaps because of the jungle vegetation. However, as our fear intensified and spread like a contagion, so did the pungency. I swallowed hard to tamp down a wave of nausea.

The confusion created by our unexpected guests exploded in my brain. Their demands sounded garbled and distorted until a sense of survival came to my rescue. I latched onto non-verbal clues: the swagger and cocksure demeanor of the captors. That's when I realized two important details. Their guns were loaded, and they would feel no regret using them.

"Oh my god, oh my god," said the blonde in a tremulous, little-girl voice. She repeated her prayer over and over until it became maddening, like the drip of a faucet.

"Be quiet. You want to get us killed?" asked Max.

"Oh my god, Oh my god, Oh my god." Her useless rant continued. Her whiney voice, her helplessness grated on my nerves until Max said what I'm sure we were all thinking.

"Shut up. Just shut up." His jaw clenched; a vein pulsed on his temple.

Max's harsh tone throttled the girl back to reality. Her voice trailed off, smothered by throaty sobs.

Alec was next to me, but I dared not look at him head on. Only with a sideways glance did I notice his eyes flitting from one side of the excavation site to the other. Was he calculating a chance for escape? Or was he assessing our poor odds of surviving the next five minutes?

The dark-skinned invaders were dressed similarly in military-issue camouflage with loaded ammo belts draped across their chests or around their waists. Their lethal-looking, high-topped black boots made me shudder. One swift kick could shatter a leg. But for all their sameness, one stood out. He was bigger and grander than his compatriots, with a barrel chest like a pro-wrestler. His uniform was of better quality and pinned on his camouflage vest were metal trinkets and gold stars. That didn't make sense. Nor did the large gold chain clamped around his thick neck. Why would someone decorate themselves with shiny jewelry and insignias of rank when dressed in camouflage? Maybe he didn't care because a bright red bandana encircled his bald pate along with a pair of expensive Ray-Bans on top of his head. He fit the perfect caricature of *el jefe*, the leader of a guerrilla unit.

The blonde finally ceased her sobbing. This welcome relief brought my attention back to the other students. That's when I realized one was missing. Hadrian. Was he able to slip away in the initial confusion? It had happened so fast. Lucky for him.

As the soldiers strutted around, one stopped and pressed a gun against the head of a student. The soldier screamed inches from the young man's face. *"Levanta los manos. No hablar."* I understood his demand. Every villain I'd ever seen on TV demanded the same. The student turned the other way and attempted to protect himself by pulling his shirt over his head. The tyrant mocked his victim and then walked away, pleased with his success.

A different soldier, one with a Fu Manchu moustache, silently counted heads, not once, but twice. Then, he vanished into the jungle and moments later returned dragging Hadrian by his camera strap. Hadrian clutched the leather noose with both hands, throttling back and forth, to maintain a breathing gap by the slightest of margins. His wheezing gasps ceased when his face was forced down in the mud. Fu Manchu struck

17

Hadrian on the back of his head with the butt of the gun. Blood splattered and dripped onto Hadrian's white tee-shirt. The photographer reacted by scuttling to the newly excavated pit as if the nine-inch hole would protect him. His actions made Fu angrier. We begged for the beating to stop. It did when Hadrian lay motionless. Shattered camera pieces were everywhere.

"Te mataré la próxima vez," said Fu. The bloodied weapon simplified the translation. The soldier wouldn't hesitate to kill.

As I tried to make sense of this new reality, I remembered the prophetic words of the flight attendant on our flight from Panama City. She had described the gangs that roamed the national park. Some transported drugs and victims for the slave market. Others were paramilitary groups with no allegiance to any country. All were trying to make a profit.

That's what drew my attention to the two unarmed men. They didn't fit in with the others. Their dirty clothes were not military. They hung in shreds from their arms and legs. The younger one, a teenager, stared at the ground, his body shivering even in the heat and humidity. He flinched every time one of the soldiers screamed or attacked a student. The other one had dark hair streaked with a heavy dose of gray. The length of his unkempt beard suggested he had been a captive for some time. He was more fearless than the younger one, stealing a glance every so often before resuming his earthward stare. I felt something in common with these two. We were scared to death.

The imposing leader began frantically pacing around the site. With each pass, he closed in on Hadrian's cocooned body, his boots inches from the young man's head. I gasped. There, tucked in Hadrian's side, was the metal coin box, half-buried in the mud, as if trying to return to the safety of the grave. The leader stopped and turned; our eyes met. Startled, I lowered mine hoping to keep my discovery a secret. Hadrian's chest rose ever so slightly. He was alive.

Up to this moment, *el jefe* remained silent. But when he spoke, his surprisingly perfect English included a pronounced lisp. It was almost comical coming from such an imposing figure. The monster sounded like a four-year-old. To compensate, he swaggered and waved his gun to remind us of the power he wielded. "I am El Leon, the Lion. Thith ith my kingdom. You will addreth me ath Your Magethty," He continued extolling his self-importance while creating a cartoon-like persona.

Alec leaned towards me and murmured, "His Majesty has frogs and spiders for subjects."

Unfortunately, there was nothing wrong with the thug's hearing. A scowl crossed his bloated face. His eyes widened, his dark skin made the whites, whiter. He moved threateningly toward Alec, flourishing his revolver. "Thpeak up. We all want to hear."

Perhaps foolishly, Alec stepped in front of me glaring at our nemesis until El Leon shoved the muzzle into Alec's chest, pushing him aside like a shower curtain. "Maybe the thenorita will enlighten uth." He placed a surprisingly soft hand under my chin and raised my face towards his. "Tell me, what did your boyfriend thay?"

"Leave her alone. I—"

"Thut the fuck up before you join your friend." He nodded toward Hadrian and turned his attention my way. "I want to hear from the pretty thenorita."

What lie could I tell that would be believed? I looked at Hadrian, blood still oozed from his scalp, and then at Alec. "I'm sorry. I can't hear very well. I'm not sure, he—"

El Leon stuck his palm toward my face. A demand for silence. He surprised me by returning his revolver to his holster, stepping back, and slapping Alec's shoulder as if they had always been friends. A grim smile showed El Leon's even white teeth. Was this a token of leniency, an opportunity to explain ourselves? That we meant no disrespect to the gang's territory?

While my thoughts were about redemption, El Leon's smile vanished. This game was far from over. Alec had inadvertently revealed a weakness. El Leon knew I meant something to Alec, and I could be used.

El Leon nodded to another soldier, and with little warning, he pivoted, and rammed the butt of his rifle into Alec's mid-section. He doubled over, gasped, and collapsed. I bent down and cradled his head, begging him to breathe.

"Oscar!" shouted El Leon.

The same soldier grabbed my arm so tightly I thought it would break. He dragged me across the excavation site, causing me to lose my balance and trip over Hadrian. Oscar continued to pull me along like a rag doll until I found myself next to the blonde. She put one arm around my

19

shoulders, and then pushed the hair out of my face. I searched for Alec. He remained on the ground, his gasps for air, less intense, his eyes locked on mine.

Then I remembered Hadrian, hoping I hadn't caused him more pain. His body lay motionless, legs curled fetal-like; his features hidden behind a curtain of matted hair. One arm was tucked into his chest. The other pinned under his body. That's when I realized the slight change in Hadrian's position. It must have happened when I tripped over him; he took advantage of the chaos when all eyes were on me. That's when the box with the ancient coins must have disappeared.

❦

"Are there any Americanth here?" El Leon demanded.

No one answered.

I stared at the ground as if that would mask my nationality.

El Leon walked slowly in and around his prisoners like a bloodhound sniffing for an American scent. His gun, unleashed again, was used for closer inspection. When he came to the blonde, he fondled a lock of her hair, brought it to his face, and sniffed. "American bitch."

The frightened girl shook her head violently. "No, I'm not American. I'm Scottish. We're all from Scotland."

"Theñorita, if you tell me who ith an American, it will go better for you."

The blonde groveled, repeated her rant, desperate to be convincing.

Frantically, I wondered. *Who in this group knew where I came from?* Alec and Max, for sure. But did I casually mention it to anyone else? My stomach clenched: Hadrian. On the long flight from Scotland, we sat across the aisle from one another. When he learned I was from the States, he talked about his plan to live there after graduation. He peppered me with questions about New York City. When I mentioned that I once had an apartment to rent in Philadelphia, his interest shifted south. He was disappointed to learn it was already claimed by my best friend and her husband. I didn't think Hadrian would give my dangerous secret away, but maybe someone else had overheard our conversation.

"We're all Scottish," said Alec. "We're teachers and students on an archaeological dig." He sounded almost normal, although one hand still pressed his gut.

El Leon turned and waved his gun again. "Who'th in charge?" he screamed. His voice had risen, falsetto-like.

For a moment, the jungle stilled. The howling monkeys, the cicadas, and the bellbirds stopped to listen.

"One more time." His voice low, edged with steel. "Who ith the leader?" *El Jefe* fumed and stomped in my direction. He grabbed the blonde by her ponytail. "My men will enjoy her." He shoved the blonde toward Oscar who sniggered while dragging her in the direction of the nearest tent.

Alec stood. My heart dropped.

El Leon cocked his revolver toward Alec. "You again. I'm getting tired—"

"I'm in charge." Max glared at El Leon. "I'm responsible for this group. Let the girl go."

Max had found his 'Spartacus' moment.

"You're coming with uth."

El Leon motioned with his gun for Max to stand next to the two slaves. Then the brute scanned the team.

"You," he yelled at the blonde.

The girl cried out as Oscar nearly threw her beside Max.

El Leon turned, scanning the remaining team members, looking for another. "And you. Get up."

Who did he want?

"I thaid, get up, or I'll kill your boyfriend."

El Leon stared directly at me.

I looked at Alec. His fists hardened, his nose flared, an animal ready to spring.

To avoid Oscar following orders, I quickly walked over to Max and the blonde.

"Your thoelatheth. Untie them."

"My what?" I asked.

"The thtringth in your thoeth!"

"I don't understand."

"Theeth thingth!" he muttered in frustration while pointing at his bootlaces with his gun barrel.

The two slaves used our laces to tie our hands behind our backs. Discreetly, I turned my wrists hoping to find some slack. Instead, the laces tightened and cut into my skin.

El Leon pointed at the blonde and addressed those remaining behind. "If anyone followth uth, I promith you I will thlit her throat firtht." Then he ordered his men and the slaves to prepare to leave. We were lined up single file: the blonde, me, and Max. Oscar guarded the rear.

Before El Leon gave the command to start, he turned and stared at Alec. "Your girlfriend will earn her keep. Everyone knowth an American hothtage bringth in loth of cath." He turned to look at me. "You will make me a rich man."

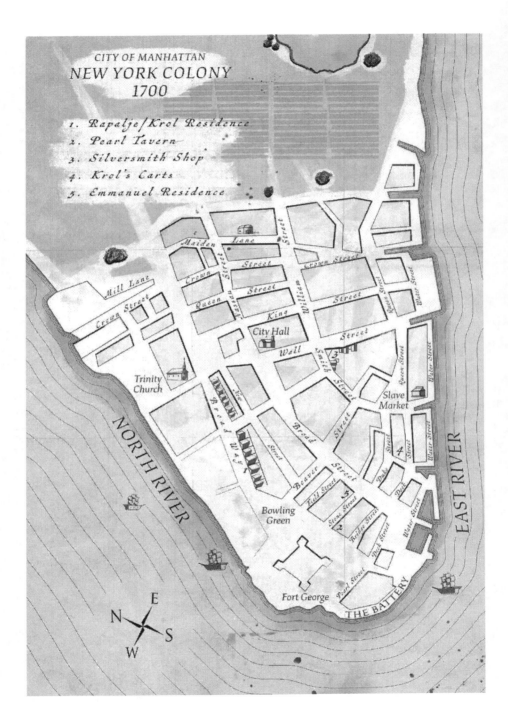

CITY OF MANHATTAN
NEW YORK COLONY
1700

1. Rapalje/Krol Residence
2. Pearl Tavern
3. Silversmith Shop
4. Krol's Carts
5. Emmanuel Residence

CHAPTER FOUR
DAUGHTERS
MANHATTAN 1707

THE GRAVEMARKER WAS appropriate for someone young. It was carved in the shape of a headboard and gave the appearance that the precious child was merely taking a nap. But this was an eternal rest, and neither the shape of a headstone nor the tranquil surroundings of the Trinity Church graveyard, could give comfort to the parents. They would grieve the rest of their lives, until it was time to join their little one in perpetual slumber. I knew that to be true. Alain and I had lost our precious daughter almost eight years ago, shortly after we arrived in Manhattan.

Now, surrounded by sandstone slabs, I was reminded of the ancient standing stones found all over Scotland. The difference was that no one knew for certain who erected those monoliths and could only guess their purpose. Devoid of any engraving, no clues were available to explain their circular placement and the few oddly situated outliers. Some thought that the henges marked the location of a cemetery or were meant for a long-forgotten religious rite. My father believed they had a more sophisticated purpose: a solar calendar. Four times a year, the sun's rays glanced off the stones in such a way, that they announced the start of a new season. Like the markers in the churchyard, the standing stones reminded the living that others had come before them.

I often visited this burial ground which until recently had been a garden. The adjacent building, representing the established Church of England, was built a few years ago. I wondered if the architect purposely positioned the church's entryway facing the North River. It offered a most pleasing prospect.

As I often did, I knelt by the headboard-carved stone; the oldest one in the graveyard. My hand lightly patted the moss-covered chiseled edge as if the young proprietor still needed comforting. My fingers followed the lines and circles of the etched epitaph, picking up damp grit along the way. I whispered the etched words which I knew by heart.

HEAR. LYES. THE. BODY OF.
RICHARD. CHVRCH
ER. SON. OF. WILLIA
M. CHVRCHER. WHO.
DEIED. THE. 5 OF. APRIL
1681. OF. AGE 5 YEARS
AND. 5. MONTHS.

The double-sided headstone was most unusual for one so young. The back side had two raised reliefs: skull and crossbones and a winged hourglass; symbols to remind the living that life was fleeting. The intricate carvings were a sign of great wealth.

I never knew five-year-old Richard or the Churcher family. But I felt a strange connection to him. His grave became a place to mourn my own child who had no lasting marker to remind the world of her short life. That was often the case for the poor. Their passing hardly mattered. If they were fortunate, their resting placed was marked by a wooden cross, lasting only a season or two. For a newborn babe, with impoverished parents, there was nothing. Therefore, I pretended our daughter was interred in a place like this: peaceful and well maintained.

The headstones planted around Richard Churcher gave clues to the lives of the deceased. One, a few feet away was for a married couple. Their clasped petrified hands celebrated their eternal wedding vows. Another headstone, off by itself, had a carved acorn above the owner's name. It represented a mighty oak and the strength of the man who slept six feet below. On others, place of birth was proudly proclaimed by a Tudor rose or a Scottish thistle. As in life, the adult memorials loomed protectively over the smaller childish ones, and the wealthy flaunted their status with symbols in sunken or raised relief. However, there was one message all had in common. No one would escape the inevitable.

A brisk wind, with a hint of early summer sweetness and the promise of a coming storm, was welcome on this unusually warm day. It blew from the direction of the river and found its way around the churchyard, and like mourners, the grass and leaves bowed respectfully. Thus, at Master Churcher's grave, I prayed that my daughter, Rebecca, knew everlasting serenity. I often thought of her and how we came to be in this place.

Almost eight years ago, Alain and I felt like we were the lucky ones We had barely escaped with our lives from Caledonia, the Scottish colony on the Isthmus of Darien. The Company of Scotland, created to finance the endeavor, sold shares to establish an outpost and a trading route to control the lucrative commerce between the Atlantic and Pacific Oceans. But the ones who paid the most were the colonists – with their lives. They were either buried at sea or in the muddy graveyard in New Edinburgh. That's where Alain lost his kinsman, our dear friend, Filib.

After abandoning the colony, our ship, the *Caledonia*, limped into Manhattan on August 4, 1699. Expecting only a short stay and a chance to purchase stores, we were due to sail home. I was anxious to reunite with Alexandra, our eighteen-month-old daughter who had been left in the care of Alain's sister, Davina. Alain feared the return-crossing. I was heavy with our second child, ship's fever still raged, and food barrels were almost empty. Many sailors had deserted, and the vessel needed repair. Alain believed a stormy sea would destroy the ship before St. Kilda was sighted. *Caledonia* was a floating coffin.

To save ourselves, we pretended that my lying-in was imminent, and although no others were permitted to disembark, Lieutenant-Governor John Nantan approved my staying at a nearby inn. He even provided the services of a midwife.

Our second daughter, Rebecca, was born shortly after *Caledonia*'s sails disappeared in the morning mist. From the moment I held our infant daughter, I knew she was not long for this world. Her breathing came too fast and uneven. She gulped for air as if she were starving. At times, her breathing became almost imperceptible.

The midwife said nothing. Her grim face and head shaking were enough.

"Can I hold her?" I asked nervously. I longed to embrace my infant daughter.

27

Alain lowered Rebecca into my arms. "She's a wee one. But is as beautiful as her mother." His words could not mask his troubled look and forced smile.

At first glimpse, my baby appeared like any newborn. Her blue eyes were slits, as if we had disturbed her nap. Her head was covered with a soft haze of light brown wisps; eyelashes so fair it was as if they were missing. I saw right away what had alarmed Alain and the midwife. Her petal-soft skin had a bluish tint. Her lips and tiny paper-thin fingernails were even bluer.

The midwife mumbled something about restoring the balance between the humours of the body. "Mrs. MacArthur, perhaps if the child suckles, her condition will improve."

"Do you think it's too soon? She seems so weak." I knew that babies were born knowing how to suckle, but I worried it would impede Rebecca's breathing.

"Oh no, my dear. Sucklin' is soothin' and the foremilk is best." She hesitated and then added, as it was an afterthought. "And for the mother as well." She took Rebecca and laid her on the bed. "Here, let me help you."

While the midwife loosened the strings of my shift and propped a pillow behind my back, she shared a diverting story.

"Many years ago, when the colony was Dutch, the night watchman, Ebenezer Parkman had a fever and a bad case of the wastin' sickness. Everyone believed his time was short. The reverend was called for, and prayers were said. Mr. Parkman's wife, who was still nursin' her boy, Jonas, decided to wean him and provide nourishment to her husband instead." The midwife picked up Rebecca and placed her back in my arms. "There now, just hold her head and point her in the right direction."

As I held my breast with one hand and the baby with the other, I asked, "What happened to Mr. Parkman?"

"The man recovered. He lived another thirty years."

The midwife's story gave me hope. For a moment. But instead of feeding, Rebecca gasped.

"Try again. Sucklin' is nature's gift, but some babies, especially the tiny ones, need encouragement."

This time we were almost successful, but then nothing. She continued to wheeze, her breathing short and desperate. "Rebecca's turning bluer," I cried out. "Her lips are almost purple." I bent down low over the baby's mouth. "I don't think she's breathing."

28

The midwife seized the child, laid her at the foot of the bed and quickly uncovered her. "Sometimes the wee ones forget to breathe. The cooler air will revive her."

When that didn't work, the midwife rocked Rebecca while pacing, patting her back as hard as one could with a newborn who weighed almost nothing. "Come on, child. Another wee breath." The midwife glanced my way, but then quickly diverted her eyes so I wouldn't see her fright.

"Let me," said Alain, reaching for Rebecca.

He tried the same routine: pacing, patting, and begging. When he stopped, and buried his face in the baby's tiny body, I knew she was gone. Rebecca, my second daughter, named for my mother who died giving birth to me, never had a chance.

The sing-song voice of my youngest child, Sally, melted away the painful memory of Rebecca's death. Here, in the Trinity Church graveyard, Sally was reciting a recently learned nursery rhyme. I knew she would want me to hear her. The often-read letter from Davina, stowed in my pocket, would have to wait.

Lavender tis blue, dilly...silly
Lavender tis green
When I am a...big girl...silly...milly
Mama...shall be Queen!

When I chuckled, Sally stopped gathering the hairy-stemmed blue forget-me-nots. She stared at me, wide-eyed, and when she realized the reason for my laughter, she came running to give me a hug, bringing along her childish scent. Damp curly tendrils stuck to her neck and one spiral attached itself to a rosy cheek. Excited and breathless from her play, she asked, "Do you like my song, Mama?"

"Are those the words your father taught you?"

She paused considering my question. "No. I changed some." Her brow furrowed. "I hope Father doesn't mind. I like my words better. Dilly is such a silly word, and I don't want to be a king. I'd rather be a girl and you are the queen."

29

When Sally finished her explanation, I reluctantly released her to gather more flowers. To my child, this garden of death was a pleasant place. The harsh reality of life had not yet invaded her innocence. I shuddered when I remembered those harrowing days, shortly after Rebecca died, when we were just starting out in Manhattan. Desperately poor with barely enough coin to rub between our fingers, we sought our way to survive in our new home.

The satchel grew heavier and more cumbersome the longer I wandered the narrow streets, searching for the silversmith's shop. I shifted the coarse linen bag to the other hand which helped until the drawstring tightened around my wrist, leaving a mark, and numbing my fingers.

The hunt for the craftsman began unexpectedly with Bertram White. He was the owner of The Pearl, a tavern where Alain and I had rented a room. Moving to The Pearl and away from the inn where we endured our tragic loss had been Alain's idea. Finding new lodgings didn't take long. Manhattan was awash in taverns and inns. It seemed like every fourth or fifth structure offered drink, food, and lodging.

Mr. White worked hard to ensure The Pearl was profitable. His establishment was open until the wee hours of the morning and cultivated a faithful crowd who came for the latest news, the camaraderie, and a full mug. Bertram was a shrewd businessman. He knew that success also depended on avoiding certain topics like his association with the infamous Captain William Kidd. A year ago, the pirate was tried and hung at the Execution Block along the River Thames. Mr. White knew to be discreet but discarded good sense when tempted by a pretty face. I overheard his vulgar whispers to the butcher's wife.

The Pearl always had customers: sailors, soldiers, pimps, merchants, solicitors, and a large clumsy fellow nicknamed, Gallumpus. They gathered around wooden slabs set on wobbly trestles, toasting each other with full tankards, or banging their fists to make a point. The boards were dark-stained, and the plank flooring was drenched with sloshed ale especially after singing a chorus of their favorite song. The air reeked and it penetrated everything, snaking its way through the cracks in the ceiling to our chamber. My clothes and hair smelled of The Pearl.

Customers argued politics, the cost of doing business, and the danger of trans-Atlantic shipping especially when there was news of a floundering. Their favorite topic, which became even more heated and often led to fisticuffs, centered on the quality of the local whores. Was it Esmeralda or Simone who was the more imaginative? Or was Esmeralda guilty of cheating her customers by promising more than she could deliver? Disputes arose about which bawdy houses ran a clean operation or which were responsible for giving an honest fellow the clap.

The latest gossip centered on the new governor of New York, Edward Hyde, Lord Cornbury. His Lordship shocked the colony by appearing before the General Assembly dressed as a woman. It was said that he pretended to be his cousin, Queen Anne. Cornbury's response to the accusation was, "You are very stupid not to see the propriety of it." He might have gotten away with his indiscretion, but the governor had been seen at various times, similarly dressed. This tittle-tattle was fodder for his political enemies.

The innkeeper always joined in chin-wagging with his patrons. He snickered while he provoked their disagreements, encouraged their quarrels, and proposed more drink. He imbibed as much, or more, than anybody, and still turned a profit.

If I happened to walk near when Mr. White was particularly perverse, he delighted in making me the victim of his crude remarks, taking advantage of Alain's absence. "Mrs. MacArthur. And where is your fine husband today, eh? Perhaps he'd like to join us?" Mr. White knew Alain worked on the pier from early morning until dark. But before I could answer, Mr. White responded with a query. "Is he keeping the butcher's wife company? She's very accommodatin'. Not the usual hedge-whore."

"Bert, you'd know about that," cried Gallumpus while readjusting his eye patch without letting go of a full mug.

"Maybe you should give the mistress here, a lesson," suggested another.

"Nah," replied Bert. "Her husband will know somethin's 'up'." His hand went to his groin and grabbed whatever he could find. "Mr. MacArthur will wonder how his wife became so skilled, so attuned to his wishes…so quickly, eh?"

That's how it usually went. I blushed, and the customers fell over laughing. I wondered why crude men, like Captain Pennecuik, the master of the ship I sailed on to the Scottish colony, and now Mr. White, had a

31

habit of grabbing their crotch. As a rule, I avoided Mr. White, but at times, like today, it was impossible. When the innkeeper saw me with my satchel, he became threateningly curious. I quickly diverted the coming taunts by asking for directions to the silversmith's shop.

"How would I know anythin' about a silversmith? Do I look like a rich man?" He gestured like an actor toward his three customers sitting in the shadows. Benches were strewn helter-skelter, and the floor was littered with dried leaves and something unrecognizable. "Does this mean I might get paid, eh? Your needin' a silversmith, and all? The rent is overdue. I'm not runnin' a charity house."

Sneers and chortles poured from the threesome. One banged his tankard hard on the table, drenching his friend's breeches. The offended man reached for his sword only to clutch at air. The innkeeper wisely demanded weapons be relinquished before any drink was ordered.

The lack of Mr. White's sobriety and the encouragement from his friends, made it impossible to reason with him. I considered telling Alain about the innkeeper's effrontery, but we were at his mercy. He was willing to wait for payment, although our debt grew larger. But I had a plan, and perhaps starting today, I wouldn't have to endure this much longer.

I hugged the satchel closer.

"Hey, whatcha got there?" asked the one-eyed monster as he thrust back the bench scraping the wood planks. "Give it here." Was he pretending just to get a laugh from the others? "Don't run away when I'm talkin' to you."

As I turned and stepped into the street, I heard his partner say between chuckles, "I think her man's been pimpin' her out. She's made him so much coin she has to get the excess melted down." Both men laughed even louder. The scraping of benches was accompanied by a loud thump.

"Hey!" Bertram White stood at the door. "The silversmith. That way." The tavern owner's forefinger aimed east. "A word of warnin'. He's one of them, the deceitful race." The innkeeper spat on the stoop and wiped his red nose with his shirtsleeve. When he turned to go back in the tavern, he barreled into two men running out.

Raindrops dripped off the silversmith's sign, splattered on my hood, and ran down my back. Myer Myers, Master Silversmith was inscribed above an engraved hammer and anvil. The smith's shop was barely large enough for the customer already engaged with the shopkeeper.

I waited my turn, until a fashionable older gentleman with a pointed beard and curled mustache emerged to the tinkling of a bell. He hurried down the street taking large strides skirting puddles and a young mother scolding her children.

When I entered the shop, the bell continued its toll as I was greeted with a familiar lemony scent. It reminded me of my father's home and the fragrance of cleaned silver in preparation for my wedding. The smell originated from a small bowl set before a young-aproned boy. Standing over him was an older man. Master Myer Myers, I presumed.

"Here, Jacob. Don't forget to do this part of the yad. The tarnish between the grooves is the hardest to remove."

The implement being polished was eight inches long and on one end was a tiny hand with an outstretched forefinger. I recognized the pointer immediately. It was used by rabbis and scholars when reading the Torah. Its purpose was to keep the oil from one's fingers from touching the sacred parchment. My father used a yad for the same reason when he read his ancient books.

"Which should I use, master?" A pile of various cloths of different textures, some dark with tarnish, filled a basket.

"The softest one. Dip one corner in the salted lemon juice. Rub gently. Here, let me show you." The master nodded while he explained the most elemental lesson for an apprentice about to spend years learning the art of creating functional pieces of silver. "Silver is a soft metal, and the English are known for the finest silver in the world. Treat it with care and reverence." A moment of patient silence existed between student and teacher, until the older man's gnarled hand patted the youngster's back. "That's it, Jacob. Next, you'll polish the crown, the breastplate, and the finials."

Finished with his lesson, Master Myers turned. "Ah, may I help you, Mistress?"

"Yes, I have something." I opened the satchel and slowly revealed the heavy candlestick. I placed it in the man's opened hands.

He nodded as his fingers glided along the ribbed column. "This is a handsome piece of workmanship." While he continued his examination, his eyes diverted momentarily to assess my stained petticoat and dirty mules. "Where did you come by such a beauty?"

"My father gave it to me. A wedding gift. I used to have another. They…this one…was meant to usher in the Sabbath. At sunset—"

"I'm aware of when Sabbath candles should be lit," he said while fingering the engraved hallmarks. "Hmm! Edinburgh. James Penman. Fine artisan. I know his work." The master's attention shifted to the fluted sconce. "What happened to the other? My wife lights two candles."

"I left it in Scotland. With my daughter." I couldn't tell him that the other candlestick was used as a weapon to stop my brother from killing Alain who was trying to save me from a forced marriage. And in the process, it fell out of my hand and ended up in my father's. Remembering the events of that horrible night almost blinded me to the meaning behind Master Myer's words. But now I understood Bertram White's disparaging remarks. The silversmith and I were members of the 'deceitful race.'

"What can I do for you? With this?" He nodded while placing the candlestick on a small table near two others awaiting repair. There was no question which was the most magnificent.

"Would you be interested in purchasing...or...melting—"

The bell clanged wildly. Alain burst in the tiny shop. "Lass, there you are. I've been looking everywhere." He stopped when he realized we were not alone and squeezed my arm gently when he saw the candlestick. "What's this? What are you doing?" Alain must have noticed the surprised look of the master and his wide-eyed apprentice. "Excuse me, sir. I didn't mean to barge in." He looked at the candlestick again. "Anna, we need to talk." He grabbed my hand and pulled me outside. The doorbell dinged our exit. "I went back to the inn to find you, and Bert said you ran off, something about a Jew silversmith." Alain put his arms around me and pulled me in. "I was worried, I don't trust that innkeeper."

I stared into his eyes. "We owe Mr. White his rent. And the midwife. Did you see the look she gave when you offered her a shilling?"

"I don't care. I won't let you sell the candlestick. It's all you have from your father."

"Alain, he didn't mean for me to have it for our marriage. You know that."

"I will provide for you. It was a promise I made when we married. You will always have my protection, and I will not have you selling your possessions."

"But how? We have nothing. We know no one. If I wasn't so weak...from Rebecca...Mr. White is always asking me to do his laundry. He's—"

34

"It's not clean sheets he's after." Alain reacted the way he always did when angered. His fists clenched and the scar on his face reddened. "I'll find more work." He placed a hand on his sword. "Get the candlestick and come home."

We re-entered the shop and while I made the satchel heavy again, Alain said to the silversmith, "What would you give me for this?" He pulled his sword out of its sheath.

"No," I pleaded.

"It's made of steel by one of the finest swordsmiths in Scotland."

Mr. Myers peered over his eyeglasses. "I have no doubt. It seems to be of fine workmanship. But I only deal with silver and gold. There's a swordsmith just down the street. He may be able to help you."

Alain replaced the sword in its leather home. "Thank you, sir."

As we turned to leave, Master Myers said, "If you're looking for work, I know someone who is interested in hiring a strong young man. To do heavy lifting. And handle a horse and cart." Myers eyed Alain's physical promise.

"Who do I talk to?"

"On Dock Street. My friend Joris Krol needs a cartman. He just lost a worker. Man broke his arm in a brawl. It's a good wage you'll make. And if you work hard and are reliable, Joris is looking for someone to manage his workers, someone with sound judgment and discretion. The job comes with a small house."

Alain put his arm around my shoulder and drew me close. "I have a wife and debts."

Myers nodded his head and grabbed his hat from a peg by the door. "Jacob, watch the store while I take Mr....uh—"

"MacArthur. And...you've already met my wife."

When we arrived at Joris Krol's shop, the yard in front of the stable was bustling. Three workers prepared the two-wheeled carts for the day while another brought out the horses. Most were tired looking; their sagging backs bespoke their limited usefulness. One horse, about to be harnessed, neighed loudly, and reared up after his handler punched him in the head. Other workers, the cartmen, dressed in their telltale frocks, leaned against the stable doors, waiting for the boss and their daily assignment.

Myer Myers looked around, searching for his friend. "Mr. MacArthur, my apprentice is untested. He cannot handle much more than polishing a simple object. I must return. Tell Joris that I sent you."

35

"Bless you, sir. For your kindness." I didn't know what else to say to the man that may have saved us. I squeezed his hand and felt the callouses of his trade.

The men shook hands, and when the silversmith was about to leave, he paused. "A bit of advice. Keep your distance from Catarina."

"Catarina?" asked Alain.

"Joris' wife." With that he nodded his head, turned to me, and tipped his hat. "One more thing, my dear. Take care of your precious candlestick. It's an excellent piece of workmanship, worth more than I could ever pay, and is meant to adorn your home and welcome the Sabbath bride. It's worthy enough to remain in your family; an heirloom to hand down to your children's children. Perhaps, someday, it will be reunited with its mate." He nodded his head again, and disappeared among the growing number of vendors, sailors, shoppers, tradesmen, laborers, fishmongers, a water carrier, and a whore hurrying to her next client.

My thoughts returned to the graveyard. Playing with the flowers, Sally recited a new nursery rhyme over and over. Her preoccupation was my chance to reread Davina's letter. I snatched it from my pocket and devoured her words which I knew by heart.

May 1, 1707

Dearest Anna & Alain,

I hope this letter finds you & precious Sally in good health. Before I go any further, & describe the events that have befallen our family, please be assured that Alexandra & I are in the best of health. Your daughter is a curious & talented young girl, almost a woman, & I have no doubt that it won't be long before suitors are wearing down our threshold to vie for her favors. She has the promise of great beauty, & in that way, she is like her mother.

It is with sadness in my heart that I must inform you of the untimely passing of our beloved father. It happened quite suddenly, just after Father Drummond's fortnightly visit when he announced a renewed purpose in life: to save me & Alexandra from our unmarried state. During a heated exchange with our father, on which I must confess I eavesdropped, an agitated Father Drummond banged his fist on the table to control the conversation. He stated that the union of two souls was the Lord's plan, & that my spinsterhood was ungodly. But worst of all, I was setting a poor example for my niece, especially one fast approaching marriageable age. Our father answered heroically. He would not allow the priest to interfere & dictate who & when I should marry. Or Alexandra. Although marriage prospects for a nine-year-old are a bit premature, or so I thought. But the 'saintly' Father Drummond does not share that vision.

We were relieved when the priest announced his departure. I looked forward to two weeks of relief from talk of the devil. But later that evening, Father suffered an apoplexy. When he revived, his speech was strained, & he had no movement on his right side. Three days later, he joined Mother under the elm.

That was a month ago, & now it seems that Father Drummond has redoubled his efforts. Believing, more than ever, I'm in need of a man's protection. I do not, & I have no intention of marrying until I am ready. My hope is to find the same kind of love & respect that exists between my dearest brother & my beloved sister.

Based on these unfortunate circumstances, my concern is now for Alexandra. What if something should happen to me? There would be no one left to protect her.

Sally's outbursts of anger at the blue petaled flowers forced me to put Davina's letter away. The circlet kept breaking, and after the last attempt she threw the wilted flowers on the grass and snarled. I offered my help, but she stubbornly refused. Sally was a strong-willed child, and I believed that this strength saved her during our first years in Manhattan when it seemed like the world was consumed with sickness and death. Instead, I held out my arms, and she came and nuzzled close. It didn't take long for her to lay her sleepy head in my lap while I caressed her plump cheek and kissed her fingers. The peacefulness of the quiet graveyard could not quell my frightful memories of almost losing Sally.

The all-too brief early morning chill was encouragement enough to burrow under the counterpane. The comforting odors of goose down, male musk, and dawn filled the room. It was the first time, in nearly three years, since Alain and I had arrived in New York, that I felt content.

The aroma of fresh coffee, burnt toast, and warm tarts coming from the house next to ours reminded me how hungry I was. Our landlady, Catarina's busy hearth invaded my cocoon. No longer could I put off the inevitable. I threw back the cover to begin my day.

I peered into Sally's cradle at the foot of the bed. She was still asleep. I wondered if the delicious smell would awaken her appetite. My throbbing breasts indicated it wouldn't be long before a meal far outweighed the comforts of her dream world.

Born three months ago, her name Sarah meant princess. We called her Sally, in memory of my dear friend who was murdered to save me from my treacherous brother.

A sound sleeper, Sally was not bothered by her squeaks and groans. But I found them disconcerting. After the devastating loss of Rebecca, any unusual sound brought me running to her cradle. When she was first born, I swept her in my arms to ensure nothing was amiss. Now, I was slowly learning to accept that Sally was a healthy babe. But sometimes, the old fear crept back, and I sat by her cradle at night and watched her. I would run my finger along the soft bottom of her foot, and much to my delight a sleepy smile appeared while her little body wriggled. Only then would my anxiety evaporate. Alain chided me for fussing so. He reminded me that Sally's lusty cries, that woke us in the middle of the night, were a testament to her good health. But then, I caught him looking in on her, too, stroking a pink cheek, for no other reason than to ensure all was well.

When Rebecca died, the midwife tried to console us. "You're both young. Before you know it, you'll be callin' me again."

At the time I was too distraught to think of an answer until I recalled something my father once said. He had a cache of wise sayings that tended to put life's greatest challenges into perspective. His explanation of a parent's love was my favorite. "My children are like the fingers on my hand. If I lose one, can I say it doesn't matter because I have four left? The same goes for the loss of a child. Nothing can compensate for the grief."

That described exactly how I felt about Rebecca. She would always be in my heart. The smell of her newborn skin, the curl of her tiny toes, and the blue pools of her eyes were seared into memory, for the rest of my days. And on Fridays, at sunset, when the candlestick was aglow with the flickering Sabbath candle, my hands hovered over the imagined heads of two missing daughters, while I blessed them both.

If the delicious smells emanating from the Catarina's kitchen didn't awaken the little one, then perhaps the tang of strong lye soap would. Up and down Broadway Street, serving girls, slaves, or poor matrons scrubbed their front stoops with a mixture of river sand and soap made from wood ash. The lower half of their aprons and skirts darkened as they scrubbed on their hands and knees. Using a stout rag or brush, they erased the grime and muddy footprints leftover from the day before. Once satisfied that their stoop was a credit to their housewifery, they poured buckets of water to remove the remaining grit. Cleaning the stoop and maintaining a tidy home was very much a Dutch custom. Even those who were not Dutch, joined in. A good first impression spoke volumes about the qualities of the matron of the home.

Before the baby awoke was the best time to wash the stoop. I grabbed a bucket, a cake of newly made soap, and a worn-out brush. Around my waist, I tied a still-damp, stained apron and scooped a half cup of sand from another bucket.

Ready to open the front door, Sally's soft whine stopped me. I waited, and then nothing. Perhaps she returned to her sleepy world. I touched the knob again and was greeted with another whine. This one was louder. My breasts ached and the top of my shift felt damp. As much as I wanted to get this chore completed, Sally had given me enough time off this morning. I returned my tools and went over to her cradle.

Staring at my babe, my eyes played tricks on me. For a moment, I thought I saw Rebecca in the cradle. The bluish skin. The deepening purple on her lips. I shook my head to dislodge Rebecca's ghost. In her place, Sally writhed and moaned and began to howl like a dog on a night with a full moon. When I lifted her, I immediately noticed her body was hot to the touch. My cool hands caused her to shiver and retract. I undid the

39

swaddling blanket and found tiny blisters covering her stomach. One was creeping up her neck.

I paced the room with my sickly child. Nothing seemed to soothe her. She wasn't interested in food, and only nodded off when she exhausted herself from crying; the calm lasted but a few minutes. Her cries became moans, and her glassy eyes stared helplessly. I returned her to the cradle and covered her lightly with a swaddling cloth when she began to tremble.

As much as I found it distasteful, our landlady, Catarina Rapalje, Joris Krol's wife, was my only hope. Catarina was a domineering woman who reigned over her home and her husband. She was proud to be Dutch and rejected English customs, like refusing to take her husband's surname, even though the colony hadn't been Dutch for thirty years. She was born Catarina Rapalje, and she declared her headstone would be engraved the same.

Our house, situated behind the landlady's, faced her kitchen entrance. The aroma that enticed me earlier was now nauseating. I found Catarina bending over the Dutch oven. Cooking was usually a chore she left to the help. With a burnt-edged cloth she tilted the hot lid.

"Mrs. Rapalje," I interrupted. "Forgive me. My daughter is sick."

The thin woman stiffened and, with an exaggerated motion, replaced the lid with a thud. She cleared her throat when she turned, her hands resting on non-existent hips. Her face, powdered white, the latest fashion of the upper class, was startling and comical. The heat from the hearth or her rising anger coagulated the powder along the deep grooves that radiated from the edges of her mouth and along the furrows of her forehead. Her face appeared to be melting.

"Please. My baby, Sally, is sick with a fever. She's burning up." The frantic tone in my voice as well as my tears, I hoped would soften the woman's demeanor.

Catarina sighed heavily with impatience followed by an unusual noise in the back of her throat. "Does your child have the pustules?"

I nodded.

She quickly put the burnt cloth to her nose and mouth. "Don't come any closer. Fever is spreading through the town. Two dead on this street. The undertaker was busy this morning. You must leave."

Stepping backward, I felt for the door. "What should I do? I can't lose her."

"Get a doctor," she muffled the words through the cloth. "Isn't that what you do when someone is sick?"

Of course, a doctor. But where? I couldn't think straight. "Could your maid show me?"

"I have no idea where that good-for-nothing is. I've been calling for her all morning. My stoop has not been cleaned. What will the neighbors think?"

"I'll clean your stoop when I get back. Please."

I could sense a self-satisfying smirk under the cloth. I knew she would love to lord over me while I scrubbed her stoop, forcing me to redo areas I had already cleaned. To ensure her sense of superiority, she lowered her mask, smoothed her apron, and with much fanfare, fluffed her skirts. But when she noticed the cloth was white with powder, she awkwardly hid it in her pocket and checked her cap to cover the growing bald spot.

"No. My girl has too much to do. She's as lazy as they come. Dr. Smith lives just down the street toward the English Church." Her forefinger aimed in the direction. "You'll know which house it is. It's on the corner and it's not as grand as mine. Now leave."

I had no choice but to go. My arms ached as I carried Sally passed the stately homes that fronted Broadway. Many were in the old style with gabled roofs and slender colored bricks. One of the finest homes was that of Alain's employer. But there were also the modest homes of bricklayers, shopkeepers, and emerging craftsmen. The doctor's Dutch-styled house was two blocks away. It was easy to find because Mrs. Rapalje was wrong. His was the finest house on Broadway.

The stoop had just been scrubbed. A young slave, her hair covered with a kerchief, poured a bucket of clean water to wash away the sand. Her apron was splattered and dripping.

"Excuse me," I asked. "Is Dr. Smith at home?"

The girl stood, arching her back, her black skin shiny with sweat. She wiped her brow and upper lip with the edge of her damp apron. "The doctah ain't home. Come back t'morrow." She leaned on the tips of her toes, peered at the bundle I was carrying, clicked her tongue, and returned to her bucket.

"Please. My daughter has a fever."

I pulled back the blanket to show the woman. She didn't recoil. Perhaps she was used to the sick showing up at the doctor's door.

41

"Your baby ain't t'only one. There's a heap o' sickness goin' on." She waved her hand, a gesture to prove her point. "Dr. Smith is tendin' t'others far worse than your little one. You has t'wait." The woman resumed her watery chore and forgot I was there.

I had no choice but to retrace my steps. Sally began to moan again, but now accompanied by a deep rattle in her chest. I clung to my baby and burrowed my face in her fevered body. Her breath had the stench of death.

It was useless to go home. Instead, I headed toward Joris' shop where Alain worked. Along the way, cartmen lined up on street corners, waiting for the cry from merchants, shopkeepers, and tradesmen, that meant employment, When I arrived, Alain was nowhere in sight, and the shop was empty. I looked in the stable but found only one cart hidden behind bales of straw.

Disheartened, I trudged northward and then turned into a smaller cobblestoned street, trying not to turn an ankle on the uneven surface. Some of the shop signs creaked in answer to the slightest breeze. A familiar sign, the hammer and anvil, engraved below the name of the proprietor, reminded me that this was the place of a kindred spirit. I placed my hand on the doorknob.

The jingling of the bell provided a feeling of relief, the first since my confrontation with Catarina. Instead of Master Myers, I found his apprentice Jacob, clad in a leather apron, protective sleeves, and a knitted hat, standing over a table scattered with the tools of his trade: a planishing hammer, wire, a file, and snips. More hammers and saws, of all shapes and sizes, dangled from hooks within arms' reach. The young man, a head taller since my last visit, was in the middle of a delicate operation, attaching the handle to a silver teapot. Nearby, four cups awaited his attention. The bell interrupted his work. He turned to the door.

"Good day. May I be of service, Mistress?" Before I could answer, he said, "I beg your pardon…um…I remember…you were in the shop a year…two years ago. Your candlestick. Master Myers still talks about—"

"Yes. I'm Anna MacArthur. Is the master in?"

"I'm afraid he was called away. I'm not sure when he will return. Could I—"

"No. Thank you." I knew it was expected of me to say I would return, but that might be too late. I couldn't leave. "May I wait here until Master Myers returns? I must see him…I'm afraid I need his help. Again. But this time—"

The doorbell tolled. Myer Myers entered with a flourish bringing in the pungent odor of fresh dung, compliments of the horse-drawn cart that had passed moments before. He hung his broad-brimmed felt hat and replaced it with a smaller red cap hanging on a hook nearby. Then he turned to face me.

"Jacob, have you helped this young woman?"

"Master Myers. I don't know if you remember me."

He looked at me closely and then he added, "Of course. And your husband, Mr....um...MacArthur. He took that job...working for Joris Krol. Yes. Yes. My friend cannot stop thanking me for recommending your husband. Joris claims he's a wonder, and I hear he's managing the cartmen."

"We are grateful, sir. At times, my husband helps with deliveries when there's a shortage of workers. Some are too ill to work."

"Yes, I'm afraid the fever has stricken many throughout Manhattan. It's a nasty business." He leaned forward, and for the first time, noticed the sleeping bundle in my arms. His tone softened. "How can I help you today?"

I hesitated. I didn't want to be rude, but I was anxious to announce the reason for entering the shop. "I am in need of your help. For my child. It's the fever." I bit my lip to forestall their trembling. "I didn't know where else to go. Sally needs a doctor."

While Master Myers did not come closer, he did not flinch, draw back, or demand that I leave. Instead, he turned to his apprentice, whispered in the lad's ear, and the boy tore out the door. The bell swung wildly in his wake.

"Jacob will see if the doctor is home."

"I went to the doctor earlier. His slave told me that he was seeing other patients, and I would have to wait my turn." I peered down at Sally and pressed my lips against her forehead. The back of my eyes filled with tears; one caught in my throat. "My daughter...cannot...wait."

"Hmm. We must be talking about two different surgeons. Baruch Emmanuel possesses no slave. In fact, he abhors the very thought of owning a human being no matter how some interpret the Bible. You must be referring to the doctor who resides near Trinity."

"Yes, that's where my landlady, Catarina Rapalje, told me to go. She ordered me to leave her home once she found out my daughter was ill."

43

"Hmm. That sounds like Joris' wife. Well, whatever is wrong with your daughter, Dr. Emmanuel will tend to her, and if he is not home, his wife, Deborah, is a competent healer in her own right."

The doorbell sang out again. Jacob plunged into the shop like a whirlwind and nodded to Master Myers.

"Just as I thought. Baruch will see your child. Jacob will show you the way."

I could not dam my tears any longer. Along with my runny nose, I wiped the corners of my eyes with the edge of Sally's swaddling cloth.

The silversmith offered a handkerchief to staunch the flood along with more reassurances. "You can rely on the good services of the doctor. His home is but a short distance away."

I offered my gratitude and quickly followed Jacob. If it had been an appropriate gesture, I would have kissed the man's whiskered cheeks. The doorbell pealed with our departure, and Sally's cry joined the chorus.

"Anna!" Alain called as he brought the horse and cart to a halt and looked up at the sign. When he noticed Sally whining miserably in my arms, he asked, "What's wrong?"

I had little time to explain. The distance between Jacob and me had grown. Alain started up the horse-drawn cart as we followed the apprentice's diminishing figure to the doctor's surgery.

Baruch Emmanuel was not what I expected. I envisioned a wizened old man exuding years of stored-up medical knowledge, a scholar like my father. So, I was taken aback when a tall young man opened the door and extended a hand in friendship.

"Hallo. Velcome. *Commen.*"

His thick German accent did not surprise me. Although, the Jewish community remained small, an increasing number of Ashkenazim from Central and Eastern Europe made Manhattan their home.

Behind the doctor, stood a well-endowed woman with dark curly hair; a plain but pleasant face peeked from under a lace-fringed cap. She appeared to be the same age as the doctor. I supposed this was his wife, Deborah, but when he addressed her as, *meine leibe,* I knew for sure.

Alain and I entered the Emmanuel home and immediately my senses came alive with the aroma of yeasty bread and something baked with cinnamon and sugar. We were ushered to the surgery just off the entranceway. Although it could have held more furnishings, what was there gleamed from a recent polishing. The fireplace was swept, and everything was orderly.

The doctor, taller than Alain but much thinner, placed my daughter gently on a table and like an onion peeled back the swaddling cloth. The odor from a wet-filled nappie overcame the aroma from the kitchen. The doctor paid no mind and bent low to scrutinize Sally's body, pressing his ear to her chest, stretching out her arms and legs. He turned Sally onto her stomach and pulled out a glass to further examine the pustules. Her howls announced the discomfort of the cooler air and the unfamiliar touch.

The doctor straightened, covered the baby lightly, stroked his chin, and paced around the table. As he spoke, he was cautious with his words. "Your daughter is not vell. Of this, you know. *Gelbfieber*...ah...Yellow Fever, is afflicting hundreds."

Hearing the words 'Yellow Fever' from a doctor was frightening. I could feel the blood drain from my face, and Alain noticed my reaction. He put his arm around my waist to steady me. Or perhaps, he was also searching for support.

"I've treated many patients. I'm familiar vith the symptoms: fever, body aches, tiredness, a rash. The illness gets its name from the yellowness in the eyes and skin." He reached down and uncovered Sally again. "Your child does not share the inflammation that is plaguing the city."

"I don't understand," said Alain. "She has a fever."

"That's true." Dr. Emmanuel pointed to Sally's stomach. "Do you see the pustules on her torso? They are creeping down her legs and across her arms."

I was almost afraid to ask. "Is it smallpox?"

"No, no, no. Mrs. MacArthur. That I'm sure of. If it vere smallpox," he continued, "Sally vould have pustules on the soles of her feet, her palms, and every inch of her body." As if Sally wanted to prove his point, she stretched out her tiny fingers and wrapped them around the doctor's forefinger. "Vhen did you notice the pustules?"

"This morning. Shortly after she awakened."

The doctor gently pulled his finger from Sally's grip and walked over to another table near an open window. He dipped his hands in a bowl and rinsed them with water from a nearby pitcher. Deborah offered him a cloth. "*Dankeschön, meine Liebe.*" He smiled at her, and after wiping his hands, he continued. "That confirms it. It's not smallpox. The pox doesn't show up for two to four days after the start of a fever. And it's not the yellow fever either. Did your child vomit this morning?"

"No. But she isn't hungry."

"That's to be expected. A feverish brain has more important things to do than vorry about an appetite. I believe your daughter's fever is easily explained. She has a common childhood ailment. One, ve all suffer - a rite of passage. Chicken pox. If you and Mr. MacArthur had it, there is no vorry of your contracting it."

I hadn't noticed the doctor's wife had left the room until she returned with a small packet of herbs which she placed in my hands. "Steep the chamomile leaves into a strong tea. Let it cool, and then soak a cloth in the tea and gently vipe your baby. It may help vith the itching, and the coolness vill lessen her fever. If that doesn't help, put *das kind* in a tub of cool vater vith the chamomile leaves. Uncooked oats vill help as vell." Deborah placed her hand on my arm. "Let us know if the child does not improve in a few days. Ve are alvays here to help. Our community is small, only thirty families, but ve vatch out for each other. And vonce your daughter improves, please come back. You and your family vill be velcome."

I hesitated a moment. Should I mention that Alain was not of our faith? Would the Emmanuels care? What about Myer Myers? Would they be so hospitable if they knew? I only had my father as a guide. He acted politely to our Christian neighbors and those he dealt with in business. He invited them to dinner or offered a night's lodging, as any Scot would do. But there were limits. Father would never eat at their table, nor would he stay in their home. I couldn't blame him for his caution, knowing the desperate times when his family had to run for their lives because they were betrayed by their Christian neighbors to the Inquisitional Court. My father remembered the past with a saying from the Talmud: *He who has been bitten by a snake is scared of a rope.*

I nodded but chose to remain silent and hoped Deborah could not read my thoughts. And that is how I met two more members of the Jewish community.

46

"Mama, can we go home now?" Sally rubbed her eyes and yawned. Her sweet voice returned me to reality. Her face stared into mine as the remnants of an unfinished flower bracelet fell into her lap.

Davina's letter, safe in my pocket, poked at me as if a reminder that Alain and I still had to discuss its propitious contents. The earliest my sister-in-law would receive our reply would be the end of the year.

As I prepared to leave, I brushed off the purple petals that clung to Sally's skirt and the few that drifted to mine. Then I spit into a handkerchief and wiped off the dirty smudges from my daughter's cheek. "Hold still now. Don't you want to look pretty for your father?"

Sally pulled back and wrinkled up her face. "I don't like having spit on my face."

"Just one more bit. On this side." I held her chin and turned her head.

"Mama, why are you smiling?"

"I have wonderful news."

"What is it?"

"I'll tell you. On our way home. It's getting late. We'd best be off."

Sally plunked her hand in mine and pulled to hurry me along, but I tripped on Richard Churcher's grave. My foot was ensnared in an exposed tree root. The recent rains must have unearthed it. As I untangled myself, I imagined the young boy's spirit was trying to detain me. He didn't want to be left alone.

As we walked away, hand in hand, I turned and eyed the child's gravestone once more. It always made me realize how fortunate I was to have Sally. And now, this welcome news from Davina, I replayed the rest of her letter in my mind on our walk home.

> *I don't know if my father had a premonition that he had little time left in this world, but shortly before he passed, he told me about my sweet sister's secret. Please be assured I have told no one, not even Alexandra. I shudder when I think what that despicable priest would do if he knew the God you prayed to. Therefore, I fear for the child's future. Who she marries should be a matter for her beloved parents. Perhaps the time has come for Alexandra to be reunited with her mother's faith.*

If you wish, Alexandra might set out in the late spring or early summer when the seas are calmer. Before I make any arrangements, I await your instruction in this delicate matter.

Your loving sister,
Davina

CHAPTER FIVE

A GALAXY OF WEBS

DARIEN NATIONAL PARK

I HAD NO idea where we were or where we were going. Were we near the coast, heading inland or was our destination south to Columbia or north to Costa Rica? The dense brush anchored into every inch of living space not already taken by the innumerable trees, eliminated any sense of direction. The jungle teemed with chatter, rare flora and fauna emitted fragrant scents and fetid odors. Everything was wet: the leaves were glossy; the ground was spongy; and the air was heavy with dampness. The incessant rain stair-stepped its way from leaf to leaf, thus creating muddy pools for the benefit of smaller species in this biome. But perilous to those who'd turn an ankle. Each time we hacked our way to the next small clearing, what was discovered looked exactly like what we'd just left.

At the start of our trek, when I still felt emboldened, I'd glance over my shoulder to make sense of this unusual world. But that brought on angry words, threatening gestures, or a shove or two from Oscar. I learned, soon enough, to look ahead in this forced march of a never-ending déjà vu.

Once, I learned from my dad about using a wet finger to locate the direction of a breeze. Whichever side felt the coolest suggested where the wind was coming from. Perhaps, an easterly would hint the nearness of the coast. I raised a saliva-covered finger. Nothing. I should have known. Not even the slightest breath stirred the leaves.

Our forward march was hard work, made treacherous with lace-less hiking shoes. Cutting our way through thorny brush, slippery moss-covered rocks, fallen tree limbs, and the exposed roots of the strangler fig limited our progress to a few feet at a time. The only thing I knew for certain was we hadn't gone in circles. Our path never crossed one recently hacked.

At times we were forced into waist-high swamps, wading through nose-clogging clouds of gnats and mosquitos. This reminded me of a swarm of midges, the no-see-ums of Scotland, which attacked Alec and me during an early morning hike on Skye. It was like a scene from a horror movie. The "wee beasties," as Alec referred to them, relentlessly bit, dotting our skin with hundreds of small red mounds. The itching that followed was torture.

Our captors ordered us to stop, not to rest as I had hoped, but for a temporary standstill so that a few thick branches could be bound together. With little effort, the unit's gear, previously carried on the backs of the men, was transferred to the primitive raft. This promised speedier forward progress but would also hasten whatever Fate had in store at the end of the road.

Once we continued, every muscle in my body rebelled. I needed rest and food, but more importantly, sleep. I found refuge in the past, and memories of my dad provided a welcome diversion along with a warning. I remembered our hikes to Watkins Glen or Bear Mountain. Dad always reminded me to stay hydrated; never to start out without a full thermos. "Dehydration," he cautioned, "can bring on dizziness and confusion, a deadly combination in a remote area." Dad's advice was now a cruel irony. I was in a rainforest, and my throat was parched like the desert.

In an odd way, I was grateful for my captors. Undaunted by the jungle, their lack of hesitation suggested they knew exactly where we were and where we were headed. The slaves and Fu Manchu were at the front, followed closely by El Leon. Fu oversaw the slaves as they slashed a path with machetes. The moment either one stopped to wipe the sweat from their eyes or arch a sore back, Fu became relentless, shouting murderous threats that needed no translation. The madness was becoming commonplace.

Before we left Scotland, Max assigned readings to prepare us for Darien. Much of the information was not a surprise, what you'd usually expect in a rainforest: bamboo, mangrove, rare orchids, bougainvillea, pumas, anteaters, spider monkeys, and brightly plumaged birds. I found the articles on the poisonous plants and animals most intriguing. While I didn't worry about encountering the tiny dart frog, whose venom would cause an upset stomach, I was concerned about its predator, the fer-de-lance who lived under rocks or piles of leaves. I rationalized that the snake wasn't known to go after humans; it chose to flee rather than fight. But that didn't lessen my fear because there were also scorpions, fire ants, and wild pigs to worry about. Consequently, my eyes were glued to the forest floor. From behind, I noticed the blonde's head lowered too. Now, I wished I had skipped that part of my education. Sometimes it's better not to know.

Anna had written about the dangers of this area in her journal. She described a colonist dying shortly after being pierced with the sharp needles of the chunga palm. Her vivid account of the large hairy botfly made my skin crawl. Anna had witnessed a doctor pulling a botfly maggot out of the thigh of William Paterson, one of the colony's leaders. In the late seventeenth century, it was believed the female botfly deposited her eggs into human flesh. But modern scientists learned the mosquito and the botfly worked symbiotically. The botfly laid her egg on a mosquito who transferred the egg into a human to hatch. I would have preferred if the botflies and chunga palm were extinct, but unfortunately, I discovered on the internet they were alive and well.

My ancient ancestor also described the fast-growing plant life which reappeared a day or two after being cut. That was also verified by the Scots in the second expedition in late 1699, four months after the first expedition abandoned the colony. They found the newly built Fort St. Andrew over-grown by jungle. A bleak reminder that our trail would soon disappear. Alec might never find me.

It was almost sunset; dusk was gaining momentum. The early evening brought a chill to the air made worse by my damp skin and clothes. My legs ached. If we came upon a flat, dry surface, I planned to beg for a five-minute rest. But fallen tree trunks were water-logged, and rocks were either moss-covered or lay partially hidden under piles of saturated leaves.

The thought of rest was squelched by an ear-piercing cry. I froze, afraid to turn around. I envisioned a puma hidden in the brush, closing in on its prey. Us.

Max came from behind and stood by my side. Another lower-pitched scream, more of a whine. His hand touched my arm in a protective gesture. I didn't move away.

A few paces in front stood the blonde. Her back toward me, her body stiffened and then shuddered. Before I could ask what was wrong, her bound hands began to swing wildly at her head. Again, a sharp animal-like scream.

"Get it off me," the blonde screamed while she continued to thrash about.

The soldiers rushed over, pointed their guns, and yelled for us to get back.

"I've been bitten. Help!" Her pitiful pleas meant nothing to the soldiers. Their glares remained the same - menacing.

I forced my voice to stay calm, even toned. To lessen her fear, and my own, I spoke slowly. "What's…wrong? What…happened?"

When she turned, I had to swallow the bile lodged at the edge of my throat. The top of her head, her face, and chest were shrouded in a white cocoon of gossamer threads. A hairy eight-legged beast, with at least a six-inch span, gripped the remnants of its former home.

Perhaps it was instinct, or Max felt the need to protect a student in his charge. He sprang at the girl and swiped the spider, forcing it to tumble to the ground and scurry toward the safety of the brush. But Oscar was too quick. He snatched one hairy leg. The spider wriggled from side to side, trying to pull itself up and fend off the giant attacker.

Oscar roared at the insect's antics and offered his prize to the blonde who screamed again. The soldiers laughed when Oscar dropped the spider and stomped it with his boot. All that remained was a huge muddy imprint. The victor clenched his fist in the air, and the other soldiers nodded their approval and slapped the warrior's back. He gloated with his heightened stature, even though he'd done nothing but vanquish a weaker enemy and bully a defenseless young woman.

I turned my attention to the blonde. "Don't open your mouth." I pulled the sticky threads away from her face. "And hold your breath while I get this stuff from your nose." She pursed her lips and whimpered as my bound hands wiped around her nostrils. Some of the filaments were caught in her eyelashes. I gently tugged on the golden tipped hairs. The cobweb clung like glue to my fingers even after I wiped them on my pants.

Just then she shrieked.

I jumped back. "What is it?"

"Something's crawling."

"It's nothing," said Max. "Nothing's there. You're feeling pieces of the web Hanna is pulling off your hair. You're okay."

While I worked on the blonde, El Leon approached. I thought his lethal glare was for me, but it was squarely placed on Oscar. In a heated exchange, El Leon shoved Oscar several times while dressing down his lieutenant. At first, Oscar was defiant, argumentative, but then his demeanor changed from boastful champion to compliant underdog. Did this suggest El Leon mistrusted Oscar? Was he trying to gain the advantage with the other soldiers? Was this his first attempt at a coup? I met Max's eyes and gestured with mine. Did he notice this weakness within the unit?

To reinstate his authority, El Leon barked harshly to the blonde and pushed her along. The girl resisted by crumpling onto a soggy log and convulsing into sobs. The leader looked around at his men. His failure to control a young female wasn't helping and played right into Oscar's hands.

I had to do something. I preferred to be El Leon's prisoner. Oscar had a mean streak in him "Please, Your Majesty. Give us a minute." I sat down beside my patient. Wetness seeped through my pants. I wanted to put my arms around her, return the same comfort she gave me back at the site. "I know you're frightened, but I'm not sure how long I can hold them off," I whispered. "We need to go." She pulled back and stiffened again. I added, in what I hoped was a reassuring tone, "The spider is dead. Oscar killed it."

The girl's sobs quieted to a whimper. "I've been bitten. On my back."

I turned to El Leon. "If you untie our hands, I can help get her moving."

The leader motioned to Oscar, but the man hesitated. His gaze went to each of his compatriots as if considering if this was the right time to fight back and dethrone El Leon. I held my breath. It was a moment when the leadership of the unit was in crisis. But Oscar acquiesced and cut the shoelaces.

Relieved, I pulled back the collar of the blonde's khaki shirt baring one shoulder. What I saw made me recoil. Considering what we just experienced, the large purple-winged dragonfly tattooed on her pale skin was too real looking.

Max came over to examine the blonde, lightly touching the area where the spider bit into the flesh. It was turning an angry red. "Feels like a couple of raised punctures. Like a mosquito bite," he said.

"Its fangs dug into me."

"You'll be okay," said Max. "It's inflamed and will itch a wee bit, but in an hour the discomfort will lessen. Most spiders aren't poisonous."

Was Max just saying that to calm the girl down? I searched his eyes for the truth, but he turned away.

"I wish we had a first-aid kit. Hydrocortisone cream," I said.

"Let me see if I can find some clean water to cool the skin." Max looked around until he found some nearby funnel-shaped leaves filled with rainwater. He pulled a handkerchief out of a pocket, dipped it in the leaf, and did the same with several others until the cloth was soaked. He wrung the cloth so that the water dripped over the reddened skin. The blonde's shirt immediately darkened with streaks down her back. She must have felt some relief because she stopped crying.

"Thath enough. Get up. We need to move. It'll be dark thoon."

Oscar stepped to El Leon's side; the almost-coup forgotten. He raised his gun in support in case we didn't cooperate. Then, Oscar motioned angrily to the soldiers, and they resumed their places. The slaves picked up their machetes to continue their battle with the rainforest.

I eased the girl into line and laced my arm around her. Walking side-by-side would not last. The path quickly narrowed. Max fell in behind us. As we resumed our forward march, I looked up and saw there were spider web galaxies everywhere. Each was guarded by a similarly gruesome-looking beast.

"Hold my hand," I said. "Don't look up. Look straight ahead. We'll get through this together."

It was still dark when I heard an alarm clock. The buzzing was annoying. My hands swatted the air above and then around my head, searching for the snooze button. A few more moments of precious sleep was all I wanted. But then the introduction of a new sound, a relentless swishing and gurgling, even more maddening because of its unrelenting cadence. Forcing my eyes open, I bolted up. The new sound did not turn off.

Was this a nightmare or reality? I thought about pinching myself. No. I was awake. I was sure of that now. Like turning on a light switch, I realized the buzzing came from mosquitos and early-morning flies, and the rhythm of the swishing came from rows of visible whitecaps, breaking on the beach as they had for centuries.

I had no recollection of our coming to the coast last night. Maybe it was dark and there was no moonlight, or I was too tired to care. After the excitement of the blonde's encounter with the spider, the rest of the evening seemed like a fog; I was so tired. All I wanted to do was sleep.

But now, the last of the night sky gave way to the promise of a new day hinted at by splotches of silvery gray and smoky blue. Then, swaths of pink and coral, haphazardly added, turned the sky fiery red, the sea a blazing furnace. This reminded me of my Dad's corny sayings. He had one for any occasion, and this was his favorite from his days in the Navy: *Red sky at night, sailor's delight. Red sky in morning, sailor's warning.*

Sleeping next to me was Miranda, the girl I'd nicknamed 'the blonde.' Everyone knew that except her. How could she be so dense? Curled up, fetus-style, Miranda used a fallen log for a pillow. Several ants already hard at work crawled on her shoulder, another poked out of her hair. I wondered how many insects I attracted through the night.

I glanced over my shoulder. Max was within arm's reach, snoring away. I shuffled over to create a wider gap. I wanted no misunderstanding between us.

Like a jigsaw puzzle, this made no sense until the framework of yesterday's events took shape. Parts of the last twenty-four hours slowly surfaced: armed intruders, Hadrian beaten, hostages taken, Alec left behind. I reacted viscerally. My breathing quickened and the visible pulse on my wrist throbbed, which explained the pounding in my head.

Evaporating darkness revealed other sleeping forms, soldiers sprawled around us, in no apparent order. The one who was meant to be on guard, snuffled softly with a revolver in his hand, aimed at no one.

Anemic rays of morning sunshine now reached the outskirts of our camp. I scanned the tiny beach where my captors had chosen to spend the night. Again, I looked over at Max. No surprise he'd chosen to lie next to me instead of Miranda. Maybe I was wrong about him. Maybe I should have been grateful for the protection he willingly offered. But I knew he would take it as an invitation; one I had no intention of advancing. Instead, I found his constant nearness maddening, at times repulsive. The only other person who noticed this was Oscar. He snickered at my discomfort, like when Max reached for my hand or stood beside me. And now, Max was inches away. Another opportunity. One that became easier with Alec not around. It was better not to dwell on Max. It only made me miss Alec more.

My attention focused on the slaves, as they, too, began to stir. Not knowing their real names, I nicknamed them Old Man and Young Guy I could've just as easily called them Tall Guy and Short Man, because that was the extent of what I knew. We were warned not to talk to the two men. It wouldn't have mattered; I never heard them use English. In fact, they didn't speak, except to each other.

I wondered why they didn't try to escape. This was the perfect time of day. The sun wasn't fully up. The guard was still asleep. The beach was surrounded by jungle on one side and water on the other. The slaves could have easily slipped into the forest, hidden instantly. Instead, Young Guy lay there rubbing one foot with the other, whispering to his partner.

I thought about escaping all the time. This was a good time for us as well. Our hands were no longer bound. The waves would cover our footsteps. I could snatch the guard's gun before he knew what was happening. And if Young Guy and Old Man supported us, our numbers would equal the soldiers. But success was almost impossible. For one, El Leon was missing, and Oscar had just awakened. He sat up and stared at me with a cruel smirk.

Miranda stirred with little throaty snorts. At least she wasn't crying. The spider's bite peeked through the edge of her shirt. As Max predicted, the reddening had lessened.

With the sun completely above the horizon now, my stomach grumbled. Yesterday, we lived on a cup of sugared water and a bowl of rice peppered with insects which made the blonde turn green and get sick behind a tree. When Max shoveled handfuls of the rice into his mouth, mumbling something about protein in between swallows, I almost joined her. I refused to eat and hedged my bets on today's breakfast. But I had a feeling the morning meal was either going to be much of the same, or nothing.

Max opened his eyes. As if he had dreamt my thoughts, he whispered, "Make sure you eat this morning. If you don't want the bugs, take them out. But eat. I need your help," he gestured toward Miranda, "with her."

Except for the sleeping soldier with the gun, everyone was stirring. The slaves tended the fire and heated the water for the rice. Oscar wiped off his machete and picked up his gun. He tiptoed over to the sleeping guard and placed the barrel near the man's temple. Oscar bent over, put his finger to his lips, gesturing to the rest of us, and then he screamed, "Bang, bang," into the man's ear. The soldier jumped to his feet. Oscar and his friends laughed until tears streamed down their faces. The embarrassed soldier quickly bent over to pick up his weapon, and Oscar's fist landed on his face. Blood spurted from the man's nose and dripped down his chest. He checked the blood with his dirty T-shirt and spit something from his mouth.

El Leon returned in time to see what had occurred. He handed a string of fish to the slaves, walked over to Oscar, and propelled his fist into the man's mid-section. As Oscar bent forward, El Leon threw another fist into Oscar's face knocking him to the ground. He reached for his holster but stopped. He was no match for the big man, and especially not at this inopportune time when El Leon had the advantage. The other soldiers turned away, ignoring Oscar. His loss of stature doomed their support.

Work in the camp resumed. The slaves scaled and gutted the fresh fish, placing them in rows on a flat hot rock near the fire. When they began to sizzle, the air was filled with a delicious aroma. Meanwhile, the soldiers repacked their gear. It didn't take long. They traveled light.

Oscar was still on the ground. His eyes darted from man to man. For a moment, our eyes met, but he quickly looked away, back to his former comrades and then to the forest. When he thought no one was watching, he quietly maneuvered himself closer to the trees, and then disappeared. Perhaps he needed to relieve himself, more likely he wanted to lick his wounds. I hoped he was gone for good.

I sat next to Max while we ate. It wasn't because I wanted to, but I'd seen him talking to El Leon. I was curious.

"Max, what did you say to El Leon?"

He didn't answer at first. Just smiled.

"Did you find out where we're going?"

"Sort of, but His Majesty wasn't very forthcoming. Had his mind elsewhere. He got angry with me for bothering him. I thought he was going to slug me like he did Oscar. But finally, he said something about a Kuna village on the other side of the bay." He nodded in the direction he meant. "You can't see it from here. It's hidden in the jungle."

"Did he mention what's going to happen to us?"

"No, but I gather that whatever it is, will be in that village. Just a hunch. El Leon is in a hurry to get there."

Now it was my turn to offer some information. "Oscar's gone."

He chuckled. "Good riddance. One less."

"Do you think anyone will find us? Rescue us?" The word 'rescue' caused Miranda to turn around. Her eyes wide with hope.

"I doubt it. Finding anything or anyone in this jungle is nearly impossible."

I sighed heavily knowing he was right. Miranda looked the way I felt. Ready to burst into tears.

When we started moving again, El Leon stayed in the back of the line. Glancing over my shoulder, I watched him walk backward, gun raised, protecting the rear. Each time we stopped so the slaves could slice through more brush, El Leon walked up and down the line, scanning the jungle. He was taking no chances on a revengeful Oscar.

Miranda walked in front of me, her shoulders shaking like she had the hiccups, still reacting to Max's gloomy assessment. Tired of consoling, I ignored her. It distracted me from thinking.

I didn't agree with Max. I believed our chances had increased greatly in the last couple of hours. With Oscar gone there were four instead of five armed men. The slaves could join us or stay neutral at best. The weapons, however, remained a problem. We needed a way to solve that.

I continued to keep busy creating different scenarios. Alec could come to our rescue. Or maybe Oscar would return and kill El Leon. The combination of the two, although highly unlikely, would make our situation more favorable. But if I knew one thing about Max, he probably hoped for another solution – that we'd never see Oscar or Alec again.

CHAPTER SIX

THE KUNA

FIVE HUTS AND one dilapidated shed were lined up along the white sandy beach. The sparse number of dwellings could barely meet the definition of a hamlet, let alone a village. Interspersed among the homes were tall, elegant palms. Their fronds waved a lonely welcome in the offshore breeze.

Adjacent to the shore was a weather-beaten pier and, at the furthest end, a slatted outhouse. Many of the wooden slats were missing or broken, and the open door, hanging haphazardly on a loose hinge, framed a primitive toilet that was nothing more than a hole that emptied into the sea. Tied up on the pier, two *cayucos* bobbled on the incoming tide. Besides the swaying fronds, the waves were the only other movement.

The huts teetered on stilts intended to prevent flooding and to keep out snakes, pumas, and others of their ilk. A log ladder leaned against each hut. Its position was akin to a welcome mat. An upright ladder meant welcome; a ladder turned down signaled privacy. I knew this from reading Anna's three-hundred-year-old description of her visit to a Kuna village. It appeared that not much had changed.

The largest home was closest to the water and furthest from the outhouse. The fortunate residents had the best views and less stink. It had a flat thatched roof and lacked walls like the other huts, but the addition of a circular windowless room made it unusual. Either the add-on was needed for a growing family, or the homeowners wanted to show off their wealth and status.

At first glance, the sleepy village looked deserted until one large dog slinked out from behind the shed. It stopped in its tracks; a paw froze in mid-air. A chorus of growls rumbled between curled lips and bared fangs. The mongrel's warning came too late. In an instant, the dog barreled towards us, its jaws slashing the air, saliva spewing. Course hair spiked along the dog's spine, meant to make him appear bigger, more menacing.

I had only seconds to save myself. Running was useless. The sea, the jungle, or the outhouse offered no shelter. The dog would pounce before I even took a step.

But El Leon did not flinch. In fact, he took a step forward waving a wet bag in front of the oncoming beast. As if on cue, the dog stopped; its vicious barking succumbed to whimpers. The air filled with a terrible stench from fish that had been left out in the open too long. El Leon reached in the bag, grabbed a handful of leavings. The dog sniffed wildly and licked the offering while El Leon talked gently, as if the dog was a loving pet. When he walked toward the pier, the dog followed and waited impatiently while the remaining contents of the bag were upended. The animal slurped, gobbling down skin, fish heads, and bone.

With the excitement over, Fu and the others sat on nearby logs. I ran my dry tongue over parched lips as I watched them raise their flasks. I turned away, sat against a palm, and scanned the five huts instead. I had the uncanny feeling we were being watched. I wondered how long it would take for someone, the leader perhaps, to make an appearance. Would he be decked out in regal fashion: tattoos painted on his chest; a silver cone covering his penis; or a wide-brimmed plumed hat? Anna's description of Chief Andreas. Perhaps like Andreas, the present-day chief would be accompanied by naked armed guards and many wives.

I tried licking my lips again, but it only made me thirstier.

Then the most unexpected thing happened. I shook my head. Was I hallucinating? A symptom of dehydration? Alec appeared. He walked out from behind the shed. His hands were raised. The feeling of joy, relief, and terror overwhelmed me. I got up and took a few steps toward him. "Alec! What are you doing?"

"Stay back, Hanna."

"Are you crazy?"

"I said, stay back."

"Ah. Your boyfriend has come to save you. Isn't that nice? Superman saves the day." El Leon waved his gun and darkened his tone. "Get back, or I'll kill him."

I didn't know what to do. My heart pounded. Or was it breaking? One thing I knew for sure. Nothing was going to stand between me and Alec. Not El Leon's gun, or Oscar, or— Wait! Something was wrong. El Leon spoke without—

60

With no time to finish my thought. Max loomed in front of me and grabbed my arm. Furious, I twisted out of his grip, but when I tried to run, my legs felt heavy, like they were mired in quicksand. I could hardly move.

I snarled as Max reached out again, but I pulled back at the right moment and thwarted his attempt. Like El Leon, Max was not going to deny me Alec.

Then Hadrian emerged from the jungle. Miranda muffled an outburst, but Oscar grabbed her too. She was helpless like me.

Amidst the confusion, a dozen armed men dressed in khaki police uniforms appeared from behind the huts. Their guns were raised. A shot was fired. El Leon fell. A bullet had pierced his chest; blood curled around his medals. Fu and the others dropped their weapons and surrendered.

I rushed into Alec's arms. "Alec, Alec. I love you. I love you." I buried my face into his chest. He rubbed my back, but surprisingly he was silent. I pulled back, looked at him, and then glanced over at El Leon's body. "He's dead."

Alec nodded. "You know what medals worn on camouflage are called?"

"Huh? What are you talking about?"

He raised one eyebrow and smiled. "A target."

I continued to hold on to Alec, and smothered my hero with kisses, afraid he would vanish into thin air. And much to my dismay, he did.

Because that's not what happened. But I wish it had.

Something touched my shoulder; not once, but twice. It was Miranda. She whispered my name. I opened one eyelid, followed her pointed finger, and then rubbed both eyes to ensure I wasn't still dreaming. A young girl, twelve or thirteen years old, poked her head from behind a stair-log. Her full skirt partially hid another, much younger girl, who was pressing a rag doll against her chest while filling her mouth with her thumb. Both girls mirrored each other: brown skin, dark eyes, straight black hair, and blunt-cut bangs framing round faces. They wore white blouses with an intricate design. Besides age and height, the only difference between the two was a ring in the nose of the older one and a green parrot perched on top of her head.

61

Another child, a young boy, dressed in shorts and a T-shirt, peered out from a smaller hut. His appearance was the opposite of the girls: white alabaster skin and thick strawberry blond hair. This little guy looked like he had just stepped off a plane from Sweden. He jumped from the ladder and walked over to the girls, placing a protective arm around the youngest. His behavior said he belonged; his looks suggested otherwise.

"Albino," whispered Max. "They're common among the Kuna."

I was about to question him, but more residents emerged from the jungle, the huts, and even the shed. But it was the three who descended from the largest home that caught my attention. The first was a heavy-set man with greying hair and a jovial face, dressed in ordinary pants and shirt. He was followed by an ancient woman with a wrinkled face that almost hid her dark eyes. The man offered her no assistance. She needed none. The third was a young woman. Perhaps the man's daughter or wife. She was in the final stage of her pregnancy. She was also an albino.

Two folding chairs were brought forward. The man and old lady were seated on their thrones facing the community; the young woman stood behind. The man was introduced as Javier, the *Sahila,* the spiritual and political leader. No name was given for either woman. After a few minutes, the old lady nodded off.

Javier motioned to El Leon. "*Nuegambi use be noniki.* Welcome. You back so soon. How long you stay?" It was not surprising that Javier could converse in English. Adventure tourism in the national park was an income producer; the Kuna had learned enough to get by.

"One night. Maybe two. Until I get word from…Marcuth."

I noticed that El Leon carefully chose his words; trying to avoid those with an 's.' But when it couldn't be helped, he would slow his speech, placing emphasis on the syllable that didn't strangle his tongue.

The chief scowled; his tone had a dark edge. "Marcus? Bad man. I don't want him here." Javier gestured with his hand to indicate the village. "He cause trouble last time. We want no violence. No corruption."

"There will be none, Javier...onth I deliver the girl," he looked my way and continued, "we're out of here."

"I still don't like." Javier glowered. The old lady opened one eye. "Why this one go to Marcus?"

"American. They will pay much to get her back."

"I'm not an American," I said. "I'm Scottish. Check my passport." And then I realized the proof was back at camp.

"What about the other two?"

"They'll go to the…highetht bidder. The blonde will bring in many men." El Leon tried to touch Miranda's hair, but she recoiled.

"Chief, Sir," Max interrupted and continued before El Leon could stop him. "I'm Dr. Jones." He extended his hand and took a step toward Javier. "I could be of service to you and your—"

Fu Manchu lunged forward, threatening to shove the butt of his rifle into Max's mid-section.

Javier stood, ignored Max, and spoke to El Leon. "You pay me to stay here. Twenty US for food. Ten more for shed. For sleeping."

El Leon pulled out a wad of greenbacks. The old woman opened the other eye and smiled a toothless grin.

Max, Miranda, and I sat under a large palm. Our plates were filled with Red Snapper, sweet, mashed plantains, coconut flavored rice, tortillas, and hard-boiled eggs. Just the smell reminded me how hungry I was after a diet of rice, insects, and sugared water.

"We must do something before Marcus arrives," I whispered. "Who knows how many men he'll have. Our odds will be worse."

"Maybe someone will rescue us," said Miranda, and then she mumbled something about Hadrian. Did she have the same dream?

Miranda mentioning Hadrian didn't surprise me. They hung out together. She always volunteered for assignments that included him, especially when it took them away from camp, like digging a trench for a latrine. They would do anything to be alone, but I was grateful they signed up for the nasty chores.

"Maybe Alec," I offered.

"Don't count on it," said Max. "Your boyfriend doesn't have a clue where we are. And without a weapon…he's probably packed his bags and is on a plane back to Edinburgh. He didn't put up much of a fight when you were taken hostage."

Max was so predictable, so maddening. I knew he'd say something hurtful as soon as I mentioned Alec. I could've hit back and said that Alec loved me. And that I loved him. He would never leave without me. But what was the use? Max was bull-headed, self-centered, and wrong.

We ate our food in silence. But not for long. Young Guy moaned while squeezing and rubbing the toe box of his wet canvas sneakers. His mouth twisted in pain and deep furrows lined his forehead. Getting no relief, he angrily tore off his sneakers to attack his torment. He didn't have to go to that much trouble. The shoes were shredded. It would've been easier to access his foot by flipping over the rubbery sole.

His exposed feet were swollen and blistered, his toes black and blue. The blotchy skin on the bottom barely hung on the raw flesh. His feet were ghastly. Dead looking.

Old Guy whispered while fanning his nose. Both became agitated; the younger man shook his head. Tears flew off his cheeks. The argument ended, but the younger man didn't stop scratching.

"Looks like the poor lad has trench foot," said Max. "I can smell the sweet stench."

I smelled nothing but decomposing leaves and the acrid odor of unwashed bodies. Probably mine. "I thought trench foot was when your feet were constantly cold and wet. It's hot here."

"The problem is the dampness."

"He should put his feet closer to the fire, dry them out."

"Won't fix the problem. You must warm them gradually. It can take months to heal. He needs dry socks and shoes."

I remembered the first time I ever heard about the ailment. My eleventh-grade history teacher, Mr. Haas, had shared stories about his grandfather who fought in World War I. The elder Mr. Haas had lost three toes from nerve damage caused by trench foot. He was lucky. If the condition had been worse, like Young Guy's, amputation was the only remedy.

I stared at my feet, encased in socks and hiking shoes, still damp twenty-four hours after trudging through swamp and puddles.

"Don't worry. It doesn't happen overnight." Max hesitated while glancing at El Leon nursing a bottle of beer. "I have an idea. It's a long shot, but trench foot might be part of the plan."

"Huh?"

"Do me a favor. Say my name. Not Max. Dr. Jones." He leaned in close and squeezed my hand. "Loud enough so El Leon can hear you. Make it convincing, especially the doctor part." He must have read my hesitation as indecision, and added, "Do it now while there's time."

This was an easy request. I preferred a return to a formality between us. "Okay, here goes," I whispered. "Dr. Jones," I shouted, "hands off. Don't touch me again, Dr. Jones." My plea sounded corny, especially emphasizing his name.

Miranda stared at us, Fu smirked, and the younger slave stopped scratching.

Max edged closer to El Leon, whispered something, and both men chortled. The boss man nodded and returned to his beer. Max walked over to the slaves and conversed quietly. Then he got down on his haunches to inspect the younger man's feet.

"What was that all about?" I asked after Max returned.

"I wanted to talk to the slaves. I told El Leon I could help the younger guy. With his foot."

"How's that? You hold a degree in podiatry?"

He chuckled. "I am a doctor."

"You're a Ph.D. who unearths dead civilizations."

"Of course. But El Leon heard you call me Dr. Jones."

"Really? I thought he was a smart guy."

"He's a smart thug."

With more relief than Max would know, I said, "Okay. From now on, you're Dr. Jones again."

"The slaves are from China. They paid cash to some cutthroat guide who promised to take them to the States, but once they crossed the border, six months ago, from Columbia into the Darien Gap, they were robbed and sold off to El Leon."

"Do they speak English?"

"The older man does. He was a professor at a university in China. He learned English from a colleague so he could gain entrance into the US. His son needs medical attention quickly or he's going to lose one or both feet."

65

"Why'd they leave China?"

"The professor was put on a watch list after he made a few unfortunate remarks about the government. He knew it was only a matter of time before he'd be incarcerated in some Chinese gulag, so he fled with his family in a container ship, and that's how he ended up in Colombia. Shortly after they met up with the so-called guide, his wife was raped and murdered, and the daughter was sold off. She's probably dead, or worse."

The awfulness of his tale left me speechless. My mouth searched for a hint of moisture; I found only bitterness.

As the sun went down, Javier directed us to our accommodations: the shed. It had one small window, four weathered walls, and a door that seemed permanently ajar. When we entered, I immediately smelled the dampness of a dirt floor and heard critters scramble from their siesta. The lack of electricity meant no light; the darkness made the four hammocks appear ghoulish.

El Leon took no chances. He ordered Max's hands bound first. When it was the blonde's turn, and mine, Javier said, "Not them. They come with me."

El Leon frowned. "No. They…thay here."

Javier drew in a deep breath. He appeared taller. "My village. My law. They come."

"Not the American. Too valuable."

Javier hesitated. "I make deal. You keep blonde."

The soldiers snickered, and one grabbed his crotch. Miranda's eyes went wide. We all knew she had little value in terms of ransom for El Leon to care.

Javier didn't care either and gestured for me to follow him.

"I'm not going anywhere," I said. "Not without her," I stared directly at Javier. "You want me. She comes too."

I glowered at Javier. Miranda rushed over and grabbed my hand. El Leon hesitated, then nodded. I breathed again and wondered if I had made the right decision. Did I just trade one monster for another? Instead of entertaining El Leon and his soldiers, were we now facing an equally bad situation? Javier and his men?

When Miranda and I entered Javier's home, the young pregnant woman, who turned out to be his wife, met us. Her eyes were lowered, her hands rested on her enormous belly. Fearing the worst, I wondered if she knew the evil we were about to endure. Her pale face showed no sign of empathy, nor was there an offered hand, touch, or smile to show she understood.

"Go. Máyli, will show you." His voice proffered no redemption either.

We followed the young albino. Miranda tugged on my arm to slow our progression to what awaited us in the next room. I was desperate to think of something to say to Máyli, to save us, one woman to another, to appeal to her husband, beg him not to do this. But she moved quickly, and there was no time. In seconds, we were in the round section of the house, the part with no windows. Surprisingly, the air was cool, but little drops of sweat trickled down my spine.

It took a moment for my eyes to adjust. Seated in the center, haloed by the soft light of a lamp, was the wrinkled lady. She was surrounded by bolts of colored fabrics, tiny scissors, and spools of thread. Her hand held a threaded needle while a young girl, the one I saw with the parrot on her head, sat by her side. She had been speaking in an unfamiliar language to the girl; her voice trailed off when we entered.

On a low table in front of them was a square of orange fabric with an intricate design in green, yellow, red, black, and white. The old woman was showing her work to the girl. I noticed similar designs on the front and back of the midriff of Máyli's puffy-sleeved blouse. Her exposed arms had lesions on her bleached skin.

When the ancient lady looked up, Máyli introduced the woman. "Javier's grandmother. She is the oldest member of our community. Her knowledge of *mola* is unsurpassed."

Grandmother? *Mola*? I was confused. Then I realized I'd better speak, or my hesitancy might be considered rude. "Oh…I'm Hanna. And this is—"

"Miranda. Pleased to meet you." For the first time since our becoming hostages, the blonde smiled.

The old woman pointed to the floor. *"Nuegambi use be noniki."*

"My husband's grandmother says welcome. Please sit. She speaks Kuna only. I will interpret."

Relieved, I thanked her. "Should I re-introduce myself?"

"Yes. In Kuna. It will be considered great respect. Repeat my words. *An nuga* Hanna."

I did.

"An yeel itoe. An nuga Breseide,*"* said the woman.

"My husband's grandmother says she is happy to meet you. Her name is Breseide."

If eyes could twinkle, the old woman's did, and her face broke into a toothless grin doubling the number of wrinkles. Then she returned her attention to the fabric and her student.

"The young woman is my husband's grandmother's great-granddaughter. She is now of marriageable age, the right time to learn *mola*. It is a Kuna word to describe the stitched design worn on our clothing." She pointed to the appliquéd piece on her blouse.

Calloused fingers from decades of sewing touched my arm. Breseide was ready to begin. She brought out five squares of fabric, all the same size, but each a different color. She placed one on top of the other and then basted a geometric design that held them together. Following the stitches, she slit the top orange piece with a pair of tiny scissors to expose the next green layer and folded in the orange cloth and secured it with tiny invisible stitches. Once that was completed, she slit the green material, exposing black fabric, and tucked and sewed the green.

"This is an art Kuna have known for centuries. *Mola* is a reminder of long ago when we painted our skin."

"Tattoos?"

"Yes. When missionaries came, forced Kuna to wear clothes, so the body painting hidden."

"So, you now create the designs and put them on your garments? Um…blouse."

"Yes."

"My ancestor, Anna, came here as a colonist three hundred years ago. She described the tattoos of Kuna in her journal."

Breseide rethreaded her needle and handed the fabric to the young girl. With a bony finger she pointed to where the work should be continued, and then turned to speak to Máyli. I tried to grasp what was being said by the tone in the old woman's voice and the look in her eyes.

"My husband's grandmother wants you to know that Kuna once fought over *mola*. Long ago, when she was the wife of the *Sahila*, Kuna were at war with Panama government. They wanted Kuna to become more western and give up the *mola*. We refused and started a revolution. Kuna people won, and a treaty was signed that allowed us to remain separate – with our laws, council and, most importantly, with our traditions."

"What year was that?"

"1925."

I looked at Breseide. That would have made the old woman, who still earned her keep by creating artwork and teaching the next generation, at least one-hundred-years-old. Miranda looked surprised. She must have done the math, too.

"Why did you save us from the shed? Why bring us here?"

"My husband's grandmother wanted to meet you. An American. She wants to know why you left your country to come here."

I told them about Anna, the Scots' colony, and the journal with the entry about Filib's death. I added in the details about the archaeological dig and that we were looking for a specific artifact, the knife that Filib used to commit suicide. I told her as much as I could: where he probably died, and how the Indians tried to help.

Máyli translated for Breseide who shook her head and every so often would click her teeth. *"An nue gapie,"* said the old woman.

"My husband's grandmother is tired. She offers you rest in this house. No worries. You will be safe."

"How do I say, I am happy. Thank you."

"An yee ito dii. An nuedi."

I repeated the Kuna words. The young girl covered her giggles.

Máyli helped the old woman shuffle to a mattress in the corner of the room. The young girl lay next to her.

Miranda and I crawled onto a pallet in the opposite corner. It wasn't long before I heard the soft snoring of the others in the room. I thought the blonde had fallen asleep too, but I was wrong.

"Hanna? Are you awake?"

"Yes." Although I was tired, I had trouble sleeping. My thoughts were filled with the events of the day and Alec. Was he safe? Did he know where I was? Maybe he was waiting for the right moment. Like in my dream.

"I can't sleep either. I'm so scared."

"Maybe Breseide won't let Marcus take us away. I think she likes us."

There was silence from Miranda, until she rolled over, facing me. "I hope so, but I'm not counting on it." I heard her sniffle and then one or two whimpers. "My mother…Mum begged me not to come to Panama. She had a premonition that something terrible would happen. My plane would crash into the ocean. I'd get some jungle disease and would have to be airlifted out. Or some terrorist attack in the airport." I could feel her smile in the dark. "Well, she was almost right on the last one. Hadrian wanted me to join him. Said it would be a trip of a lifetime." She hesitated again. "I guess everyone understands…you know…we're together."

"Well, it's not a well-kept secret. I mean who volunteers to dig a latrine?"

It was good to hear her laugh. "Do you think we'll get out of here?"

"Yeah, I'm sure of it," I lied. "Hadrian and Alec are probably waiting for the right moment to raid the village."

"Hm. I guess you're right. I hope so. Thanks, Hanna. I wish I was strong. Like you."

Those were her last words before I heard breathy gulps of air. I thought about her mother's sense of foreboding. No surprise. The Scots were a superstitious lot, but that's what made them so interesting. I was glad that I could ease her fears, and maybe my own at the same time. Because one thing I knew for sure. Max was dead wrong. Alec would come - no matter what.

The next morning, Miranda and I awoke to the smell of cooked fish and coconut.

"Nuwedi, Good morning,*"* said Máyli balancing a full tray.

"Nuwedi," I repeated, carefully eyeing the food-laden bowls.

"I'm hungry," said Miranda, licking her lips.

"In my language we say, *An uku itoe."*

Miranda reproduced the odd sounding words.

Máyli placed the food on a low table and handed out wet towels while she explained the different parts of the meal. "The drink is *coco de agua,* coconut water. Very refreshing." Next, she pointed to a plate of uniformly cut mango and bananas. Then, she whisked away dripping lids unleashing clouds of aromatic steam. *"Oros,* rice, *madu,* bread, and *tilapia.* The *skungit,* lobster, is for my husband's grandmother. It is considered sacred food, forbidden for outsiders. I will bring you cups of *cabi."*

"No need to translate," said Miranda. "I'd love some coffee."

Máyli, Breseide, and the girl joined us for our meal. Except for the looming threat outside, we appeared like old friends, catching up on our lives. Máyli told us her child was due in a couple of weeks. She had miscarried twice but was hopeful since this babe was almost full term. I also learned that the Kuna couldn't run away from the problems of the twenty-first century. Rising seas threatened. In another year or two, they would have to move further inland.

"Why is this room different from the others?" I asked. "All the huts are open to the outside."

"My husband's grandmother and I reside here. The sun's glare bothers her, and I am a moon child. I must shield my skin and eyes." She gestured toward the scaly growth on her upper arm and the one at the base of her neck.

"Your eyes?"

"Yes. Like my skin, my eyes lack color. I am not blind, but my eyesight is poor." Máyli patted her engorged stomach. "I do not know if my child will be like me. But Kuna love our babies no matter what. Moon children are considered a special gift." She lowered her gaze and smiled as if it was nice to remember her specialness.

Our talk lasted for an hour; It was nice to forget the danger outside.

"I know it is soon time for you to leave. But my husband's grandmother would like to talk to you, Hanna."

"Leave? When…why are we going?" Miranda's little girl voice returned. She put an uneaten piece of mango back on the tray and wiped her wet fingers on her sleeve, forgetting the towel.

"My husband says Marcus will arrive soon. But first—"

Breseide tapped the arm of the young girl and pointed to the corner where they slept. The girl returned with a jewelry-like box and a rolled up *mola.* Breseide smiled broadly as she retrieved a small metal object from the box and showed it to me.

I'd only seen 17th century buttons from pictures. This one was likely from a man's jacket, used for decorative purposes or functionality. Women's clothes didn't have buttons; ribbons, pins, or laces served the same purpose.

"How did Breseide come by this?" I asked.

Máyli interpreted. "It has always been. For as long as my husband's grandmother can remember, she has owned this. It belonged to her many grandmothers. We are a female-centered community. Property is passed down through our mothers."

"Does Breseide have more?"

A wrinkled hand reached into the box again and several more buttons and two pox-faced musket balls filled her palm.

I couldn't believe the treasure. We were the third archaeological group to come to Caledonia and the prize was stored in a box.

"Tell Breseide she has many valuable items. People like me, and Miranda, archaeologists, have traveled thousands of miles to find what the Scots left behind."

Máyli spoke to Breseide. The old woman nodded.

"My husband's grandmother understands. She knows why you and your friends have come. She has seen others dig in the earth."

Breseide offered her toothless grin and held up a coin. It looked like the ones we had unearthed just two days ago. I returned her smile. The Kuna had been archaeologists long before the field became a scholarly pursuit.

The old woman returned the artifacts to the box. My sense told me it was time for Miranda and me to leave. I wanted to thank Breseide for her hospitality and asked for Máyli's help in translation. She taught me how to say goodbye, *Degi malo*.

But Breseide shook her head. She was not done. She pushed the rolled *mola* in my hands. Was she offering me a gift? *Molas* are considered a one-of-a-kind artwork and tourists pay a lot to get an original. This piece was not only authentic, but it also appeared old. I looked at Máyli for translation.

"My husband's grandmother wants you to open."

Breseide motioned for me to go on. Clicking her tongue impatiently.

The *mola* was stiff and heavy, made with many layers of material but that did not explain the weight.

I slowly unwound the cloth, round and round, until all that was left was the prize it uncovered. In the very center of the *mola* was an ancient *sgian-achlais*.

A Scottish dagger.

CHAPTER SEVEN
SWEET MARY MCBRIDE
NOVEMBER 15, 1708

I HAVE ALWAYS treasured this journal. It once belonged to Alain's mother, but with her passing, my father-in-law, Laird MacArthur, presented it to me as the new lady of Thistlestraith. Within these pages I have told the story of my marriage, our perilous journey to Caledonia, & how we came to the colony of New York. However, I must explain my long absence. I couldn't bear to write about the loss of Rebecca. No words can adequately describe my broken heart. But the healing effects of time, plus the joy that Sally has brought to my life, has renewed my courage to continue with my story.

We received another letter from Davina. This one was dated May 28, 1708. Alexandra was ill and missed two spring sailings. Davina assured us that our daughter's condition was not life-threatening. We concurred with Davina's decision to wait until Alexandra improved. After my own experience, even the strong & vigorous had no defense against ship's fever.

In the meantime, there were other reasons for delays. Davina hired, what she thought to be, a suitable traveling companion, a single woman of about twenty years. The woman backed out when she discovered she was with child. Another chaperone died in a tragic carriage accident. Now, the search is on for a third. Questionable conditions on board another New York bound vessel caused Davina to reconsider. Its cargo was mostly convicts & prisoners-of-war banished to the colonies. Another letter dated two months ago, described a scurrilous captain & his offer to protect Alexandra. My sister-in-law said his manner was forward & offensive. No female companion could protect Alexandra from the captain.

It has been more than a year since we first received Davina's proposal. Perhaps, it will be another year before we can embrace our daughter. Meanwhile, our life continues with unexpected twists & turns & reversals.

The position of a cartman did not require any proficiency or years of apprenticeship. Brute strength, not intelligence, was enough. But when cartmen had earned a reputation for boorish behavior and fist-fighting, a series of laws, enacted when New York was still New Amsterdam, regulated the workers and their fees and required them to accept liability. As a result, the cartmen gained respectability especially after earning the title of Freeman. The law included other requirements. Joris ignored all of it.

"Doesn't that worry you?" I asked Alain one evening. "Surely, someone in the Council or the local constable will suspect Joris."

"Aye, I used to be concerned when I first started working for the man. Maybe confused is the right word. I didn't understand what was going on. I always thought carters had to be licensed and own their cart and horse, with no debt. They worked for the city. There's no middleman allowed."

"But Joris owns the carts and horses and the men work for him."

"Aye. Now you understand my confusion. I've learned that things are not always what they seem. It works for Joris, though. He keeps the workers and the government happy."

"By breaking the law? Is that what you mean?" I asked.

"When the city awards a license, the cartman must do the city's bidding. One day a week, he must haul dirt…garbage…from householders to the city dump. At any time, if there's an emergency, the Council can demand his services and the use of his cart. The licensed cartmen cannot refuse. And fees must be whatever the law says it is. A lot of men don't like being told what to do, and some can't afford a horse and cart. Joris fills their need."

"How does he get away with it?"

"You know the numbers painted on the carts, the ones assigned by the city? Joris assigns one of his workers to paint numbers on his carts, to make them look authentic. As long as he doesn't hire an African or some vagrant, no one knows the difference."

"Someone will catch on."

"I don't think so. Joris pays the government plenty to look the other way. Every month, a well-dressed fellow comes by and has a private meeting with Joris. He doesn't stay long, but one time, when he was about to leave, Joris handed him a thick packet, and the visitor quickly stuffed it inside his jacket. They shook hands and the deal was done."

"What deal?"

"Protection. To carry on an illegal business."

"You'll get thrown in gaol."

"Not to worry, Lass. Joris has been operating this way long before I arrived. Besides, he owns the business. Not me."

Employment as a cartman was fortuitous for Alain and his employer. Once Joris realized that my husband was a skilled horseman, a knowledgeable farrier, and a capable manager, Alain was placed in charge of handling the workers. He was responsible for hiring and dismissing those who showed up late or drunk, insulted customers, or wagered on the speed of their nags. He worked to establish a good relationship with local merchants, the churches, and because Joris charged less than what was proscribed by law, his carts were chosen for lucrative building projects. Alain assigned loads, created a delivery schedule, and filled in when a worker was let go. He convinced Joris to pay the men fairly, and in turn, the unlawful cartmen worked harder and elevated the business to meet the needs of the burgeoning city. Joris Krol declared, discreetly of course, he had hired the best foreman in Manhattan; a major reason his wealth had tripled. In turn, Joris was generous with Alain and offered us a small house behind his. But Caterina, Mr. Krol's wife whined bitterly and blamed her husband's generosity for her frugal household budget. This was the reason, she claimed, she couldn't afford to dress in laces and fine woolen fabrics or manage a proper home for an up-and-coming businessman. A second maid, a gardener, or even better, the purchase of a house slave like Dr.

Smith's, would be an improvement. That, she believed, would secure her place in society. Catarina did not abide by the old Dutch tradition: make a fortune, but do not flaunt it.

Alain's close relationship with his boss also increased his contact with Catarina. At first, she rarely visited her husband's shop, but once Alain took over management, she found excuses to do so, especially when Joris was out of town. On other occasions, Catarina demanded my husband personally deliver a case of wine or a newly ordered crate of dishes from London. Any of the cartmen could have done the job, but she insisted that only Alain treated her packages with care.

He complained about Catarina's forwardness: a brush of her hand against his or one that boldly touched his leg. When Alain stepped back, she'd apologize as if it was an accident. Once, she pretended a dizzy spell. I inadvertently witnessed the scene when she swooned right into his arms. Forced to keep the lady from falling, he promptly deposited her on a barrel near the horse shed and asked one of the other men to keep an eye on her. Catarina was not pleased.

"She was up to her old tricks today," said Alain as he sat at our table while I stirred the contents in the stew pot. "Catarina came into the shop, leaned over the counter, revealing what only her husband should see."

"Were you tempted?" I chuckled, glancing at my own décolletage, covered with a scarf tucked around the neckline.

"I'm serious, Lass. How would it look if Joris walked into the shop, just as his wife was pouring out her…um…?" His fingers fluttered toward my chest. "Or purposely positioned herself so she could rub against my leg? She would not hesitate to place the blame on my shoulders. That I'm sure of. Sometimes I think she orders baubles on purpose so she can come to the shop or demand delivery. I bet she orchestrates her husband's absences. The woman's insufferable. The boss deserves better."

"Maybe you should tell Joris. Prudently, of course."

"How can I? How do I tell my benefactor about his wife's unseemly behavior? A cuckolded husband would do anything not to be the subject of ridicule. He would turn us out, and then what? We need the income, and now with Alexandra coming, we need another room. Just the other day, Joris promised me a bigger house if he wins a hauling contract from Trinity Church."

I looked around at our tiny but comfortable home built in the Old Dutch style which included separate bedchambers, away from the cooking and eating area. Our present arrangement, with one sleeping quarter was sufficient for now, but it would improve if we had two. But contracts take time, and nothing came of Joris' offer. Catarina continued to place herself in front of Alain.

One day, our fortune changed. Joris was kicked in the head by a horse.

The funeral was well attended. Alain's boss had a large family, and he was known by many. Forty years ago, Joris had arrived in New York with five siblings who were now scattered in all directions. One brother lived near Albany; another owned a tavern in Brooklyn. A younger brother was a successful tobacco planter up north along the river. One sister married well. Her success was mirrored in the richness of her clothes, the gems on her fingers, and the height of her hair. Catarina hated her sister-in-law, ignoring the woman the moment she arrived. There was one other sister the family never acknowledged. It was rumored that the madam owned a bawdy house. Catarina could not risk her social standing, although it had gone down a peg or two. Widowhood often turned women into social outcasts.

When Joris' son and his wife arrived, Catarina spoke a few obligatory words of welcome and left to speak to others. Catarina didn't trust her son who inherited the family business, so she was practical when necessary, and thus pretended graciousness. She needed to protect her future.

Alain and I attended the service and interment at Trinity Church. Catarina and Joris were Dutch, but not too Dutch. Catarina insisted her husband's remains be interred in the cemetery controlled by the elites of the Church of England. Rather than show remorse over the loss of her husband, Catarina could not restrain her tongue. She boasted about the choice burial plot near other wealthy departed and the expense of her husband's double-sided headstone. She claimed it would serve as a beacon, a reminder of a worthy man who was responsible for the prosperity of Manhattan. Her son knew better than to restrict the funds for such a showing.

Alain continued managing the cartmen, and the business thrived as if Joris still sat at his desk, poring over the accounts. Occasionally the new owner, Joris' son, would come unannounced to the shop, but he always seemed genuinely pleased, and let Alain run the business. The son was more than happy to leave it that way.

Despite all the ugly words and warnings Catarina said about her son, he did not throw her out of her home, but provided a generous pension every month so she could live in respectable widowhood. Much to Alain's delight, the seduction became less fervent, and then ceased. He had no idea why.

I joked with Alain that maybe Joris' ghost had returned and threatened his wife with nightly haunts unless she behaved. Or maybe her son was aghast at his mother's rudeness at the funeral and hinted he would reduce her stipend. I had no proof what prompted the change for the better, until an incident occurred a few weeks later.

When I walked around the city, either to market, to meet with Deborah Emmanuel, or to the shop where Alain worked, I avoided the street where The Pearl was located. Today, it couldn't be helped. A wagon filled with chipped stone overturned blocking my usual route which forced me to pass The Pearl. I should have thought better, but my mind was not on Bertram White or his tavern. We had received another letter from Davina, and I was anxious to share it with Alain.

From the depths of the inn came loud singing and the constant banging of a drum. A chorus of male voices belted out a vulgar tune, one I'd heard before when Alain and I roomed at the inn. One singer would start off with a four-line verse, followed by a refrain sung by all. Then a volunteer would create a new verse followed by the same response. This was accompanied by singers banging on the table with their fists or empty mugs to compliment the lustiness of the song. Today, the beating of a drum was added, although it never kept pace with the rhythm. I was sure the participants were so drunk they would not recognize their own mother if she walked through the front door, naked.

Sweet Mary McBride's legs a spreadin'
A lass who's in need of my beddin'
She swishes and sways, says "ooh" as we lay,
Sweet Bonnie's dreamin' o' weddin' day.

Fill-er up, fill-er up, fill another cup,
Fill-er up, fill-er up, I need another cup.

Sweet Mary McBride's gone asea,
No happier captain can there be.
She swishes and sways, says ooh as they lay,
Sweet Bonnie's wishin' o' weddin' day.

Fill-er up, fill-er up, fill another cup,
Fill-er up, fill-er up, I need another cup.

Just as I tried to hurry by, Bertram White stomped out the door. "Ah, Mrs. MacArthur. Do you miss me and my fine establishment? Come back for a visit, eh?" As he spoke, he staggered closer.

I made the best of a bad situation. "Good day, Mr. White. I'm on my way to see my husband." I hoped that by mentioning Alain, the menace would not be so forward. I was wrong.

"Really? Your husband's shop is not on this street. Perhaps, you're needin' somethin' eh?" His croaky chuckle was ominous. "Come inside. You know I'm still lookin' for someone to wash my laundry." He leaned closer as he offered employment with a wink. His fiery breath almost singed my hair when he reached out to touch me. "These lovely hands would serve me well, eh?"

"I must be on my way. My husband—"

"I'm not interested in your husband." His fingers circled my wrist, but before his grip tightened, I twisted my arm and stepped back. He went for my arm again, but this time he was faster and stronger, and before I knew it, I was being pulled inside the tavern.

I looked around for something to fight back with or someone who would help me. But the young boy who swept the floors and cleared the tables couldn't risk his boss's anger, and it was too early in the day for the cook. The singers in the rear of The Pearl, surrounded by darkness, were

80

too loyal to Bertram. Besides, none were sober enough. Instead, they cheered Bert's conquest.

My only course was to fight back, kick the man in the shins like I once did to my brother. But my skirts wrapped around my legs, and instead, I tripped and fell. My attempt to fight angered Bert, and he renewed his effort to drag me toward the stairs.

"You bastard. Let me go."

Bert responded with another grisly chuckle.

The singers, stopped mid-verse, and came to witness the entertainment. One-eyed Gallumpus gestured to help his friend. Another suggested that Bert just carry me off and be quick about it. A fourth was about to speak but then passed out, crashing from a table, to a bench, to the floor.

The last man, the drummer, placed his instrument down and walked over. "Now Bert. Don't harm the lady. She's a pretty wee thin'. Treat her nice-like, and maybe she'll come around tae yere way o' thinkin'."

"Get back to your drummin'." Then he screamed to his young helper. "Fill Davey's tankard, and keep it filled 'til I return." Bert hauled me to the first step.

The drummer placed a hand on Bert's shoulder. "Let the lady go. I ken her husband. He won't like ye treatin' her like this."

I glanced over at the man. The bottom half of his face was covered with a trimmed gray beard and his hair was neatly pulled back into a leather thong. He looked out of place with his fine clothes and felt hat.

"Her husband won't mind sharin' her," growled Bert. "Now get back to your drinkin' or get the hell outta here."

"I canna do that. My conscience would bother me for the rest o' me days, havin' a good time while the lady's in distress."

"I don't give a horse's ass about your conscience."

All at once, two things happened. Bert pulled me harder up another two steps, and then he slumped on top of me. Was he going to rape me in front of everyone? But his body was heavy, lifeless. Someone had knocked him out. Quickly, I untangled myself and headed for the door while the other men rushed in to check on their friend.

The drummer said, "Let 'im be. He needs tae sleep it off." Then he turned to me, took off his hat, and in a familiar voice said, "Mrs. MacArthur, we meet again."

The drummer had familiar squinty eyes, surrounded by deep furrows, and a grin I knew all too well.

Cook Davey Innes had reentered my life.

CHAPTER EIGHT
A VERRA ELIGIBLE BACHELOR

PHYSICALLY, I WASN'T hurt. However, my fingers trembled, and my teeth chattered uncontrollably, as if I was standing in the middle of a snowstorm. At the same time, my shift was soaked. I tried to regain my dignity, but the events that led up to the assault, played in my mind. I blamed myself for my predicament by foolishly walking by The Pearl instead of looking for a safer route, even if it would have taken me longer. My guilt turned to rage and brought on tears I didn't want. They were a sign of weakness, and that, I was convinced, was the flaw that had led to my attack. I wished more than anything for a dirk, one like Filib's. I imagined thrusting it deep into Bertram's throat, twisting it, draining my enemy's life blood. I felt satisfaction in his abstract suffering.

I vowed that Alain would never learn what transpired. The Highlander in him, with his deep-rooted sense of salvaging my honor, would chase my attacker to the ends of the Earth until he placed Bertram White's remains at my feet. I would not risk Alain's life. I had not forgotten what happened to Harley back in Scotland.

I had almost forgotten Mr. Innes when his hand gripped my arm, steadying me. A look of concern in his face, eyes narrowed, the usual smile, now grim. I fought to regain my composure. Weakness was a curse.

"Mr. Innes, what in the world? You are the last—"

The former cook of the *St. Andrew* and the *Caledonia* led me away from the inn's doorway and an unconscious Bertram White and the crowd that had gathered. I noticed two middle-aged matrons, holding tightly onto their market baskets while glaring at my attachment to Mr. Innes One stiffened and whispered behind a raised hand to her companion; the other tittered mockingly. I imagined they thought me a temptress or worse, deserving the assault, for I was a woman walking the streets unescorted, tempting the worst of men.

"Let's be away from this place," said Mr. Innes as he eyed the two. "We can get reacquainted without these annoyin' gnats nosin' intae our business." His description of the two women was said in a loud voice. Then he growled at the one who laughed. She quickly picked up her skirts and rushed off, leaving the other alone and friendless.

Innes and I hurried along the busy street, heading in the direction of the pier and the East River. Others going in the same direction, or the opposite, stepped aside to let us pass. Men tipped their hats to acknowledge Mr. Innes. I wondered about this unusual respectability, and then I noticed his coat and breeches were made of fine wool. His hose was silk, the silver buckles on his leather shoes sparkled, and a large gemstone set in precious metal encircled the middle finger of his right hand.

I had no idea where Mr. Innes was taking me until we ducked into a dark coffeehouse, the perfect place for conversation and to catch my breath. Several customers seated at nearby tables nodded toward Innes. Apparently, he was well-known; I wondered why I had not bumped into him before today. He gestured toward an empty table in the rear. Being the furthest from the fireplace and the other occupied tables, it offered the most privacy.

The owner, wearing a grease-stained apron, welcomed us effusively. From one hand dangled coffee mugs hooked on his fingers. In the other, he carried a pot of coffee. As part of the entertainment, he placed one mug on the table and held the pot high in the air, directing a fountain of steaming brown liquid into it. After the second was filled, the owner accepted Mr. Innes's gratitude and looked around for his young server. He grumbled at the boy's tardiness even after a plate of warm biscuits, a buttered loaf, and a pot of jam were set on the table. The lad sped away and returned with a cone of hardened sugar. With a knife, he deftly chiseled a portion into chunks. The coffee, strong and bitter, needed an extra lump of sweetness. The warm mug felt comforting. That and time lessened my trembling.

The owner and his helper retreated as their tasks were completed, creating an atmosphere of privacy and seclusion. Every so often, one of them eyed our table, to see if we needed their service. It appeared Mr. Innes had developed a rapport reserved for the rich.

At first, there was silence between us - two old friends. I was grateful for the peace and serenity and the old familiarity of Mr. Innes' companionship. Then, slowly, in between sips, I shared all that had happened after we said goodbye on the deck of the *Caledonia*. Once I concluded my story, our cups were promptly refilled, and more warm biscuits appeared. My friend added sugar to his mug, and while he waited for his coffee to cool, the master storyteller began his tale.

"Don't start yere bleatin'. I canna stand tae hear a female cry. I have no choice. Don't you see? I've got tae get off this death trap." Cook Innes pleaded with the nanny goat he had stolen in Port Royal so the ship's crew and passengers could have milk with their porridge. "I'm sorry I canna take ye with me, ye make tae much o' a racket."

With a pat on the goat's head and a tickle under her goatee, Cook Innes grabbed his woolen cap, the one which brought him luck, a small bag of hard biscuits, a flask of whisky, and silently slipped into the streets of Manhattan, the night before the *Caledonia* was to sail to Scotland. Three other crew members deserted the same night, but each went a different way. The cook preferred to be alone.

The next day, Innes still wasn't sure where to go. He knew no one, unless he counted the middle-aged spinster, he encountered on the streets of New York shortly after the ship docked. Gerta had just emerged from a shop, her market basket full, when a runaway horse harnessed to an empty cart came close to trampling her. The unattractive woman ended up flat on her back, the contents of her basket tossed everywhere. Quickly, Innes ran to her side and inquired about her injuries. Seeing she was more shaken then hurt, he helped her to her feet and retrieved her lost goods. Innes surprised himself by behaving like a perfect gentleman and not taking advantage of the situation. He didn't have to. Gerta did. She complained about feeling weak, on the verge of fainting, so she could hold onto Innes' hand longer than necessary. Twice she had to apologize when she leaned her body into his.

Innes wasn't oblivious to Gerta's overtures. He was experienced in the ways of women. But he was also interested, especially when she mentioned her wealthy father and the large farm he owned north of Manhattan. Innes had considered farming, and Gerta could be the answer. All was going well between the two until a much younger and much prettier sister showed up. Gerta, realizing a change in Innes' attention, backed away, flung a few ripe tomatoes at his head, and walked out of his life, never caring to see him again.

But Cook Innes couldn't forget Gerta, especially her rich father and the farm. It didn't help matters that the vision of the younger sister remained and reignited his lust for a wife and a litter of children. If he couldn't have one sister, he'd take the other. Even Mrs. MacArthur had said he would make a wonderful father. Smiling at the pleasant memory, he imagined sitting in front of a cozy fireplace, in his very own home, surrounded by a wife preparing the evening meal, while he bounced a child on each knee, regaling them with his tales of sea life. Of course, he would have to clean up the stories a bit, and tone down the language and the discrepancies so as not to subvert young minds. But he wanted his offspring to think of their father as a heroic seaman, like a sailor on the *Argo,* accompanying Jason on his many quests. Not a common cook.

If his dream was to succeed, he first needed to make amends with Gerta, rekindle her affections, and somehow get to the sister. That would require a pretty bauble or two.

Innes inquired about a position with Mr. Joris Krol, the proprietor of a newly organized hauling concern who was looking for a certain type of worker. With his lucky cap in hand, Mr. Innes found Joris Krol seated behind his desk, peering over his glasses, immersed in his books. When Innes proudly offered his services, he was stunned by the response.

"I'm not sure carting will suit you. I'm looking for men, stout workers who can load and unload carts quickly and control the horses pulling heavy shipments." Joris said this while his eyes evaluated Innes' physique. "You seem a bit old for that sort of thing."

Innes' looked up as if he could see the gray hairs standing at attention. "Mr. Krol, sir. I'm a bit younger, and a helluva lot more robust than I look." He apologized when he realized his poor choice of words. "Sorry, sir. But ye see, gray hair on a young head runs in my family. My da turned white before he was twenty but was still strong enough tae work on the ships all his life. Strong as a bull in more ways than one," he said with a wink, "if ye get my meanin'. And my older brother turned gray by the time he was thirteen. Even my mum—"

"Where did you say you worked last?"

"I didn't, sir. I sailed on a merchant ship. Ship's cook, I was."

Joris looked up from his writing.

Innes stopped talking, waited for a response, and then realized he had better fill the void with words. "Not many believe cooks have tae do lots o' difficult chores and heavy liftin'. The big iron pots can weigh hundreds, maybe thousands o' pounds, filled tae the brim with steamin' porridge, and the captain demandin' his breakfast be brought tae the deck, weather permittin'. The captain liked tae take in the fresh air while he ate. The pot was heavy, and none o' the sailors could lift it. But tae me it was as light and sweet as a virgin bein' carried tae her weddin' bed." Innes eyed Mr. Krol to see if he was captivated by the story.

"Why are you no longer with the ship?"

"Well, truth be told, sir, the captain hated my cookin'. He said I made the lumpiest porridge he'd ever tasted. And he tired of spendin' his days in the head and leavin' the bridge in the hands o' the first mate. He detested the man and thought me and the first mate were in some kind o' alliance tae keep the captain busy. Ye know, with his business." Innes pinched his nose to make sure Joris understood his meaning. "Then one night, the captain awakens, a hollerin' and a screamin'. The whole crew came a runnin' onto the deck, wonderin' if the devil himself had come aboard. All of a sudden, the captain's dashin' up the ladder, and at the same time fiddlin' with his fly, and pullin' at his pants. He's yellin' my name over and over as if I was a whore he had just enjoyed." For effect, Innes stopped momentarily, shook his head, and tsked in sympathy for the afflicted captain.

Joris had stopped writing long ago. His eyes rested squarely on the storyteller.

In a conciliatory tone, Innes asked, "I could stop if ye like, unless ye want tae hear the sad endin' o' this tale?"

"Yes, go on."

Innes sighed deeply. "I'm sad tae say the poor captain didn't get tae the head in time. He crapped so bad, the seam in his pants burst, leavin' the man naked like the day he was born." Innes stopped his tale to let the far-fetched facts take their usual effect.

Joris swallowed hard. "Then, what happened?"

"Well, as ye'd expect, the captain was hoppin' mad. I don't blame him, even after he threw me into the brig and banished me from his ship the minute we arrived at our next port. The last image I had o' the man was him standin' on the bridge with a blanket wrapped around his waist held up by a cinched belt. His final words tae me…I'm ashamed tae repeat…but he suggested I sign on tae cook for the Frenchies."

Joris let out a throaty chuckle. "That's quite a tale you tell. All right. I guess I'll try you out for a week and we'll see how you manage." He scratched his chin whiskers and returned his attention to the papers on his desk. "At least you won't be cooking," he mumbled to himself.

Innes worked for Joris Krol for six months, and once he earned enough, he traveled north and found Gerta. He was more than delighted with the size and richness of the farm and that nothing had changed; Gerta was still unmarried and her appearance had not improved. The former cartman begged forgiveness, and Gerta gladly accepted the few gifts he purchased.

It didn't take long for Innes to learn that the prettier sibling had wed the month before and had moved to Albany. Now, Gerta was the only daughter still living under her father's roof. Her plain broad face and severely crossed eyes meant that unless Innes proposed, she'd never find a suitor. Therefore, he swallowed his pride and quickly found himself a married man.

Farming was not what Innes thought it would be. The work was tedious and boring, the hours long. It was nowhere near the excitement of going to sea and discovering new and exotic islands along with the welcoming charms of the local women. At least that's what he remembered.

Gerta worked hard to be an attentive wife, an able cook, and a caring partner. But she could not make up for his disappointment as a landsman. It didn't help that the newlyweds lived with Gerta's father, so they were rarely alone except when the old man checked on the livestock each evening before retiring. It was then that Innes tried to converse with Gerta, but his wife's cross-eyed gaze unnerved him. Her eyes seemed to be everywhere except on him.

The coffeehouse owner returned with another plate of sliced fruit cake and a fresh pot of coffee.

"I stayed with Gerta for five years. We had no children, and her father's health failed. She spent all her time takin' care o' him. Feedin' him, wipin' the spittle, and helpin' him at the pot. He became the child we never had, and I felt I was in the way. So, one mornin' I left. For good."

"How could you? Your wife needed you?"

"I ken it sounds bad, but Gerta actually told me tae go. She said I'd be happier on my own. I asked if she was sure, but her screamin' convinced me. I begged her tae let me stay, but she forced me out the door."

I wasn't sure about the truthfulness of his story. Davey Innes could tell the biggest lie with the straightest face.

"Sometimes thin's just work out for the best. Maybe Gerta found some happiness, carin' for her father and not bothered by the likes o' me. At least I gave her respectability – being a married woman and all. I like tae think that." Mr. Innes pulled out a pure white handkerchief from an inside pocket and wiped tears from dry eyes. "But now I have another chance at happiness. I've found someone else. Someone who'll warm these old bones."

"That's bigamy. You're still married to Gerta. You'll be thrown in gaol."

"Nah. Dear Gerta met her Maker a year ago, in the springtime. Luckily, it was during the thaw, a month after her father." Innes took a deep breath before announcing the most important part of the story. "I inherited the house, the land, and a box filled with silver coins." A smile grew on my friend's face, wrinkling the skin around his eyes. Slowly, he folded the handkerchief and replaced it in his pocket. "And ye know what that makes me? A verra eligible bachelor."

CHAPTER NINE
FEBRUARY 1709
BETROTHED

CATARINA TAPPED HER foot and took short, shallow breaths. "Joris was a fool. He may have promised you…many things. A larger home will not, if I have any say in the matter, be one of them. My husband was generous enough with you. And your wife."

I couldn't see Alain's face from where I stood, eavesdropping outside the cartmen shop, I imagined him clenching his fists and his scar flaring while straining to keep his voice even toned but rich with sarcasm. "Mrs. Rapalje, how may I help you on this bright, cheerful day?"

"Are you listening to me? I'm not here to discuss the sunshine or how jolly I am."

I almost giggled. Obviously, Alain hadn't bothered to look out the window. Raindrops were spitting on my hood, and the thick cloud cover turned everything gray and dreary, much like the difficult woman demanding my husband's attention.

I wondered what prompted Catarina's foul mood. It might have been a stoop not cleaned to her liking or a delayed order of a set of new silver teaspoons from Master Myers.

"Mr. MacArthur," she said in a low voice. "On more than one occasion, I have tried to be pleasant to you. I showed interest in your accomplishments and even complimented your efforts to Joris. Instead of showing your gratitude, you rebuffed me like I was some common woman." In a more seductive tone, she added, "I could have made your life so much better. If you'd only agreed—"

"Mrs. Rapalje, I am a married man. I gave Anna—"

"Yes, yes, yes. We all said those silly little words. God won't strike you dead if you don't keep your end of the bargain. In the end, that little strumpet you bedded—"

"I'll not have you disparage my wife."

"Oh, you mean the Jewess? You think I don't know your Anna's a Jew?"

"Which God she prays to is none of your damn business."

"True, but that doesn't mean I have to keep you on and allow your family to live in a home I own. Besides, Joris overpaid you. I told him so, right before he died." Her tirade paused. I imagined her grinning from ear to ear while flakes of face powder drifted onto her dress. "Most men of your caliber would have gladly accepted my offer. You could have had anything you wanted, including a larger home."

Now my fists clenched. My nails dug into my palms.

"I always appreciated Mr. Krol's kindness, but I am no thief. I worked hard for your late husband and will continue to do so for your son. I've earned every benefit. Nothing was taken or given without merit. I've toiled, without complaint, to ensure this business was a success." I heard him draw a deep breath. "But I will not soil his memory with your indecent suggestion, nor will I repudiate the promise I made to the woman I love." Another hesitation followed by a loud thud. "Now get your—"

"Alain," I interrupted as I entered the shop. The two adversaries were feet apart. "I was on my way to market," I lied. "You won't believe who I met." From the corner of my eye, I saw Catarina's glare.

"Hmph." Catarina skirts swished, forcing clumps of dust to escape from under a cabinet. "Mr. MacArthur, my son may stop by today. Tell him I have an urgent matter to discuss." Then, as if she remembered the earlier discussion, she added after clearing her throat. "If this was my shop, and I was the boss, you would be lucky to be employed as a cartman."

"But it isn't, Mother. The business is mine. Mr. MacArthur will continue to work for me." Catarina's son appeared at the front door. His sleeves were rolled up and strands of light brown hair had worked free from a thong. "He has earned my gratitude. And you should extend yours as well."

Catarina swallowed hard and patted the edges on her lace cap to ensure the bald spot was concealed. At first, she appeared startled by her son's retort, but then straightened her back and plumped her skirts. "Joris could have chosen a more competent manager. If your dear father would have listened." Then she turned abruptly to her son. "Now you hear me out, you good-for...I helped your father with this business since the day you were born. It's more than just hiring the workers. I know who to pay—" She stopped, and like a changing tide, her demeanor and tone softened and became contrite. "I know a gentleman, someone with a sterling reputation and knowledge about almost everything. He's successful, rich in fact, and doesn't need the income. He offered to work for us...for me. He's beholden for my many kindnesses. All I have to do is ask." Her beady-eyed stare turned to Alain. "He doesn't need a house."

I wondered if Alain and Mr. Krol were thinking the same thing I was. Who was this paragon? Someone she met at church? Catarina rarely attended, although she could have used a lesson about humility and covetousness. Maybe a friend introduced her and gave a glowing recommendation. That couldn't be it. Catarina had no friends.

"Mother, it is because of Mr. MacArthur that we are doing so well. You have two maids and a gardener in your employ. If you want a slave, we can see to that."

Joris' son may have only come to the shop once or twice a month but appreciated a healthy balance sheet. "Did you know that most merchants seek us out? We have earned a reputation for dependability. Our men don't get into drunken brawls, and if they do, they are let go immediately. The next time Trinity Church, or any church for that matter, needs hauling done, the lucrative contract comes here. The profits pay for your dresses, your powders, and the fine roof over your head. We...You have Mr. MacArthur to thank."

For a moment Catarina seemed at a loss for words. She fiddled absentmindedly with her ringed fingers. "Well...my dear friend...he—"

"Mother, why are you really here? I don't mean to be rude. Mr. MacArthur and I have accounts to work on. There's a large shipment that needs scheduling, and Peggy is expecting me home by the weekend."

"Your wife can wait. I bet she would be horrified to hear her husband talk to his mother in such a manner. And since you are wondering, I came to check on my order. I'm expecting new fabric and laces. My dressmaker grows impatient. Have you forgotten your mother's needs?"

For the first time, the younger Mr. Krol noticed my presence. I had come at the wrong time. Caught in the middle of a family feud, my cheeks warmed and mirrored his red ones. Remembering Davina's letter, I plunged my hand into my pocket and felt comforted by the folded pages.

"Mother, I will keep an eye out for your shipment," Mr. Krol said more contritely. "As soon as it arrives, I promise, I will deliver it to you myself. Shall I have one of the men see you home?"

"No. That won't be necessary. Besides, I'm late to meet with my friend." And with great emphasis on her final words, Catarina walked out the door while tossing out one more clue: "He shall walk me home."

Minutes later, Mr. Krol grabbed his snuff-colored coat, black felt hat, and bolted out the door.

Alone at last, Alain reached for my arm and pulled me gently toward him while he leaned against his desk. He kissed my wrist, my neck, and my eyelids. "Does my touch still make you tremble? After all these years?"

I said nothing but leaned against his solidness as my answer. Grateful for our few minutes of privacy, I was mindful that at any moment, someone could burst through the door with news of a busted wheel or a runaway horse.

"I miss you, lass." He lifted my chin so my eyes would meet his.

"Alain. I heard what you and Catarina were talking about."

He looked at me, and the old scar blazed. "I won't let that...woman...talk like that about you."

"You mean that I'm a Jew?"

"No. Yes. You know what I mean. Her disparaging comments. She knows how to get under my skin."

"She's not the only one in Manhattan who feels that way. The first Jews in Manhattan were almost expelled." I could have gone on and, like my father, talked about the sad history of my family. But this was not the place.

"I'm afraid I might be the cause for Catarina knowing your identity. I mentioned it to Joris once. I wasn't thinking."

"No matter. We couldn't keep it a secret forever."

He snuggled my face. "You smell good. Like after a spring rain." A smile grew. "Along with a wee bit of Sally."

"You mean I don't smell like you and your men who must bathe in *Odeur de cheva?*"

Alain pulled me closer. "I have a funny story to tell you about horse stink."

I barely had a chance to ask him what he meant when his lips covered mine and I was engulfed in a divine, intense need to stay exactly where I was, for as long as I could. I willed myself to remember this moment: the feel of Alain's strength as it rippled through his body and migrated to mine, the briny taste of his lips and tongue, his scent that defined his strength and masculinity. We stayed entwined while everything else evaporated around us until the door burst open.

"Mr. MacArthur, sir." Filling the doorway was one of the cartmen. A big man, well suited for the job. "Sorry. Didn't mean to…interrupt…you with the missus."

Alain stepped back. The edges of Davina's letter poked me through my petticoat.

"Mrs. Krol's, I mean Mistress Rapalje's crate has arrived. I figured that's why she was visitin'. I thought you'd want to know."

"I'll get right on it and…or… if you see Mr. Krol, let him know."

The worker was gone as quickly as he arrived.

I returned to Alain's arms, to resume our closeness. But when Alain's hand fumbled into my pocket and discovered the letter, the precious moment was gone.

"From Davina?"

"Yes. She has found another woman willing to look after Alexandra. She's an older woman, a widow and is anxious to come to Manhattan as she has a relative living here."

"Does Davina say when the ship sails?"

"She's not sure but expects to have good news shortly. For all we know, our daughter could be in the middle of the Atlantic right now."

I tried to sound excited, but the thought also filled me with dread. After more than two-hundred years, trans-Atlantic sailing was still fraught with danger. I'd heard so many awful stories, including what I experienced myself.

Alain plucked the letter from my hands and brought it close to the window. His lips mouthed each word. As he read the letter, his face transformed into exquisite happiness. He reached out and brought me into his arms again, crushing my lips, and the letter between us.

The door burst open again, and the same man returned. He cleared his throat, not once, but twice. "Mr. MacArthur. Excuse me sir, madam, for intrudin' again." The man fumbled with his cap like a supplicant begging forgiveness. "Mr. Krol needs you right away. He says, to come quick, sir."

Once again, I stepped back while Alain grabbed his hat from the wooden peg. "What's the problem?"

"It's his mother. She needs rescuing. Mr. Krol is ready to fight for her honor."

"Show me the way," cried Alain as he rushed toward the door behind the worker. Then he stopped, as if remembering something. He turned and pulled me close, resuming the interrupted kiss. When we both came up for air, he said, "Stay right here until I return." With that, Alain was gone.

Some wives adhere to their wedding vows and obey their husband's every wish. What was true for others was not for me. My relationship with Alain was not between master and subservient spouse. I usually followed Alain's good advice, if it made sense, and there was a good reason to do so. But not this time. I had to see what was going on between Catarina, her son, and whoever was despoiling the widow's honor. I rationalized it was my wifely duty to make sure my husband didn't sustain any injuries when he marched onward to save his boss and the boss's nasty mother.

※

I didn't have to go far. Catarina's screams gave away her location. What I found was quite a sight.

Catarina's son was sprawled on the ground. Alain bent over Mr. Krol, pressing a cloth against his face to dam a river of blood that stained the front of his shirt and waistcoat. The injured man alternated between breathing heavily through his mouth and moaning. Whenever Alain readjusted the cloth, what appeared was a grossly crooked nose and eyes that were turning black and blue.

On the other side of the yard, Catarina knelt on the ground next to her mystery suitor, her skirts pillowed around her. She rocked to and fro, patting the brow of a gray-haired man; his left arm bent in an unnatural angle. He whimpered every time he flinched.

"Mr. MacArthur," said the older man, "ye didn't have tae wallop me. I was only givin' the lady a light peck on the cheek. I've the right."

That replay of events stirred Catarina's son into an upright position. He might have bolted after his adversary if it weren't for Alain holding him back. Instead, Mr. Krol spoke with an odd nasal tone. "You have no right…to touch my mother. Have you no decency? And she a recent widow." Then he moaned again and lay back on the ground.

"I didn't realize it was you," said Alain. "I was trying to protect Mr. Krol."

Joris' son said to Alain, "You have an odd way of coming to my rescue. I'm sure my nose is broken."

My head whipped from man to man. Not only was I taken aback when I realized the man being caressed by Catarina was none other than Davey Innes, but it seemed that Alain was the cause of injuring both men. Still incredulous, I took a few steps closer. Mr. Innes had been elegantly dressed an hour ago; now his coat was ripped, the hem stained with mud. His silk hose was dirty, torn, and one drooped around his ankle baring a hairy leg.

"Ah, Mrs. MacArthur. Ye're a sight for these sore eyes. I beseech ye tae put in a good word about my stellar character. Tell this good man, that he has nothin' tae fear from Cook Innes."

"Cook?" Catarina looked up from her nursing duties. "Davey. Beloved. Who is this Cook person?"

"Umm…nothin' my sweets, just someone Mrs. MacArthur and I kent years ago."

It was evident from the way Catarina held my friend's head close to her flat chest and the loving words they used to address each other; theirs was more than a casual acquaintance.

"Mother. Who is this…reprobate?"

Catarina stood up, smoothed her skirts, and helped bring Mr. Innes to his feet. She took his good hand and the two of them faced her son. "This is Mr. David Innes. My betrothed."

"Your what?" Mr. Krol pushed the cloth away from his face. "Father's grave hasn't gone cold yet." Mr. Krol turned and glared at Mr. Innes. "How dare you fiddle with the heart of a woman who has suffered the greatest tragedy any woman can experience? You have taken advantage of my mother, sir."

"Oh fiddlesticks," said Catarina. "David did no such thing. I'm a grown woman, and I gave myself freely to this man. Mr. David Innes will be my husband."

My friend raised a finger and mumbled "Davey." He appeared to object to the formality of his given name. But he relented when Catarina glared. It was useless to argue with his strong-willed wife-to-be.

"Furthermore, this is the man you should hire to manage our business." Catarina glared at Alain. "Not this good-for-nothing." Then she turned to her son. "You can give us your blessing and stand up for me," she continued, "or you can go home to that wife of yours and wallow in her charms." Catarina lightly touched her betrothed's arm. "David, let's get you to a surgeon and then home."

A smile crept over Cook Innes' lips. The worry lines on his forehead smoothed. His eyes moistened. He enjoyed Catarina's defense.

"I know a good doctor," I said.

"Not that murderer, Dr. Smith," screeched Catarina. "He has more dead patients than living. He will not touch my David. I won't be a widow before I'm married."

"But you are a—" began her son.

"No, not him," I answered. "Dr. Emmanuel's surgery nearby. Mr. Krol, you should probably see the doctor, too."

Catarina looked at Mr. Innes's limp appendage, and although I didn't offer, she replied, "No need for you to show us the way. If your doctor is as good as you say, we will have no trouble finding him." She turned to her son. "You…you might as well join us. Come, David."

Alain came over to me and whispered. "Dr. Emmanuel is a Jew…You know what Catarina thinks."

"Baruch Emmanuel can handle the Grand Inquisitor."

As the three walked away from the once chaotic scene, Cook Innes turned and gave me one last look. He placed his collapsed hat on his head, offered a crooked smile, and shrugged his shoulders as if to suggest, his life as a landsman hadn't turned out the way he envisioned. However, it wasn't all bad. He ended up a rich eligible bachelor, and now he was about to embark on an interesting and challenging chapter in his life. No matter the difficulties he would experience with Catarina, I looked forward to the spectacle, and if I knew Cook Innes, it was going to have a surprise ending.

CHAPTER TEN
A MAN OF FEW WORDES
DARIEN NATIONAL PARK

WHAT I BELIEVED had been buried in the sand or lying at the bottom of the ocean, now rested in my hands. The knife was in remarkable condition thanks to the *mola*. The shroud had sheltered it from the damaging effects of humidity and salt water.

I couldn't help thinking about the possibilities, that this was Filib's knife. The one he used to end his life. Anna witnessed the tragic scene and documented it in her journal. At the same time, I feared the knife had come into my hands too easily. Common sense raised red flags. Hasty conclusions could tarnish my budding reputation. Envious colleagues would take much joy in discrediting a rush to judgement and declare the find nothing more than a trinket left by a modern-day adventurer.

Uncovering the dirk's authenticity would take real work. It began with Máyli's words: *For as long as my husband's grandmother can remember, she has had these possessions.* The age would be simple to determine, and if proven to be three centuries old, that would make it a priceless discovery. Whether it was Filib's or not.

A month before I left for the dig, Alec and I had found a swordsmith in Skye. Forging weapons was a lost art; but there were still a few smiths honing their craft in Scotland. We spent an afternoon with one master and watched the fiery birthing of a dirk. In Anna's time, they were created from broken swords. The smith joked that it was an ancient form of recycling. A Highlander, who couldn't afford a full sword, could still purchase a lethal weapon for less.

The smith's shop had a showroom with several glass cases filled with dirks and swords. The most startling difference were the handles. They were made from various types of wood, different grains and colors; most were intricately carved. One caught my eye. The smith placed the dirk in my hands as if it were his first-born. I turned it over and around while he pointed out the single-edge blade, the false edge at the end, and the efficiency of the Celtic knots carved into the wooden handle.

Holding Breseide's knife, I thought it much more stunning than the modern-made one back in Scotland. My fingers curled around the dark wood, bog oak or ebony, feeling the ridges of the sculpted handle ending in a flat pommel. The design had a practical application. It prevented the user from losing his bloody grip in the heat of battle. The tang, or blade, most likely steel, was fitted into the handle.

I remembered something else.

"Do you see this flat ring on the pommel's end?" The smith held out a dirk he had just taken from another case. The ring was a shiny piece of hammered silver. "That's where the new owner can order an engraving. Some like to give their weapons a name. Like 'Sweet Revenge,' 'Demon Hunter,' or 'Head Trimmer.'"

I chuckled. "Why give the weapon a name?"

"Many a warrior would spend more time with their weaponry than they did with their wives and children," said Alec. "Naming them added a familiarity, like a closeness one has with a pet."

"Some chose a special trait to boast about their prowess," said the smith. "Perhaps something they were known for. Like…um… 'Knight of the Blade' or a religious man might inscribe, 'Soldier of God.' The only limit was the number of letters that could fit on the ring."

Now, five thousand miles away from the smith's forge, I turned the knife over. The ring was tarnished and dirty. Rubbing my finger over the metal, I could feel the worn edges. Perhaps an engraving. I was reminded of the four engraved letters on the key I found in the safe deposit box four years ago: RBOS - the Royal Bank of Scotland. That's what led me to Anna's story and brought me to this place.

A soft cloth would do, but not the ancient *mola*. I tugged on the edge of my T-shirt and began to rub gently so as not to scratch the metal. I didn't get far. A man's booming voice and heavy footsteps came from outside the room.

"Máyli, bring the women." It was Javier.

Miranda looked at me; her eyes brimming, saucer-like. She reached for my hand. Hers trembled. I had seconds to think how to get out of this.

"Máyli," I said. "Please ask Breseide if I can take the knife outside. I want to show it to my teacher, Dr. Jones. I promise to return it."

When Breseide nodded, I tucked the heavy coiled cloth under my arm and climbed down the wobbly log-ladder. Miranda, Breseide, the young girl, and Máyli followed.

Coming into the blinding sunshine, I squinted and shielded my eyes. Dark figures standing in front of the hut were edged like a corona during a solar eclipse. Slowly the shapes materialized into Javier, El Leon, his men, and Max. And others.

Marcus had arrived, and he wasn't alone. Two brutes were right behind him, and a young woman, about my age, stood by his side. Curiously, my focus wasn't on Marcus. I was drawn to the woman and her Bob Marley T-shirt. Many of the gift shops at the Panama City airport had them on display. Now I regretted not purchasing one. It might have provided a connection between us. Perhaps some needed sympathy points, because around the woman's waist hung a wide leather belt, and on the side, slipped between belt and pants was a large revolver.

The woman's almond-shaped eyes crawled all over Miranda and then me. Her glare never wavered while she leaned in and whispered something to Marcus. Their eye contact and his smile made it clear she was important to him.

El Leon stepped forward. "Itth been a while, Marcuth."

Marcus drew back from the woman. He looked slightly annoyed at being interrupted. "Huh? What'd you call me?"

The woman snickered and brazenly sauntered toward El Leon. "Mr. Bossman. How can we do business with someone who can't talk? How can we trust what you – 'thay.'" She turned to her audience and burst out laughing before edging closer to her boyfriend.

El Leon pivoted. His men stood like statues. His gaze shifted to Javier. Reputation was everything. Then El Leon glared at Marcus. The air was tense with expectation. I wasn't the only one who was startled when El Leon clapped his hands and a huge smile lit up his face. "Come on, man. Cut the playing around."

Marcus and the woman joined in the merriment. The two leaders embraced, slapping each other on the back. The rest of the men joined them. This must have been normal banter between the two leaders.

"So, my friend," said Marcus, "I hear you have something valuable to sell. It had better be worth going out of my way to come to this dump." Javier glowered, but the big man responded by spitting at Javier's feet.

Pointing to the two slaves, Marcus added, "And not those two scrawny slant-eyed chickens."

"What I have ith worth the trouble. Hothtageth."

Marcus smirked. "Hostages, man. Hostages. Learn to speak." He wiped his mouth with the back of his hand. "Is that all? I can get all the hostages I want."

"No, no, no," said El Leon patiently. "An American."

Marcus turned, found Miranda. He leered at her in a creepy manner, undressing her with his eyes. Then his attention settled on me. "*Americano*? Is this the one?" he asked. "I'll give you two thousand US. And if you throw in the blonde, I'll give you five hundred more. Somebody will buy her to liven up their days and nights."

"Nothing doing. You could get fifty-thouthand for the American alone."

"You're loco." Marcus pointed at his head and made circles with his index finger. "Maybe a couple of years ago, but not today and only if the American has rich relatives. If not, I get nothing but heartache. Meanwhile, I have to feed her and fight with my men to stay away." He stopped and thought for a moment. "Three-thousand dollars." He chuckled again. "My friend, think how many beers and whores you and your men can buy."

"The girl ith prime. Americanth pay. And you know it."

Marcus stared at me and slowly licked his lips. His girlfriend was not amused. Then he turned toward El Leon and said with a devilish smirk, "What ith that you thay? Thpeak clearly. Your men need a new *jefe*."

The woman laughed. This time El Leon's soldiers snickered and didn't stop when he glared. He was losing control and all because of a malfunction of Mother Nature.

Marcus grew impatient. He came over and yanked my wrist so hard I dropped the *mola*. He twirled me back and forth. "Nice. Not damaged. At least from what's visible." Then he placed one finger under my chin, pushing my face skyward. And another finger played with my lower lip to inspect my teeth. I could smell his stench and my fear. "Thirty-five hundred. Not a *centavo* more. That's all—"

Just then, Fu Man Chu yelled, "Oscar, *Hombre, aqui.*"

The haggling stopped, followed by shouts and the clicks of guns. Marcus forgot I existed and turned.

Oscar stood on the edge of the jungle. His clothes were ragged, his hair stuck out like he had been electrocuted, and dried blood painted his face. He staggered, glassy-eyed, mumbling something while waving a gun with twisted fingers.

The Kuna backed off. One frantic parent shushed her toddler while creeping backwards toward a hut. The teenaged boys and men moved in front of their women.

Fu continued. *"No seas idiota. Baja tu arma."*

Oscar continued to babble nonsense. Was he high or was something else agitating him?

"Tu madre folladora," El Leon cursed.

Nothing deterred the deranged man from coming closer.

El Leon raised his gun, faced Oscar, and fired. In response, a barrage of shots went off; some in the air as warning; others deadly. A bullet whizzed by my head and thumped as it embedded itself in palm bark. The firing ended with a women's scream. Three were slumped on the ground.

It didn't take long to figure out what had happened. The smoking gun in Miranda's hand told the story. When El Leon hit Oscar squarely in the chest, Fu avenged the death of his friend. In the confusion, Miranda grabbed the woman's gun and shot Marcus in the head. The girlfriend screamed while cradling his crumpled body.

That's when Alec emerged from the jungle armed with a rifle. He was followed by Hadrian carrying a stout club. As they approached, Alec's eyes warned me not to react. "Fu. Tell your men to put down their weapons. You're outnumbered."

"By what. The jungle? The monkeys? The spiders?"

"Give it up. Every man here will take you down." Alec swept his hand in a gesture that encompassed the onlookers.

Fu Manchu didn't budge even when the other soldiers threw down their weapons and disappeared. Tall Guy and Short Guy, now unafraid, joined the Kuna.

"But I still have this." Fu pointed his AK47 into the air and spun in every direction. "I could kill fifty before anyone took a step in my direction." His arm muscles tightened as the gun flashed rapid popping sounds. Spent bullet casings flew. The smell of burned motor oil was everywhere. Fu paused to reload, his actions quick and flawless. Silence filled the void. He raised his rifle, ready to fire. A primitive cry stopped him.

It was Javier.

Breseide was on the ground. Blood turned her gray hair red.

"Abuela, mi abuela."

Máyli rushed to her husband's side and pressed the old woman's lifeless hands to her face, wailed pitifully, and kissed them. No longer would they create the beautiful *mola.*

Javier's eyes narrowed like an animal ready to spring. He came toward me. I backed away. I begged him to stop. But the enraged man kept coming.

"No!" yelled Alec. He ran toward me, but there was no way he could get between us in time.

I covered my head in preparation for a mighty blow. Still confused, I had no idea what I had done.

Javier bent down for the *mola* at my feet. The knife's wooden handle clearly winked from the hem of the cloth. Javier grabbed the dirk, and with the quickness of forgotten youth and the rage of a madman, he propelled it with deadly force into Fu's neck. The murderer was dead before his body hit the ground next to Breseide's *mola.*

Several of the Kuna gently placed Breseide's body in a hammock and slowly carried her toward Javier's hut. They were followed by several women chanting a dirge. All but one entered. The lone singer took her post, guarding the log-ladder and continued her lament while Breseide was prepared for the Afterworld. Others milled around the hut waiting patiently to pay their respects.

Alec and I took our cue from the mourners and distanced ourselves until we found some privacy on the edge of the pier. Still stunned, I held onto Alec. To touch and be touched, gently, with compassion, the absence of cruelty, the very essence of humanity, convinced me the nightmare was over.

It was later, in the early evening, when we shared stories.

"How did you know where I was?" I asked.

"We followed as soon as we could. The newly hacked leaves and brush were like breadcrumbs. And then, Hadrian found a fresh boot print in the mud."

"That was Oscar's. He smashed a spider."

"Spider?"

"A spider bit—"

I told Alec about Miranda, the spider, Oscar's difficulties with El Leon, and Oscar's disappearance.

"That must have been when we bumped into him. We found Oscar asleep, curled up against a log. He was easy to capture and disarm, and he was furious with El Leon. It didn't take much convincing to get him to talk. I made him an offer. If he led us to this village, I would give him a gun to kill El Leon."

"But what would have happened if he turned around and shot you?"

"Aye. I worried about that, but Hadrian suggested we give him an empty gun. Oscar was so filled with hate, he never noticed. His confronting El Leon was meant to give Hadrian and me time to figure out what to do next, which of course, it turned out we didn't need. Everything went our way, except the death of the old lady."

"Hadrian!" I almost forgot. "How's he doing?"

"He'll survive. El Leon's men scared him more than hurt him. He has a thing for the blonde, so he insisted on coming."

"You mean, Miranda."

"Aye." Alec raised an eyebrow. "The blonde has a name. She's one brave lassie."

"I wonder if she'll ever get over killing Marcus. Will she go to jail?"

"I doubt it. There were enough witnesses to corroborate her story and what Marcus had planned for her. Besides, in this part of Darien, the Kuna rule, and that means Javier. He wanted Marcus, El Leon, and their ilk done away with. You could say Miranda did him a favor."

"It's sort of funny, in a weird way."

"Funny?"

"Her mother predicted…never mind."

"What?"

I took a deep breath. Something else needed to be said. "I have to tell you about Max."

"Shh! Not now." Alec pressed his hands against the small of my back drawing me closer. Our touching continued. His lips, searching and hungry, quickly found mine and lingered there. He pulled back for a moment. "Finish your Ph.D. As soon as possible." Then we resumed where we left off.

The roar of the plane's engines during take-off made talking difficult and the noise stayed at the same level for the forty-mile flight to Panama City. But that was a blessing. After all that had happened in Darien, there was much to mull over; best to be alone with my thoughts. Besides, once Alec and I boarded our connecting flight to London we would have the opportunity to catch up. For the first time in seventy-two hours, I wasn't afraid of the next ten minutes. It felt strange not to feel frightened.

For some, the murderous events had turned in their favor. The Kuna were rid of the gangs that plagued their community. The two slaves regained their freedom. They were offered room and board and kindness. Young Guy's trench foot was nursed by the young girl who was Breseide's student. She was most attentive. It would be several weeks before he could travel again. Young Guy didn't appear to be in any hurry to leave.

We stayed long enough for Breseide's wake. Since Javier's grandmother was a woman of stature, the little village swelled with nearby Kuna coming to pay their respects. The women wrapped Breseide's body in her hammock, securing it with a rope-like umbilical cord. The villagers sat around regaling stories of her life. In this way, they affirmed Breseide's many accomplishments so she would be welcomed in the Afterworld. Two women chanters chronicled her journey.

The burial took place on the mainland. We did not attend. We had a flight to catch. But Máyli noticed my interest in Kuna burial traditions and was gracious to share.

"My husband's grandmother will be buried inside a small house. It will have everything she needs for her new life. Kuna women will keep her home clean, ensure she always has fresh food, and will provide gifts. She will not arrive empty-handed in the Afterworld."

I thought of the many civilizations that practiced the same belief. Perhaps the ancient Egyptians really had made their way to the New World, bringing their ideas of life after death.

105

"My husband's grandmother's hammock will hang in the grave, and a *tabla*, a wooden board, filled with gifts and personal items, will be placed above her body."

"Hung in the grave? You mean she won't be buried." I was confused.

"Her hammock will never touch the Earth. Then a mound of dirt, meant to look like the belly of a pregnant woman, will cover the *tabla*." Máyli's hand rested on her enlarged belly.

"What kind of presents will she bring?"

"Before her death, my husband's grandmother chose a gift of great value to show respect. Something the ancestors will recognize."

Only one gift could come with such an important woman and fit that description. Filib's knife wrapped in a *mole*.

We settled in our seats for the thirteen-hour flight with a short layover in Toronto. Miranda and Hadrian sat behind us. The rest were scattered around the plane.

Max had to stay behind. One of the students came down with a severe stomach bug and had to be hospitalized. As the person in charge, Max was responsible until the patient was no longer pot bound.

"I'm sorry the lad is sick, but I have no regrets that Max had to stay behind," whispered Alec.

I smiled as I watched the jungle below grow distant, and the trees merge into a solid green mass. I pulled down the shade and rested my head on Alec's shoulder. I couldn't help but reflect on the last time we were on a flight together. We had just met, and this handsome Scot caught my interest from the first moment I saw him.

Remembering Jess' advice for overcoming jetlag, I tried to get some sleep. But Alec wanted to talk. "It's a shame you couldn't convince Javier to give you the knife, Did Breseide offer it to you as a gift?"

"No. She just wanted me to see it. After I told her about Anna and Filib. Good thing Hadrian still had his small digital camera with him. He took lots of pictures."

"You know, I had brought the box of coins with me. Just in case I needed to buy your freedom. Maybe I could've bought the knife."

"I doubt Javier would have sold it. The dirk had been in Breseide's family too long." I paused and swallowed hard "Filib's knife is right where it should be. With its rightful owner."

"How are you so sure it was Filib's?"

"The dirk matched the swordsmith's description for a seventeenth century weapon. However, I'd still like to return to the smithy, show him the pictures, and get his expert opinion." I hesitated before going on and grabbed a tissue from the pocket of my sweatshirt. The next few words were hard to say. "But that's not the only proof I have. Remember the smith said that the ring was often engraved to suit the owner. Well…Breseide's…Filib's dirk was engraved with an important clue…*A Man of Few Wordes*."

"Shakespeare. What does 'Henry V' have to do with Filib's knife?"

"On the end of the pommel, the silver ring. Once Máyli had cleaned the dirk for the burial, I saw the inscription. I'm now positive it was Filib's. Anna mentioned several times in her journal that the little Scot spoke only when necessary." I dabbed the tissue in the corners of my eyes. "Máyli let me hold the dirk one last time. It felt like a long-lost relative about to slip away. Forever. I wrapped my fingers tightly around the grip and tried to commit it to memory." I wiped my cheeks with the used tissue. "Alec, I have no doubt that I am the descendent of Anna and Alain. That makes Filib my relative. I have never felt so close to him as when I held his knife."

Alec took my hand, opened my fingers, and pressed my palm to his lips. They were soft and warm. He hesitated a delicious moment before speaking. "Shakespeare's words. The rest of the quote is fitting as well."

"Which is?"

"And men of few wordes are the best men."

CHAPTER ELEVEN
THE ICING ON THE CAKE
NEW YORK - 1709

I REACHED FOR the journal on a shelf above the worn oak desk. It was my favorite place to write. Not too close to the hearth, to be baked like the bread in the oven, but satisfying with a late winter storm raging outside. Above the desk, the panes on the only window in the room were partially snow covered, precisely on the diagonal as if God had used a straight edge. Although the window could be drafty, especially when the winds blew out of the north, it was worth the pleasing prospect. Tree branches and leafless bushes were brushed white with a clear dark edge for emphasis. A thick blanket covered the path between our house and Catarina's.

A batch of quills lay haphazardly in the desk drawer, waiting to be pruned. Several shorter ones were donations from local crows and hawks. The longer ones were goose or swan. I selected a white quill and silently thanked the bird who offered up its elegant flight feather. The nib had already been cured and cut into shape, but the downy barbs needed scraping with a small knife. A manicured quill would prevent stained fingers and ensure the paper to remain clean of blotches. The other end of the long feathery spine needed shortening to avoid a poke in the eye. Sharpening the hollow shaft was the last step before the pen was ready. In a way, I felt sorry for forcing the quill to write words that were most inauspicious.

> *March 2, 1709*
> *Another letter from Davina arrived today, overshadowing the previous one. Events beyond our control have delayed Alexandra's sailing. My heart is heavy.*

I tugged at a handkerchief hidden in my sleeve and wiped my eyes. Two tears escaped and rained on the freshly written words. Turning back pages, I recalled the dated entries about Alain and our children. I was reminded of a decision made long ago, when we left newborn Alexandra before sailing to Caledonia. This journal was meant to be hers. Our time apart was a festering wound; the journal was part of the healing.

I unfolded Davina's letter and reread it, searching for an inference, a hint, that somehow, I had misinterpreted her words. But I was only fooling myself. Her message was clear. I picked up the pen, dipped it into the inkwell, and continued where I'd left off.

Parliament has commandeered all available ships. They are needed to transport thousands of Germans who have recently made England their refuge, a result of war, high taxes, starvation, & bitter cold in their homeland. It is said that the extreme cold has frozen birds in mid-flight. Queen Anne intends to ship three-thousand Palatines, as the Germans are called. They are meant for Carolina, but word has spread around Manhattan that Governor Hunter wants the immigrants to settle in the pine forests along the Hudson. Living on the edge of the frontier, they will serve as a bulwark against the French & pay for their passage by producing pine tar for the British Navy. Once their debt is erased, the Palatines would be granted farmland.

The government's plan has promise, but sadly, it has prevented our daughter from sailing. Meanwhile, Davina secured a room in Edinburgh so they are closer to the port & can take advantage of an opportunity. There is another benefit. They are further removed from Father Drummond.

I have met Germans, like Deborah & Baruch Emmanuel. Their countrymen have been living in Manhattan for many years & are known for their excellent baking. Catarina said that they use their feet to knead the dough for their rye bread. I don't believe her.

I placed the quill in the amber jar, fanned the page until the ink dried, and then closed the journal. As always, I pressed my hand along the embossed thistles on the cover before securing the two leather strips. After returning the book to the shelf, I tugged on the ends of my shawl when another wintry gust rattled the plate glass.

Three months later, on Wednesday, June 12, Catarina and Mr. Innes were married. This first month of summer was the perfect time for weddings. After a long cold winter, many had taken their first bath of the year. Now, the air was not so thick with human stink. Instead, the fragrance of roses and lilacs filled the void.

Only two others, besides the bride and groom and Reverend Vesey, attended the ceremony. No one knew who they were, but they served as witnesses. One was described as a young man wandering the Trinity cemetery until the Reverend persuaded him to a higher calling; the other, a newcomer to Manhattan, was prodded to delay his stroll in exchange for a shot of whisky. Not even Catarina's son made it to the nuptials, and according to rumor, probably initiated by the bride, that was exactly how she wanted it.

After a night of consummating their marriage, the bride and groom prepared to share their happiness with the community. A wedding was an opportunity to display a family's wealth; in this case, two healthy purses. This was manifested in the overflow of every manner of abundance.

Much of Manhattan was invited, including Alain and me. The feast, set in and around a tavern, incorporated the traditions of three cultures: Dutch, English, and Indian. Although not intentional, the different food associated with these groups had intermingled enough, resulting in new and delicious flavors.

The Dutch were known for their love of sweets. It was no surprise that the dessert table was the centerpiece. Guests licked their lips from the smell of cinnamon, burnt sugar, nutmeg, and ginger. Loaves of *kock*, a Dutch honey cake, were surrounded by trays of marzipan, candied almonds, cookies, cinnamon bark, and pastries. *Olie-koecken*, deep-fried balls of dough, stuffed with raisins, apples, and almonds, and then dusted with sugar, was a favorite of Alain's. Wisps of steam suggested they were still warm from the frying pans of melted lard. I declined even a taste.

Expensive turtle meat, imported from Philadelphia, was the main ingredient for a soup meant only for special occasions. Along with thyme, garlic, bay leaf, and tomatoes, the soup bubbled in large black cauldrons. When almost ready, I watched the cooks add the last ingredient, a generous amount of sherry. The mixture of spices, herbs, and alcohol was intoxicating.

Close by were baskets loaded with assorted breads, white rolls, pumpkin, and gingerbread along with pots of fresh churned butter and cheeses. I wasn't surprised to see that rye bread was conspicuously absent.

On another table, trays of herring, a traditional fish for the Dutch, were set besides platters of duck, goose, and pork, along with dumplings, roasted squash, and another Dutch favorite, cole slaw. Meat pies, an English specialty and the groom's personal favorite, were also in abundance.

The bride and groom arrived amidst a flutter of handkerchiefs and shouted hurrahs. I wondered about the genuineness of the hearty congratulations. It was no secret Catarina was detested. Some of the women were jealous of her wealth. Most agreed that the groom could have done better. Therefore, the loud cheers were probably in anticipation of the feast and the numerous bottles of Madeira and English porter. That was in addition to the casks of apple brandy and bowls of lemon and orange rum punch. The floating rinds were the only proof they were part of the recipe. The alcohol far surpassed the mountain of food.

This was not a joining of two young people. Nor was it the first time either had said the sacred words, giving their pledge. But it was a second chance for companionship, happiness, support, and financial security. No matter what the age, a wedding was a blessed event, although this one didn't share the excitement, freshness, and expectation of virgin participants. Some guests took advantage of the newlywed's maturity. They whispered behind fans or hats, heads lowered, close to another's ear. Their eyes and hand gestures suggested their vulgar talk. Bouts of raucous laughter confirmed it.

"Never met the groom. He seems like a likable fellow," said a rotund fellow supporting his weight on a cane. "But he has to be a loon to marry a woman that looks like that."

"Well, he can just put a blanket over her face and carry on," chuckled his companion while making lewd pelvic gestures.

The first man's wife put a finger to her lips and chortled. "Let's not be rude. Besides, we came for the feast. It's been the talk of the town for days."

What barely caught the eye of the men became the focal point for the female guests: the bride cake. It was situated on a table encircled with fresh flowers. I moved closer and joined several matrons who scrutinized every inch of the double-layered cake with almond and white icing.

"I helped make my Cousin Daphne's cake for her wedding," said a dour woman who looked old enough to have made many bride cakes. "If you ask me, they were grander than this. Daphne's took at least three pounds of sugar and an equal amount of butter."

Her companion, a slightly younger version, but still hard-faced, circled the cake and came so close I thought her nose would dent the hardened glaze. "The icing is thin on this side. It's barely covering the lumps. The currants, almonds, and citron weren't chopped fine enough, and the baker was too cheap to make enough icing to hide the cake's flaws."

"Do you think Catarina will notice? Maybe I should point it out to her."

"Nay. Catarina will just make a fuss. She'll send someone to drag the poor baker out of his shop, and demand he return her money."

"Mmph. Even so, this cake must have cost a pretty penny. But what does it matter? Catarina has found another rich husband." The woman sighed. I imagined she was thinking that marrying two wealthy spouses in one's lifetime was an amazing feat.

"True. But her first was rather plain looking. And this one, rough in his appearance, and his manner is rather indecent. Even my Harry says he's a bit vulgar. Spends his time with riff-raff at The Pearl and flaunts his wealth as if he just came into his money."

"Well, Catarina is not asking us for our opinion. Nor would I give it. She'd bite my head off. Besides, marriage is nothing more than a business proposition. As it should be." The woman held up her fan and tittered behind it. "What does it matter? Tis all the same under the covers."

Catarina and Mr. Innes greeted their guests. There was handshaking from the groom and forced smiles from the bride while swishing the rich fabric of her gathered skirts, like a young girl. Above the waist, the bodice was adorned with a graceful sweep of expensive lace that also cascaded from the sleeves. The groom was most debonair in a fine grey wool suit with the whitest silk stockings and gold buckles on his one-inch heeled shoes.

Mr. Innes held his wife's hand and gently steered her in one direction or the other. His doting on her did not last. When a guest complimented Catarina's attire and announced her a beautiful bride, Innes tenderly picked up his wife's hand and kissed it. Catarina jerked away, wiped the back of her hand on her skirt, and hissed, "Control yourself." Then she cracked a smile and rapped him gently with her fan. When laughter exploded from the guests, Mr. Innes retreated to a bottle of whisky only to change his mind and head for the punch bowl.

Catarina continued talking as if nothing had happened, but I wondered how much she paid attention to the conversation around her. The entire time, she patted her hair to ensure no wayward strands escaped and adjusted the lace cap to mask the bald spot.

"I gather ye think me a wee fool." Mr. Innes stood behind me, a cup of punch in each hand.

"Well, maybe more than a little," He answered his own question while offering me one of the cups.

I tasted a drop and winced. The fumes almost toppled me.

He grinned. "Only take wee sips. I've heard that someone's added a bit more rum than the recipe calls for."

I eyed the other cup. "Are you going to drink that?"

"Nay. I prefer whisky. This here's for Catarina. She's a wee bit nervous, causin' her fickle temperament. As her lovin' husband, it's my duty tae take care o' my wife's needs."

I cleared my throat trying to erase the taste. "That's understandable. A new bride. The excitement. You know—"

"Now Mrs. MacArthur, that's verra nice o' ye tae say about the new Mrs. Innes." The skin around Mr. Innes's eyes crinkled as he chuckled low in his throat. "But you and I both ken how Catarina can be. Mmph. Let me say this politely, being that yere a lady and all. My wife is a scheming, heartless, and domineering bitch, and the only reason she agreed tae marry Davey Innes, ship's cook, thief, deserter, and all-around rascal is because o' my recent good fortune." He paused and took a deep breath. "But don't ye worry about me. I ken what I've gotten myself into."

113

"Well then, why did you marry Mrs. Rapalje? There are many women who would gladly consider you."

"Remember, I told ye about my plans o' domestication. Well, it didn't work out the way I hoped. The first time. Now I have tae settle." He nodded and raised the remaining cup toward his wife. "The fact is, I don't want tae live alone and I surely don't want tae go back tae sea. Catarina is a difficult woman and challenges my manhood, but she'll keep me company, maintain my house, and tae tell ye the truth," he lowered his voice to a whisper and leaned close, "she's not so bad at night."

"What? Mrs. Rapalje?" I covered my mouth and giggled.

"And they'll be none o' that Mrs. Rapalje. She's Mrs. Davey Innes from now on." He smiled once again and looked at the punch aging in his hand. "Now don't you go sayin' anythin'. We're old friends – you and me – we can trust each other with our secrets."

I smiled. I loved talking to the old cook. He made my heart glad. "Of course."

"Besides," he sniggered, "I have plans for that woman. And I can guarantee this. It will please everyone, including yourself."

"What are you —"

"David." Catarina shrieked from the other side of the tavern. She was standing next to Alain and her son which was most unusual.

"Coming, my love."

"Get me some punch," Catarina said. "A full cup."

Mr. Innes' face beamed. "Duty calls. I need tae get her soused before she notices the icin' ain't perfect."

"You know about that? How—"

"O' course. It was too temptin'. I licked off a swath with my fingers earlier this mornin'. Tae tell you the truth, I ate more than I should have, so I spread the rest o' the icin' with my fingers tae cover it up." Then he leaned toward my ear again. "After a cup o' this flamin' brew, I could punch a big fat hole in the bride cake, and she'd think it was as pretty as can be."

As my friend went off to his wife, he got waylaid by guests wishing him congratulations. He glanced back, winked, and raised the cup. That's when I knew for sure. Mr. Innes had reinforced the punch.

I looked for Alain and was surprised to see he was following Catarina out the open tavern door. How strange. I made my way quickly through the throng of guests and was delighted to see Dr. Emmanuel and his wife, Deborah. They were probably invited by Mr. Innes after the good doctor treated his arm. I greeted them quickly with a promise to return. I was on a mission. I needed to save Alain from Catarina.

Hearing angry voices, I found Alain and Catarina at the rear of the tavern. This time I didn't eavesdrop. Catarina stood tall, her back straight, and lips pinched. "Now that David and I are wed, it is only right that he takes on Joris' business. It befits David's status in the community and as my husband."

As much as I liked Mr. Innes, I was tempted to reveal his sordid past. Maybe then his money would not appear so shiny.

"Your son owns the company," answered Alain. "Not Innes. I don't answer to anyone else."

"My son is a good-for-nothing. He will do what I say. Besides, he only comes to New York to check up on you. With David in charge, my son can stay in Brooklyn permanently. He's a lazy sort." She stopped and smoothed out the lace on her sleeve. "And I won't have to put up with his good-for-nothing wife. Unless there's a funeral."

I was alarmed by Catarina's pronouncement. She was a viable threat to Alain's livelihood along with the small home that came with the job.

"Does Mr. Innes even want the business? He has spent many years at sea. I can't imagine him sitting behind a desk."

"My husband wants nothing more than to please me. He finds great joy in my happiness." She nodded toward Mr. Innes who was approaching with the ordered cup of punch. Her lips cracked a smile, and she responded with a stilted wave. He, in return, pursed his lips, and nodded toward the upstairs room and the privacy it would offer.

Catarina shook her head and turned back to Alain and spoke quickly. "I expect you and your family to move out by the end of the month."

"Your son will decide. Until then—"

"I don't think you understand me." She lowered her voice to a gruff whisper. "If you aren't gone, I'll tell my son about your rude inappropriate behavior. My son may not love his mother as he should, but he won't put up with a common laborer acting in such a foul way." Catarina didn't wait for a response. She turned to her husband who had just arrived, smiled prettily, and nodded coquettishly.

On a day when Catarina had the greatest motive to be generous and congenial, she could not deny who she was: vindictive and cunning. In no time, the bride transformed from shrewish Kate to tender Bianca.

CHAPTER TWELVE

ALEXANDRA

CATARINA'S THREATS WERE forgotten shortly after she left town with Innes. But my fear came roaring back whenever I noticed someone who reminded me of her. That happened three days ago. I saw a woman, from behind, who looked and walked like Catarina. She was thin, held her head in a haughty manner, and swiveled her hips with each step so that her skirts swished. I followed from a safe distance, until she stopped in front of Catarina's dressmaker's shop. My heart raced, and my palms grew sweaty. But when the woman turned to greet a friend, her powder-free face lit up with a welcoming smile. The two women embraced, hooked arms, giggled like young girls, ignored the shop, and continued down the street. Of course, that could not be Catarina. She had no friends.

Yesterday, Mary, Catarina's maid, a tall woman about my age, confided in me. "A messenger arrived with a letter from the mistress. She and Mr. Innes are expected to arrive home in a few days." The maid wrung her hands to control their shaking. In a timid voice she added, "I need this job. My mum can't take in laundry anymore. She's got the ague. But I can't abide working for the Mistress. It's been wonderful since she went away."

Mary looked around to see if anyone was watching while she handed me the folded letter. An inelegant hand scratched out a long list of chores. When I handed it back, she said, "There's more on the other side."

Carriages were rare in Manhattan, so every rumble had me flying to the window. Late in the afternoon, a coachman stopped in front of Catarina's house, got down, and checked the horses. No passengers got off, and no baggage was removed. After he tightened the harness, the carriage disappeared down the street. Mr. Innes and his wife did not come home that day.

Two weeks passed and Catarina and Mr. Innes still hadn't returned. And every day I wondered if this was the last time Alain and I would awaken in our warm bed. I adjusted the blanket to cover my shoulders. The July morning was still cool. I considered hiding under the counterpane if it would block out my worries and the constant reminder of Alexandra's absence. I prayed Alain would bring some encouraging news from the port captain, but each evening I was greeted with silence on the matter. After a while, I stopped asking.

That's what made this morning so different.

"I got some news yesterday." Alain said as he bunched up his pillow. "No, lass. It's not about Alexandra." His deep sigh sounded off-putting and purposeful. "A messenger came by the shop. Mr. Innes and Catarina are expected later this week."

My fingers pulled the blanket tighter. "I guess they'll toss you…us…out now," I said. "They won't even be grateful that you ran the business while they were away."

"Mmph, I didn't mention this…I didn't want to get your hopes up. Before he left, Mr. Innes asked me to stay on. He said we would talk once he returned."

"Really! Maybe Innes will want—"

"I'm not counting on anything, Lass. Mr. Innes…he's married to a strong-willed woman. He wants her happy, and you ken he has his own way of doing things."

I rolled toward Alain and lowered the blanket.

"Do you ever wonder how Catarina got her son to give up control? The work wasn't hard. Besides, you did it all, and he liked the job you were doing. The business remained profitable."

"Aye. I'm betting she lied like a thief caught red-handed. Catarina probably told her son that Mr. Innes would run everything. Her son didn't need to leave his home in Brooklyn. I'm sure that was very tempting to Mrs. Krol. Without lifting a finger, her husband would be assured a lifetime income." Alain rolled toward me and propped his head on one hand. The other fiddled with the strings on my shift. "As much as I liked Joris' son, he was not ambitious. And certainly, no match for his mother."

No longer secured, the shift slipped, baring one shoulder and one breast. Alain leaned forward and kissed the exposed skin. His lips felt warm, and his tongue tickled. He paused and offered a final explanation, "If the younger Mr. Krol had a choice between gazing into his wife's

118

beautiful eyes, caressing the softness of her skin, and never worrying about an income, why wouldn't he? I ken I would."

"I don't think so. I mean, yes, you would gaze into my eyes and touch me in a way that I adore. But you are also responsible. Never ruthless, but resolute, strong-minded." I ran my hand along Alain's ribs and then traveled to the knobs on his spine. I moved closer to place little kisses on his lips, his neck, and then sunk lower to the cleft in his chest. When I began to play with the curly red hairs around one nipple, he reached for my hand.

"Now who's being ruthless?"

Alain moaned when I returned to our conversation. "Regrettably, many of your sex are not man enough to stand up to Catarina. They do her bidding and cower in her sight."

"Aye. She's man enough for many of them."

"Alain, I hope I'm not like that. Like Catarina."

His hands went around my bottom and pulled me closer. His lips within touching distance of mine. "You are definitely not man enough."

I made a gallant effort to pull back. "You aren't being serious. Would you make an unjust decision to please me? Would our marriage blind you to what is right?"

"I can't think of that now. I have something more delightful in mind."

The other half of my shift surrendered. But before I did, I wondered how men could compartmentalize their lives so effortlessly. For the moment, it didn't matter to Alain that he might lose his livelihood and our home. Instead, only one thing was important to Alain – what went on in our bed. It checkmated reality. Every time.

Two days later, three trunks of diminishing size were stacked on Catarina's stoop. At the same time, Sally and I returned from a visit with Deborah Emannuel, we watched the maid grunt and tug at the smallest one. Its size belied its great weight. When she saw me, she gestured toward the house. Her mistress was home.

I decided that because of my friendship with Mr. Innes, I would speak with him, and as soon as possible, in a place where Catarina couldn't eavesdrop. Alain suggested the back room where he worked. But the next seven days passed with no sight of Mr. Innes,

With few options remaining, I went to Catarina's house. Mary opened the door slightly, framing her body. Her eyes brimming, she sniffed into a handkerchief. Before I could say a word, the door jerked open, nearly knocking the maid backward. Catarina drew her wrapper tightly around her waist, although it was big enough to circle her twice.

"Mrs. Rapalje. Excuse me. My husband was wondering when he might expect Mr. Innes?" I stepped back, expecting a sharp retort. Would she be upset at how I addressed her? Her maiden name was what she preferred when she was married to Joris. But now, she had a new husband. Why hadn't I figured this out first?

"What? You're still here?" Catarina dragged a handkerchief across her nose which leaked like a faucet. Her red eyes and baritone voice indicated she was ill which added to her poor disposition. "Mr. Innes is at the shop and has been every day since we arrived home." After a bout of coughing, loud enough to awaken the dead at Trinity, she blew two long nasal foghorns. "Every day. From now on," she mumbled after sneezing into the wilting handkerchief. "As he should be." She walked away from the door which Mary closed behind her. It did not muffle another bout of coughing.

Mr. Innes never came to the shop, that day or the next. Alain decided to search for his boss, and I suggested the coffeehouse or The Pearl. I cringed at the thought of Alain speaking to Bertram White. Suppose he mentioned our last encounter. No. Not even Bert was that stupid to tell a husband what he tried to do to a man's wife.

Speaking to Mr. Innes was forgotten because the next day, the port captain had news. A ship from Leith, *The Molly,* had entered the harbor. The news arrived by messenger. In minutes, I gathered a few stale biscuits, grabbed Sally's hand, and flew out the door.

We arrived at the pier as the crew of *The Molly* prepared to tie up the ship. Living in Manhattan, I was used to the rows of merchant and English naval vessels docked along the East River. The pier was a noisy place, filled with the shouts of men ordering goods to be loaded and unloaded. Cartmen offered their horse-drawn carts to haul the contents of the bowels of the ships to local merchants. Ships' crews worked quickly and shouted curses at strollers or the curious to get out of their way. All were anxious to quench their thirst at the local tavern and a romp with the local entertainment.

The saturated hulls of the ships creaked and scraped as they rose and fell with the tide. The air was marinated with the odor of boats. It's a smell that's hard to explain, but unforgettable. A combination of rotted fish, salt, mold, unwashed men, and linseed oil used as a wood preservative. I remember Duff, a crew member on the *Saint Andrew*, describe it thusly: "Tis a jumble o' rum and piss."

I scanned the deck for an eleven-year-old girl that matched the sketch Davina had sent more than a year ago. She would be easy to find, her presence out of order amongst the world of men. But I had to wait. Passengers were ordered to stay below until the gangway was set, and the official representing the port captain came on board and cleared the ship. Perhaps, this very moment, Alexandra was looking out one of the port holes, searching the crowd, searching for her parents.

Looking around at those standing nearby, there was a man and woman about my age clutching each other. The woman had tears in her eyes and the man, perhaps her husband, patted her hand. Were they waiting to be reunited with a family member, too? Would Alexandra think they were her parents? I would not have blamed her. It broke my heart that she didn't know us. It was possible she could have walked right by not knowing who we were.

The Molly was alive with activity. Deckhands scurried everywhere. Those on the boatswain's gang let out the bow, stern, and spring lines. They began as thick coiled snakes and jumped to life as they unraveled. Once secured, new passengers, the local rats, braved the tightrope and dashed aboard. They were on a mission, in search of food, and were known to eat anything, including their own waste. These cunning rascals would not be missed. It was said that rats outnumbered Manhattanites.

Shouted orders were accompanied by good-natured bantering between the crew and their counterparts on the pier. The sailors were in a jolly mood; they had reached safe harbor after a profitable sailing. On the top deck, in the center of what looked like organized confusion, stood a tall man. His straggly blond hair covered the epaulets of a short jacket. He constantly pushed his hair back when it dangled in his face. A scarf was tied neatly around his neck. I could think of better uses for it. Sailors kept running to him to get their orders, and then dashed around the ship to convey them to others. This had to be the quartermaster in charge of deck operations. I didn't see the captain anywhere, or anyone dressed to look the part. Perhaps he was working on the last entry in the ship's log in preparation to meet with the port official. After spending months on a ship, I was familiar with the routine.

One crew member, a skinny young lad, about twelve years old, slid down the ladder from the top deck without touching a rung and disappeared into the deck below. Moments later, he reappeared and scurried back with the quartermaster's cap.

Leaning on the rail were several crew members ogling the crowd. One young fellow smiled wide and waved to someone he knew. A pretty girl returned his gesture. Their sweet encounter was greeted with rude comments.

Two of his shipmates stared in another direction. A short fellow with a bloody scarf covering a bruised head pointed to a group of women dressed like birds in bright colors. Feathers decorated their hair and heavy rouge reddened their faces. "Ladies," he yelled while leaning over the railing. "Where's my Lilly? Have you seen her? Tell her Jack's back in town and Mighty Zeus's achin' for her." This prompted crude laughter.

"She's no longer working," shouted a young woman in a red dress cut purposely to reveal her charms. "Ran off with an officer. At least that's what he called himself."

An older woman stepped forward and lifted her dress to her knees. "Jack, I'll take care of Zeus. He'll get his money's worth."

The sailor squinted at the woman. "Zeus might be a bit too much for a grannie." Then he dragged an older sailor toward the railing. "Maybe he'll do."

"Not interested. How about a discount, Jack? Half what these other ladies charge?"

"Sounds like a bargain," shouted a sailor standing next to Jack. "If you don't take her offer, I will. Besides, looks to me like she's got plenty of experience. Might know a trick or two the younger ones don't."

"Get to work." The haggling was cut short by the boatswain. "Or you'll have extra duty before you spend a night off this ship. Now git." The crew grumbled as they retreated, the women looked downcast until their attention turned to another larger vessel about to dock. But the older whore stopped short and released a loud snort when the boatswain winked at her. Her evening's work held promise.

Two crewmen lifted a wide plank and carried it to an opening in the railing. With a mighty heave-ho they directed the board to two others waiting on the pier. This served as the gangway, a bridge, for passengers and crew to disembark. Its placement increased my anxiety.

"Why is it taking so long? The ship was tied down an hour ago."

"Anna, it's been thirty minutes."

"What's going on now? Can you see?" Standing on tiptoes, I depended on Alain when it came to looking over others.

"The official representing the port captain just went on board. He has to clear the ship and make sure there's no contagion."

"Contagion?" I had forgotten. Ships were often floating coffins. Once ship's fever spread, there was no way to stop it. When Alain and I sailed to Caledonia, many were buried at sea. No matter if they were crew or passenger, no matter their age or sex. It was like the Angel of Death came on board.

"The officials are a bit more cautious these days. There's talk about fever from Poland and the Baltic."

"This ship is from Scotland," I said. My voice desperate.

"It doesn't matter. Everyone is being careful. Parliament is considering a new law to quarantine a ship for forty days. Even the cargo will be burned, especially if it's yarn, blankets, or wigs. It's devastating for shipping companies. Indemnity doesn't make right a ruined reputation."

"Forty days. You mean Alexandra could be made to stay on board for forty days?"

"Aye. Just keep your eye on the flags on the halyard. If a Yellow Jack is hoisted, that means quarantine. We won't know until the official inspects the log. The captain must account for every soul who boarded the ship in Leith. If the number is less, an explanation must be in the log."

Just then, the same official came up topside, followed by a well-dressed man in a blue and red coat with gold epaulets and buttons. On his long curly wig sat a large, plumed hat. No doubt, this was the captain. The two men conversed and then parted. I looked carefully to see if anyone had a yellow flag in hand. Thankfully, none was visible.

The first to come down the gangway was a passenger, a young man. He limped with the aid of a crutch and had difficulty managing the horizontal slats nailed into the ramp meant to prevent slippage. When he lost his balance, and almost toppled into the water, the crew could not contain their laughter. The young man glared back at his tormentors, but they ignored him, waiting for the next victim.

There weren't many. This ship, it appeared, carried mostly trade goods: hogsheads of beer and crates of whisky bottles and tools. In between the mountains of barrels, crates, and wooden boxes, one piled on top of another, I caught a fleeting image of a powder blue dress billowing around a young girl's legs.

Speechless, I pointed at the apparition.

Alexandra.

I tugged at Alain's sleeve. "There she is. Look. She's walking to the gangway." A vision appeared. Light brown hair braided and pinned. A raised hand shading her eyes, searching the crowd on the pier.

Alain said nothing. His eyes were on our daughter.

"There's your sister," I said softly to Sally as I picked her up so she could see. Sally waved, but I wasn't sure Alexandra saw her.

"Our child has become a beautiful young woman," I said to Alain. I felt like I had just given birth, and I couldn't stop staring at what I had brought into the world. It was like living in the age of miracles, the stories my father used to tell me long ago.

Instead of focusing on Alexandra, Alain pointed in another direction. "What's she doing here?" His tone turned urgent and angry.

Nearby, stood a large man, and next to him was Catarina. She said something to the man and then pointed directly at us. I didn't know him, but Alain did.

"That's the constable for the Dock Ward. What's Catarina up to now?" growled Alain. His eyes narrowed, his fists clenched, and his scar reddened.

And then, Catarina melted away.

"Mamma? Papa?"

"Alexandra?"

"Yes."

I stepped forward. Not an ocean, but an arms-length away. Should I embrace her? Would she allow me? We were like strangers until my daughter rushed into my arms and we hugged for what seemed like forever; I couldn't let her go. Not even to Alain. We stood there connected, mother and daughter. I could barely breathe, and I didn't care.

"I'm Sally. Your sister."

Only Sally's sweet childish voice was able to part us. I held Alexandra's face in my hands to get a good look at her. Wisps of soft curls framed her face. Arched dark eyebrows enhanced soft brown eyes. Long eyelashes brushed translucent cheeks. I could see hints of my father in her face.

Alain rushed in for his turn, and Sally hugged them both. How wonderful to see my family united. For the first time.

"Mama? Papa? This is Claire White." Alexandra turned to the woman standing behind her. "My companion."

The small woman was almost hidden by Alexandra. She stepped forward and we shook hands. I had almost forgotten about Claire and expressed my gratitude for keeping our daughter safe. "Would you care to have a meal with us, Mistress Claire? Perhaps stay for the night until you find lodging?"

"That won't be necessary. I'll be going to my brother's establishment. He's a widower and is expecting me. I'll be taking care of his household, at least until he remarries. His second wife died many years ago. Such a fine man, proud to be a freeman, and look," she fumbled in her bag and brought out a letter. After unfolding it, she pointed to the writing, "Such a fine hand. Wouldn't you say?" She held the letter close to her face. "I'm not sure where he lives. He mentioned something…something about a pearl or Pearl Lane. The writing's smeared."

Alain and I looked at each other. "Is your brother Bertram White?" Alain asked.

"Why yes. He's my baby brother, and he begged me to come. I could hardly say no to family, and then when I was offered this opportunity to escort your fine daughter to the very city where my brother lives, it's as if God himself ordered me to go. So here I am. Do you know him? Can you show me where he lives?"

125

For someone who seemed shy at first, Claire made up for it, speaking profusely.

"Of course. It's not out of our way...the least we can do," said Alain.

"Thank you, sir. I will miss your daughter. She's a lovely young woman, and she's safe now. My job is at an end, and another is about to begin. Oh, and by the way, your sister Davina gives her happy regards to all."

"Thank you, Claire," Alain said as he looked at me and winked.

"Mama? I almost forgot. I have a letter, too." Alexandra reached into her pocket and pulled out a sealed note. "I'm sorry it's creased but you can see that the wax is not broken. I put it in my pocket this morning. I didn't want to forget to hand it to you the moment I got off the ship."

I took the letter. Her eyes suggested she was proud to accomplish this task that had been assigned to her.

"Davina? I wonder what news she has. Maybe she's getting married or Father Drummond has found her."

"No. No. It's from *Grand-pere*. It's from your father, Mama."

I looked at the unopened letter. It felt odd, like its author reaching out from another time, across eons of space. "Thank you...Alexandra." I stared at the letter, lost in its possibilities, and then returned to my daughter. "Let's get you home and Mistress Claire on her way. I'll open it later." I tucked the letter into my pocket, but I could feel it throb against my skin.

"Mr. MacArthur. You sir. Stop." It was the big man, the official, who had been standing next to Catarina. He appeared from behind.

"Yes. What can I do for you, Constable?"

"I have a warrant for your arrest."

"What? On what charges?" Alain turned toward Catarina who kept her distance.

"For defyin' an ordinance. Offerin' illegal employment for cartmen and operatin' an unlawful shop."

"There must be some mistake. I don't own the business." Alain pointed toward Catarina. "She does."

"That's not what the lady says. You two can sort that out in a court of law. I'm only doin' my job."

The constable took Alain by the arm and began to pull him away. He tried to wrestle free, but the fellow was strong, the right man for the

126

job. "Mrs. Innes warned you'd be difficult. Like it or not, you're comin' with me."

As Alain was pushed and pulled down the street and disappeared into the crowd, I noticed Catarina's glare. She had not moved. But the smile on her face had. It grew steadily and cruelly. Suddenly, she turned, and the last thing I saw were her skirts swishing as she walked away.

PART TWO

CHAPTER THIRTEEN
KILMUIR – 2008

THE KILMUIR CEMETERY was located on a bluff at the tip of the Isle of Skye's Trotternish Peninsula. Once, the graveyard was adjacent to a sixteenth century church, now only waist-high stone walls protected the dead. Visitors were rewarded with panoramic views overlooking the expanse of the Atlantic Ocean. Out there, somewhere in the distant blue, were the Outer Hebrides, the islands of Lewis and Harris and many more. Beyond that, the New World. Shielding my eyes from an unforgiving glare, magnified by the glassy sea, I couldn't help but think of Anna. Had she felt the same emptiness I was experiencing? The prospect of an uncertain future?

Alec promised to take me to Lewis and Harris one day. He extolled the beauty I would find there. "The white sand beaches equal to those found in the Caribbean. Their beauty is in their barrenness. The pristine water just as turquoise." He described the trip as easy, a ferry ride from Ullapool on the mainland. "As long as the sea isn't rough, and you don't mind spending many hours on board."

"Is there food on the ferry? Is it any good?"

"It's not fine dining, but much better than what the airlines offer. There's a bar too. If you don't like what's on the menu, whisky will fill your stomach." He chuckled as one playful eyebrow arched.

"I'm not sure. Pitching and rolling on a boat is not my idea of fun. I mean, are the Hebrides really that beautiful?" I wondered at my hesitation. When I first came to Scotland, I couldn't wait to explore everything: the highlands, the castles, the one-track roads. Perhaps I was becoming too cynical, or burned-out, taking it all for granted, like some Philadelphians who never ventured beyond their neighborhood to see the Liberty Bell.

"Absolutely. You'll see. Nothing like it. It's a simple drive from Lewis to Harris. They're connected, you know."

I didn't. But now our plans were put on hold. Some things in life were beyond our control.

Alec's father had died.

As Mr. Grant's condition worsened, the family knew it was a matter of time. Alec's father had an incurable disease; his muscles were turning into stone. There was no cure, no treatment, and surgery only made it worse. The progressively debilitating disease robbed Alec's father of mobility and speech. The prognosis turned grim when his jaw clamped shut and his lungs began to harden. Stalwart to the end, Mr. Grant made his end-of-life wishes known to his family. No heroic measures. No stomach tube or breathing apparatus to force air into solidifying tissue. At one point, he broached the idea of ending his life, but Mora, his wife, a strict Catholic, wouldn't hear of it. Church doctrine did not condone relief from his long-time suffering.

It didn't matter. He got his wish. One morning, Alec's father did not awaken. Mora praised God's benevolence.

At the cemetery, the newly dug gravesite was surrounded by ancient stone markers patiently waiting to welcome the newcomer. The dark wooden casket was covered with eucalyptus, aspidistra, and purple roses. The creative florist had arranged the foliage and flowers to resemble a thistle, the national flower of Scotland. Silent mourners huddled together, seeking the support of each other as they faced the ugly reminder that life is brief. The words spoken by the priest offered some comfort as they drifted away with each breath of wind that floated up the bluff.

Mora, dressed in classic black with a simple strand of pearls, an anniversary gift, was flanked by her two sons: Alec and Iain. As Alec's fiancée, I stood next to him, at the end of the line-up, locking my arm in his. Kate, Iain's wife, and the newest addition to the family, stood between Mora and Iain. Her hand played nervously with a gold chain that had escaped the tartan scarf draped around her neck. The scarf flapped like a flag along with her long dark hair.

The first and last time I saw Kate was more than three years ago, when Alec brought me to his home to meet his parents. Iain urged Kate to lure Alec, her old boyfriend, back into her arms. When Alec ignored her flirtations, she turned toward more fruitful territory, the younger brother. Kate's family had had connections with the Grants since she was born, and it was always assumed that Kate would marry Alec. But Fate had other plans. Iain saved the day when he proposed. The couple wed two months later.

Alec and I had good reasons not to attend the nuptials. The first was timing. We were on a planned archeological dig in Panama. The second was personal. Before his engagement, Iain came on to me, even though he knew Alec and I were a couple, and then lied about it. The third reason was geographical. Iain and Kate eloped and married in Paris. Regardless, both families rejoiced to be lawfully united.

The same family warmth did not extend to my relationship with Alec. I felt like an outsider, a usurper, only tolerated. I believed most of the Grant family, except for Alec's father, would be just as joyful if I returned to the States. Alone. When I mentioned my concerns to Alec, they sounded petty and childish, but he always allayed my worries and said he didn't care what his family thought. We would always be together. Until death do us part, he'd tease.

Now, at the cemetery, the reality of the Rite of Committal for a beloved family member was no joking matter. The earthy scent from the freshly dug grave was a bleak reminder of the man inside the box.

When Alec learned that his father's condition worsened, we rushed to his side. As it turned out, we arrived the day before he passed. We were the last to see him awake and have final words. Alec told me later, that my being there pleased his father.

A hospital bed, set up in the downstairs library, had a chair on either side for family vigils. Evidence of the last sacrament was strewn about on one cloth-covered end table: used cotton balls, a crucifix, a small bowl of water, candles, a plate with torn bread, and an empty glass. The tools for treating the sick were scattered on another table: a clipboard, a box of tissues, latex gloves, and a water bottle with a limp straw. Directly across from the bed was a clock with large digital numbers. Alec's father requested the clock. He wanted to keep track of the minutes and the hours. For what end was too depressing to contemplate. On the patient's bed, attached to the side railing, golden-colored urine dripped into a bag. Every so often a whiff of ammonia swirled about the room, a stark reminder that at least one bodily system still functioned.

Alec motioned to the nurse seated quietly in the darkest corner of the room. "I'd like a few minutes alone with my father. If you don't mind."

She nodded. "My name is Charlotte. Call me if your father needs me." Charlotte looked at her sleeping patient and then made for the door while pulling her sweater tightly around her. That's when I noticed the drapes flapping by a window in another corner of the room. It was opened several inches.

"Charlotte. Why is the window open?" I asked, while crossing my arms to keep warm. "It's cold outside." I walked over to the window and began to close it. Even in the summer months, it could be chilly on Skye.

"No. Please don't. Mr. Grant requested that it remain open." She hesitated before explaining. "Many of the old ones prefer it."

"To be cold?" I looked to Alec for an answer.

"It's okay, Charlotte. Thank you. I'll explain."

The caretaker took one long look at the window and then at Alec. She smiled slightly and grabbed the pitcher of water. "This needs filling. I'll be right outside. If you need me."

When the door clicked, I whispered, "Explain what?"

"It's a Scottish tradition. When someone dies, a window or door is opened so the soul can escape. Sometimes, when someone knows the end is near, they will ask for the window to be opened so they can hurry God along."

A tiny shiver spiraled down my spine. I didn't have a response. What could I say? I remembered Grams, the night she died. She wanted the same, the waiting to be over. To move on.

The window was forgotten when Alec's father opened his eyes, exposing their hollow blueness: glassy and tearing. I came closer and Alec grasped his father's hand. A faint smile crossed the man's parched lips.

"Da, do you want some water?" Alec asked.

His father blinked.

"Here. Let me help." I put the straw into the glass and trapped the water with my finger over the open end. I pulled the water-filled straw out of the glass and brought it to the patient's mouth. But I let go too quickly and one side of Mr. Grant's face and his pillow got wet. The second attempt was more successful. Again, Alec's father blinked his approval.

"Da. Are you cold?"

He blinked twice.

"Do you want the window open?"

He blinked once causing a tear to spill and disappear in his hair.

"Alec, do you want to be alone with your father?"

"No. My father wants you to stay. I want you to stay."

Mr. Grant blinked again; the almost imperceptible smile returned. I approached the other side of the bed and ignored the chair. I leaned over the rail and cradled the patient's frail hand. The nurse who attended my grandmother told me that the warmth of a human touch is what a dying person wants most. Besides, it was the only gift I had to give.

Alec ignored the ominous signs and chatted about everyday things with his father while I remembered the last time we were together. He was the only one who treated me with kindness and generosity from the first day we met. He greeted me with a smile and was delighted in my relationship with his son. When we announced our engagement, Alec's father could not contain his joy. He truly made me feel welcome. Now, my one ally was leaving me.

We quickly succumbed to silence when the patient drifted off to sleep. I patted Mr. Grant's hand for the last time, nodded to Alec, and headed for the door. If Alec was feeling the same as I did, when Grams died, I knew he'd want a few precious minutes alone with his beloved parent.

The graveside service included the Lord's Prayer, the Twenty-Third Psalm, and a short eulogy by a cassocked Father Wilson. Then, the priest recited a final prayer from Numbers: "Receive the Lord's blessing. May the Lord bless you and watch over you. May the Lord make his face shine upon you and be gracious unto you. May the Lord look kindly on you and give you peace." He waved an aspergillum, generously sprinkling the coffin with holy water and added, "In the Name of the Father, and of the Son, and of the Holy Spirit." A chorus of Amens followed and Catholics like Mora, Alec, Iain, and Kate made the sign of the cross. All heads were bowed, except mine.

"What's the water for?" I whispered to Alec.

"It's a way of saying farewell. Father was greeted into this world with baptism. And now the holy water reminds us of his salvation." Alec turned and leaned toward his mother who was sniffling into a handkerchief. Alec wrapped one arm around Mora and returned his attention to the funeral.

This was all so foreign to me: the funerary mass at the church, the hymns, knowing the appropriate time to kneel or stand, praying the rosary, and now the Rite of Committal, the interment. I had never attended a Catholic funeral, baptism, or communion. My ignorance was a reminder of my insular upbringing and made me feel like a stranger. Alec, along with the rest of his family, had a deep religious bond. But I was the broken link in the chain. No matter how much I tried, I could never make it whole. Now, standing at the outer edge of the family, I sensed remoteness, even though Alec was squeezing my hand.

When Father Wilson concluded the service, Alec, Iain, and his mother took a few steps toward the casket. Mora put her fingers to her lips and then touched the wood. She plucked one of the roses and pressed it to her chest. Then Kate and I were motioned to approach, and after watching Kate take a rose, I did the same. We were followed by other mourners until only the greenery remained. Alec and Iain guided their mother to a waiting car, stopping now and then to greet family and friends anxious to offer their condolences. Although there was a meal of consolation back at the house, some preferred to extend their sympathies now so they could dive quickly into the food and whisky.

Kate and I stood alone with our roses. Neither of us sought to comfort the other; to ease the awkward moment. But that didn't last long. Not for Kate. She was swarmed by her parents and siblings, and the rest of the extended family and friends offering a mixture of condolences and congratulations.

I smiled and pretended I didn't care and turned to look around the ancient cemetery. I couldn't help but notice a monument that towered over the rest; a granite Celtic cross marking the gravesite of Scotland's favorite heroine, Flora MacDonald. Even I knew her story. Flora was renowned for hiding Bonny Prince Charles when he fled the English after his failed attempt to place his father on the throne in the mid-eighteenth century.

"They say she's buried in a shroud from a bedsheet slept on by the Prince."

"Huh." I turned, wondering about the voice behind me. A familiar one along with the extension of a much-needed friendly hand. "Ira. Dr. Mason. How nice. Thank you for coming. It feels like ages since I last saw you."

"Ah. Too long. I hear I will soon be addressing you as Dr. Duncan."

"I'm afraid so," I scoffed. "And I owe some of that to you. Encouraging me to pursue my degree so I could remain in Scotland."

"If that brings you happiness, my dear, then I am pleased to be partially responsible."

We walked away from the milling guests. I smiled but didn't respond. As was evidenced today, happiness could be fleeting. And then I remembered and put my hand on Ira's. "I'm so sorry to hear about Esther. You know Alec and I would have attended the funeral, but we were stuck in Panama." Another gust of wind flew up the bluff and sailed across the cemetery to play with my hair. I quickly secured the curls under my hat. "So much has happened while we were away."

"No problem, my dear. Jewish funerals happen quickly. Your card and donation in my wife's memory were appreciated. Esther was quite fond of you." Force of habit caused Ira to check on his cap; he tapped it when he found it perfectly situated. "By the way, I heard you made quite a splash for yourself on the dig. Where the old Scots failed to create a colony."

"Yes. It all turned out for the best, although it was a bit traumatic. Sort of Indiana Jones-like. Imagine finding Filib's dirk after all those years. I still can't believe it sometimes."

"It proves Anna's story. Right?"

"That was the best part. I was able to confirm her journal was authentic, an important historical document."

"What do you intend to do with it?"

"Already done. It's now a part of the National Archives."

"Good choice. It belongs to you and Scotland."

"I was told I could visit the journal anytime I wished. Like checking out a relative in a nursing home."

"You did the right thing, my dear. A precious artifact needs to be preserved for posterity."

"I agree. It was hard to part with Anna's journal, though." I remembered the painful moment when I touched the cover's embossed thistle and the worn binding for the last time and placed my inheritance into the hands of a curator. "Alec came with me. I couldn't have done it alone." I needed to change the subject before I started to cry. Of course, this being a funeral, no one would have suspected the reason for my sadness. "It's nice of you to have traveled across Scotland to be here for Alec. It will please him. Have you seen him yet?"

"No, I arrived too late to greet the family, but not for the service. Alec and his father had a special bond. I've heard you liked the old man as well. May his memory be for a blessing, my dear."

"Thank you. What a lovely thing to say."

"No need for thanks. In my tradition, to comfort the mourner is considered the greatest *mitzvah* - good deed - one can do. I should be the one thanking you."

"I know what the word means. Like a *bar mitzvah*."

Ira smiled. "So, when is the big day for you and Alec? Marriage is also a *mitzvah*."

"I don't know. It feels like we've been engaged forever. Three years now." I glanced over at Kate; Iain had rejoined her. "For some, that would be forever." I gestured toward the newlyweds who were talking to Father Wilson. He looked comical trying to tame his cassock against the wind. "They married shortly after they got engaged, leaving Alec and me far behind. Maybe we're too comfortable with the way things are. That's the downside of living together. What's the rush? We have everything but a priest's blessing and the legal paperwork."

"Ah. Are you planning on converting?"

"What?" I hadn't realized I had included the Catholic Church in our marriage plans. "It would make life easier." I stared back at my future sister-in-law still playing with her necklace while placing a hand lightly over her stomach. Tears welled in my eyes again. "Maybe Alec's family would be more accepting."

"I'm sure they will love Alec's choice. But how do you feel about conversion?"

"I don't know. I hadn't thought much about it until now. Hmm. Converting from what? That's the question. I wish my parents had given me something to start with."

"Anna did."

"Anna? I'm not sure—what did she give me? Oh, you mean the candlesticks?"

"Yes. And her journal. This might sound a wee bit speculative coming from an academician who prides himself on sticking to the facts, but maybe Anna is reaching out…the only way she can."

Ira made me laugh again, but I couldn't help thinking that maybe my heavenly grandmother was urging Anna on. I wouldn't have put it past her.

Silence engulfed us as we walked arm in arm along the stone wall and stopped by a most unusual ancient gravesite, a carved effigy of a knight. It was old but in excellent condition.

"This is the well-known marker for Angus Martin," said Ira. "He married a Danish princess and sired seven sons. It's believed he stole this fantastic carved slab from the island of Iona."

"Really?"

"It's a good story, but there's no proof. You know, my dear, we historians stockpile a lot of useless facts."

"So, Alec reminds me all the time."

"Well, I must confess I did my homework before coming here. This is an ancient graveyard inhabited by many interesting characters."

We walked further until we came to another unusual marker. I stopped cold. The chiseled name was Charles MacKarter. "Is that another spelling for MacArthur? That was Anna's married name. Do you think there's any relation?"

"Possibly. The MacArthur clan was quite distinguished and proud at their peak five hundred years ago. Claimed they were descendants of King Arthur."

I leaned closer to read the epitaph:

HERE LIE THE REMAINS
OF CHARLES MAC
KARTER WHOSE
FAME AS AN HON
EST MAN AND
REMARKABLE PIP
ER WILL SURVIVE THIS
GENERATION
FOR HIS MANNERS
WERE EASY AND RE
GULAR AS HIS
MUSIC AND THE MELODY OF
HIS FINGERS WILL

138

"That's funny. The carver didn't finish his work," I said. "Almost half of the stone is blank."

"Maybe he was afraid he wouldn't get paid. MacKarter's son and heir drowned shortly after his father's passing."

I took hold of Ira's arm again as we returned to the thinning crowd.

"Professor?" I stopped and faced my friend. "You have given me a lot to think about."

"I have?"

"About Anna. Reaching out. Conversion. Which way to go and...Alec. His family constantly reminds me of our differences in religion, history, and national pride. They don't say it to my face, but I can see it in their eyes and mannerisms...their distance. But I come from a distinguished clan, too. I have Scottish blood in my veins. And Jewish. Anna and Alain were...are my family. You have never let me forget that." I leaned over and planted a kiss on his whiskered cheek. "It was good to talk to you, Ira."

"Happy to help, my dear. Please, call on me any time. With Esther gone, my life and home are terribly empty these days. The Friday night dinners, the smell of chicken soup, the glow of the candles, and the chatter around the table, I'm afraid, are delights of the past."

"We should have you over. I'd love to light my candlesticks again. If you would show me how. The prayers, I mean. Do you think that would be okay? Is there a rule against it?"

He chuckled. "No, my dear. I would be happy to stand in for Anna and instruct you."

"I'm only sorry the invitation has taken me this long. Of course, the lovely Friday night tradition must continue. Grams would have wanted that."

"I think Anna would, too."

Our simultaneous laughter turned heads, including Alec's. He grinned as he came running over.

"There you are. I should have known Dr. Mason would steal you away."

I unhooked my hand from Ira and grabbed onto Alec.

"You'll join us at my parent's home, for something to eat and drink, won't you Professor?" asked Alec.

"Of course, he will," I answered instead. "It's a *mitzvah* to do so. I have it on good authority - to comfort the mourner."

"I'll be happy to, my dear. I want to pay my respects to the family by drinking a glass of *schnapps* in memory of Mr. Grant."

I must have looked puzzled.

"Whisky. There's only one important fact that will make you a true citizen of this great country. The Scots make the best."

CHAPTER FOURTEEN
DOORS CLOSING - DOORS OPENING

THE COMMUNITY WHERE the Grants lived was a quiet one. There were no strip malls, office buildings, or apartments. Houses were a brisk walk apart, and there were more sheep and Highland coos on the one-track roads than cars. Strangers rarely entered the peaceful enclave. Philadelphia, my hometown, couldn't have been more different.

But today, the serenity was put on hold. At first glance, it looked like the Grants were having a grand celebration: a wedding or a baptism, perhaps. A number of cars were parked bumper-to-bumper on the grassy edge of the gravel path leading to the house. Swarms of men and women, young and old, greeted each other with handshakes and hugs. Guests stood before the front door or wandered around the boxwood hedge into the gardens. Quickly, it became apparent that this was not a happy event. All were dressed in somber colors: black, gray, or navy dresses for the women; semi-formal attire for the men. Instead of laughter and casual conversation, hushed voices were muffled behind white handkerchiefs, dabbing teary eyes or a runny nose.

Arriving guests walked quickly as if they were late for dinner. Children ran ahead but did not shout their arrival. Women carried their potluck contributions in silver-foiled casserole dishes, sealed cake plates, or napkin-covered baskets. All accepted, without question, the orders of an elderly woman who, like a traffic officer at the busiest intersection in Edinburgh, directed the placement of each donation. This included two teenage boys carrying trays of Scottish salmon and sliced venison. This was a funeral luncheon. The food and the guests, even those who were already into the whisky, were there to support the family who had just lost a loved one.

The close-knit community always coalesced when needed. Alec told me that several ladies of the Skye Garden Club, most childhood friends of Mora's, stayed back at the house, rather than attend the funeral. This was to insure all was ready when the mourners returned. The women were easy to spot. Each was gray-haired, or nearly so, and fluttered like butterflies in their colorful print aprons. Their first chore was the tradition of covering the mirrors throughout the house, believing a funeral was a time of inner reflection, not of one's outward appearance. Then they moved onto the buffet. Mourners would be hungry. Stacks of silverware, napkins, and plates were strategically placed along with trays of local cheese. Homemade shortbread and candy dishes filled with tablet were set on a sideboard, reserved for desserts. With the help of a few strong arms, crates of local whisky were opened and made ready. Pitchers of water, needed to enhance the whisky's flavor, were placed nearby.

We arrived after Iain and Kate and found them engrossed in a conversation with her family. They never acknowledged us. Perhaps that was by choice. Either way, it was for the best. Our strained relations were publicly awkward.

A garden club lady, the traffic officer, rushed over to greet Mora and help with her hat and coat. The woman backed off when Alec beat her to it. With a few whispered words to her son, Mora ascended the stairs and disappeared. Alec's eyes followed her every step. For one who hadn't always described his mother kindly, I was surprised by Alec's concern.

"Should I go after her and see if she's okay?" he asked.

"Give her some time," answered the gray-haired matron. "This has been a long day, a long week. Mora needs a good cry. A chance to brush out her hair and make some minor adjustments. The mirrors are covered so she won't be long. Now you go and greet your guests and get something to eat. I'll see to your mother."

"Thank you, Mrs. Adair. And thank the other ladies as well. Their kindness is appreciated."

Mrs. Adair's lips barely smiled; her eyes were wistful. She nodded and walked toward the stair and retrieved a handkerchief from an apron pocket. After pressing it to her eyes, she blew her nose, and grasped the bannister.

"Mrs. Adair is a wonder. Your mother is lucky to have such a good friend." She reminded me of Gram's friend, Estelle Shasta. Women like Estelle existed everywhere.

"She lost her husband six months ago. Pancreatic cancer. He didn't last long. Mom stayed with her throughout the ordeal." He hesitated. His forehead furrowed. "Maybe that's a better way to go. My father suffered too long."

"I'm not so sure about that," I said. "To go quickly or linger. Your father's mind was sharp almost to the end. He maintained a sense of humor and got to watch his family prosper and grow. Your earning a doctorate, teaching at a prestigious university, and Kate coming into the family. And me." I forced myself not to look at the new bride. "I've heard it said that even those with full-time nursing care, like your father, prefer life to death."

As if on cue, Charlotte, the nurse, side-stepped her way through the crowd while balancing a plate of venison, black pudding, berry salad, and a buttered roll. She nodded, but when it was clear her aim was an empty chair on the other side of the room, we continued where we left off.

"You're probably right. That's a good topic, though, to use when experiencing one of those awkward moments with Father Wilson. I can hear the good Father's answer. *It depends on the dying man's salvation status. There is no good death unless one has accepted the Catholic faith.*" Alec's eyes followed an aproned lady wiping spilled tea on the floor. "Mom's going to need her friends once everyone goes home."

"Are Kate and Iain leaving, too?"

"No. But Iain won't be much help, and neither will Kate. She'll be visiting her family or shopping on the mainland. It's the free meals and board—"

"I hope you don't mind," interrupted Mrs. Adair. She must have finished taking care of Mora. "I put together a plate for each of you. Salmon, buttered cabbage, cherry tomatoes, and sliced cucumber. Would you like a roll? Butter? I couldn't fit it all on the plate." She unloaded two napkins draped on her arm and announced she would be right back.

"Mrs. Adair," I said. "I thought I saw some celeriac mash. It's become one of my favorites."

"I'll get you some, dear. I have been given strict orders from Mora that you and Alec are to be fed."

"Really?" I asked.

"She said the two of you worked so hard to look after Mr. Grant, plan the funeral, and take care of everyone else. Mora's grateful. It's a difficult time, to lose a beloved family member like your father. This is when the best in us comes out." She patted my hand and motioned for me to eat. "Oh, and would you like a drink? Tea? Whisky, perhaps? My husband liked it with a few drops of water. I'll be right back." She was gone before we could answer.

"That was nice of your mother. To be concerned."

Alec said nothing. His mouth full.

For the first time, except when I was around Alec's father, I felt acceptance. Maybe things weren't as bad as I imagined. When Mrs. Adair returned with the drinks, I took a sip of the whisky. I never cared for the taste but welcomed its spreading warmth.

A burst of laughter and glasses clinking shattered my thoughts. The source came from the circle of friends surrounding Alec's brother and Kate.

"Seems like when one door closes, another opens," said Mrs. Adair. "It's the cycle of life and there's no escaping it. Congratulations to your family. It's time you had some good news." Then Mrs. Adair disappeared into the kitchen.

Alec and I stood alone. Facing each other, our eyes connected. Alec put his free arm around me and pulled me close. I wondered if he saw Kate telegraph her condition at the cemetery. When she had placed a light hand on her still-flat stomach. She and Iain had assured the family's future; something Alec and I had failed to accomplish. I wondered if Mora knew. She had to. The feeling of acceptance vanished.

"I guess I should wish them congratulations," said Alec. "I'd rather ignore Iain, but it wouldn't be fair to Kate. I'll be quick about it. You don't have to come."

I was about to answer when Father Wilson joined us.

"Father, excuse me," said Alec. "I must speak to my brother and his wife. I'll leave you in good hands. With Hanna." Alec walked away, but not in the direction I thought. He stopped to refill his whisky glass.

I put down my unfinished plate and glass. "Father, the eulogy was lovely. It was nice what you said."

"Easy to do for a man like Alec's father. Caring. Generous. He was the kind of man who wouldn't think twice about running into a burning building to save someone. I wish there were more like him." The priest stopped, looked at his glass, and swallowed hard. "You should hear the things I say when the deceased is not so good. Lying doesn't come easy to a man of the cloth. Nor should it. But sometimes—" He chuckled. Father Wilson's laugh sounded like wind chimes in a slight breeze. "He really liked you, you know. Thought you were great for Alec." He took another swig. "Men don't lie on their deathbed. Even the not-so-good ones."

I wanted to tell Father Wilson that there were other good men. My dad died trying to save a co-worker and a friend from a building about to collapse. "I've been meaning to speak to you, Father. You know, I'm not Catholic. I was raised outside of religion, but I had a Jewish ancestor generation ago."

"Yes, I've heard."

"It doesn't mean my family was totally irreligious. In her own way, Grams was spiritual. She believed she was connected to something more, bigger than herself. The past. Her family. It meant everything. She felt this tremendous obligation to her ancestors and needed to hand that down to me." I sighed deeply. "It's hard to explain."

"Spirituality can mean many things to many people. All I know is that when one accepts Jesus Christ, into their heart, that is truly a feeling of divine spirituality. Only then, can one find peace within themselves. Maybe that's the spirituality you are seeking."

I wasn't sure if Father Wilson understood Gram's version of spirituality. It had nothing to do with Jesus Christ or God or Buddha, for that matter. "Alec and I have been engaged for a long time." I stopped, careful not to suggest that our religious difference was the reason, but Iain and Kate, just feet away, were a living example of how similar backgrounds greased life's cogwheels. "We have a wonderful relationship. Hit it off from the moment we met. We love each other, and Alec has never suggested that religion was an issue. But I'm wondering—"

"If sharing the same religion will make it easier? The answer is yes. I see it all the time. The compatibility factor goes up. More so if children are a part of the picture. It's less confusing. Both parents on the same page."

"But shouldn't there be a better reason to convert? Shouldn't I feel an affinity toward Catholicism? That somehow a gap needs filling. In other words, shouldn't I want to be a Catholic even if I had never met Alec?"

"Why yes, of course." Father Wilson looked around and suddenly became distracted. "I'd love to go into this further, but it's hard to do it here. Besides, I see Mora has returned, and I promised to check in with her. Could we meet sometime and delve into all of this? Then I could answer your questions about the steps toward conversion."

"Of course. We live near Aberdeen, so it will have to wait until Alec and I return in a few weeks."

Father Wilson shook my hand, wished me well, and then sped toward Alec's mother. After a few hushed words, they headed for the library, closing the door behind them. While I rubbed my hand from the priest's icy grip, I prayed our conversation would remain confidential. I

145

also wondered if Father Wilson was the right advisor. Would he understand my situation? Or would he not be able to see past official church doctrine that Catholic should marry Catholic? My conversion was the only way to achieve that goal. It's what his superiors and his flock expected. I needed to find someone else.

"I took the liberty of bringing over some *Schnapps*." It was Ira. He carried two shot glasses and offered one. "*L'chaim*. To Life," he said and quickly swallowed the contents in one gulp.

"*Sláine.*" I managed a sip.

"*Slainte. Mhor agadi.* Great health to you."

I considered another toast but changed my mind.

"Forgive me for eavesdropping on your conversation with Father Wilson. If you're looking for someone to chat about Catholicism, a little closer to home, might I recommend my friend, Prescott? You remember, Reverend Prescott Walton. He joined us for dinner. The Sabbath dinner when you brought your candlesticks."

"Wasn't he a Presbyterian minister?"

"Yes, but born a Roman Catholic, and converted when he married his wife."

"Sort of the same situation I'm considering. Yes, I remember. I asked him if there were any secret codes that only Catholics used to identify others of their faith. I asked that question in reference to Anna's journal and her attempt to navigate in a non-Jewish world. Now that I think back, that was an interesting conversation. Yes, I recall Reverend Prescott. Quiet, but nice." Raised voices sailed across the room. I refused to look away. "Would he consider talking to me?"

"I'll be happy to ask. He can at least answer your questions, and then, if you decide to move forward, you could contact Father Wilson. Or maybe Prescott could recommend someone else."

"I don't think Father Wilson will do. I'd rather someone who isn't so intimate with the family. Not that I don't trust him. Clergy are supposed to keep conversations private. Right?" I stared at the closed door to the library. "I would feel awkward sharing my intimate thoughts with a priest who's also a family friend."

"I'll speak to Prescott and let you know."

"Perfect. Alec and I will be home in two or three days. I have to submit my dissertation and Alec has his classes and—" Loud voices sailed across the room. Alec's, most of all. But before I went to rescue him, I had

146

to make sure Ira understood one thing. "Please don't tell Alec about our conversation. I need to figure this out on my own before I say anything."

"Mum's the word, and—" Now Ira noticed the disturbance. "Seems like Alec is upset about something. Too much drink and bad blood between brothers is an unhealthy mix."

A young man in a kilt stood with outstretched arms between Alec and Iain. His stance and taut calf muscles, along with a thunderous brogue, showed he meant business. "Enough. This is not the time or place. You both have had too much to drink."

"I'm not drunk," shouted Alec.

"He's just jealous. I got the girl…he wanted." Iain gestured with an empty whisky glass in one hand. The former contents dripped from Alec's face to his shirt.

"That's not what this is about, and you know it."

"Do I, Brother? Why else…would you put your…hand…on my wife?" Iain turned away to console Kate.

Alec lurched for his brother, but the young man stood in his way. "One of you is a liar," yelled Alec. "If it's not Kate, then it's you."

"I don't know what the…f-f-fuck you're talking about." Iain slurred his words.

"It doesn't belong to you. I don't care what you told Kate." Alec broke free and started again for his brother.

"Alec, no." I grabbed his arm, missed, and got a handful of shirt sleeve. "What are you doing? Stop it."

Iain looked at us. "Yeah, listen to your girlfriend and…fu…off. The two of you." Iain grabbed Kate's hand and jerked her away. She turned her head, our eyes met; hers said nothing.

Silence engulfed the room. "Alec," I whispered while everyone stared. "Come outside. You need to cool off."

I took Alec's hand as we walked into the garden. When we neared the shore of the bay, we stopped. "Alec, what's wrong? What's gotten into you? I know you and Iain don't get along, but why were you going after him?"

Alec said nothing at first. The silence felt like forever. "It had to do with you."

"Me? I don't need my honor protected. I don't care what your brother says. And I certainly don't want you to get hurt."

"My brother said nothing about you."

"Then what was it? From the beginning. Please."

Alec took a deep breath. "It's to do with Kate. She was with her family. Talking about the baby. They were congratulating her. And then, she showed them."

"Showed them what? Alec, I'm confused."

"A chain around her neck. She pulled it out and showed them. A gift from Iain. She said he gave it to her when she told him she was pregnant."

"A necklace? Who cares?"

"Hanna. You're not listening. On the chain was…the ring. The one stolen from my apartment. That night. Kate has Anna's ring."

CHAPTER FIFTEEN

TRUST

MANHATTAN

IN A MOMENT, my life changed.

Like a common criminal, Alain's hands were bound in front of his children and the crowd on the pier. He had no chance to offer a defense, and therefore was presumed guilty. The burden of proving his innocence would be his because Catarina wielded power through her purse and position. My husband's shame was mine as well, his dishonor, a burden on our children. Our lives would be tainted forever.

As the constable dragged Alain away, I begged the man to tell me what would happen to my husband. Instead of answering, he grunted and cursed and shunted me aside. I was left with nothing. I had no idea where Alain would be incarcerated or for how long.

Alexandra's eyes went wide with fright. My poor child had lost her father once again. She grabbed my hand and turned her face inward, into my arms, as she sought protection amidst the chaos. Sally grabbed my skirts and clung to one leg. She begged her father to come back and soothe her tears like he had always done before. But he never heard.

When Catarina's dirty work was done, she snaked her way back through the crowd. The gap she created was quickly refilled with onlookers, hoping for another round of entertainment. I glared at those who remained to witness my family's downfall and recoiled at their harsh words.

"Serves her right," snarled a middle-aged matron to her husband. "And she has children to care for." This was the same couple, that, moments before, I thought Alexandra might mistake for her parents.

Her husband looked my way, his eyes wandering over my person from head to toe, evaluating my condition and status. "The wife has done nothing wrong. Tis her husband who was arrested."

"Mmph." The wife turned toward her husband and hooked her arm in his. "That's what you get when you choose unwisely and marry a scoundrel. A decent woman would have had more sense."

"The court will decide on his guilt or innocence. Not you, my dear. Come along. Let us not make a spectacle."

I watched the two slink away. If it had not been for Sally and Alexandra, I would have put the scold in her place. The world had no shortage of Catarinas.

Other spectators followed their lead, but as they passed, women gathered their skirts and swished them away, as if my misfortune was contagious. A few souls nodded in sympathy and then averted their eyes so as not to further my embarrassment, for the sake of my children.

Left alone at the water's edge, I hadn't felt despair like this since the days before my proposed marriage to an unwelcome suitor. As I held onto Sally, her cries turned into throaty whimpers. Alexandra regained her composure and tried to look brave. "Mama...what about...Father? What should we do?"

I put an arm around my eldest and pulled her close. "I don't know, Alexandra. I do not have an answer. Not yet."

She nodded; her lips quivered. This was a painful moment. The truth can be terrifying as well as a necessary bridge to trust. The loss of which was irreparable. By its very nature, trust was fragile as a gossamer thread, impossible to repair once torn apart. Children know when they are being fed lies. I would not do that to her.

The reality of our situation was frightening for me as well. Was Alain about to be locked in some dank place with rats for cellmates? We would need help from a solicitor. But where would I find one? Would I be permitted to see my husband? Would he be fed? I felt around in my satchel and found the hard biscuits. I wish I had thought to give them to him. But first, I had to see to my daughters' well-being. Our home was not the place. Catarina could throw us out on the street at any time. Perhaps she had already started to do so. I envisioned Mary emptying our wardrobe and drawers and stripping our beds. Counterpanes, shirts, stockings, and smocks tossed into the street, trampled to a muddy pulp by hooves and wagon wheels. Feathered mattresses and pillows, exploding like birds, soaring once again, to the skies.

I had to find a suitable place for Sally and Alexandra. But where? Then, I remembered – Baruch Emmanuel and his wife, Deborah. The doctor had always treated us with kindness and took good care of Sally when she was ill. I had much in common with the Emmanuel's: co-religionists and we were new to this land. But first, I needed Alexandra's chaperone to help with my plan.

"Mistress Claire!" The woman turned reluctantly. She was distracted by someone on the ship. I raised my voice and called again. "Claire!" She walked toward me while glancing over her shoulder, touching her lips, and blowing kisses. Mistress White seemed enchanted by one of the *Molly's* crew, the tall sailor, the Quartermaster. He pushed his stringy hair out of his face, grinned, and made no attempt to hide his interest. I sensed Claire had done more than keep a watchful eye on Alexandra during the trans-Atlantic voyage.

"My husband said we would take you to your brother's place. I intend to keep that promise."

Claire's voice turned desperate. "That's most kind of you, Mrs. MacArthur, but my things are not off the ship. I'm waiting for my friend…that sailor I was talking to…he promised to help. I can wait. You have enough to worry about. Please, go along with your daughters."

"That's not possible." I was not letting Claire off so easy. I needed her. "I would never think of leaving a woman, especially one new to our city, on the docks. I will request your baggage be delivered to The Pearl. I am sure your um…friend knows where it is. All of the sailors are frequent guests of your brother's establishment."

"But I wish—"

"It's no bother." Straightening my back, I looked down on the shorter woman. "Pickpockets line the streets in wait for new arrivals. They will offer their assistance and leave you lying in an alley, penniless or worse. You took excellent care of my daughter, and I will return the favor. Now, come along. I'm sure your brother is anxious to greet his sister."

Claire realized no excuse would change my mind. Besides, I had plenty of arguing left in me, and enough reason to do so. She sighed heavily and tucked in the few loose curls; their enticement was no longer needed. That's when I noticed her hands. They were short and thick like a man's, and no ring would ever make them feminine looking. I also thought I saw a callous or two. This was good news for Bertram White. He was about to get strong hands to do his laundry.

Our first stop was the Emmanuels. As I had expected, they welcomed my daughters, and then Claire and I continued to The Pearl.

I hoped that by delivering Bertram White's sister, she would serve as an excuse to enter the tavern. That is where I expected to find Mr. Innes entertaining his friends with his crude ballads. I had to let him know what Catarina had done. He was the only one who could stop her before she did any more harm. Claire's presence might minimize her brother's incivility toward me.

As we approached The Pearl, shouts and raucous laughter could be heard. A drunken sailor stumbled out the door, followed by another, and together they collapsed in the middle of the street. Bertram appeared, his hair, Medusa-like, his lips thin and taut against bared teeth. He gripped the kerchief of a third crewman, shaking him violently while screaming into his ear.

"If I ever catch you or your friends in my establishment, I'll horsewhip your arse so bad you'll never take a shit again without remembering this day. Now git the hell out o' here." The tavern owner kicked the man hard in the rear so that he toppled over his comrades.

"Is that my—" asked Claire.

"Yes," I said. "That is your brother."

"Oh my." Claire said something more, but I never heard another word. The beating of a drum and the vulgar words of a tavern ditty were music to my ears.

Mr. Innes made some inquiries and found that most prisoners were taken to City Hall, located on Wall Street. The newly built structure was three stories high, topped with a cupola and a weathervane. The triple arched entrance faced Broad. Centered on the second floor was a set of double doors that led to a large balcony used for public speeches and declarations. On either side were three long windows. The architect's attempt at symmetry appeared purposeful; perhaps a reference to maintaining the fragile balance of the scales of justice. It was an imposing building, meant to remind one and all of the government's supreme authority.

My friend took my arm and directed me across the street toward the entrance. I was grateful for his calming strength. "Mr. Innes, how is it that you can spend hours drinking with your friends and show no sign of intoxication?"

"Aye, others have remarked about my amazin' sobriety. Some have even complained. They say it's no fun drinkin' with a sober man."

"Is there a secret? An herbal tea? A magic potion?"

He chuckled as we were about to climb the City Hall steps. "Aye, that there is."

"Well?" I glanced at the building and stopped.

"I take small sips and make sure there are lots o' opportunities tae waste my drink. I clash my mug wi' others and smash it on the table, sloshing the ale so there's more on the floor o' the table than the mug. Then, like a good drunk, I pretend to stumble and demand more, for me and my friends, and repeat the process. By the time our mugs are filled a third o' a fourth round, my comrades are tae drunk tae notice whether I'm drinkin' o' no." He gave me a curious look and winked. "I know what ye're thinkin,' and I'll bet ye want tae know why."

I nodded.

"I'm not as young as I used tae be, although I'm told by some that I still have a pretty face." He smiled wide and a few toothless gaps, more than I remembered, stared back. "You see, I still like the company o' the friendly drunks. They're more sociable than the woman who warms my bed. But my insides can't take the spirits anymore. So, I pretend. No one's noticed. O' at least they aren't sayin'."

We stopped talking when we entered City Hall. A silent reverence seemed appropriate. The first room, the Governor's Hall, was a large reception area flanked by additional rooms. A fire engine filled one, and another served as a storage area. A third room caused my heart to beat wildly. The word dungeon was carved on a sign. My fear must have been plain on my face. Mr. Innes reassured me that this was for hardened criminals who committed capital crimes like murder and treason.

We took the stairs to the second floor and found a man sitting at a desk in front of the large room where the Supreme Court sat. When he did not acknowledge us, Mr. Innes cleared his throat and inquired where the prisoners who committed small crimes were kept. The man pointed toward the stairs, past the smaller Mayor's Court, and another sign: Debtor's Prison.

"Alain's not a debtor," I whispered as we ascended to the garret.

"Perhaps yere husband's in a separate cell for small crimes. Better than bein' gaoled wi' murderers in the cellar. It's a rather unhealthy place, even for one as robust as Mr. MacArthur."

"And if he's not here—"

"Then I'll find out where he's been taken." As we approached the attic, Mr. Innes put one finger to his lips. "Let me take care o' this."

In a chair propped against a wall was a man fast asleep. His head drooped on his chest and then bobbed ever so slightly in time with his snoring. His chair almost toppled when he awakened with a start, the moment Mr. Innes and I walked across the room. I concluded this must be the goaler. He yawned, rubbed his eyes, and asked gruffly about our business. Innes' explanation included wild gesticulating. Whether this was done intentionally, I could not say, but the goaler's eyes followed Mr. Innes' ringed fingers like a cat waiting to pounce on a mouse. His fine woolen clothes with real silver buttons supported the goaler's assumption.

While the two men talked, I glanced around the room. In the central area were three small high-placed windows and an alcove to the side with another window. This allowed for enough daylight so that candles were not needed, a savings for the taxpayers. In each corner of the room was a cell which was secured by a thick wooden door with a square opening that allowed for monitoring the prisoners. Glimpses of daylight suggested that each had the same small window. I edged closer and found the first two cells empty. A third was occupied by an elderly man. If this was where the debtors were held, it appeared that the good citizens of Manhattan were paying their creditors. In the opposite corner of the room was a fourth cell.

I glanced over at Mr. Innes. He and the goaler were still engaged but my friend must have sensed what I was about. He took one step to his right so that he blocked the goaler's view. Then, Innes reached into his jacket and held up something shiny.

Edging closer to the mystery cell, I peeked in and tried to make sense of the two gray shadows on the floor. One was asleep on a bed of straw, undeterred by a rat that scurried and sniffed around his gray head. The other, leaned against the wall and appeared to be asleep as well.

I took a chance. "Alain," I whispered. The seated man stirred but did not look up. "Alain," I repeated slightly louder.

154

"Hey, what's she doin'? Stay away from the prisoners," yelled the goaler.

"Anna!" A hoarse voice called from the cell.

"Get away I say, or I'll lock you up, too."

"Now don't git yereself inna pickle, man. The lady means no harm." Mr. Innes reached into his pocket and jingled the remaining coins until he caught the goaler's attention again. "Surely, we can come to some kind of arrangement." He revealed another coin which he fingered like a magician adept in legerdemain, and then slipped them into the goaler's palm. The man bit down hard on one, dropped them into his pocket. And then opened his palm again. Mr. Innes grumbled a few "hells" and "damns" and reluctantly offered another, and then another.

The goaler patted his bulging pocket. "I need to piss. Tell her to be quick about it."

My attention returned to the cell. Alain's white fingers were wrapped around the splintered edge of the door opening.

"Alain, I brought Mr. Innes. He's going to get you out of here."

Alain's fingers reached for mine. "The children?"

"I left them with Dr. Emmanuel and his wife. They are safe for now. I couldn't take them back to our house. I didn't know what Catarina would do."

"Mr. MacArthur. Don't ye worry none. I'll take care of Mrs. MacArthur and the bairns. They won't want for nothin'. As for Catarina. That woman doesn't know when tae leave well enough alone." He mumbled a few more salty words and shook his head.

"You see," I blurted out. "Everything will be alright."

"Have ye been told anythin' about a hearin'?"

"No. But the other fella," Alain gestured to the man sleeping on the straw, "he's been here for two months. Says he hasn't been given a court date and has no idea what charges were brought against him. I'm afraid I won't be out any time soon."

"Mr. Innes will get you out. Isn't that right, Mr. Innes?"

"I'll talk tae the constable. He and I have had a few drinks taegether. He likes my singin'. Says my songs are entertainin'. We have an understandin' of sorts. When ye have wealth and property, people pay attention." His wink was a reminder of my old friend, the cook. "I'll give ye two lovebirds a bit of privacy, but don't take tae long. That goaler will be back soon. He knows there's more coin in these pockets and will want

155

to lighten my load." Mr. Innes turned and spat on the wooden floor. "I've seen his kind before. He won't be satisfied until he sucks me dry."

Alone, for a few moments, I described the events at the pier after Alain had been taken away.

"Anna. I will need someone to represent me in court. Someone who knows the law."

"Mr. Innes—"

"I'm not sure Innes knows the right people. Yes, he has money and maybe…but I'm not hopeful."

I wanted to beg Alain not to give up. Right now, hope was all we had. I unlatched his fingers from the door and pressed them against my wet cheek. When I kissed them, I noticed two jagged nails and dried blood from a fresh cut on his thumb. Then I reached in my satchel for the biscuits and passed them through the small window. I cupped Alain's face and touched his lips. "Be brave, my love."

"Go now, Anna. This is no place for you. Kiss our children for me. I will be—"

The prison door crashed open. A rough-looking man, I'd never seen before, filled the space.
"What are you doin' here?"

"The goaler allowed this woman tae see her husband," said Mr. Innes.

"What? I'm the one in charge. I run this gaol and I didn't give you permission."

"But the other man—" said Mr. Innes.

"My assistant. A pisser if I ever knew one. Probably fed you a story so he could get you to part with a coin or two. Now get out or I'll have you arrested. As you can see, I have plenty of room for you and the lady."

Mr. Innes took my arm and we hurried down the stairs and out the building. We did not stop until we were a block away.

"What will we do now?" I asked.

Mr. Innes took out his handkerchief and wiped his forehead. "I'll talk to the constable. If that doesn't work…well…I have other means." After wiping his upper lip, he returned the handkerchief to an inside pocket. "Let's go, Mrs. MacArthur. Your bairns are probably wonderin' where ye are."

But as we got further away, slivers of doubt arose and chipped away at the promise I had made to Alain. I began to realize that there was little my friend could do to save my husband. For the very first time, since the day I met Mr. Innes almost fifteen years ago, I feared he did not have a solution.

CHAPTER SIXTEEN
STRANGER IN A STRANGE LAND

DEAR PRECIOUS ANNA,

From the time I was a little girl, my father and I had a close relationship, a result of many hours spent together in his library. Even today, if I closed my eyes, I could smell the old books, the beeswax candles, and his mint tea. While he pored over his ledger for hours and answered his many correspondents, I would gather his books, sort them by size and thickness, and arrange them into tidy stacks. I pretended I was the curator of my father's books and ordered them so he could find them easily. Father praised my efforts, offered me a sweet, and called me his Precious Anna. But one day, that all changed. Nathan, my older brother, decided to join us. He scoffed at Father's words, stamped his feet, and pushed me down. Nathan screamed that I was neither precious nor industrious. Father said nothing. That was the first time I realized my brother did not love me, and that Father would not protect me.

It has been many years since I have seen or spoken to my father. His poor judgement and inaction bound me to Maurice, a Frenchman, a man I did not love, and who, like my brother, used brute force to get his way. I was left with only one choice. To escape on a cold wintry night from the only home I had ever known.

That action and Father's inaction unleashed a chain of events, including the death of my best friend, Sally, and Alain killing my brother.

Now, Father's letter lay heavy and stiff in my hand. Once, I vowed that he was dead to me, and banished him from my life. But this missive, if I dared to read on, brought me to the precipice of his resurrection. There was no doubt in my mind that Alexandra would ask if I read it. She would want to know what her grandfather had written. I would not lie to her. Therefore, I read on, but reminded myself, that at any time, I could condemn these pages to a fiery death.

It is my fervent hope that Alexandra has safely reached the shores of the New York colony & that you are in good health. Please let me explain how your daughter came to be the carrier of this letter.

More than a year ago, a woman arrived at my door. She introduced herself as Davina MacArthur, the daughter of a friend & client. She moved to Edinburgh to be closer to the port to find ship's passage for Alexandra. Davina told me about your voyage to the ill-fated colony & your safe removal to New York. It grieves me that my prediction about Caledonia came true. Davina also wanted me to know I had a granddaughter.

At my invitation, Davina & Alexandra came to live under my protection. This arrangement has been good for all concerned. Davina felt safe from Father Drummond's disturbing advances. With Old Simon dead, there was no one to run my household. I was pleased when Davina agreed to do so.

I have pursued the education of your daughter. Alexandra has a bright & nimble mind, like her mother; but unlike you, foreign languages are effortless. Her fluency in French already surpasses mine. The same could be said for her grasp of my business. My granddaughter has quickly learned contract language & double-entry accounting. She will never hide behind a screen. I have learned my lesson the hard way.

With Davina's permission, I have instructed Alexandra in the ways of our religion & the history of our family. Davina thought this was what you would have wanted. I hope that pleases you.

My heart is broken with Alexandra sailing away, but I find solace in Davina's presence. Now, I am afraid I am about to lose her, too. She has taken up with a fine young man, Colin Grant, the son of another client. It will not be long before Davina has her own home & little ones to care for.

Before ending this letter, it is of the utmost importance to write the following. I contemplated putting what needs to be said at the head of this letter, but I was afraid you would not read on.

Your foolish father begs forgiveness for his poor judgment. I was wrong to force you into a marriage you did not want. My blindness has caused untold suffering. Every day, since that terrible night when you left, I beg the Almighty to forgive my sins. I deeply repent my actions.

Jewish law requires that the one who has been hurt cannot be forced to forgive. But by the law that I hold most dear, I must confess my sin before you & God.

In closing, I offer fatherly advice. The Torah mentions many times about the plight of the stranger in a strange land. Our forefathers arrived in Egypt as outsiders, & then, four hundred years later, escaped to find refuge in an unknown place. We have been wandering ever since, & you are not the first in our family to do so. Seek out your brethren. They are hidden in plain sight. They will offer you their help & hospitality. We have been taught how we are to treat the stranger.

On the next Sabbath, imagine I am placing my hand on your head while I offer God's blessings. I will continue to write. I hope that someday you may respond.

Your father

I walked to the fireplace, pulled back the screen, and placed the pages on the burning log. In moments, it flared before settling into ash. My father never mentioned Alain's name.

❦

"I have bad news," said Mr. Innes. Standing in the center of the Emmanuel's front room, he fidgeted from one foot to the other, twisting the brim of his hat between his fingers until it had a permanent curl. Baruch Emmanuel excused himself, offering us privacy, but I begged him to stay.

I had never seen Mr. Innes like this. Even in the worst of times, he offered a ray of hope with his infectious smile and a humorous rejoinder.

Now, he avoided my eyes and shook his head. His chin bobbed on his chest. He focused on his buckled mules as if his shoes were another conversant. For the first time, he looked old and frail.

"My drinkin' companion, ye ken the constable I mentioned. I spoke tae him. Pleaded with him. He wilna help." Innes began to sniffle, leaving dark streaks on his sleeve. "He refused...he wilna get yere husband out o' gaol. He says your husband has tae go before the judge, and he has no idea how long that'll be. I'm sorry...Mrs. MacArthur...I have made your husband's situation worse." Mr. Innes found a handkerchief and wiped his eyes.

Worse? I wondered. How could this be? Mr. Innes was the luckiest man I knew. He always came out unscathed, no matter what the situation. On the voyage to Caledonia, he had escaped Captain Pennecuik's wrath and ship's fever. When we arrived in New York and he jumped ship, he talked his way out of a noose. And his marriages brought him unearned wealth to last the rest of his days. I wanted to grab him by the collar and shake him. With a forced calmness, I asked, "How much worse?"

"I thought my drinkin' partner was a friend, such a jolly fella, especially after he had a few. We sang taegether and he'd buy me a round and I'd do the same for him. I thought I could confide in the man. We always got along."

"Mr. Innes, please. What happened?"

The former cook hesitated and then tried to conceal a gaseous stomach from a recent previous meal. "Believe me, Mrs. MacArthur. I tried my best. I even drank a wee bit o' ale with the man."

I glared at Mr. Innes. No more prologue.

"Well, it's like this. I asked him, polite-like, if he kent your husband. He said he did. Said Mr. MacArthur was a model prisoner. Verra quiet. Didn't give the goaler no trouble. Not like the others. I thought that was a good sign, your husband bein' so well behaved, so I asked if there was anythin', I could do tae lessen the gaol time. I assured the constable that this was between him and me, a personal transaction. The constable looked at me, puzzled-like, a look I had never seen before, like he didn't ken what I was talkin' about. Then his face turned angry when I held out three coins in my hand. At first, I thought it was because I had misjudged the size o' remuneration. I retrieved more from my pocket, but that made him angry as a hornet. He accused me o' bein' a spy for the government. 'Always on the lookout for dishonest workers,' he said. I assured him that wasn't the case. I was a friend tryin' tae help another. Then, he accused me o' bein' a rascal, and worst o' all, a cheat. A veritable stain against my character. Never have I been accused o' dishonesty. Not by captains and shipmates, tavernkeepers and the few whores I've been acquainted with." He stopped and took a deep breath.

"Mr. Innes...the point."

"The constable told me he kent I was a scoundrel because I pretended tae drink while encouragin' others tae imbibe even more. He accused me o' workin' for Bertram White. He also called me a liar and a lot o' other names I wouldn't say in front o' a lady." Remembering that Baruch was in the room, Mr. Innes turned, "O' in the presence o' a gentleman. But I'm no rascal. It's my fragile stomach."

Innes shook his head harder. "After the Constable accused me o' attemptin' tae bribe him, he said he had a mind tae throw me intae the dungeon with your husband." When Mr. Innes finished, the room became silent. I had to think. I saw frightening images of Alain languishing in that dank prison for months, even years, with hardened criminals, wasting away from lack of food and fresh air. My daughters, especially Sally, would forget their father's face. We would be forced into poverty, living where we could, begging for scraps, trying to avoid the only profession open to a woman during harsh times.

Our conversation ended with a rapping at the door. Deborah quickly answered and gestured for the guests to enter. The first was Master Myer Myers. We nodded our greeting. Then a second unknown man crossed the threshold. His unusual height forced him to lower his head to avoid the lintel. When he straightened, he acknowledged me with piercing black eyes in a face framed with dark curls. A felt hat made him appear even taller. His ominous appearance, at first alarming, contradicted Baruch's broad smile and jolly welcome.

Abraham Haim de Lucena, the minister of the Jewish community in Manhattan, appeared to be a nervous sort. His right cheek twitched as he continually looked back at the opened door. As if he was expecting someone else.

While introductions were made, I knew better than to extend my hand in greeting, especially to a religious man. That was something my father had taught me. *A commandment from God*, he would say, *an unrelated man and a woman should never touch.*

"But Father," I would argue, "It's just a welcoming."

"Yes, but a handshake can convey much more. Whether it is limp or firm or if one grasps too long or relinquishes rather quickly, it might communicate something unintended."

That sparked another memory; the day I met Alain. Father extended his hand in greeting. Mesmerized by the handsome Highlander, I wanted to reach out and touch him, too.

"Mrs. MacArthur." The minister interrupted my thoughts. "My Rachel will be here any moment. I invited her to come. I hope you don't mind, but she misses female companionship. I wanted her to meet you, another young mother." As if they had rehearsed this, his wife entered the room. "Ah, there you are, Rachel. Please come. This is Mrs. MacArthur."

The young woman smiled and nodded during introductions. Her hair was covered with a fine linen cap and half of her body seemed to be hidden by a coverlet. From its depths came the soft mewing of an infant. Later, I learned this was Samuel, their first born. But the most noteworthy feature about my new acquaintance was her height. The top of Rachel's head came to her husband's elbow. Rachel extended her hand, but the baby squealed. She laughed, readjusted her load, and followed Deborah to another room for privacy.

"Please, everyone, have a seat," said Baruch. "Anna, I have shared your husband's unfortunate situation with our minister and Master Myer. They are eager to help any way they can."

I looked at each man in turn, but someone appeared to be missing. With all the commotion of the new arrivals and introductions, we were one short.

"It seems your friend has left us," said Baruch. "He slipped out the door after Rachel arrived. Maybe he vill rejoin us later."

I had also noticed. Mr. Innes looked increasingly uncomfortable, fiddling with the buttons on his waistcoat while glancing at the door. Maybe he realized a sad truth; he had promised more than he could deliver. While his resources were more than adequate, he lacked sophistication and the right connections.

"Mrs. MacArthur." Master Myers was the next to speak. "The minister and I are not proficient with the legal assistance your husband needs, but we may be able to bring in someone who is."

"I am grateful, sir, and I will gladly accept your help. But please forgive me for asking why? We barely know each other."

"It is our custom to help our brethren in time of need," said Minister de Lucena. "You see, my ancestors and twenty others fled Recife when the Inquisition arrived. They fled to Dutch-controlled Manhattan, but on the voyage, they were taken advantage of by pirates and forced to sell all they owned to pay for their passage. Petrus Stuyvesant, the governor at the time, was no friend and ordered the Jews out of his colony. With nothing but the clothes on their backs and no one to help, they were in a desperate situation. Until some of the influential owners of the Dutch trading company, fellow Jews, came to their defense and ordered the governor to stand down.

"Since the time of Moses, we understand what it is like to be a stranger in a strange land. When one of our own is in trouble, we rush to their aid and offer all we have." He sighed deeply and pressed his fingers on the twitch. "It is a sad fact that the oldest hate in the world forces us to wander the world."

I hesitated, hoping that the truth would not seal Alain's coffin shut. "My husband…is…not of our faith."

"That is no matter," said the minister. "He is the father of Jewish children. He is a man of flesh and blood who has been wrongly accused. He is your husband."

"My daughters and I are grateful, sir."

Girlish giggles and a baby's squeal from the next room interrupted the seriousness of our conversation.

Master Myers smiled and cleared his throat. "Do you know Mr. William Burnet? A barrister from England. Practices law mostly in the high courts."

"The name is not familiar. My husband and I would not mix in the same circles."

"He's highly regarded and has all the right connections. He even claims King William was his godfather."

"But that's in England. That might help little here."

"Mr. Burnet is destined for great things in the colony. There is talk that he will be appointed governor."

"Then he will want to be paid. Handsomely," I added.

"Not to worry. I have it on good authority that Mr. Burnet is not opposed to accepting his regular fee."

"Sirs, I am sure he is quite capable. But my husband and I are in no position to pay for his services. With Alain in gaol, my daughters and I are beggars. We cannot go home again and are dependent on the good will of others."

"Anna," said Deborah who had reentered the room. "Please do not think of your staying in our home as charity. You may abide here as long as you wish. I will care for your children while you deal with matters regarding your husband."

Just then a small face, Sally's, appeared from behind Deborah's skirts. She smiled shyly and ran into my arms. How fortunate to be young, oblivious to the perils of the world, and content in her present circumstance.

"I know," continued Deborah, "that if Baruch and I fell on hard times, others vould be there for us."

"We are a small community," said de Lucena, "a determined people who know how to survive."

"Mr. Burnet will not do this for free."

"Yes," said Myer Myers, "but each of us in the community gives a monthly allotment to our benevolent association. We help the widowed, the orphaned, and the bride without a dowry. We will help you."

I was familiar with the charity. My father often gave to a similar fund in London.

"I have one more question. Why would Mr. Burnet do this? For Alain?"

"Mr. Burnet has provided many services for our community. Wills, legal disputes, and simple contracts. He does not do it out of love for the Jewish people. We pay him well."

"But why will he help my husband?"

"Mr. Burnet likes a challenge, and a case like your husband's could be most profitable. That is another one of Mr. Burnet's assets. Perhaps, the best. He has no conscience when it comes to taking or giving bribes."

CHAPTER SEVENTEEN
UNSPOKEN WORDS
SCOTLAND

THE SKY OPENED. Alec and I were driving in the middle of a ferocious rainstorm. Wind buffeted the car, swerving it back and forth, from one edge of the lane to the other. Streams of water snaked across the road. Alec reduced his speed, gripped the steering wheel, his knuckles taut and white. Fat raindrops thumped and pinged against the windshield. The wipers, working at high speed, couldn't keep up. Their rhythmic swish added to the racket. The healthy baritones and sopranos blaring on the classical radio station, couldn't drown out the noise outside. However, it magnified the silence between us. Alec had barely uttered a word since we left Skye.

I don't recall exactly when Alec fell into a silent funk. Maybe it was before we left the Grant home earlier this morning. But then, I remembered his asking the usual questions before starting a six to seven-hour drive across country: *Are the sandwiches packed? Did we forget anything? Do you need the toilet one more time?*

Alec's silence must have started when we entered the main road, heading northeast toward Inverness. The reason, I believed, was simple. He was furious with his family, and I would have to wait until he was ready to share what had happened.

I knew only the bookend facts. It started when Alec discovered Kate had Anna's ring. And it ended when his mother promised to speak to Iain and Kate and get the ring back. Any attempt to pierce Alec's protective armor, and get hm talking, to discover what had occurred in between, was so far unsuccessful. I tried innocuous conversation starters like: *Do you mind listening to Tosca? Would you like me to drive a bit? Wasn't it nice to see Ira?* I thought mentioning his colleague and mentor would spark some exchange about the current semester or the search for a new department head. Maybe I would have had more success if I was direct, while maintaining a caring voice, and said: *What the hell happened with your family in the library?*

Alec's silence offered an important lesson. The longer it went on, the harder it was to end. Whoever said *silence is deafening* knew exactly what they were talking about. I had to break the stalemate. But first, I needed to think.

Our initial plan was to stay three or four days after the funeral: to help Mora empty closets; return the library to its original state before it had been converted into a hospital room; and remove all evidence of the luncheon. The garden ladies attempted a clean-up, but there were serving pieces, tablecloths, and good silver that needed Mora's attention. The floors begged a sweeping and the kitchen needed a thorough cleaning. But after the kerfuffle over Anna's ring, Alec's response was short. "We're out of here as soon as we can pack."

I understood Alec's anger was reinforced with a healthy dose of embarrassment. He was mortified that his brother treated me so brazenly, thought nothing of committing a crime, and never apologized. That, I believed, was the cause of his silence.

Our eastward progress slowed considerably due to weather conditions. That allowed time to make a mental list of safe topics. The one that was foremost in my mind concerned my dissertation. It was due a week from now. My writing was based on Anna's journal and how her experience added new information to what was previously known about the Scottish colony, Caledonia. The manuscript still needed a few adjustments and some minor corrections to the bibliography. Editing was never-ending. Alec had gone over the rough draft and had made many suggestions. In addition, he had described the process of defending my thesis. First, my work would be distributed to other Ph.D.'s who served on the dissertation panel. After reading, they would question my research and conclusions, and I would respond and defend my work. Alec promised to help me anticipate the questions for the dreaded interrogation.

I glanced over. His eyes were glued to the road. This was not the time or place. I tucked the conversation piece away and let my mind wander again.

Our destination - the tiny seaport town of Johnshaven, along the North Sea - was still hours away. We chose our flat for its location: the picturesque, white-washed homes, the smell of the sea, the weather-beaten fishing boats lined along the docks, and the quaintness of the town's name. It was a temporary move until I found a teaching position. Two weeks ago, when I spoke to my old college roommate, Jess, I discussed the possibilities.

"I'll have to get used to calling you, Dr. Duncan," said my friend.

When I mentioned the possibility of a position in the States, she replied, "What fun. We could shop, hit the bars; like we used to." But the upbeat tone of her voice sounded tired and forced. "And I'm dying for you to meet Jeremiah."

The baby's soft murmurings, clearly heard on the phone, reminded me of the contrasts of our lives. Jess was now responsible for a new life. Her pretend exuberance could never revive what we once had. It's not that we couldn't be friends, we would just be different. My circumstance had also changed. I wasn't the same girl who flew off to Scotland, at a moment's notice, almost four years ago. Now, I was planning to take a sharp left down a whole new career path.

"Wait," Jess said. "Would Alec leave Scotland? Give up his position at the university? Or would you come...back...without...him?" She wavered. I thought it was due to the baby. "Wait a minute. What's going on with you and Alec?"

"I'd have more choices in Boston, New York, or California. Maybe a position at Penn. It would be fun to teach at our alma mater." I surprised myself with my response. Until recently, I thought Scotland was my home. With Alec.

"Stick to Philly or New York. We would be closer." Jess' husband had just secured a lucrative position at a large gastroenterology practice at Jefferson Hospital in Philadelphia. "Wait. You didn't answer my question." I could feel Jess' determination - to pin me down. "Would you leave Alec?"

"No...of course not. Maybe...he'd consider looking for a position in the States, too."

What was this new uncertainty I was feeling toward Alec? That never happened before. I told myself our lives were busy: Alec's father's illness; his family; my dissertation; and new responsibilities at work for Alec. Maybe there was a reason we were engaged for so long. And now the ring. Another distraction. I glanced at Alec again and wondered if he remembered to get the ring from his mother. We left so quickly, that I forgot. I hoped he didn't.

※

My thoughts returned to the present. The monsoon weakened as we neared Inverness. If conditions outside and inside the car had been better, I would have suggested the longer route, my favorite one, along Loch Ness. The upper end of the Great Glen was a gorgeous drive.

"Do you want to stop for something? A local cafe?"

I turned quickly. Startled, I had become used to the silence. "We have sandwiches. Your mother made them."

He grunted, "A peace offering."

"Do you need a break?"

"I'm fine with driving. But a cup of tea and a scone would be nice. How about you?"

"Sure." What I really wanted to say was, *Finally. You're talking Now, stop holding out on me.* But maybe Alec's suggestion to stop was truly an olive branch; his way of saying he was ready to talk.

A coffee shop paired with a parking spot didn't materialize right away. We drove around the streets of Inverness until we found just what we wanted. A partial sun had emerged which was perfect, but the couple of outdoor chairs and tables, set up outside the café, were still wet. We chose take-away cups, a bag of warm scones for Alec, teacakes for me, and headed for the riverside walkway. Alec's continued silence was punctuated by the quick footsteps of a runner and the plodding squeaks of an elderly lady. I glanced back when we passed. She reminded me of Mora's friend and our encounter yesterday.

※

Mrs. Adair found me in the kitchen. It was the best place to keep busy and hide out. After Alec told me about the ring in the garden, he stormed off to the library where his mother and Father Wilson were still sequestered. Family confrontation was no place for a future daughter-in-law. One of Dad's often repeated sayings boomed in my ears: *Blood is thicker than water*. I did not see what happened later, but Mrs. Adair did. With little provocation, along with gentle guiding, she offered the details. "After Alec left the library, Mora's voice pierced right through the closed door. I heard her order Father Wilson about as if he were her personal assistant. Mora demanded Iain and Kate come in, and if they refused, Father Wilson was to 'drag them by their ears.'"

"Did the priest do as he was told?" I asked, still wondering what Mora and the priest had been talking about before the ring became an issue. The whole situation was odd.

"One bit of advice you should know about your future mother-in-law. No one dismisses her. Many have learned that lesson the hard way."

Now that was an interesting tidbit I'd like to know more about. "And Iain, does he dismiss his mother? Would he refuse?" I could visualize Alec's brother walking off in a huff.

"Of course not. Iain puts on a show. Puffs out his chest. Tries to convince others he's more than he is. But he's no match for his mother. Only Alec is her equal. And she knows it."

Mrs. Adair was a font of information about the Grants. I had to learn more. "Then what happened."

"I'm not one to snoop or gossip, but the walls are thin, and I couldn't help but hear loud voices and someone pounding a fist on a table. I wasn't the only one to notice. The guests were uncomfortable, the sober ones, at least. Many picked up their empty casserole dishes and headed to their cars." Mrs. Adair lifted the apron over her head and patted her permanent silver curls. "I saw Alec while I was clearing the buffet table. I thought he was looking for you. I tried to tell him you were in the kitchen, but he was too fast and headed to the garden." She began to fold the apron, but when she remembered it was soiled, she stuffed it into a tote bag. "Kate came out next. She looked angrier than a hornet in late summer. She ran up the stairs to her room and slammed the door so hard that the empty whisky bottles in the dining room rattled."

"And Iain?"

"I never saw him, but based on the look on Kate's face, I think he was wise to let her be. Poor dear. I think she was too angry to cry, although it probably would have helped. She kept clutching a chain around her neck the entire time. Funny, I noticed her fiddling with it all afternoon and showing it to her girlfriends and her parents. It must have meant something. Maybe a family heirloom."

If only Mrs. Adair knew how close she came to figuring out the family squabble.

"Whatever the issue," continued the older woman, "maybe Iain has learned his lesson."

"What lesson is that?" I felt silly prodding this woman with short questions. But I had to know what she thought.

"*A craw will no wash white.*" I must have looked puzzled because Mrs. Adair quickly translated with a smirk. "A leopard cannot change its spots. And never get between a woman and her jewelry."

We carried our food until we found a dry bench along the River Ness. Alec had introduced me to teacakes, a Scottish dessert favorite, about a year ago. It was like a s'more minus the campfire. Many a teacake helped me get through a tough section of my dissertation. I quickly unwrapped the treat; a creamy marshmallow-like fluff on top of a shortbread biscuit, smothered in milk chocolate. I couldn't get enough of them.

While Alec sipped his tea and munched on his scone, he was no longer silent; but his chatter avoided his family. *Is your drink hot? How's the teacake? Inverness Castle is right up the river.* Usually, Alec's last statement led to a cascade of historical trivia, interesting or not. But not today.

That left it to me. "Alec. I'm sorry for being blunt. But I have to know what happened in the library." I chided myself for apologizing. There was no need, although the confrontation between the family was inadvertently my doing.

"I apologize, too…for my silence," he said. "Every time I revisit what happened, I get angry all over again. Of course, you should know."

"Why didn't you come looking for—"

"I did. I went back to the garden. I wanted to tell you we were leaving. But you weren't there. I started back to the house, but I got waylaid by my mother."

"Mrs. Adair didn't tell me."

"She wouldn't know. She wasn't in the garden. She didn't hear my mother."

Based on what I was learning, I wasn't so sure I agreed. Mrs. Adair seemed to make it a habit to be in the right place at the right time.

"Iain admitted he was responsible for taking the ring. Well, not him, but he got someone else to do it. Didn't even try to lie."

"Stealing it is more like it."

"Mmph. He felt it was a precious Scottish heirloom. Part of the nation's history and must remain here. It's what he believes. Scotland belongs to the Scots. He was afraid you'd go back to the States and take it with you."

"Why didn't he suggest I donate the ring to a museum? Not that I would have, at least not yet."

"You're thinking rationally. My brother's form of nationalism has robbed him of all reasonableness."

"I could better understand his motive if he had donated it himself. But he gave it to Kate, pretending it was something he bought for her. Maybe that's why she was so angry. She's realized she's being played a fool."

"Don't go so easy on Kate."

"Believe me, I'm not. But there's one thing that's curious. If a man gives a woman a ring, she'd want to wear it." I glanced down at the round diamond on my left ring finger. I loved it the moment Alec surprised me with a proposal at Martyr's Memorial in St. Andrews. Stretching out my fingers, I said, "Can you imagine putting this ring on a chain and hiding it? No woman would do that unless she had good reason. A very good reason."

"When my mother demanded the ring, Kate ran out of the library."

"Mrs. Adair said she saw Kate looking pretty pissed off. Ran to her bedroom and slammed the door."

"Yeah," Alec scoffed. "Don't part a woman from her jewelry."

That was the second time I'd heard someone say that in the last two days. I rolled the teacake's silver foil wrapping between my palms and deposited it into the empty paper cup. Alec finished the last of his tea. It was almost time to go.

"Alec, did you get the ring?"

"No, I'm sorry. We left in such a hurry. But don't worry. My mother said she'd get it once Kate cooled down. I'll get it the next time I go home."

"Did anything else happen. I mean after Kate ran out of the room?"

"Yes. But let's get going. We have a long drive. I'll have plenty of time to tell you."

Mora asked her son to sit with her on the only bench by the yew hedge. She knew making demands on her first-born would not work. Alec was smart and confident, strong-willed, and candid. Even as a small child, he was curious but careful before accepting anything. He was not easily intimidated

Alec obliged his mother. At first, there was silence. A chill came off the water. Neither Mora nor Alec noticed.

"Mother, Hanna and I are leaving shortly." Alec thought his mother might reach over and touch his arm and offer some gesture of motherly affection. But she didn't. He wasn't surprised.

"I know you're hurt about the ring," Mora said with almost no emotion. "We need to discuss this."

"I'm not hurt. I'm furious." Alec clenched and unclenched his fist. Something he had always done since childhood. "How could Iain break into my apartment and then make excuses for his actions? And don't tell me that technically he didn't do it or maybe he's blaming it on Kate. Which line is he feeding you now? And how did he find out about the ring anyway?"

"The first time you brought Hanna to the house. It was at dinner. Remember? You and Hanna talked about finding the ancient safe deposit box in Edinburgh. It all made sense to Iain when he bumped into you and Hanna outside the bank."

"I shouldn't have to fear my brother. Neither should Hanna."

"Alec, I'm not excusing what Iain did. It was wrong. I'm upset with him. And so is Kate."

"Yeah! She won't get to keep the ring. By the way, who stole it?"

"I don't know, and I doubt if Iain will say. Probably someone from that political group he hangs around with. Unfortunately, your brother is no longer a child. I can't send him to his room and forbid him from associating with certain friends." Mora hesitated while straightening the pearls around her neck. "But I need to know what you intend to do about this. Are you planning to contact the police?"

"It has crossed my mind. It would serve Iain right. A day or two behind bars would scare the hell—"

"Excuse me, Mora." Mrs. Adair stood behind his mother. She looked like she was going to curtsey. "I don't mean to interrupt, but the ladies have cleaned the best we could, and we are ready to head out. Is there anything else I can do for you?"

Mora stood, brushing the front of her skirt as if it was full of breadcrumbs and then clasped her hands. "Thank you, Maddie."

Mrs. Adair looked like she wanted to hug her friend but held back.

Mora's standoffishness extended beyond her sons. Finally, she said, "I don't know what I'd do without your friendship."

Madeline Adair nodded, walked back to the house, and never looked back.

Mora turned to Alec, straightened her back, and stated the real reason for her talk with her son. "Do not press charges against your brother. You'll regret it. Someday, after I'm gone, you'll only have each other. And if you do this, and your brother is arrested, there'll be no going back. It will always be between you."

Alec clenched his fists again. "What about his stealing from me? From Hanna? Iain's the one who's crossed a line."

"You're correct. But Iain's about to become a father. Marrying Kate, and now the baby, he has taken on a lot of responsibility. It won't do for my grandson to have a father with a police record."

"If it had been the other way around, would you have asked Iain to go easy on me? Would you have been as concerned for my responsibilities with Hanna?"

"You would never have behaved like Iain. It's not in you. Besides, you have Hanna. She's no Kate."

Alec looked at his mother not knowing how to take her last statement. Should he be angry? Bewildered?

"I wish Iain and his wife happiness," said Mora, "but I'm not hopeful. Kate is immature, financially irresponsible, whiny, and, I know this sounds unkind, she's not bright. Right now, her youth and sexuality are what's keeping Iain interested. But all of that will fade after children come along."

"I never knew you felt like that about Kate. I thought you preferred her; wanted me to marry her."

"I've learned a lot since Kate moved in. She's a spoiled girl and annoying like a gnat. It doesn't matter how many times you swat it, it keeps returning." Mora sat on the bench again, facing her son. "But you have found a woman, a true partner, who loves you and your faults. She's an independent sort but will stand by you no matter what life throws your way." Mora's eyes became moist as they searched the shore of Staffin Bay. "I imagine Hanna's the kind of person who doesn't need entertaining. Spending a cozy evening together at home is enough." She brushed an unaccustomed tear from her cheek, stood up, and finished her summation. "Kate doesn't match up."

Alec was stunned, but wary, and wondered if this was his mother's attempt to get Iain off the hook. Butter up his relationship with Hanna and he would forget about calling the police. But this was his family and that mattered. "Okay. I'll do as you ask. But Hanna and I are leaving as soon as we finish packing. I can't stay as long as Iain is here."

"I understand. Please give my apologies to Hanna."

"Maybe you should tell her yourself.

"I will."

"I mean how you feel about her."

Mora never said another word. She walked toward the house, never looking back.

CHAPTER EIGHTEEN

SACRAMENTS

REVEREND PRESCOTT WALTON must have been at least seventy years old. But he looked years younger. His skin was fair and smooth, and his one or two age spots could have been mistaken for youthful freckles. The few creases radiating from the corners of his eyes, deepened only when he smiled broadly or laughed boisterously. Dark lush eyebrows, that had not thinned, gave him a more youthful appearance, and a full head of light brown hair meant no tell-tale comb-over like other men of a certain age. It was only when I sat on the sofa, and he on his Chesterfield, that I noticed streaks of silver, highlighting his natural color. Detection depended on the tilt of his head and the angle of the afternoon sunlight spilling into the living room.

"You realize, you do not have to convert to be married in the Catholic Church," said Reverend Prescott. His tone was serious but empathetic, his voice hoarse and his eyes watery. Prescott had a terrible head cold but insisted on our planned meeting. He pulled out a white handkerchief, dabbed his nose, and sniffled. I had the feeling he wanted to blow hard but considered it impolite. "No need for you to be baptized, either. If Alec is a Catholic in good standing, there is no problem."

"Is that how it was for you?" I didn't want to pry, and if I was, I would apologize. *It was easier to ask forgiveness than permission.* That was another of my dad's many kernels of wisdom.

"No. The church was strict back in those days. It was believed that intermarriage weakened the bond and adversely affected the children. By extension, that would result in less faithful. Besides, marriage is one of the sacraments."

"I understand that a sacrament is something holy and therefore marriage is considered sacred," I said. "But I'm not sure I totally understand the Catholic meaning of sacrament."

The Reverend reached for his cup of tea which had been sitting in a mismatched saucer on an end table. The scent of lemon and honey filled the air, and after slurping noisily, he said, "Sacraments are the bond between the individual and God. They are gifts from the Almighty, allowing the faithful to become One with the Body of the Church and serve as a way of communication and the offering of eternal life. They are signs of grace from God."

I must have looked puzzled. Prescott took another sip and put down the delicate cup. "Let me explain it another way. Imagine you are on a road trip. You have a destination, and in this case, it is the bond between you, the Church, and God. To get there, you must take the correct route and there are stops - sacraments - along the way. First stop is baptism, where promises are made that the child, or the convert, will follow the Catholic tradition. Then the Eucharist, also present at Communion, where Catholics renew their baptismal promise by taking bread and wine. Through transubstantiation, they believe it transforms into the body and blood of Christ. It's not only food for the body but for the soul and thanking Jesus for coming into your heart. Next, is reconciliation, or confession and recognizing one's responsibilities, and maybe a need for change. The next sacrament is a juncture, either marriage or holy orders. The final stop is anointing the sick or last rites. It's intended to bring peace and comfort to the sick and those who are terminally ill.

"Hanna, this is a lot to take in at one time. A born Catholic enters their first sacrament without knowing it and takes on the others gradually. They are taught the sacraments by their parents, godparents, and at Sunday School. It's almost second nature."

Prescott's summary brought on more questions. Could any sin be erased by confession? Even murder? How could an educated person believe in transubstantiation? Eternal salvation? Did Alec? Was he secretly striving for God's grace, and by marrying me, would he miss the boat? I sort of understood what my dad meant when he called organized religion a bunch of mumbo-jumbo forced on humanity to keep the masses compliant.

"When you converted, weren't you afraid that you wouldn't achieve the sacraments and gain eternal life?" I asked.

"Well, the Protestants only believe in two: baptism and the Eucharist."

"Please don't take this the wrong way, I mean no disrespect, but to an outsider it appears you took the easier way out."

I was relieved when he chuckled, but it ended in a bout of coughing, a quick exit to fetch another box of tissues, and a refill of tea. "Now, where were we?" he said when he returned. "Yes. I'm sure you have many questions, and I'm probably not the right person to answer them all. If you'd like, I could find someone, a priest perhaps, for you to talk to." Suddenly, Prescott's demeanor changed. His eyes grew pensive, his voice grave. "I was born a Catholic but converted to marry my Helen. Given the circumstance and choice again, I would not hesitate to do the same. Helen was my grace and our love a blessing."

I remembered that his wife had passed shortly before we met at the Mason home over three years ago. But from his downcast eyes, I was afraid that my questioning exhumed a fresh sorrow.

Prescott excused himself again. His absence gave me an opportunity to survey the room. Evenly spaced on the mantle were pictures of children and grandchildren posed during family get-togethers, holidays, weddings, and graduations. Evidence of lives well-lived. Crocheted doilies were strategically placed on cushioned headrests of two side-by-side chairs set in front of a darkened hearth. I imagined Prescott and Helen spending their evenings sitting together; the glow of the fire flickering in their eyes: she, knitting a pair of socks for him; he, working on Sunday's sermon while puffing an unlit pipe. It was an idyllic illustration that I'd seen in an old edition of *Lassie Come Home*, a favorite book from my childhood.

When Prescott returned, we resumed our talk. But now it was more mechanical, lacking emotion. "If you don't mind my asking, why did you convert? I know the reason was because of your marriage, but since you were baptized, you were…are technically a Christian. Why go one step further?"

"I didn't feel a pull toward Catholicism. Just went through the motions and did it because my parents expected it of me. But I found a greater affinity to Helen's church, and I thought it would make us a stronger family unit. There are more choices today. Maybe you and Alec would consider a Humanist wedding. It's quite popular and perfect for a couple in your situation. It's gaining in popularity and outnumbering church weddings, although neither the Catholics nor the Protestants will admit it."

"Yes, I have heard about that. But I'm still not sure."

Prescott sat back in his chair and steepled his fingers under his chin. "Let me ask you a question. If conversion is not required for a Catholic marriage, then why do you want to do it?"

"I thought it would help. With Alec's family. His mother is very devout, and I think it would bring harmony. Especially, if…we have…children."

"Ah yes. Little ones always make a difference. I've counseled many interfaith couples trying to find their way just as you are doing. They think they can make decisions about religion after children come along. What they don't realize is - it's harder. So much emotion surrounding religious upbringing. In-laws, who might have minded their own business, become vocal and interfering when grandchildren are baptized in a different faith. You're right to figure this out before you get married."

Prescott retrieved his hot tea. It was a reminder not to forget my own, but after ignoring it for much of our conversation, it was cold.

"What does Alec think? I'd be happy to talk to both of you. As I've said, I've counseled many young couples, and some were a lot less level-headed."

"Alec says he's fine with a civil marriage. But I wonder if he will feel that way ten years from now, or when we have a family, and he realizes that his religion does matter. Maybe my conversion will solve that problem."

"I see. Well then, what's stopping you? Is that some hesitation I'm hearing in your voice? Is something else bothering you? I hear your dissertation is coming soon. You're dealing with enormous pressure."

"The defense is in a few weeks. But I have some preliminary meetings at the university tomorrow. It's a busy time." I wavered with what I was going to say. "I'm wondering if my hesitation about converting has something to do with Anna. Like I'm haunted by a distant Jewish ancestor." I scoffed. "Does that make me one? Jewish, I mean." I felt a sense of guilt, like a blanket I couldn't shake off on a warm day.

"Ira would be a much better person to talk about your Jewish heritage, but unless you converted, you are not Jewish. The only other way to become Jewish is through the female line of your family. Matrilineal descent. And even if all of Anna's direct descendants were female, each generation producing another daughter, which is highly unlikely, your father put a stop to it. He could not pass Anna's Jewishness on to you."

"Why through the female line?"

"It's more accurate. One always knows who the mother is, but not the father. Especially, in time of war and upheaval when rape is the order

179

of the day. This is an ancient tradition that has helped the Jews survive when they should have gone the way of the Philistines and the Sumerians."

"So, it's possible that my father's mother was Jewish, but I'm not?"

"Correct, but highly improbable. Too many generations between your grandmother and Anna."

"Any suggestions for me, Reverend? How do I sort this out?"

"Keep questioning and exploring. Ask Alec to take you to mass next Sunday. There's a Catholic Church on The Scores in St. Andrews. See what goes on. To be fair, it might take a few Sundays."

"I know where it is. It's close to Martyr's Monument." I could feel a smile broaden when I thought of the stone obelisk.

"Maybe you'll get to meet the priest. I've heard good things about him, but I don't know him personally to make an introduction for you. And you might want to have that chat with Ira. You know he'll love talking your ear off on the subject if there's a hot pot of tea and a tin of biscuits. Might be a good idea to bring Alec along. Like marriage, you're in this together."

The next day, the meeting at the university went well. My mentor and I went over some last-minute changes for the manuscript and we discussed the process of defending my dissertation. Dr. Susannah Oliver, who was ten years older, was the youngest member in the department. I was glad to work with someone who still remembered the torturous process.

"Everyone is nervous at this point. So much is riding on doing well. But I wouldn't worry, Hanna. You've done your homework, and it's excellent. The faculty is quite impressed in what you've been able to achieve in just over three years."

I wondered if that included the illustrious professor and notorious womanizer, Dr. Jones. Thankfully, he was on sabbatical this semester, researching a new book. Rumor had it that he was living in Sri Lanka with a former student, and the juiciest part of the gossip was that she dumped him. Maybe he was searching for a new roommate. I was glad he was preoccupied and wouldn't be present at my defense.

Dr. Oliver held up the 95,000-word manuscript. "But first, this has to go to the examiners."

I took a deep breath. It was overwhelming. "Could they make me redo whole sections or the entire thing?"

Dr. Oliver assured me again that all would go smoothly. "I've checked your work many times. I'd never let anything go to the next phase without it passing the smell test. Don't forget, my reputation is on the line as well."

That didn't make me feel any better. Now, we would go down in flames together.

"In two weeks, you'll meet with the examination board. This is sort of a preliminary defense. It's good practice for the real thing. You will be questioned on how well you know the topic, your methodology for choosing the research, and if your thesis advances new knowledge in your field. Of course, they'll be looking for any flaws we missed. Let's hope we got every comma correct."

"Really? They look for commas?"

"Let's just say it depends on the examiner. Some are picky. But commas are an easy fix. What you don't want to hear is that your sources are unreliable, or you need more evidence to support your thesis. Consider this first step like a conversation. You get to discuss your work with others who are interested in the same topic."

Dr. Oliver gave me additional advice, but I knew no matter how much was said, I was on my own. Earning a Ph.D. was the ultimate prize in the academic world, and defending a dissertation separated the wheat from the chaff.

⚜

When the meeting ended, I hurried to the carpark and quickly aimed my car south for Johnshaven. I still smiled when I thought how we decided to move to the little seaside village based on its quirky name.

"Look," I said to Alec after pointing to the map. "There's a town called Johnshaven. It's between St. Andrews and Aberdeen. What a cute name. Let's see if a flat's available."

Alec raised one eyebrow. "It's Johnshaven." He pronounced it as Johns Haven not the way I did, John Shaven.

My faux pas became a frequent inside joke. Alec would say something like, "Let's go home to John Shaven" or he would mispronounce the name at a nearby gas stop. "Are we near John Shaven?" The locals would frown and mutter under their breath until Alec corrected himself. Some of the old-timers were not amused.

Rolling hills on one side and the North Sea coastline on the other, the A90 and A92 motorways were the quickest routes home. The sea, the color of slate, was topped with whipped whites that splattered on the beach. Evergreen signs popped up every now and then, announcing new routes to access passing villages. Halfway through my forty-five-minute drive, I passed the quaint harbor town, Stonehaven. Alec and I often stopped there for dinner. The pier was lined with sightseeing boats, yachts, and fishing vessels. One of our favorite seafood restaurants was located just off the boardwalk, a few yards from the center of town. I was reminded that another visit was due; reservations were a must, especially during the summer months when the town swelled with visitors.

Perhaps we would do this when we visited nearby Dunnottar Castle. In all the time we lived on the east coast, we failed twice to see the famous ruin. The first time, it was overrun with tourists. We couldn't find a spot to park at the head of the path. Since Alec and I preferred the medieval castle to ourselves, we postponed our visit for late fall or winter. But off-season had its drawbacks. Opening times were shorter due to less daylight, and we were at the mercy of Mother Nature, especially when there were high winds. The location of the castle on a rocky point jutting out into the sea and its steep snaky path made it dangerous.

Today, the sky threatened a storm. Virga was off in the distance, dark clouds consumed lighter ones, and the air held a pungency of damp earth. Except for a couple of tandem trailers and a motor home, there were few vehicles on the road. Nothing like the traffic jams in Philadelphia and New York. It was peaceful and quiet; a chance to think. I remembered my fear when I first drove in Scotland. But it didn't take long to get the hang of the steering wheel on the right side. I wondered if I went back home, would it be an easy return to the left? Maybe I should choose a large city with a good public transportation system.

There it was again. That nagging thought of going home.

The tandem roared and filled my rearview mirror. I quickly got behind a small white car and when it was clear, I stepped on the gas and sped around. Before I knew it, the white car replaced the truck in the mirror. I tried going faster, but the car matched my speed. I rolled down the window and waved the driver to go on. But the car stayed where it was, too close. I solved the problem by losing the driver when I took a turnoff for gas and a cup of coffee. When I got back on the road, I checked my watch. I'd be home in fifteen minutes, probably before Alec.

I thought about what to make for dinner, and that depended on what could be defrosted quickly. I was glad to be preoccupied with innocuous thoughts other than religious conversion and my dissertation. Another sip of coffee and a recheck of the mirror. A second white car trailed behind. Like the first, too close. Again, I rolled down the window and waved the car on, and again, the driver stayed where he was. *Holy crap! What are you waiting for?* When I sped up and slowed down, the driver mimicked my speed. A roundabout was ahead. I slowed to enter. Three exits. Mine was the second. Would the driver choose a different one? He didn't and continued to follow.

I tried not to panic. White cars were not unusual. Neither were drivers heading in the same direction and choosing the same exit. Except, his refusal to pass, even when I drove slowly, just under the speed limit, was odd. My exit was coming up shortly. Another roundabout. I didn't bother with a turn signal. Why let the driver know in advance where I was heading? A different driver, in a gray car in the next lane, honked. But I didn't care. I waited until the last possible moment, turned on my signal, but continued around the circle twice and then swerved left at my exit and sped down the road toward Johnshaven. A check at my rearview mirror. I breathed a sigh of relief. It was empty. Maybe it was my imagination. I'd rather think about dinner.

Alec cupped his hand under my head. His fingers running through my hair aroused every nerve of my body. I shuddered and a torrent of stored-up craving spread its warmth. Alec gently guided me toward his lips, soft and supple, the scent of wine lingering and intoxicating. But this was not a night I longed for tenderness. I wanted to be taken, quickly, completely, as if I needed punishing for the doubts I'd had recently.

Impatient, I mounted and immediately felt his heat, his longing between my legs. Alec's labored breathing and groaning drowned the storm outside. Lightening lit up his face, arms, and torso. A sheen glistened on skin stretched smooth over taut muscles. The flickering light, undaunted by slightly opened window blinds, created eerie images on the walls.

Slowly, I lowered myself toward Alec, my hair caressed his chest and face. Covered him with a veil of ringlets. Caressing his eyelids, ears, and chest, I kissed him long and hard until his body gave in and trembled in defeat. Nearby thunderclaps were barely noticed. Our love making continued until we were satiated. Exhausted, we lay loosely in each other's arms.

Stillness hung over our bed. The storm had subsided. The last gasps of rain spattered against the window; the rotting wooden frame permitted the room to grow cool and muggy. Covered by only a top sheet, Alec pressed me to his chest, his heart throbbing in my ear.

We had not made love like this in a while. I wondered if this was how it was when sailors were at sea, away from wives or girlfriends for months, maybe years. Reunions greatly anticipated. Like virgins on a wedding night, only now with the experience of each partner's likes and dislikes. But how long did that passion last? I worried that ours was dimming, and we could only look forward to unexpected moments like tonight. Maybe we had become too complacent, too comfortable. Maybe it was me.

Alec broke the silence. "There's nothing better than a hearty meal, a warm bed, and a beautiful wench. It's all I need to be content the rest of my life."

"Does order matter?"

"Not as long as you're in my bed." He turned, put his hand under my chin, and raised my face so our eyes met. "I've never wanted anyone as much I've wanted you." He sighed and rested his head on the pillow. "Sometimes, I want you so badly, it hurts." He stroked my breasts and legs and squeezed my buttocks and then playfully slapped my rear end. "I think about all of this on my drive to work. I'm distracted when I'm lecturing or attending a meeting. I rush home so I can take you into my arms. When we make love, I never want to stop. At times, I wonder if this is all a dream. Or if I'll come home and find you're gone."

I should have responded, and told him he had nothing to fear, that I would always be with him. But I kept silent, squeezing my eyes shut.

Alec lifted his head. "I mean every word. I sleep well, knowing that when I wake in the morning, you'll be by my side."

I mourned quietly. Sobs caught in my throat and became another excuse to say nothing.

"What's wrong, Hanna?"

I took a deep breath. "I don't know. There's so much going on. I can't think clearly."

"Your dissertation?"

"Yes. And other things." But rather than tell Alec what was really bothering me, I took the easy way. I told him about my meeting with Reverend Walton and my concerns about conversion.

"You want to be a Protestant?"

"No. Catholic. Would you take me to mass on Sunday? I want to —"

"Hanna, you don't have to do this. I'm perfectly content with the way things are, and I don't need the church. I need you."

"Reverend Walton said marriage is a sacrament. How could I deny you that? Your mother would—"

"My mother? This is not about her. It's about us. Our life together, as man and wife. You are my faith. What I believe in."

Alec said all the right words and I knew that he meant them. I couldn't fault him for that. But that didn't stop the lingering voice in my head. Maybe if I could put it into simpler words, so that I could understand it; perhaps that would help. But I couldn't. It was like trying to explain the taste of water. Or how a blind person sees the changing leaves in autumn. The doubting was difficult to explain, but there, nonetheless. And it refused to go away.

CHAPTER NINETEEN
MAYBE MORE, MAYBE LESS
1709

A LADDER WAS the only way to reach the attic. That was how my daughters and I accessed the uppermost level in the Emmanuel home where we washed and slept and comforted each other. Two beds, a chair, and an old chest of drawers filled the space in the rectangular-shaped garret which had a musty smell like damp clothing or rotting wood. The odor was most pungent after a good rainfall. We had even less room to move about once Alexandra's trunk arrived. It filled one corner and, when closed, served as a table to set out our brushes and hairpins.

When I wished for privacy for myself or my family, I wrapped my shawl around the top rung of the ladder. This messaging, suggested by Deborah, indicated that we wished no visitors. The Emmanuels were most respectful.

Today, I put out my shawl. I hoped to write to Davina and let her know of Alexandra's safe arrival and to thank her for all she had done. I wondered if I should share our frightening news or if I should tell her that Alexandra carried a letter from my father. Perhaps, she already knew about the letter. After gathering my quill, ink, and writing paper, I set to work.

The first words were easy: *Dearest Davina. Alexandra arrived safely. Your brother & I are forever in your debt.* What came next was not. The words needed to convey the correct meaning escaped me. Lost in thought, I never heard the creak of the ladder. Nor did I realize Alexandra had reached the landing.

"Mama, forgive me. I don't mean to interrupt your letter writing." Alexandra stepped closer. The glow of the candlelight caught the curly strands of her hair creating a halo. She pulled her wrap tightly around her shoulders. The room was not cold, but something had caused my daughter to sense a chill. "I overheard your conversation with the minister and Dr.

Emmanuel." Alexandra lowered her eyes; her lips quivered. "I fear for Father. What will happen to him?"

I lifted Alexandra's chin until our eyes met. She looked so much like my father. I wondered if he recognized his mirror image. "Then, you know that Minister de Lucena, Master Myers, and Dr. Emmanuel are doing everything they can to get your father out of gaol."

"But we do not have the money. I heard you say so."

"Then you also heard that the Jewish families in New York have offered to help. This is what Jews do when one is in trouble. Perhaps a generous benefactor has already come forward."

"Do you mean that funny man who is your friend? Mr. Innes?"

"No. I'm afraid not. I don't know if I will hear from him again." It hurt to even think about Innes walking away without saying a word.

"But that means we will be indebted to many. Yes?"

I shared Alexandra's concern. We would never know whom to thank or to whom we owed an obligation. We would suspect everyone. Every time we were introduced, we would wonder. And if word got out and gossip spread, as it often did, so would our shame.

Alexandra went over to her trunk and rummaged through her things until she found what she was looking for. "Here," she said as she handed me a white handkerchief wrapped around a solid object. From the feel, I could tell it was metal. By the way Alexandra handled it and the reverence in her voice, I knew it was something special. "Auntie Davina gave this to me. Before I boarded the ship. She thought it would keep me safe."

I unfolded the cloth and a gold cross necklace with a raised image of Jesus Christ was revealed. A rope-like gold chain was attached, and it continued around the perimeter of the crucifix. It was not heavy, but it was solid and clearly of great worth.

"Perhaps this could pay for the man who will try to get Father out of prison."

"But it is yours. Your aunt gave it to you to remember her by."

"I love Auntie Davina. But I don't need a remembrance." She added with a whisper, "Perhaps I will return to Scotland someday. Besides," she continued in a normal voice, "Grandfather instructed me that a Jew does not wear such a thing. He wanted me to return the necklace. I lied and said I would, but I never did. I kept it hidden in the handkerchief." Tears welled in her eyes. "I am sorry I lied to Grandfather, but I couldn't hurt Auntie

Davina's feelings. She only wanted to keep me safe…on the voyage. Was I wrong to lie?"

I hugged my daughter who now sobbed softly. "No. Not at all." Her pain brought back the memory of when I lied to my father. It was necessary to save myself from an unwanted marriage. I also understood my father's disapproval of Davina's gift, but there was a time to accept the generosity and, just as important, the intention of a gift. The cross was a precious family heirloom, one that Davina should have handed down to her children. Not mine.

"Did you know it belonged to my grandmother? Alexandra Cora Campbell MacArthur? I have her name."

"That makes it even more special."

I brushed my daughter's tears away with the cloth. "I don't think we need Auntie Davina's cross just yet. Put it in a special place…until we do."

Alexandra pulled back and closed my fingers around the cross. "No. I want you to have it. Please. If it will help Father."

Seeing the earnestness in her eyes, I could not refuse my daughter's offer. "Thank you, Alexandra. This is kind of you."

I folded the necklace back into the damp handkerchief and slipped it in my pocket. I would use it only if necessary. The candlestick would go first.

A week later, a hearing was held at City Hall. My husband was one of six prisoners who shuffled into the Mayor's Court, the Court of Common Pleas. The Mayor or the Recorder served alternately as judge; today it was the Recorder's turn. The room was sparsely filled. None of the six were accused of a sensational crime that would attract a crowd of the curious. Except for Alain's crime, the cases were of the mundane variety; petty thievery and a failure to pay debts.

The judge went through the motions of doling out sentences. As each prisoner was called, he pushed back his powdered wig and squinted over his spectacles. I recognized the second man to face the judge: Alain's cellmate. His dirty clothes barely fit a shrunken frame. A ragged beard, concealing half of his face, caused him a bit of discomfort. He continually scratched his cheeks and chin and when he started to rub his head, the goaler took two steps back.

The debtors' cases took less than ten minutes. The man charged with stealing was another matter.

"John Cooper," called the clerk.

The prisoner waddled forward to the sound of muffled titters. When the judge asked, "Where are you?" and peered over his raised platform, a raucous outburst disrupted the usual sedate proceedings. He pushed his spectacles up the bridge of his nose. "Oh, there you are. Stand tall, will you?" More laughter swirled throughout the room.

"I am standing, your Judgeship."

That was true. But the diminutive thief had an unusual body. His limbs were short and disproportionally misplaced with his average sized torso. I could not help staring at him even though I had seen people with his condition. This was the first time I had the opportunity to observe in detail.

"Mmph. If you say so. Let's get on with it. John Cooper, you are accused of stealing two pies from Annabelle Janssen's window ledge. How do you plead?"

"Not guilty. I didn't steal nothing."

"You didn't steal anything."

"That's what I said, your Judgeship."

"Your accuser says differently. Annabelle Janssen, would you step forward?"

A young woman arose from her seat in the gallery. She was a few years older than Alexandra and plain in dress and appearance. There was not much remarkable about her until she stood in front of the judge. That is when her height was most noticeable. While most women were on the shorter side, like me, Miss Janssen, I believe, was taller than any man present. Her gaze was fixed on the judge as if she were going to extreme measures to avoid looking at the defendant.

"Now, Miss Janssen, tell the court what happened."

Annabelle cleared her throat and glimpsed back at the older woman sitting next to an empty chair. "I had just finished baking two fruit pies - just the way my mother taught me - for my sister's wedding feast. I put the pies - apple and cinnamon - on the window ledge to cool. The next thing I knew, they were gone."

"Did you see or hear anything?"

189

"No, sir. Pies don't say—" The courtroom burst into laughter again and Annabelle looked confused until her eyes widened. "Oh, you mean…no, sir, I heard no one."

"Did a neighbor or a friend see you put the pies out to cool?"

"Only the flies and gnats." Annabelle waited for the laughter to die down. "I had to keep shooing them off the crust – the pies smelled that good – or there would have been none left for the wedding guests. It's my mother's recipe, you know."

"No, I don't. But the pies were important. Is that right?"

"Yes, your Judgeship. My mother planned on serving a lot of food. She told my father she didn't want the guests gossiping that we were too poor to do right by my sister. You see, it took a while, but my older sister finally got a husband. Just in time. And I wanted to help, being her devoted sibling, and the pies…well, they smelled so good."

"Is it possible an animal, a dog, or a rat could have run off with the pies?"

"Oh, No, sir. The window ledge is this high." The young woman held up her hand to indicate it was the height of her shoulder and being that she was tall it was quite substantial.

Silence filled the courtroom at first, and then slowly, a wave of laughter rolled in.

"Young woman are you trying to tell me—" The judge stopped short. "Mmph." He removed his glasses and shook his head. "Case dismissed. Mr. John Cooper, you are free to go."

The witness turned to leave. "Not you, Miss Janssen." He returned his glasses and stared directly at her. "Now I can't say what exactly happened to your pies. Maybe it's true that a thicket of flies attacked your precious delicacies. But here's some advice. The next time be careful. This way you won't accidentally push the pies off the ledge, hide that fact from your mother, and accuse an innocent man."

Annabelle Jansson and her mother fled the courtroom.

Alain was the last to be sentenced. I steeled myself for what was to come. Mr. Burnet had warned me earlier this morning as we neared the arched entrance of City Hall.

"Incarceration is never good for one's health, Mrs. MacArthur." He said this as his cane tapped noisily on the cobbled street, keeping time with his words. "Most come out for the worse. My job is to get your husband discharged before the damage is done."

He explained that confinement was not punishment, but a holding place until the hearing. "Mr. MacArthur can expect a harsh sentence, whether it is the stocks, mutilation, whipping, or execution."

I froze and must have turned pale.

"Forgive me, my dear, but I'm trying to be honest. Severe punishment is intended to discourage the accused from repeating the offense and to deter others. Execution," he went on, "is rare in the New York colony. The last man hanged was Jacob Leister and that was over twenty years ago. His offense was treason; much worse than your husband's."

When Alain's name was called, my nightmare turned real. My husband stood, straightened his back, and stared directly at the judge. There was no smile, no acknowledgement; only the scar on his face seemed to darken.

As Mr. Burnet rose, his chair scraped the wood floor. He cleared his throat and placed one finger between his tight collar and his neck. "Your Honor, I ask for leniency for Mr. MacArthur. He was employed by his accuser's deceased husband, Mr. Joris Krol, and in good faith, Mr. MacArthur maintained the business during a period of mourning."

The Judge repositioned his spectacles, shuffled some papers in his hands, and then stared at no one in particular. "That's not what it says in this complaint. Your client was told repeatedly that his services were no longer needed. But he persisted."

"I'm afraid, your Honor, that there was some confusion after the death of Mrs. Rapalje's first husband. Mr. MacArthur was employed by Mr. Krol, and upon his demise, Mr. MacArthur stepped in, only to keep the business thriving."

"Maybe so, but that still doesn't account for the fact that running an unlicensed cart shop is against the law. It's common knowledge."

"If that's the case, then why aren't we trying Mrs. Rapalje and her son? The younger Mr. Krol inherited the business."

The Judge shuffled more papers until he found what he wanted. "Says here that Mrs. Rapalje did not know what her husband's business was about, but once she realized its unlawfulness, she begged Mr.

MacArthur to cease and desist. Says here, in her statement, 'I'm only a simple woman. Joris Krol provided for me like any good husband. I didn't feel it was within my rights to question him.' Mrs. Rapalje thought the matter had been settled when she left Manhattan with her new husband. When she returned, she was horrified that Mr. MacArthur continued without permission, unbeknownst to her or her son. She also claims that Mr. MacArthur was forward and possessed a menacing character."

"Sir, my client did—"

"Mr. Burnet. Would you like me to add lewd and lascivious behavior to the complaint?"

Before Mr. Burnet could answer, the Judge said, "I thought not. Now, Mr. MacArthur, did you or did you not run the illegal carts? Yes or no, will suffice."

"Yes."

"Correct, Mr. MacArthur. There is no excuse for breaking the law. An example must be made. Those who wish to make their livelihood as a carter must be licensed. Therefore, you are to remain incarcerated until you have satisfied a fine of thirty pounds."

Gasps, including mine, hummed through the courtroom. Thirty pounds was a huge sum, equal to the yearly wages of a skilled worker. Enough to purchase five horses or fifty stones of wool.

"If the fine is not paid in full immediately," continued the Judge, "Mr. MacArthur will be returned to his gaol cell and starting tomorrow he will commence to work it off."

❀

After Alain was taken back to his cell, Mr. Burnet and I hurried from City Hall. Shocked by my husband's punitive sentence and the dismal future that lay ahead for my family, I found the shrill voices of children playing and shopkeepers' crying to passing customers, maddening. While everything appeared normal, my life had come to a screeching halt. Mr. Burnet grabbed my arm and steered us through the melee. We did not stop until we arrived at the Emmanuel's front stoop.

"Your husband's hearing went exactly the way I expected."

My heart stopped beating. "You expected this?"

"Yes, Madam. This particular judge, I know him well. He prefers to come across as the supreme defender of British common law and order, and all that. He doesn't want to be thought of as soft."

"I cannot afford Alain's fine. How long will it take him to work it off?"

"A year. Maybe less."

I wondered if Mr. Burnet was playing with the truth to lessen my anguish. His probability of *maybe less* than a year had a frightening companion: *maybe more.*

"Is there not someone who could help with a loan?" asked Mr. Burnet. "Your fellow Hebrews?"

"There are only a few families. Their paying your commission is more than generous."

"I hear you have a friend who has the capital." He chuckled. "Isn't he married to the woman who accused your husband?"

"Yes. We are old friends, long before he met Mrs. Rapalje. I have not seen him for a while. He may have left for his farm up north."

"Any family back home in Scotland?" asked Mr. Burnet. "Your people always seem to find resources."

"My husband's sister is unmarried, and my father lives in Edinburgh. We have not spoken in many years." That was not entirely true, of course. Was it providence that my father chose to write at this time? Father would argue that it was not Fate or fortune. It was God's hand at work.

"Well, do not worry. There are still other means. The right words whispered into a receptive ear plus a few extra coins and all charges will be dismissed. I've seen it before."

I prayed he was right. Confinement was a terrible punishment, not only for the gaoled, but for the family that carried the additional expense for room and board. Every meal, every comfort had to be paid for.

"You said you were not surprised with the outcome of the hearing. What did you mean?"

"Those who operate the penal system know there is much profit to be made by putting a man in gaol. Each has their hand out, from the judge to the constable to the goaler. If you could somehow find the means to modify your husband's sentence, perhaps the Judge would allow Mr. MacArthur to serve out his sentence in a private residence."

"Thank you, Mr. Burnet. I'll consider all you have advised. But first, is it possible you could find a way so I could see my husband?"

"Of course, Mrs. MacArthur. But that will require a bribe. In fact, from this day forward, everything will have a price."

After a satisfactory pile of coins had passed between Mr. Burnet and the goaler, I was at last given permission to visit my husband. The goaler banged on the cell door. The men grunted and stirred which also awakened the putrid smell of unwashed bodies, stale urine, and something else that defied explanation. It poured out the door's window, forcing me to burrow my nose in my scarf.

"Wake up. MacArthur, you have a visitor. Don't take too long now with the missus."

Alain came to the window. He placed his hand on the window's ledge. I lowered my scarf.

"Anna, what are you doing here?"

"I brought some food. Some meat and fresh bread. And a flask of ale. You must maintain your strength." I reached for his hand, undeterred by the grit and calloused skin. The cut was scabbed over. "I needed to know you are alright. Mr. Burnet is trying to get you out of here."

"How? There's no money for that."

"Mr. Burnet says he has a plan. If it works, you will be confined at home."

Alain turned and looked at his cellmates. All had faced away to offer some privacy, a silent arrangement between prisoners. He whispered. "You need money to soften a sentence. Lots of it. Could you ask Innes?"

When I told Alain about Mr. Innes, he clenched his fists. "I knew he couldn't be trusted after he wedded that witch."

"I have another idea. One that I know will work. I'm sure of it." I hesitated before going on. "Master Myers will pay me handsomely for my—"

"No. I won't have you selling your candlestick. I'd rather be in gaol for ten years."

"It's worth at least the price of your sentence. Maybe more."

"Or maybe less. But that's not the point."

194

"It may be the only way. Your life is more important to me than cold metal, and there is one more. Alexandra's."

"The battered one. The one you used to save my life—"

"Time's up," yelled the goaler. "Kiss the missus and say your goodbyes."

Alain grabbed my hands. "Anna? Promise me. You won't sell the candlestick."

I slowly untangled my hands from his. "I love you Alain. I have loved you from the moment me met. And…I will do what is necessary to save you. Don't ask me to make such a promise."

"Come on now. It's time for my dinner." The goaler picked at his teeth and spat out a remnant from his last meal—"

I backed away from the cell door. Alain's face filled the window, his hand reached out. I walked slowly, playing for time, looking back. Before I lost sight of him completely, he called out, "I love you."

CHAPTER TWENTY
THE DEVIL'S PITCHFORK
SEPTEMBER 5, 1709

THE FESTIVE TABLE was surrounded by hungry guests. The women, all modestly dressed, were seated on one side. Their long tresses swept up off their neck were captured under French lace or linen caps. A few wore head scarves, spiraled like turbans, giving them an exotic look. The men also had their heads covered with hats or kippahs. In the larger society, head covering was removed when entering a church or a home to show respect. Jewish men did the opposite but for the same reason. Their heads remained covered to show respect to God.

Children of all ages were placed near their parents. Alexandra sat between Deborah and me. My daughter adored my friend and was delighted they could be close. Sally sat on my other side and clung to my arm every time one of the more grandfatherly guests told her how lovely she looked or felt the need to explain the mystery behind the rituals.

At first glance, my attire mirrored the other ladies: clean, simple, and unassuming. But on closer inspection, their dresses were created from fine fabrics. The skirts and sleeves were tucked and pleated in such a way that generous amounts of yardage announced the wealth of the wearer. My curls were imprisoned in a plain white starched cap rather than one made of fine linen or lace. Any similarity between the other women and me ended there. I had no spouse seated across the table. Alain was still in gaol.

Rachel's table was beautifully set, reminding me of my last days in my father's home. Father had ordered his housekeeper to prepare for many guests to attend my wedding dinner. Only our best silver trays, candlesticks, tableware, crystal decanters, and the rarest of foods would do. No expense, he reminded her, would be spared. But Maurice, my intended husband, was a monster and it was only through Alain's intercession that I was saved from a loveless marriage. Reminders of Alain brought tears to my eyes.

"These are exquisite," exclaimed an elderly man seated nearby. He picked up a silver utensil next to his plate, hefted it onto his palm to determine its worth

The compliment for the newest addition to her table, caused Rachel to smile broadly. "The Italians call the tined tool, *forchetta,* and at my request," she gestured toward the silversmith, "Master Myers was kind enough to make them especially for the holiday."

"Myer, you have outdone yourself," said another. "The Almighty Himself must have sent the angels to guide your hand. I may ask you to fashion some for my table. My wife—" He stopped short when the woman seated across from him cleared her throat and glared. I wondered if she minded his boasting or, perhaps the cost for such an extravagance was well beyond their means.

While others greeted newcomers and exchanged the latest gossip, I lifted my *forchetta* and felt the smooth curved handle. While I too could never afford such a luxury, I still recognized fine workmanship. My father had taught me well. He patronized the local silversmiths, and his home was filled with commissioned pieces: pitchers, a sugar dish and creamer, a cruet stand, trays of various sizes, bottle stands, an engraved teapot, and matching cups. On the underside of the fork was the craftsman's hallmark: a double M.

"Do you think they are useful? I mean, for the young ones?" Deborah asked. "I hear that even the French court won't allow their children to use them. They say it's reminiscent of the devil's pitchfork."

"My grandfather had *forchetta*. He allowed me to use one," said Alexandra. I smiled at my daughter, envisioning her seated in my place at my father's table. I was pleased that she had fond memories.

"You see," said Rachel, pointing to my daughter. "If children can try new ways, so can adults. Besides, we Jews don't put much stock in the devil anyway." Rachel's voice held a tinge of irritation, something she rarely displayed. Perhaps, she was tired. Her eyes looked heavy and I saw her stifling her yawns. Many days of preparation, directing the cooking and baking, and managing her growing family was taking its toll. It did not matter that her husband could afford several Africans.

Minister de Lucena cleared his throat as he stood. His height alone was enough to bring a hush to the room. One or two mothers shushed the younger children or patted an arm to get their attention. Even the youngest sensed the moment and obeyed their elders.

"Rachel and I welcome you all to our home. Your presence brings us much joy. It is the first day of the new month of Tishrei when we celebrate *Yom Teruah,* the day of the sounding of the shofar." He stopped and smiled as he surveyed the number of guests at his table. Then, he nodded toward his wife that he was ready to begin. Rachel pointed to a young dark-skinned boy, whom I had not noticed before, peeking from behind a drape. The slave turned and ran to deliver the order, his bare feet smacking the plank flooring, growing fainter as he neared the back of the house.

The Seder for the New Year was about to begin. Three African women paraded into the room. Each carried a tray. Ruth, the eldest, was first. She wore an enormous apron over a striped dress that ill-fitted her ample figure. Nonetheless, she seemed to glide while she circled the guests carrying the largest tray above everyone's head. All eyes followed her until she reached the minister's seat, and with much fanfare, she placed it in front of him. The children sat up tall, some drawing back in horror. Sally, one of the smallest, asked to be lifted, and then squealed with delight. In the center of the platter was an enormous fish head. The eyes were fixed and glassy and as the host rotated the tray, the fish seemed to glare at each in turn.

The minister explained in simple terms, so that even the children could understand, that *Yom Teruah* was the 'head' or the beginning of a year. The fish head was merely symbolic. A sigh of relief exploded from Sally when I explained that she didn't have to eat it. This was followed by Minister de Lucena and the male guests mumbling a prayer ending in a chorus of Amens.

Other trays were placed on the table. On each was a different kind of food representing prosperity and good health for the coming year. Dates filled with salted walnuts filled one tray. Before a prayer was said, the minister explained that the Hebrew word for date was *tamar,* meaning 'to end.' His prayer included the hope that the wicked would end their hatred. Other platters were arranged with leeks, pumpkin, beets, beans, apples, pears, and quince.

Above the voices of the guests, Rachel called out. "Ruth, how could you forget the honey? Hurry! Get it!" Then she turned to her guests and added in a much lighter tone, "The quince is rather tart. It helps if you dip it into something sweet."

"I miss not having pomegranate," said a severe looking woman who sat across from Master Myers. I had never met his wife and wondered what qualities she possessed that would encourage a man to marry such a woman.

"It is too early in the season," said the silversmith. "By the time they would reach New York, they'd be shriveled and inedible."

"I substituted pears instead," said Rachel. "We're instructed to taste something new; a food we haven't eaten in a year. These are from my orchard, and they are rather delicious and sweet." To prove her point, her husband plucked a slice from the tray, popped it into his mouth, and dammed the juice with the edge of a linen napkin.

After prayers and samplings were completed, the Seder, the ritual order, concluded. Seeing that Ruth had returned, Rachel snapped her fingers, a signal that the dishes should be cleared so the meal could begin.

As the slaves leaned in and around the guests, I had an opportunity to observe them. Until this moment, they seemed almost invisible and silent. They took their orders through practiced gestures, and except for the young lad, they walked soundlessly in bare feet.

It was hard to tell for sure, but Ruth appeared to be about my age. The boy was her son. On several occasions when Deborah and I visited Rachel, I had seen him helping his mother. Young slaves were required to work as soon as they could handle a broom or know the difference between a weed and a carrot top. Ruth's son was always busy sweeping the huge hearths that swallowed his small figure. Other times, I found him polishing pots or running off on an errand. Once, I saw Ruth hugging her son and wiping away his tears. After she consoled him, he ran off, but I noticed he was not the only one upset. Did she worry that at any time he could be taken from her and sold on the whim of his owner? I looked at Sally and Alexandra and wondered how any parent could live with the loss. Yes, I left Alexandra for many years, but I always knew where she was and that she lived with those who loved her.

The youngest of the three serving women must have been a new purchase. I had never seen her before. The young woman's skin was lighter than the other two, like a drop of cream swirled into hot chocolate or tea. Her hair was covered with a colorful cloth and her skirt swayed as she carried the food. Of the three, she was the most nervous. Perhaps it was her tender age and her new surroundings. She apologized whenever she came close to a guest, even when it was not necessary. Her voice had a certain lilt to it that suggested she had spent time in the West Indies. I remembered the same diverting speech when our ship docked in Jamaica. But her English was perfect.

"Watch what you're doing. You foolish girl. Don't you see the honey is dripping?" The woman who sat across from Master Myers pushed back her chair and wiped her dress with her napkin.

The girl attempted to help the woman. "I am sorry, Ma-dam. Please forgive me." Then she glanced at Ruth who glared back and shook her head, causing the young woman to tremble and step back.

"What's wrong with you?" asked the woman while enlarging the distance between them.

"I am—"

"Shoo, get away. Rachel, is your girl ill?"

Still carrying a small tray with the honey pot, the young slave stepped back, stared at the floor, and waited for whatever was to come.

"Lucy, leave us. Ruth, get someone else to help serve," said Rachel.

I expected the hostess to rush to her guest's side, but instead it was Deborah who did. With napkin in tow, she tried her best to wipe a skirt that appeared unblemished. "I'm sure no harm is done. Lucy didn't mean to be careless. She's young and still learning. It was an accident." Deborah's reaction was not a surprise. She and Baruch made no secret of their dislike for human bondage.

With Deborah's intercession, the serving women slipped unnoticed to the kitchen and conversation resumed around the table about the price of tea, the Swedish empire losing a battle against the Russians, and the promising economic effect for Scotland after joining England in the new United Kingdom. The last topic caught my attention, and I would have chimed in. After all, the demise of the Scottish colony helped bring about the Act of Union. However, I was still bothered by the young, enslaved girl.

I agreed with the Emmanuels. This business of slavery was abhorrent. We Jews should have understood the ramifications more than anyone. Weren't we slaves unto Pharaoh for four hundred years? Shouldn't we understand the oppression brought on by slavery? How could a Jewish slave owner celebrate Passover in good conscience? Minister de Lucena and his wife were not the only ones. There were at least five other Jewish families who owned slaves in Manhattan. Some were seated at this table. Those who did not own slaves remained silent. I had a feeling that, like the silver forks, they would have purchased a slave if they could afford it.

Conversation continued until Ruth and another young slave named Jenny returned with more trays piled high with steaming food. Ruth's son beamed as he followed his mother carrying two serving spoons crisscrossed in front of his chest like Pharaoh wielding the symbols of power. The room was quickly awash with the sharpness of turmeric, the sweet spiciness of cinnamon, and the earthiness of cumin. Garnishes of cilantro and parsley were set around platters of stuffed vegetables and grape leaves filled with rice, beans, and lentils. Chopped meat was formed into balls and dotted with dried cherries. Fresh fish, without the head, was garnished with thin slices of lemon and chopped dill. Tea was steeped in mint, and cardamom stirred into coffee.

Under normal circumstances, I would have greatly anticipated the meal. But tonight, I barely had an appetite. The bounty set before me was difficult to rationalize while my husband languished on Spartan meals in a cold cell.

It was three months since Alain was sentenced. Except for a few visits, which came at great expense and only lasted minutes, we had not seen each other. I always brought food, but we learned early on that hungry prisoners could be a threat.

The other reason for my failing appetite was more about my vanity. Everyone seated around the table contributed to the community charity, and therefore, to my husband's defense. Perhaps they were not aware of who received assistance, but that did not stop my feeling of shame. I imagined that everyone around the table knew of my family's dire need.

The two enslaved women circled the table with their trays and served each guest personally. When the new slave was about to serve the woman, who had yelled at Lucy earlier, Ruth gestured for her to step aside. In the process, Ruth dropped a serving spoon.

"So sorry, Madam," said Ruth as she quickly picked up the utensil, wiped the floor, and backed away.

"This is intolerable. You are just as clumsy as that other foolish girl." The woman stood and stared down at her dress, swished the skirt back and forth, looking for splatters.

This time, Rachel came to the rescue. "I'm sorry, Elkanah. Ruth is usually so—"

"The seamstress just finished this dress and already it's been under attack. Twice."

Rachel stepped back and observed her guest. "The dress appears to be in good condition."

"Well, your slaves need to learn—"

"Elkanah, it was an accident." The firm voice of her husband, Master Myers, interrupted her anger. "No harm done."

As I watched the interplay between Myer Myers and his wife, I was reminded of a saying my father would recite from the Talmud. *A man without a fitting companion is like the left hand without the right.*

The woman looked around the table. Seemingly not embarrassed, she mumbled something, and replaced the napkin in her lap.

Ruth wiped the floor again and said in a low voice to her son, "Git another spoon from de kitchen. Quick, I say." By the time he returned, the guests had resumed their previous conversations amidst some stilted laughter. The young boy handed his mother the clean serving spoon and whispered something in her ear. Ruth, in turn, delivered the message to Rachel and then resumed her serving duties.

"Anna," said Rachel. "You have a guest. Mr. Burnet. He wishes to speak to you. He's waiting in the front parlor."

Mr. Myers followed me into the parlor. In all matters dealing with Alain, either the silversmith or Baruch Emmanuel was by my side. Their support was comforting. "Mr. Burnet. Good evening. Is there anything wrong? With Alain?"

"Good evening, Mrs. MacArthur." William Burnet stood in the center of the room, his hat and cane in his hand. "I came as quick as I could. I thought you'd want to know that I have news."

Mr. Burnet was endeavoring to get Alain out of gaol so the rest of his sentence could be spent at home. For those of means this was possible, and I had been told that the Jewish community would do what they could to secure that outcome. This would be a wonderful turn of events. I could just see us reunited once again: a happy family, Sally sitting on his lap, playful, laughing. Alexandra, sharing a seat, leaning in, and hugging her father's arm. But from the dour look on the lawyer's face, I feared the news was to the contrary.

"I'm afraid your husband will not be coming home."

I could not hide my disappointment, but I had only myself to blame for believing it was as simple as offering a bribe. I straightened my back and my resolve. "Then we are no further behind or ahead of where we started."

"I'm afraid there's more."

"What is it? Mr. Burnet, please." said Myer Myers.

"Not only is he to stay in gaol and serve out his sentence, but the constable threatened to transfer Mr. MacArthur to Albany."

"Albany? It's so far. I won't be able to see him. What happened?" I asked.

"I don't know," said Mr. Burnet. "I followed my usual routine in trying to solve matters like this. I have been successful many times before. The constable is usually quite happy to accept the arrangement. Normally, we haggle a bit over price - he enjoys the sport - but in the end, we both walk away feeling satisfied."

"So, why not now?" asked the silversmith.

"I don't know," the lawyer repeated. "It's perplexing. The Constable wouldn't even discuss your husband's situation. I upped my first offer, which is something I rarely do. I tried again, with an offer of a drink and a hearty meal at a local tavern, but he brushed me off and walked away."

This was odd. Mr. Innes told me he had the same experience with the constable. "Did the man give you a reason, a clue?"

"Not one that I could depend on. It was all cryptic."

"What do you mean cryptic?"

"Puzzling, Madam. Mysterious. Enigmatic." The man scratched his head as if to emphasize his meaning.

"Mr. Burnet, I know what cryptic means. But how was the constable ambiguous?"

"Well, what he said made no sense. Perhaps it will to you. He claimed to have a much better offer. Regarding your husband."

"That makes no sense."

"Precisely, Madam. That's what I just said. He told me that someone had offered him more. Much more."

"To do what?"

"To keep your husband exactly where he is. In gaol."

CHAPTER TWENTY-ONE
TO SAVE MY LOVE

I FORCED MYSELF not to look back at the building where Alain had to remain after my brief visit. Its bars and locks imprisoned what I held most dear and mocked the freedom that, until now, I had taken for granted.

I have heard it said that the eyes do not lie. It must be true. Alain could not hide his disappointment when it was time for me to leave. Our brief reunions were held at the aperture of a cell door. On either side, our bodies pressed against the thick wood as if our craving could melt it away. Through the window our fingers touched and sometimes grasped. Like starved animals, we gorged but were never satisfied.

On my way home, I thought about my visits. Our conversations were hurried and whispered and so much of what I had meant to say would have to wait until the next time. Alain inquired after our daughters; how Alexandra was fairing. He asked about our living arrangements and if I heard any more from Mr. Innes. Alain's opinion of our former friend was quite the opposite of what it once had been. I answered his questions truthfully but avoided difficult topics: my father's letter and the disturbing meeting with Mr. Burnet.

Hurrying on my way, I almost barreled into two young boys who were running from the shouts of an angry apple vendor. Further down the street, a skittish horse attempted to break free from his owner. I was so distracted that I barely noticed an acquaintance walking in the opposite direction: Mr. Krol, Catarina's son. He was the last person I expected to see in Manhattan. After his mother's marriage, he returned to Brooklyn, preferring the quiet country life to the complications of his father's business and his controlling mother.

By the time I realized it was Mr. Krol, the gap between us had become too great, and I chose not to pursue him. I had no desire to talk to the younger Mr. Krol, although he was a genial fellow and had treated Alain fairly. The sight of him rekindled my anger toward his mother.

After Mr. Burnet disclosed that someone was paying to keep Alain incarcerated, I assumed it was Catarina Rapalje. Who else would have acted so maliciously? That hateful woman had ruined Alain's life and mine. I wished we had never come to New York and, instead, taken our chances and returned to Scotland. I could not understand why Mr. Innes married her. He did not need the money.

"Mrs. MacArthur. Hello. Is that you?" The voice, Mr. Krol's, was light and friendly.

I thought to ignore the salutation and searched for an easy escape down an alley. But he was not to be put off. He called again, louder this time, situated himself in front of me, quite out of breath, and gallantly swept off his hat. "You do remember me. Karol Krol. Joris Krol's son." He never mentioned his mother.

"Of...of course. It wasn't that long-ago we paid our respects to your dear father." I too, failed to mention his mother.

"How is Mr. MacArthur?"

His query suggested he had no idea that Alain was locked in a cell a few yards from where we stood. "He is well. What are you doing in Manhattan?"

"Family business. Mother and Mr. Innes are leaving. Moving to his farm up north. Mother is not too happy about the idea. She doesn't fancy herself a farmer's wife." Karol's chuckle was not meant for me. "But Mr. Innes has given her no choice in the matter. I think she has finally met her match. Besides, she has not been well. Since mid-summer she's been mostly confined to bed."

Caught unawares, I feigned concern. "I'm sorry to hear that."

The young man chuckled again. An odd response to grave news. "Mr. Innes thinks getting her away from the stink of the city is for the best. Fresh air will do her some good and relieve her cough. But you know, Mother. She complains that the odor of farm animals won't be much better."

"You say she's been in bed for months?"

"Yes. The doctor has been bleeding her and prescribing his potions. She has not been eating and has been too frail to go anywhere or see anyone. At times, she can barely lift her head. She wants no visitors, but when I showed up at her door, she relented. Mr. Innes sent a message, you see. He thought I should know." At this point, the younger Mr. Krol became serious. "It's no secret that Mother and I have had a difficult relationship. Not the usual mother-son adoration. I am sure you are aware of that."

"I am, Mr. Krol. But she is still your mother."

"That is what Mr. Innes said. You see, Mother has been having some pains in her chest, and forgive me, she spits up blood. The doctor does not offer any encouragement. Consumption, or as he calls it, the wasting disease, will not be cured by a royal touch. The most Mother has is a year or two. The doctor prescribed rest and country air, so Mr. Innes thought that a move might be good for her."

"When do they leave? For the farm?"

"By the end of the week. For the time being, the house will not be sold. At least for now. The maid will stay on. Innes prefers to keep the property. In case, he says, Mother improves. I don't see the point, but perhaps he doesn't want to anger Mother by selling the place as if she was already gone."

"I'm sorry to hear about your troubles. Please tell Mr. Innes the same."

When we parted ways, I could not help but feel a bit of sadness as I would probably never see him again. As I watched Mr. Krol continue down the street and disappear around a corner, I thought about our conversation and the trio of valuable information that came from it. First, Mr. Innes was leaving and any opportunity to secure his help was fading fast. Second, from Karol Krol's description, Catarina could not have been responsible for Alain languishing in gaol. And third, my advice to Mr. Krol. He had suffered many cruelties from his mother; but in the end, there was still a bond between them. I wasn't so sure about Father and me.

"Catarina is ill? And she's leaving Manhattan?" asked Deborah as she poured hot water into the flowered pot and set the tea to steep. "Please, sit and join me. Have a cup of tea, at least." She gestured toward a pitcher of cream, a small plate of thin lemon slices, and a sugar bowl with the same flowered pattern as the pretty little teapot. Still-warm biscuits were attractively placed on a tray.

"Her son has no reason to lie." I accepted a linen napkin and placed it on my lap. "From his tone and manner, I doubt he even knows his mother is responsible for Alain's arrest."

"Then who vould pay to keep someone in gaol? I've never heard of such a thing."

"I keep thinking about all the people we've met in New York since our arrival. Any enemies we have made. The first midwife was not too pleased when we could not pay what she expected. But she would not have the money to bribe the constable. Then, there were the carters Alain supervised. He got along well with them, and they liked him. The same goes for the dockworkers, the shipping agents, and the farriers. How would Alain's incarceration be an advantage to any of them?"

"Vait. Vhat about the tavern owner?" Deborah poured the amber liquid through a tea strainer until the cup was filled halfway. She placed it on the delicate saucer along with a biscuit and handed it to me. "You mentioned he vas brusque and forward vith you and had vords vith your husband."

"Oh, Bertram White. Hmm. I doubt it. I mean, he would have no qualms about seeking revenge, but he's rather tight with his money." I added a slice of lemon, a small chunk of sugar, and stirred. "Mr. White is arrogant, full of swagger, but rarely acts on his words. Now that his sister is living with him, another mouth to feed, I doubt he would part with his coin."

The tea was too hot. I was tempted to blow on the liquid, but that was unthinkable in polite society. Instead, I took the smallest sip, being mindful not to slurp, and placed the cup back on the saucer until it cooled. The momentary pause in our conversation allowed Deborah to concentrate on adding a generous helping of cream and sugar to her tea. The only sound between us was the tinkling of a silver spoon against the cup. I continued to nibble on a biscuit while dwelling on the dwindling list of suspects.

"I know he's an old friend of yours, but do you think it could be Mr. Innes? Perhaps he believes his vife's stories. Husbands do cleave to their vives. Eventually." She brought the cup to her lips and sipped generously. An advantage of adding cream.

"No. I'm sure Mr. Innes would never do that. We have been through so much together. It couldn't be him." Nevertheless, what Deborah had suggested inserted itself like a tiny splinter, a minor irritation at first, that had the uncanny ability to fester.

207

Just then, Baruch and Master Myers burst into the room. They brushed the dust off their sleeves and the look of concern on their faces suggested they had serious business.

"Anna," said the silversmith. "Mr. Burnet came unexpectedly to my shop."

"What happened?" The uneaten biscuit dropped to my lap breaking into crumbs. My eyes flitted from man to man and then to Deborah.

"It's your husband. The constable, Mr. Burnet's connection, told him that your husband has been hurt. One of the other men in his cell had a knife."

"Is he dead?"

"No, he's hurt, not dead. The goaler called for a surgeon and he's being tended to."

I quickly stood. The crumbs speckled the carpet. "Can I see him? Can we go now?"

"Of course. We came to get you."

"Was it the food I brought earlier today? Did someone go after him?" Now I regretted the warm rolls, the slab of cheese, and a just-picked apple.

"No. That was not the reason. From what Mr. Burnet learned, it had something to do with a woman."

I grabbed my shawl and headed for the door

My husband was not in his cell. The goaler and one of his helpers had carried Alain to a separate room so the surgeon could attend to his wound, a cut on his leg below the knee. We found Alain sprawled on top of a table. One leg dangled over the edge and the injured one was covered with a bloodied blanket. The surgeon had just finished his ministrations and stepped back. I ran to Alain's side, cradled his head, and covered him with kisses. Baruch pressed his hand near the wound. I looked for facial clues, but there were none. He turned and left the room after mumbling to the surgeon about a private word.

This was the closest I had gotten to Alain in many months. His eyes were closed, his breathing slight. I whispered his name over and over and finally one eyelid fluttered. His dry lips curved slightly into a smile.

"You're here," he whispered breathlessly.

"Alain, my love. Are you in pain?"

"Not sure if—"

"No need to talk. Save your strength."

He shook his head. "A woman. She said I…the other prisoner."

Myer Myers had mentioned the attack had something to do with a woman. But that made no sense. I had never seen a female prisoner here. While I was trying to figure this out, the goaler began screaming at someone. He did not hold back on his choice of colorful language, and in response, another yelled back with an equally diverse collection of curse words. With one difference. The voice was female.

Alain whispered. "Eliza…Parker," and closed his eyes again. The effort exhausted him.

Female prisoners were not unheard of. They numbered far less than the men and their crimes tended to be more of a feminine nature like vagrancy, idiocy, or false reeling.

Baruch returned to the room. "Alain vas attacked by an inmate who had hidden a knife in the sole of his shoe. In a jealous rage, he vent after Alain. The voman in the other cell, a Miss Parker—" Baruch paused as a woman continued to speak her mind with a piercing voice that mimicked a stool dragged across a stone floor. "She's been sentenced for lewdness and giving birth to three bastards. Her children vere fathered by the man who stabbed your husband."

"I still don't understand. What does that have to do with Alain?"

"Perhaps ve'll learn the full story vhen your husband avakens."

"Do you think Alain's condition might encourage the constable to look at my husband's case more sympathetically now?"

"I vill discuss that vith Mr. Burnet." Baruch hesitated and lifted the blanket again. His eyes widened and his brow furrowed "There is another problem that is more urgent. Ve should know in three to four days."

"What should we know?"

"If the leg becomes inflamed and amputation is the only vay to save your husband's life."

Baruch and I were given permission to tend to Alain. The goaler welcomed our help. He preferred not to add nursing to his list of chores. He had enough to do with feeding the inmates, maintaining order, and getting in his naps.

Alain stayed in the same room. A stained cot was provided, and another threadbare blanket covered the patient. I brought some of Deborah's biscuits and sliced meat. While we talked, Baruch inspected and cleaned the two-inch wound that looked like gaping lips. He removed any remaining debris, changed the dressing with clean linen strips, and explained that the first sign of inflammation would show itself on the edge of the lips.

"You have Eliza Parker to thank for your improved accommodations," I teased Alain. Compared to his former cell, this room had a door for privacy, and he was safe from any who would do him harm. But those were the only benefits. The smell was still the same and someone had left their muddy footprints although it had not rained in two days. Clumps of mud mixed with balls of hair, lint, and a dead rodent filled the chink between the wall and the flooring. The goaler had made an unsuccessful attempt to sweep the room.

"Mmph. The wee stabbing. She was responsible for that, too." Alain had momentary flashes of improvement and remained awake long enough to speak. "Miss Eliza and a man in my cell, whom she called 'Husband,' had an argument. I do not remember all their words, but it had something to do with her past indiscretions. The woman had many."

"Is that the reason she was arrested?"

"Aye. Unwholesome behavior and three children with no wedding ring on her finger. That is how the goaler described it. The father of her children yelled at her from our cell, for getting locked up in gaol, leaving their offspring to fend for themselves. He claimed it was bad enough that she was cavorting in an ungodly manner with any man who would pay. Now she was sentenced for a year."

"How did that include you?"

Alain recoiled when Baruch's pincer retrieved a piece of cloth buried deep in the wound. Blood dribbled, soaking the corner of the blanket. Baruch stanched the flow by using a compress.

"Thank you, Baruch. It still gives me pain, but not as much." Alain spoke slowly, gratefully, but winced with each word.

The doctor smiled, wiped his instruments, and began the process of returning them to their proper place.

"Alain, please continue." His eyes grew heavy. I was afraid he would fall asleep.

"Eliza started screaming and got angry when the goaler told her to shut up. That's when she accused me of being one of her customers and suggested very strongly that I was the father of her youngest. If she was trying to provoke her lover, she was successful. The next thing I knew he came at me with a knife."

"How did she know you? She can't see through the door's window."

"Aye. When I was returned to my cell after the hearing, she called me Fire Crotch." Alain chuckled. "It's my red hair, you—"

"Yes, I know. It's hardly a laughing matter."

"Well, I'm trying to look at what good can come out of this. If it wasn't for Eliza and her unsavory character, I wouldn't have you sitting here holding my hand and kissing me." He squeezed my fingers and brought them to his lips. "Maybe this will work in our favor."

We returned to see Alain two days later. Eliza Parker was gone. I was glad we were rid of her.

Alain was still covered with a blanket, and it appeared he had moved little since we left him. But there were differences, too. None of them good. His skin was hot to the touch. At the same time, he gripped the blanket, and pulled it tighter around his shoulders. It did little to stop his teeth from chattering.

Baruch uncovered Alain's leg. As he redressed the wound, Alain awoke but his mumbling made no sense. His eyes were glazed, staring but not seeing. Without warning, he sat up and got angry and did not recognize me. I spoke gently but firmly which seemed to calm him. When Baruch finished and the chills subsided, I washed down Alain's face and arm. Once again, he slept. Baruch and I left.

"Anna, the leg doesn't look good," said Baruch on our way home. "The skin around the vound is red and swollen. It looks vorse than the last

211

time I changed the dressing. You may have to decide shortly. Before ve return."

"Cut off his leg, you mean?" I asked even though I knew Alain would not want to live if he lost a limb. He had seen others live terrible lives. One was a clansman who Alain was quite fond of, a hearty fellow, known to run fast and fight hard. He had lost a foot while stealing a cow from a rival clan. The cow's owner began to shoot, and a bullet pierced the thief's heel. Three days later, his foot was cut off at the ankle. His cattle rustling days were over; and he no longer felt complete. He avoided the company of others, especially women, and felt that life as a cripple was worse than dying. He spent many days in a drunken stupor. When I countered with – 'at least he was alive' - Alain disagreed. Strongly.

When we arrived home, Master Myers was waiting for us. I left the two men discussing Alain's situation and returned with my candlestick.

"Master Myers. I offered you my candlestick once before. You refused to accept it although you told me it was valuable. You said, if I remember correctly, that this was something I should hand down to my daughters and to their children. I listened, and as you can see, I still have the candlestick.

"You should know there is another one. My oldest daughter has the mate. So, if you will purchase this one, Alexandra's can be passed down to my descendants. Having such a beautiful object means nothing to me if my husband dies. He needs to come home so we can care for him. I do not know how much someone is paying to keep Alain incarcerated, but I'm sure my candlestick is worth more. Perhaps you can find a buyer. Mr. Burnet or one of his rich clients."

Both men stared, their faces blank. Not even a raised eyebrow.

"This candlestick is cold and has no feeling. It has no value except for the life it could save. I am willing to relinquish it to the highest bidder. If you refuse to help, I will find another silversmith. I will do anything to save my husband."

CHAPTER TWENTY-TWO

THE DEFENSE

2008

THE WHITE CAR slid in almost unnoticed. The cold fear came roaring back, and I forced myself not to react by braking. I didn't want the car barreling into my rear and to meet the driver on a lonely road. My heart pounded so hard I thought a vein would burst. I considered adjusting the rearview mirror, but I didn't want the driver to know I was watching. Instead, I scolded myself. Why didn't I have a strategy? Where was the nearest police station? Was there an alternate route? A gas station nearby? A café? Holding my breath, I waited. The driver still trailed, but the gap widened. The vehicle slowed, fell back another car length, and then, at the last minute, took the next turn-off. I breathed again, grateful he no longer followed.

Lately, it felt like every car on the road was a white car, and I couldn't help but suspect each one I encountered.

Susannah Oliver accompanied me when I met with the examiners. The meeting lasted almost two hours. I had no trouble answering questions, and it turned out there were only a few items to fix. The lead examiner announced my thesis was sound and the dissertation well-written, clear, and validated by good research. A few errors were uncovered in the annotated bibliography as well as a couple of typos, including some missing commas that were necessary for a more accurate meaning. I received a deadline to resubmit. Because the fixes were minor, a date for the defense was scheduled three weeks later.

We exited St. Mary's, the gray stone building where the Department of Archaeology was housed. The newly hatched spring never smelled sweeter. Freshly mowed grass mixed with the perfume of early perennials. The intoxicating scent, purposeful to attract pollinators, would last only a few days, at best. Like at a West Point graduation, I wanted to toss my manuscript in the air like the former plebes did with their hats. Susannah hugged and asked if I cared to grab something to eat at a nearby cafe.

"Sorry, I can't. I must call Alec. He's waiting for my news. Besides, I'm so excited I couldn't hold a cup of anything right now." To prove my point, I stretched out my fingers.

Susannah laughed. "You did a great job. That was almost as perfect as anyone could expect."

"Thanks. I owe it all to you." That sounded so lame, but what else could I say?

"No way. I give the same effort to all my doctoral students, but none have achieved what you have. I'm proud of you."

"Thanks."

"Well, make sure you celebrate with a glass of wine tonight. And here's something else to think—" A phone buzzed. Susannah reached into her pocket, checked the screen, smiled, and clicked off. "That's my friend who's the undergraduate chair for archaeology studies at Columbia." I must have given her a quizzical look. "You know, in New York City." Susannah scoffed. "Maggie's call was a reminder to mention that she is looking for someone to fill a two-semester position. A staff member's on sick leave. There's a real possibility this will lead to an opening due to retirement. By the way, isn't Columbia where you did your undergrad?"

"No. Penn. But I'd love to live in New York. I haven't been there in ages." I remembered the last time. At a bank in lower Manhattan, I emptied my dad's safe deposit box, the last of my inheritance. That's where I found the key that led me to Scotland, and Alec, and Anna. "Sounds like a wonderful opportunity." I hesitated for just a moment. "I…I have to think it over."

"Sure. No rush. It's a huge decision. Can I tell my friend that there's a glimmer of hope? It's a grand opportunity, and maybe it will turn into a tenured track position. You don't want to spend too many years as an adjunct."

It did sound wonderful. I could just see myself renting a cute little studio apartment in Harlem, the kind with the bed in the wall. Every Friday, I'd meet colleagues for dinner and celebrate the end of another work week.

We'd go to our favorite Italian restaurant, a small and cozy place with only ten tables, each covered with a starched white tablecloth and a small, shaded lamp. The kind of place where you smelled the garlic bread before you entered. Because I was a regular, my favorite spot by the big window would be reserved. The waiter, a heavy-set guy wearing a large white apron and black vest with a white napkin draped over his arm, would pull out my chair. He'd snap his fingers and his assistant would arrive smartly with a glass of my favorite red wine. No menu necessary.

"Let me talk it over with Alec. It's a lot to think about."

"Of course," but her excitement appeared to disintegrate. She had told me many times about female colleagues who had lost out on opportunities because of a serious boyfriend or family commitments. Susannah spoke from experience. She had been in a relationship. The boyfriend refused to wait while she traveled to digs in Africa and Asia. She told me how lucky I was to have found a guy who not only understood the world of academia but followed me on my digs. Although, Susannah admitted, Panama was a bit dangerous.

After saying goodbye, I walked down the cobblestoned street, characteristic of the old college area. My car was in the nearest lot, parked next to a white sedan that was much too close to the driver's side. I had to enter the passenger side and climb over the center console. Wearing a skirt didn't help. If I hadn't been in a hurry to get home, I would have waited to confront the driver. But the car, any white car, made me uneasy. Was this the same one that followed me several weeks ago? Did the driver know I'd be here today? Was he stalking me? I wish I had remembered something special about the car: a dented fender, a roof rack, or even a funny bumper sticker like *Oot and Aboot*. That one always made me laugh, especially when Alec said it in an exaggerated Highlander dialect.

I still hadn't told him about my being followed.

We didn't do much entertaining at our flat. Occasionally, one or two of Alec's colleagues came by for a drink before heading out to dinner. Nothing formal, some crackers and cheese along with a dip. After an hour, we'd be seated at a local establishment. Tonight, was different. We invited Ira for dinner.

I planned a glazed salmon, a tossed salad, and a wonderful crusty bread I found at a local bakery. Alec contributed two Scottish dishes. The first was clapshot, one of my favorites. He swore it was an authentic Scottish recipe, handed down by some ancient relative, but it was basically mashed potatoes and turnips, mixed with browned onions. chopped chives, and lots of butter. When Alec first described the dish, he said the root vegetables were bashed. Bashing was how the Scots described mashing. Alec also made a cranachan in one of the few fit-for-company glass bowls we owned. The dessert had layers of whipped cream mixed with honey and whisky, raspberries, toasted oats, and more honey. I was jealous watching him prepare it, especially when he taste-tested the cream and stuffed a fresh raspberry in his mouth.

Ira brought a chilled bottle of Riesling.

The last time we were together was at Alec's father's funeral. We barely had time for conversation and there was little privacy. Now, after my recent talk with Reverend Walton, I had so many questions. My interest turned toward Anna's religion, and I wanted Ira's point of view.

"Prescott and I met a few weeks back," I began.

"I haven't seen my neighbor in a while. Strange how you can see someone less when they only live a few doors away. How did it go?"

It was comforting to hear that Prescott hadn't reported back to Ira. Not that I would have minded, but it's nice to know that he held our conversation in confidence.

"We talked about why people convert, and the reasons are not surprising: attraction to a set of beliefs, but mostly because of marriage and children." The mention of children popped a picture into my head. Alec and I and our two freckle-faced kids walking to church on a Sunday morning. Alec, handsome as always, in a coat and tie, the children in their Sunday best. My modest knee-length dress accessorized with a single strand of pearls and a fascinator. Those we passed tipped their hats and smiled. "There go the Grants," they'd say. "What a fine family." Father Wilson greeted us warmly and made sure others saw his approval. Once inside, always in the front row, two busybodies began to gossip about my un-Catholic past. They were quickly hushed and fled in disgrace. In my peculiar vision of the future, I had achieved sainthood.

And then, a much different vision. I'm fleeing the Inquisition only to find myself in the clutches of Father Drummond. Alec tries to rescue me, but he's no match against the strength of the Church—

"You know that Judaism's founding fathers were not originally Jews or married to Jews," said Ira. "Abraham and Sarah were not Jewish. Neither was Jacob's wife or Joseph's. Moses' wife Zipporah was a Cushite or a Midianite, and Solomon married an Egyptian princess although he had the Queen of Sheba and 999 others in his harem to choose from."

"Are you saying that it's not necessary for one Jew to marry another? I'm confused. What about you and Esther? Would you have still married her if she wasn't Jewish?"

"At the time I met my wife, interfaith marriage was frowned upon, so it was almost unheard of. I like to believe that I loved Esther enough that I would have married her, regardless. But the issue always boils down to the children, and that's compounded when you are a member of a minority. The weight and the obligation toward survival is taught at a young age. You've heard of Jewish guilt? I feel it in spades."

I glanced at Alec and the vision of our two children disappeared.

"Catholics know how to pour on the guilt as well. My mother is an expert at it, but I must not feel the same responsibility." Alec reached across the table, put his hand on mine and squeezed. "I've told Hanna many times, I don't care about religion. She can raise our children any way she pleases."

"But will you feel differently someday? Five or ten years from now or when it's time for our first to be baptized? I don't want you to have any regrets that your life would have been easier with a Catholic wife."

"Why can't we let our kids decide?" asked Alec.

The words 'our kids' sounded funny to my ears, as if we had just kissed them on their foreheads and tucked them into bed. Like my father did.

"And then, they'll end up like me. *Tabula Rosa*. At least, let's give them a place to start. You had a Catholic upbringing. You know where you're coming from, you have roots. I go whichever way the wind blows, lost between worlds: Anna's and yours."

That's when I realized that no matter how I looked at the pros and cons of conversion, it always came back to Anna. At one moment, I'd feel Catholicism was the answer, and then I wondered how could I turn my back on my history. A woman I had never met had this strange pull on me. It was crazy and I couldn't make sense of it. At times, I wondered how different my life would have been if I had never found the key. I would have probably stayed in Philadelphia, married a public-school teacher, bought a fixer-upper in the burbs with a gated yard and a shelter dog. Without the knowledge of Anna, religion would not be an issue. But then again, it was because of Anna that I met Alec. Or was it the other way around. Regardless, the two were connected.

"It's better to bash this out now," said Ira.

"Prescott said the same. Wait a minute. Bash? Like in potatoes?"

"You mean clapshot," corrected Alec and Ira laughed.

"Consider coming to a Sabbath service at my synagogue, my dear. See what goes on. I'll join you. Alec can come, too."

"Prescott mentioned that as well. Except he suggested a Catholic mass."

"From the one or two Jewish converts I know, I will tell you that conversion is more than just turning on the Jewish lightbulb and switching off another. Judaism doesn't look at this casually; one can't just slough off religion like changing a hat." Ira reached up to ensure his *kippah* was still on his head. "It's not just learning new traditions and new beliefs. You become part of a people. If this is something you don't feel you can embrace fully, then you are doing yourself a disservice as well as Alec and your children. In other words, don't fake it."

"How will I know?"

"That, my dear, requires the wisdom of Solomon. But since we are lacking in that regard, the rabbis have their ways."

"Really? Will they try to scare me off with threats of circumcision."

Alec's one eyebrow shot up.

"No, of course not. A member of my congregation, a Jew-of-Choice, told me the story of his conversion. When he sought out a rabbi, he was turned away. He was so shocked that he thought the rabbi hadn't heard him correctly. Who turns away a convert? So, he repeated his request, right away, and again he was rebuffed. Now, this fellow believed something was seriously wrong. Maybe the rabbi didn't find his request sincere; or the Jewish community was taking no more recruits, the seats were full. So, he went back to the rabbi, asked again, and got the same response. Frustrated, he questioned the rabbi why he was being turned down. He stated his reasons for conversion came from the heart. Hearing this, the rabbi told my friend that he was now ready. It is the tradition of many rabbis to turn down a supplicant three times. Conversion should not be done under duress but only because of one's desire to embrace Judaism."

"Great lesson, Ira. At this point, I probably wouldn't have gone back to the rabbi after the first refusal. I guess that means I have a lot of work to do, a lot of exploration of Catholicism, Judaism, or Nothingism. Maybe I'll learn to be satisfied with who I am."

"And I will love you no matter what you choose," said Alec. I had a feeling Alec wanted to say more about the subject, but maybe after Ira left.

Feeling the need to move on, I brought up the position at Columbia.

"Sounds like a promising opportunity for you, Hanna," said Ira. "They don't come along very often. There are few openings, especially tenure-track, at St. Andrews. Universities are offering them less and less because of the commitment and the cost. I couldn't even give you a glimmer of hope, and you don't want to spend your career as an adjunct. If you do that too long, your chances of being considered for a permanent position lessen. Are you going to contact the department head?"

"Yes. I should hear what she has to say." I glanced over at Alec. His eyes were downcast so I couldn't get a glimpse of his thoughts. We were painfully aware that whatever decision was made, one of us was going to get hurt. This choice appeared to be as difficult as the religious one. Maybe even more so.

The hallway outside the large group room assigned for the defense of my dissertation was a busy place. Students walked briskly, even though shoulders slumped under heavy backpacks. Their frenetic routine was familiar. With minutes to spare until the next class, students raced the clock to grab a cup of coffee to keep them awake for the next long lecture. Or squeezed in a quick chat with friends, to find out the location of a party on Friday night. A minute before classes were to resume, faculty shut office doors. Their arms full of lecture notes and books, they headed in the same direction as their students. In moments, the hall returned to silence and I was left alone on the wooden bench outside the double doors.

I envied the students' naiveté and freshness. Most couldn't wait to graduate and move on. But I regretted ending my life on campus, surrounded by people who shared the same interests. I discovered that on my very first day as a Ph.D. candidate. I was sitting in a small conference room waiting for the professor to arrive. The others around me apparently knew each other. They were chatting and one of them told a joke about mummies and King Tut. I don't recall exactly how the joke went, but the others broke up laughing and then offered their own off-color archaeological anecdotes. I remember thinking: *I am in the right place. These people will get me.*

And now my life as a student was about to come to an end. Forever. What a bittersweet feeling.

I checked my watch. Again. Waiting was pure agony, sitting here, anticipating a decision any minute. Was it just two hours ago, when the interrogation had started? I sat at a table with Susannah, the other readers, professors I had chosen to read my dissertation, and another representing the examining board.

But we weren't alone. The room had fifty seats. Students and faculty filled the smallish auditorium and waited for me to soar or go down in defeat like a swirling plane that's just received a mortal blow.

Before the room was called to order, I breathed in deeply, and took one more look around. There were many familiar faces who had become friends. Miranda gave me a discreet but reassuring smile. Seated next to her, holding her hand, was Hadrian. We had been through so much together. Recalling the dig gave me chills. In the first row was Alec. I must have smiled broadly when he silently mouthed - *I love you.* At that moment, I wanted all of this to disappear so I could rush into his arms and tell him I would never leave him…and Scotland. Instead, I had to be content with the advice he had given me this morning: *Remember, no one knows your work like you do. You are the expert.*

"Good afternoon." Susannah called for everyone's attention. "Welcome. We are about to hear the defense of the dissertation of Ph.D. Candidate Hanna Duncan, entitled, 'The Female Contribution and New Insights into the Kingdom of Scotland's 17th Century Colony, Caledonia.'"

While the audience was reminded about silencing their phones and not talking, I saw out of the corner of my eye another spectator enter the room. Susannah stopped mid-sentence. She wasn't pleased with the interruption but since it was a senior faculty member, there wasn't much she could do. Dr. Jones had just taken a seat in the last row.

Before I knew it, the defense was completed. I took that as a good sign. None of the questions were surprising; many were the same ones the examiners asked a few weeks ago. I tried to gauge my performance by the expression on Susannah's face, but she was stoic. It wasn't until we were finishing, and I was directed to leave the room, that she offered a smile. I hoped it was not out of sympathy.

Now, I waited outside while the dissertation committee discussed my fate. My legs were wobbly, so I was grateful for the bench. Alec offered to get some coffee and disappeared down the hall. Miranda and Hadrian shared their mutual congratulations for a job well done. I thanked them for coming and after we joked about their 'inquisitions' to come, they said their good-byes and were gone. While I was glad to have reached the finish line, I still envied their run. A few professors and some other friends came over to say hello and share their thoughts. I was grateful when they left. I wanted time to decompress.

"Hanna, you did great." It was Max.

"What are you doing here? I thought you were off in Sri Lanka or was it Tanzania? Working on a book." Max's salt and pepper hair brushed his shoulders, and his jacket was slung over his shoulder. He looked great. Unfortunately. But as he approached the bench, I refused to scoot over to provide a seat. There was no way I was going to let him think I might be interested. On second thought, he probably preferred standing. It allowed him to be intimidating. Like he needed to lord over me. But Max had not changed. He came closer. Too close. Fingers poised to touch my arm, without permission.

"Where's your boyfriend?" He hesitated. His eyes searching. "No wedding ring? I thought surely you'd be married by now."

Max's presence brought back unpleasant memories. His unwanted come-ons, his uncomfortable touching, his put-downs of my relationship with Alec; and when the situation became frightfully dangerous, he was a coward.

I ignored his question and the passive-aggressive ploy he often used. I rose and looked him squarely in the eye. "Were you waiting for me to be alone?"

"I knew your boyfriend wouldn't let me speak to you."

"His name is Alec. Dr. Grant to you. And I don't need his protection. Unlike you, I'm not a coward."

"I always thought you could do better."

Why did men like Max and Iain, think that I could do better? Like I was a little girl who needed help with a decision. "With you?" I scoffed. "Let me ask you this. Why do you think the university gave you a leave of absence? I wasn't the only woman to complain. Others have come forward. The administration created a phony excuse to get you off campus. Now that you're back, every co-ed needs to be on her guard. Perhaps you should resign before you're fired."

The moment the words tumbled from my lips, I felt sorry for Dr. Jones. Not for the man, but the brilliant scholar who had thrown away his career. In the past, students clambered to be in his classes, join his digs, and bask in his limelight. Everything he had built had gone up in flames. His future was bleak. No one would buy his books or seek his advice. Prestigious universities would shred his resume, and donors with deep pockets would refuse to fund his expeditions.

"I'm sorry Hanna. You were special. I…we could've—"

"There's no 'we.' I was your student. I trusted you. So did all the others. Instead of trying to protect your students, you went after them."

Max looked around without answering. Alec's steady footfalls echoed on the tiled floor, getting louder as he came closer. Max fled in the opposite direction.

Alec handed me my coffee. "I thought he was out of country."

"I thought so, too. But I have a feeling we won't be seeing him on campus anymore. Good riddance."

"Hanna," interrupted Dr. Oliver. "Would you please step inside?"

I gave Alec a quick kiss and hurried back into the room. Susannah closed the door behind me. The chairs around the conference table were empty. Instead, the three professors and the examiner stood next to each other. Susannah took her place at the front. Their formation resembled a receiving line. Or was it a gauntlet? What's going on? Surely, I must have made some grievous error. It looked like they didn't even want to talk to me anymore. My legs went wobbly again.

Dr. Oliver steeped forward. She extended a hand. I looked at her. What was she doing?

"Congratulations, Dr. Duncan."

I stopped breathing. I walked over. I didn't know what to do. Or say. She gestured her open hand again. I took it.

"Dr. Duncan, I presume?"

"Yes. Oh, yes. Oh, my god. Thank you." I couldn't control that feeling you get right before you're about to burst into tears.

The next professor stepped forward and shook my hand. "Congratulations, Dr. Duncan." This was said again and again and again.

Alec and I walked out of the building, taking our time as we sauntered on the cobbled street, heading toward the carpark. I didn't care if it was rainy or windy or even if there was a blizzard. The sun was brilliant today, no matter what.

"We must celebrate. I made reservations at a new restaurant that I think you'll love."

"How did you know?"

"That you would pass with flying colors?"

"Yes. I mean, as soon as I came out of the room, you shook my hand and said, Congratulations, Dr. Duncan. That's what everyone in the room did."

"Hanna, this is not my first go-round at a defense. I know when a student has made it."

I kissed him on the cheek and then the lips and then snuggled closer as we walked. "You could have said something before you rushed off to get coffee." I laughed. "But it's okay. It gave me a chance to say what I needed to, to Dr. Jones."

"I'm sorry I wasn't there."

"No problem. Let's forget about it. It's time to celebrate."

We stopped at an old oak tree by the entrance to the carpark. Alec turned and pulled me in. "Where's Martyr's Monument when I need it?"

I grabbed his jacket lapels and pulled his face close to mine. "This tree will have to do." We stayed locked in an embrace and ignored the friendly chatter and titter of passing students and the distant sound of a car engine. The voices disappeared. But the car's engine grew louder: roaring, consuming, and threatening. It gunned past, leaving a puff of black smoke in its wake. The driver craved our attention. In a moment, the car exited the carpark and sped down the street. The gray granite walls of the ancient buildings could not snuff out its stark whiteness.

CHAPTER TWENTY-THREE
SCOTTISH ROSE

TWO-HUNDRED-SEVENTY-TWO STEPS.

That's how many there were on the path that snaked its way to the top of a rocky headland jutting out into the North Sea. Situated on the grassy summit, the ruins of Dunnottar Castle, the mighty medieval fortress, had guarded the northern coast of Scotland for seven centuries. This was not a hike for the weak or faint-hearted. Sturdy shoes were a must; a walking-stick was beneficial. Handicapped accessibility did not exist.

Beginning at the carpark, the flat path, bordered by tall grasses and thistles, led to a descending staircase with shallow and regular steps like those found on entering a subway. This was followed by more gently sloped ramps and another staircase. The walk started easily enough, mostly downhill, luring the tourist forward until they reached the bottom of a V-shaped gorge. This is where the warning posted at the start, made sense. The ill-prepared or unfit faced two difficult choices: return or go forward. Either way, it was a strenuous climb.

At this midway point, there was a wide landing where two paths intersected. One led to the rocky cliff tops offering astounding views of the castle and the North Sea; the other brought the visitor to the castle itself. Climbers used this respite to catch their breath and snap a few pictures. By the time we arrived, a tour guide had just finished his explanation. He held up a sign and a group of Asians followed his lead. Just as quickly, several teenagers filled the gap. A girl, dressed in shorts and flip-flops, bent over, hands on her knees, as if to catch her breath. "I don't think I can go any further. My ankle hurts and I'm getting a blister."

"Come on," urged a friend. "We're halfway there."

The girl looked at the path and blew on her bangs to get them out of her eyes. The steps toward the castle had lost their uniformity; the incline went skyward. "I can't." She held out her injured foot as if to prove her point. "You guys go ahead. I'll wait here."

"Are you sure?" her friend asked. He glanced at the others who had already started out.

"I'm positive."

The friend still hesitated but left to join the majority. The girl pulled out her phone from her back pocket and quickly became preoccupied.

I tilted my head toward our destination, grabbed Alec's arm, and said, "Time to do this."

Whether we wanted to or not, we climbed at a slower pace. Like a toddler learning to tackle a staircase, I took one steep step at a time, stopping every so often to catch my breath and take selfies with the amazing site in the background. Once the entrance fee was paid, Alec and I walked through an underground passageway, a pend as it was labeled on my map, to the top. We were richly rewarded for our efforts.

We stood on a mostly grass-covered summit that ascended one-hundred-fifty feet above the sea. Except for the natural bridge linking it to the mainland, steep cliffs encircled the peak, and like an eternity pool, plummeted into the North Sea. The cliffs were home to many seabirds: puffins and razorbills. Screeching gulls, soared overhead with the help of thermals, searching for food.

In front of us were ancient stone buildings. Some in neat rows, others stood alone, almost all were roofless. On the left was an expansive grassy area called the Bowling Green. The edges sloped inward, as if on purpose, to keep a ball or a player from falling off the cliff.

"That's funny," I said. "My dad used to take me to a park in New York called Bowling Green. It's down in the lower end of Manhattan, in the financial district."

"No surprise. The Dutch brought the game to New Amsterdam. It was popular throughout Europe."

"I didn't know it was so trendy."

"The game, also called skittles, was banned in England when soldiers preferred to play rather than learn the art of warfare."

I waited for more. Alec always had lots of information stored in that head of his. But there was nothing. Strange. I had a feeling all morning, during breakfast and on our drive to Dunnottar, that he had something to tell me.

We moved to the next area. It was a grassy quadrangle with a large cistern in the center. Buildings that looked more like small houses on a

Monopoly board, were lined on three sides. One row ended with a large chapel.

As we peeked behind stone walls, we found bunches of tour groups huddled around a guide. Bright yellow ear plugs wired each visitor to black receivers hanging around their necks. I edged closer to eavesdrop but could only hear bits and pieces of information: medieval fortress, Vikings, William Wallace, Mary, Queen of Scots, crown jewels, and Jacobite rebellion.

Again, I waited for Alec to tell me more, but instead, he nudged me forward and we encountered another group. This talk was different. Words like uplift, Silurian Period, pudding stone, and erosion suggested an earth science lesson. We stayed until we were made uncomfortable by the glares of those who paid for the lecture.

Alec and I moved on to the chapel. I knew from the brochure that this was the oldest structure. We walked along the perimeter. Four walls remained, the roof was gone, and on one end, at the entrance, was a perfect gothic archway. Above the entrance was a similarly shaped window nearly the same size. It appeared that the ancient architect attempted a sense of symmetry. Seeing a large tour group inside, we chose to walk along a narrow strip of grass between the church and a twelve-foot-high stone wall edged with white, pink, and red roses. On the other side of the wall, we discovered a grassy area and more flowers. This was a cemetery, minus the headstones.

The silence between us became awkward. I wracked my brain for something to talk about. "There's rumor that Aberdeen is going to be involved in a dig nearby," I said.

"Makes sense. The university is close."

I waited. He added nothing more. "Not far from here, years ago, some kids looking for golden treasure, came across some carved Pictish stones. It's thought that this might indicate a pre-tenth century settlement or fort."

"Mmph."

"Susannah said the archaeology department is going to put together a team. The site's on a sea stack. It would be fascinating to be involved. Susannah said I could—"

"You'll be in New York."

"Maybe. I don't know that for sure." Alec's tone was tense and curt. Was New York the root of his silence? "I'm just at the talking phase with Columbia. Nothing's settled."

"Mmph."

"If I get the job, Susannah and I could collaborate. Maybe bring some of my students to Scotland. That would be exciting."

The old Alec would have responded with a raised eyebrow. But there was nothing. Then I realized the issue between us. I was excited for my future. Alec didn't feel he was a part of it.

When the tour group exited, Alec took my hand and we silently entered the chapel. Like a bride and groom, we strode down the center of what would have been the aisle and stopped where the altar must have stood.

Alec took my hands and faced me. "Hanna. We could get married here."

"Here?"

"Yes. You can book a wedding on this site."

"You checked it out?"

"I don't want to wait any longer. We've..."

Alec didn't finish. He didn't have to. We both knew how long ago it was that Alec had proposed. He swallowed. "I have something to tell you. I need you to hear me out." He took a deep breath. "Do you remember when we met? On the plane? From that first meeting and all during the flight, we chatted effortlessly about...everything. There was something about you. The cute way you looked at me with your curls all in your face, the ease of our conversation, and how you found humor in just about any topic. I was taken with you from that moment, and I knew, that if I were lucky enough, I would someday ask you to spend the rest of your life with me."

My lips must have started to form a word because Alec held up his hand to stop me.

"When the plane circled over Edinburgh, I kept thinking of excuses, reasons to meet up with you later that day or the next. I was so afraid that you'd walk out of that airport, and my life, and I'd never see you again."

I remembered. Exactly. Alec surprised me by calling shortly after I arrived at the B&B. I hadn't expected to hear from him for a few days. If at all.

"We've been through a lot together, and I've loved every minute of it. But I'm afraid I'm losing you. You asked me to wait to get married until you got your degree. You said school was overwhelming, and you needed to complete your defense. I have been patient." Alec pulled me closer until our lips almost touched. "Hanna Duncan. I'm asking you again. Will you marry me?"

At first, I didn't answer. I couldn't. We were interrupted by the high-pitched screams of children running in from the adjacent quadrangle. A tow-headed boy chased a little girl. They took one look at us and continued their game. The boy had a rose crushed in his hand. The girl stopped and screamed as her little lover tried to put it under her nose. She swatted it, and the red petals lay crumbled on the stone floor. And then, just as quickly, the children were gone.

"Alec...I—"

"You don't have to answer this moment. I know you have another huge decision to make, and I want you to be happy. But I need to know. Will we have a future together?"

Alec stepped back, took my hand, but he could not hide the unhappiness in his eyes. As we exited the church, he attempted a faint smile, but if a smile could be described as sad, it was the one I saw on Alec's face.

Before we left, I requested to take one last look at the magnificent scenery. I got as close to the edge of the cliff as visitors were allowed. Looking down at the roaring sea, rocky monoliths broke the waves, and the rugged coastline extended north and south. I felt like I was standing on the physical and metaphorical edge of a precipice. One misstep and I would go crashing down. Which way should I go? What was the safest step to take? For the moment, there was no answer. I would have to wait and see.

❦

A few days later, Susannah sat across the table from me at the on-campus coffee shop. Her legs were crossed, and a large cup of hot chocolate was cuddled in her hands.

"Have you talked to Maggie?" asked Susannah.

"Yes. She seems nice enough. She wants me to come to New York, check out the campus, and meet some of the teaching staff. Maggie's not so sure how many will be around, since it's over the summer, but she thinks she can wrangle a few."

"I want to stay out of the process, but from what I know about Maggie, there would be no invitation from Columbia unless she was interested. My friend can be blunt and to the point, but she goes after what she wants. I admire that in her. Sounds like Maggie's keen on getting you for her department."

"Yeah. I'm…excited, too. I think."

"Hanna. Really?" Susannah stared, demanding my attention like I was still in her classroom. "If that's how you show excitement, I'd hate to see when you're depressed. What's wrong?"

I signed heavily. "I should be thrilled."

"Is it Alec?"

"No. Well, sort of. This has happened way quicker than I imagined. Alec wants to get married. He's tired of waiting. I can't say I blame him. He's been more than patient."

Susannah put down her drink and bit into a biscuit which left crumbs all over her black sweater. "Why doesn't Alec visit Columbia with you? You could stay a few days. Look for a flat. Tour New York. It could be a nice little vacation."

"I thought of that. There are some places I want to check out. About my ancestor, Anna. But Alec promised to help his mother clean out his father's stuff. It will take a week or two."

She brushed off the crumbs with a few well-directed swipes. "That long to take clothes and shoes to a charity?"

"It's more than that. There's some historical stuff his father had for years. Alec's mother wants him to look it over and figure out what's important to keep or what should be donated to a museum. There's also a Bible that has a list of names and dates for every birth, marriage, and death in the family. Actually, it's a series of Bibles and goes back quite far. His mother is hoping he'll create a family tree from the information. Now that a grandchild is on the horizon, she wants the family details in order."

"Sounds like Alec's going to be doing a 'dig' of his own."

I laughed but I wasn't in the mood for laughing. "That will keep him busy part of the summer. He's also teaching one class, and then this fall, he's taking on a leadership role in the department. It's a great opportunity for him."

"Wow! Good for Alec."

"But don't you see? How could I ask him to leave all that and live with me in New York? He's a rising star at St. Andrews. Why should he give up his job?"

"The same could be said for you. Why should you give up a position at Columbia?"

"I've asked Alec for a little more time. If…I get the job. We could see each other over breaks: Thanksgiving, Christmas. He could come to New York; or I could come here."

"What did Alec say to that?"

"He agreed. Of course. But a decision must be made by New Years. By Hogmanay."

"He gave you a time limit?" The tone in her voice made it sound like she finally found a flaw in Alec's character.

"No. I've imposed that on myself." I put the spoon down and drank the rest of the cooled tea. "I have to make up my mind."

So much distraction: Alec; the job; marriage; New York; conversion. I thought that once I got my degree, everything would fall into place; life would be simple. I'd settle into a position at Aberdeen or St. Andrews, Alec and I would get married, purchase a home, raise a family, and live happily ever after.

Why couldn't my life be as uncomplicated as Jess'? She knew what she wanted and got it. And she was happy. At least she seemed that way whenever we talked. Maybe I should call her. She always made me laugh. But then, I wasn't sure she would understand. She was up to her eyeballs in diapers and ear infections. Besides, I might be seeing her soon enough.

I was thinking about all of this when a harsh blast of a car's horn startled me. I had entered a roundabout in the wrong lane. Roundabouts were my least favorite part of driving in Scotland. I waved my apologies and let the driver pass.

Alec and I agreed to meet in Stonehaven for dinner after Susannah and I said our goodbyes. The restaurant had the best seafood, and I wanted one last visit before I left for New York. This place was our favorite; the staff had become friends.

Out of the circle, my thoughts returned to my conversation with Susannah. She was right. Alec was a great guy. She was always advising me not to let anything get in my way of advancing my career. But I'd be crazy to let him go. Delaying the marriage decision until New Years was generous; more than I should have expected or deserved. I remembered the exact moment we talked about our future. We were sitting in the carpark at Dunnottar. I rolled up the window to block out the chatter of tourists and the smell of hamburgers and chips from the concessionaire.

"We'll make this work," said Alec. "I'll come to New York whenever I can."

"I'll come…to Scotland when I'm off, too."

"No. You're going to need every moment to prepare for your classes. I remember how hectic those first years were. I'll come to you." He grasped my hands even tighter.

I was wracked with guilt. I knew what he was thinking. Would one year lead to two? Would I meet someone else?

I pulled onto the shoulder. My eyes were blurry from tears. I wiped them, blew my nose, and gave myself a moment or two before driving on. I had time. The restaurant was only five minutes away. I stared at the roiling sea on my left and the rolling hills on the right. Tears returned. How I would miss Scotland and Alec. I had grown to love this country and once, I couldn't imagine living anywhere else. I blinked and dabbed again. My eyes cleared and I noticed roses twining around a fence post. Somehow, they thrived in this harsh climate. These were wild roses. Some called them Scottish roses. They were the same flowers I'd seen at Dunnottar. The one the little boy had tried to give to his friend, red petals crushed in his tiny, outstretched hand.

The sound of tires crackling on gravel brought me out of my daydream. It was a white car. The driver parked directly behind me. The door opened. For a moment, my heart almost jumped out of my chest until I noticed large letters on the hood. 'Police.' I breathed a sigh of relief.

"Are you okay? Do you need help?"

"Good afternoon. I'm fine. I just thought I'd call my fiancée and let him know I'm on my way. Thought it best to pull off."

The officer peered in the car. I knew from news reports that Scotland Police was cracking down on reckless driving. He was probably checking my sobriety and if my seatbelt was fastened.

"Okay. Have a good day."

231

I drove on, glancing at my rearview mirror, the side mirrors and then the rear once again, every so often. Another car slid in behind. A white car. Was the officer following me? Maybe he would get off at the next exit. But he didn't. Perhaps, he didn't trust my driving abilities; or thought I was lying. The car was awfully close. I couldn't even see the headlights and then I realized it was not the police car. It was the other white car. The one that had followed me before. The one that sped past Alec and me in Aberdeen. My heart resumed its attempt to jump out of my chest. Where was the cop when I needed him? The car was inches from my back bumper. I felt a thud. *Holy Crap!* Was he trying to run me off the road? I grabbed the wheel with both hands and floored the gas pedal. For a few moments, a blessed gap widened between us. Not for long. Now, we were both speeding, and the driver was on my tail again. Thoughts of my mother, dying in a car crash, flashed in front of me. I eased my foot off the gas pedal and allowed the car to reduce its speed gradually. My grip tightened on the wheel. I prepared for another thud.

Only one more minute until I reached the restaurant. I checked again at the review mirror. I couldn't see the driver. The tinted window and lowered visor hid his features, but I had a strong suspicion it was Iain. With his deranged way of thinking, he'd love to scare me out of Alec's life. Or maybe it was Kate. No, I couldn't imagine her doing this in her condition. She'd never want to put the only Grant heir in jeopardy.

The restaurant was right ahead. I could smell it. Alec's car was parked on the side. I pulled in next to his and blew the horn several times.

Undeterred, the white car pulled into the lot. The engine idling, the driver sat there. Waiting. Waiting for what? For me? I continued blaring the horn. Alec came out, followed by a waiter.

I lowered the window. "That white car over there. It's been following me."

Alec froze and looked at me quizzically. It wasn't his fault. I never told him about my being followed. He had no idea what was going on. He must have thought I was crazy.

Another car pulled into the lot. The police car parked behind the white one, blocking it. The officer that I had just met got out and, like in the movies, he sauntered over and appeared to be talking to the driver. I still couldn't see who it was. The officer blocked my view. Then voices became louder, heated, and slurred. Male voices. It was not Kate. The officer stepped back, the door opened, and someone stumbled out.

I got out of my car and stood next to Alec. We stared in disbelief while the officer escorted the driver to the police car. The driver was not who I thought he was. It was not Iain. It was Max who tried to run me off the road. It was Dr. Maximillian Jones.

CHAPTER TWENTY-FOUR

THE REMNANTS OF ISRAEL

MANHATTAN

THE JEWS OF Manhattan called themselves The Remnants of Israel. Although the community had increased fourfold since the first Jews arrived, they still struggled to find the necessary resources to purchase a building dedicated for prayer. At first, it did not matter. The early laws of the colony forbade Jews from praying publicly. Once the statute was overturned, the dream of a synagogue became even more desirous. The community, however, began with what they could afford; a rented room near the minister's house on Beaver Street, and later, another on Mill Street.

As the Remnants continued to grow, the effort to obtain a synagogue was part of many conversations. The Manhattan Jews were jealous of their Christian neighbors. The Anglicans and the Dutch Reformed congregation had built large houses of worship, and in some cases, were outgrowing the old and building anew. So, it was no wonder that the Jews had their eyes and prayers on a larger building to include a sanctuary, a school, and a *mikveh*, a ritual bath. But the dream remained elusive. Resources were scant.

Even before the acquisition of a building for prayer, the priority of any fledgling Jewish community was the purchase of land for a cemetery. It was a communal foundation and announced to the world - *We are here.* The Jewish Manhattanites were about to purchase a second cemetery, a grim reminder of the inevitable and the Remnants' fortuitous increase from the Old World.

Ashkenazi Jews arrived from France, Poland, Bohemia and, like the Emmanuels, the German States. Newcomers sought out the nascent Jewish community which brought them to the home of Minister Abraham de

Lucena and his wife, Rachel. If they needed medical care, they were directed to the Emmanuels' stoop.

My friendship with Deborah and Rachel brought me in close contact with these wandering Jews and their new customs, traditional dishes, and foreign tongues. In addition, they improved the occupational diversity amongst the community. Many were shopkeepers and merchants. Their connections with co-religionists around the world proved an asset. French Jews brought the silk trade. An older Belgian and his son were diamond merchants. Another, whom I had never met, owned a trading ship. His wealth was a major source of gossip.

"The ship owner's name is not known to me at the moment, but from all the reports I have received, he must be successful and a proper gentleman," said Rachel. "I'm sure Abraham will make it his business to seek the man out. A wealthy Jew owning a ship in New York will not remain a mystery for long. Perhaps—" Rachel stopped, distracted by movement behind the heavy drape. Her abrupt silence encouraged a small dark face to peek out. It was Ruth's son. "What are you doing in here? Are you eavesdropping?" The little fellow stepped out from his hiding place. His eyes glued on the floor.

"Well, speak up. It's disrespectful not to respond to your elders."

The boy remained silent.

"Where is your mother?" Rachel spun around as if Ruth was concealed behind a chair or a desk. She hopped off her seat, her swirling skirts followed. "A good whipping is what you need. And no dinner."

The boy spoke in sniffles. My heart broke. This child was not much older than Sally. I glanced at Deborah. Our eyes met.

"Rachel, perhaps the boy vas caught in the room vhen ve arrived," suggested Deborah. "Not vanting to anger you, he hid. I'm sure that's vhat happened." She then directed her comment to the boy. "Isn't that so?"

The lad kept his eyes lowered. His body trembled as he nodded.

"Let me take him to find his mother." I stood and took the boy's hand and led him toward the safety and warmth of the kitchen and his mother's arms. His calloused skin surprised me.

When I returned, Rachel seemed annoyed. She sniffed and turned toward Deborah and continued her conversation as if I wasn't in the room. "Perhaps my husband and yours, Deborah, could put their brilliant heads together to encourage the man's charitable instinct. I have no doubt our husbands will be most successful. Now that we almost have enough for a new cemetery, help is needed for the purchase of a synagogue."

Rachel's suggestion was not unusual. Abraham and Baruch were the leaders of the community. But it was her tone and inflection when mentioning husbands that excluded me. After all, Alain was not a free man. Innocent or not, he was in gaol. I could not go to him and seek his protection. In a world where a woman's identity and value were based on her husband's standing, Rachel had reminded me of my situation.

"When did this shipping magnate with the golden purse arrive?" My attempt at levity did not lessen Rachel's annoyance.

"Three months ago," Rachel continued. "Master Myer's wife, Elkanah, mentioned a lady-friend of hers who met the gentleman in question. In fact, Elkanah saw them walking together. Later, when she inquired, her friend described the man as a rich elderly Jew who owned a trading ship. He told her that until his business succeeded, he was too busy; and for now, preferred to avoid any entanglements." Rachel paused when something shattered in the kitchen. She sighed loudly and strained her neck in the direction of the noise but decided the rest of her story was more important. "Elkanah's friend said the man was most peculiar, and she was unsure of his intentions as well. He kept asking her about our community and if she knew this person or that one. The woman is not Jewish, although with her dark hair and olive skin tone, many have mistaken her for one. When she made it clear that she attended Trinity Church, his manner became abrupt and he excused himself, stranding her far from home. Can you imagine? Not very gentlemanly, if you ask me."

"If he vants to know about us, vhy doesn't he just show himself for prayers?" asked Deborah.

"I was wondering the same. But still, manners or no, he is wealthy, and I am sure, Deborah, you could invite him to your home. Or I'd gladly offer him a Sabbath meal." Rachel chuckled. "I'm always looking for new guests to show off my silver forks. I will invite you and Baruch. And you, Anna. I'm sure you are curious."

To save the man's reputation, I offered excuses for his unusual behavior. "Maybe he is experiencing trying circumstances and prefers to keep his identity a secret." I wondered if Rachel would see the humor if I suggested that the mysterious man was a secret agent from a foreign government come to spy on the English. Or, worse, he'd ravished a young woman and now her family sought revenge.

"But others, newly arrived, have found us." Rachel appeared even more annoyed. "It seems odd to me." She patted the back of her head and wrapped a few errant hairs around her fingers to revive the curls. "Well, as I said, he's well-off and is about to purchase another vessel. In the meantime, Elkanah thinks he has moved into one of the finest homes in the city. If it is the one, I am thinking of, our mystery man is presently renovating it from top to bottom. Although I never saw anything wrong with the house."

"He sounds already prosperous," said Deborah. "Maybe he's not the charitable sort. By not seeking us out, there is no need for him to feel obligated to pay a yearly fee to support the synagogue. Sometimes, I find the poor more generous than the rich."

"Hmm," said Rachel. "Well, I'll talk to Abraham and insist he seek out the gentleman and accept no excuse." She took a deep breath as she readied herself to continue. "But ladies, this is the best part. I cannot keep it a secret any longer even though I promised Elkanah I would say nothing." She paused and looked at us. "The ship owner is a widower. His wife died years ago."

Rachel's promised secret reminded me of Father when I was about to repeat gossip from the kitchen maids: *Do not say something that should never be heard, because ultimately it will be heard.*

"Vealthy and available," said a smiling Deborah. "Vhat a promising combination."

"I know a couple of women who might interest the gentleman," said Rachel. "The Cohen daughter, for one. Why…she is almost twenty-eight. Rather plain and her skin is blotchy, but her family is well off. And what about Miriam? She buried her husband six months ago. It is time she married again. Hmm. I do not mind playing matchmaker." She hesitated and then grabbed my hand in excitement. "Anna, if only Alexandra was two or three years older, she could get herself quite a catch. She's such a beauty."

"As long as the bride doesn't mind an older man," said Deborah.

"Mind! Never having to worry about the price of anything. Fabulous silks and extravagant dresses. Slaves to do your bidding. Having every luxury your heart desires," said Rachel. She stopped, closed her eyes; lost in a dream she wished for herself. "I almost forgot. There is more to the little secret. And even better for Alexandra. The gentleman has a son. And the son is of marriageable age. Can you imagine? A young man of significant means and an older wealthier groom with experience. Something for everyone."

My visit and conversation with Deborah and Rachel were a needed distraction. My awful reality came roaring back the moment Deborah and I returned home.

"Anna, I'm off to see your husband," Baruch said while sorting through his medicine bag. On a table he had spread out his tools: a crooked knife, an evil-looking hook, a large needle, a thick wooden stick, forceps, leather strips, lint pledgets, rolls of linen, and a tourniquet. The tool I tried to overlook was the bow saw. It looked more appropriate for a torture chamber. When Baruch added it to his bag, my heart almost stopped.

"Will Alain…lose his…leg today?"

"It depends on the inflammation. I'm not even sure if the constable vill allow me to do the surgery. But I'm ready to offer my services."

"Do you not trust the surgeon who worked on Alain earlier?"

"No, I don't. He vas careless. He barely cleaned the vound. Although I do not think it vould have made a difference. Once the skin is broken, inflammation is almost impossible to avoid. But a cleaned vound might have made your husband's condition not so grave and there vould have been less pain."

"Are those the tools for the—"

"Yes. I vant to be prepared. I'm not called to do this sort of procedure very often." He picked up a bottle containing a reddish-brown liquid, swirled it in the light, and then placed it the bag as well. "Do you vish to come? You don't have to. It's a gruesome surgery. Quick, but dreadful. No one vould blame you if you—"

"No. I will come. If things were reversed, Alain would do the same." I reached for my shawl and as I was about to follow the doctor out the door, Alexandra stopped me.

"I want to see Father. He must be doing poorly, or Dr. Emmanuel would not be hurrying off with his bag of medicines."

Alexandra offered no pleas, nor did she use conciliatory words like 'please' or 'may I.' I was tempted to persuade her otherwise. Alain was in no condition for visitors, let alone a child. The awfulness of what might transpire was not for someone of her years. But I understood her need. Survival was not in his favor. I could not deny her the right of a final precious moment. I nodded, and we fled into the street.

The three of us walked in silence. I wondered if each was considering what we might find. Was Baruch preparing himself for the awful surgery? Rehearsing in his mind each necessary step? Was Alexandra memorizing her last words to her father? How does one choose what you will remember for the rest of your life? I had only one thought. To save my love. To give him a reason to live.

Alain was feverish and went in and out of consciousness. His leg was swollen and the redness around the wound had expanded with radiating scarlet streaks. Yellow and greenish pus oozed out of the wound and there was a rank odor that was hard to describe. Was this what death smelled like? Baruch further examined the wound, touching it lightly. He glimpsed my way, and with the briefest of movements, he shook his head.

"I won't lose my leg," said Alain as he came to, lifted his head, and then lowered it back to the table. He grabbed my arm and pulled me closer. "Do you hear me? Do not let them take my leg."

"Mr. MacArthur, Anna may have little to say in the matter. Your leg is severely inflamed. If ve do nothing, you vill lose your life."

"What will my life be worth as a cripple? What kind of husband and father will I be? I won't be able to support my family if I'm not a whole man."

"Your daughters need you. I need you," I said while yanking on a handkerchief hidden in my sleeve. It was not for tears. There was too much anger to cry. "Alexandra is here. She's downstairs…waiting to see you. She demanded to come. Are you going to deny her a father? Is that what you want? Your decision will affect your children for the rest of their lives." I hesitated a moment, allowing Alain to grasp the meaning of my words. "Alexandra wants her father. Do not take that away from her. Not again." I saw tears in Alain's eyes and considered offering the handkerchief. But I didn't. "If you prefer to die, you will have to tell your daughter yourself."

I walked out the door and slammed it behind me. The charade was over. I leaned against the wall, to keep from collapsing, and wondered if I could carry out my threat. I don't know how long I stood there. In dire situations, a minute can seem like an hour, an hour, an eternity. The door creaked. Baruch came out.

"Alain has asked to see Alexandra."

"Did…he make…a decision?"

"Yes."

"And what is it?"

Baruch took a deep breath. "Your husband's pronouncement is based on a simple premise. He loves you. And he said he vill not lose you."

CHAPTER TWENTY-FIVE

THE KISS

BLOODY RIVULETS FLOWED across the grainy oak table. Compelled by the law of gravity, the once life-giving force sought the lowest point at the table's edge and then, splattered to the floor, threatening a mound of dirty rags already stained crimson, maroon, and black. The removal of Alain's leg was gruesome.

A stranger, unaware of what just occurred, might have guessed Baruch was an artist. The doctor's apron was covered with a rainbow of reddish hues. The creases on his hands were stained and a red swath streaked across his forehead. The butchery complete, Baruch began wiping his tools, alternating between the edge of his apron and an unused cloth.

Against the wall, Alain lay on a cot. He did not groan or cry out. Blessed sleep had overcome his pain, but the fever still raged. I dipped a cloth in a bucket of cool water and mopped up tiny beads of sweat on his face. The slight rise and fall of his chest and the almost imperceptible sound of his breathing consoled me. Alain was still alive.

An overwhelming metallic smell filled the room. It was strong enough that I could taste it, as if a layer coated my tongue. I tried covering my nose with my scarf, but that did not stop the uncontrollable urge to vomit. I rushed to the bucket and added to its contents until I had nothing left. When the room began to spin, I stumbled for the door which led to the larger room with the cells. I glanced around, searching for privacy. Thankfully, the goaler's chair was empty. I rushed toward the alcove, lit by a solitary window, and leaned against the wall, my hands flat against its solidness. This was the only way to tame a world out of control.

"Anna, can I help?" asked Baruch. His voice was grave, filled with concern. "You should not have come. Even battle-hardened soldiers cannot vatch."

I continued to press against my fortress. "Alain wanted me to stay away. But I had to—" I tried taking a deep breath, but the urge was unrelenting. I cupped my hand over my mouth.

"Here. Let me open the vindow."

The rush of fresh air felt like cold rain dripping down my face. In a few minutes, the world ceased spinning. It was safe to speak. "Mr. Innes once told me that…a man can endure almost anything…if a woman is present."

Baruch placed a comforting hand on mine, his nails outlined with Alain's blood. "I'm almost finished cleaning my instruments. Then I'll get you home."

"I must stay. When Alain awakens—"

"He's going to sleep for avhile. He has had enough laudanum to knock out an ox. Ve vill come back, and I vill administer more if he is in pain." He gently squeezed my hand "You need rest as vell." He offered a comforting smile, and then returned to the room and shut the door.

Baruch was right. I was exhausted. But there was no place to rest. Nor was there time. The goaler had returned. The heavy thump of his footsteps stopped and started as he made his rounds at each cell, inspecting the contents. When he passed the alcove, he nodded, and then left me alone to struggle with the horrors I had just witnessed. I could not dismiss it. No matter how hard I tried.

Four men were enlisted to restrain Alain. One was the goaler; another was a worker in the courthouse. The other two were prisoners who agreed to help in exchange for an extra portion of meat with their dinner and a full mug of ale. Baruch slipped a few coins to the worker and gave a bit more to the goaler. Everything was for sale at the City Hall gaol.

My task was to ensure Alain drank the mixture of whisky and laudanum. I also offered heavy doses of encouragement and comfort. But from the frightened look on his face, I could never possess all he needed. His eyes darted back and forth following every movement. When the goaler dropped a basket of cloths by the table, Alain's grip tightened. When the helper returned with a bucket of water and slammed the door behind him,

Alain trembled. As Baruch affixed his apron and opened his doctor's bag, I could feel my love's heart race.

The amputation began with a tourniquet. It had a worsted binding about one inch thick. A piece of leather was attached that ended in a slip knot around a stout stick. Baruch slipped the binding above the knee and proceeded to twist the leather. Alain's breathing quickened. His eyes widened. When the tourniquet was tight, the patient surrendered and stared at the ceiling. A nod from the doctor signaled the men to take their positions around the table.

"Anna, once Alain drinks all the vhisky, place the piece of vocd between his teeth," said Baruch. Then to Alain, "Bite down as hard as you vish."

The surgery was about to start. I was familiar with the procedure. Yesterday, Baruch had explained everything.

"Are you sure you vant to know?" he asked while we sat in the parlor after dinner.

I nodded.

"I'll start by placing a tourniquet above the incision. That vill limit the loss of blood although I am afraid Alain vill still lose a fair amount. Then I vill cut a few inches below the knee and remove the leg as quickly as possible. Once it is off, another inch of bone vill be cut, leaving enough skin and muscle to serve as a flap. That vill be sewn together to cover and seal the stump."

"Is there anything you can do to make it less painful?"

"The best ve can hope for is that Alain passes out. That does not alvays happen. But I am going to remove some of the nerve at the stump. That and a dose of laudanum and vhisky vill help. The amputation vill be quick. A minute or two." His voice wavered. The explanation was difficult for him as well. "The first veek after surgery is the vorst. If Alain can get through that, his chances improve vith each day. By the fourth veek, the survival rate is greatly improved."

Yesterday, I thought my understanding of the surgery would help. Today, I realized nothing would. I pulled the mug away from Alain's lips. Thankfully, it was empty, but the raw whisky smell endured.

"Alain, stay as still as humanly possible." Baruch's voice was low but startling, nonetheless. I readjusted my position on the stool and tighten my grip around Alain's head. From my vantage point, I could see little of what was about to happen.

Baruch took a deep breath, readjusted a strap on his apron, and raised a crooked knife. "This vill be over quickly," he said. The men stared at the floor rather than the macabre scene at the foot of the table.

Nothing could have prepared me for the primal scream that erupted with the first incision. Alain's upper body stiffened and then he jerked, throwing me off balance. I watched in horror as Baruch's hands made a quick circular motion. When he reached for the saw, I prayed to the God of my fathers. When my husband lost consciousness, I whispered my thanks.

The doctor had spoken the truth. In less than two minutes, the offending leg was separated and tossed against the wall. Followed by many wads of cloth to soak up the blood.

The next day and every day for a week, Baruch and I returned to City Hall. Alain's condition did not change. Except he was alive and that was everything. While Baruch inspected the swollen enflamed stump, I attempted to feed Alain some broth. He would take a few sips, and that was only after I begged him. Once, I threatened to bring in the goaler to restrain him. Other days it did not matter. He barely stayed awake through our visit.

By the eighth day, Baruch gently reminded me that survival was difficult even for the young and healthy like Alain. I guess he did not want me to have false hopes. That is when I decided to seek out the constable.

I started with the goaler. The man bolted up in his seat when I made my request. I always seemed to interrupt his naps. His response was a pointer finger gesturing toward the stairs.

At the lower level, the constable was asleep as well. I purposely scraped my heels on the wood floor, making a racket to awaken him.

"Um, Mrs. MacArthur," said the constable while squinting out of one eye. "What can I do for you today?"

"My husband must come home."

"Yes, Mr. MacArthur would like that, would he? I'm sure all the prisoners can't wait for me to unlock their cell doors so they can go home to their wives and sleep in their warm beds. Hmm. I'm afraid I can't be so obliging."

"My husband will not survive staying here."

"That's what they all say."

"He needs my attention. For his leg."

The Constable rubbed his eyes and stifled a yawn. "Madam. Mr. MacArthur has been sentenced by a lawful court. And I'm restricted by that law. He can't be let go, to your care or to anyone else's, unless the fine and all charges have been paid."

"By charges, you mean your commission. Blood money that will line your pockets."

"Well, Madam, that's not how I would put it."

"Then tell me exactly what you mean?"

"My commissions are how I'm paid to care for your husband."

"Care! It was your carelessness and lack of controlling the prisoners that resulted in another attacking him, and now he has lost a leg as a result. Perhaps I need to contact the mayor and let him know that you have failed in your assignment. You and the goaler are asleep every time I walk through these doors, and by the smell of your breath, it's apparent you have recently returned from a local tavern."

"That's enough." Now fully awake, he slammed his fist on the desk, shaking it so hard I was surprised it didn't buckle. "I won't have you come in here, all high and mighty like, threatening my position. I'm an honest man—"

"Honest! Then what is this about a bribe you are willing to take to keep my husband in gaol? How is that the law? Even if I paid the fine, the bribe is more than I can match. And so, my husband remains a prisoner."

He raised his fist again, but instead, rubbed the wounded flesh. "That's how the game is played. The highest bidder wins."

"And if my husband dies? Be careful sir. This won't go well for you if the mayor or the governor hear of your treachery."

The constable stood, scraped back his stool, walked around the table, and came uncomfortably close. I didn't flinch or step back. Instead, I decided to lie. "Do you know who Mr. William Burnet is?" I didn't wait for a response. "He is my husband's solicitor. Rumor has it that he will be appointed the next governor of New York. He has connections in the highest places. I can assure you. He will remember you because I will not let him forget."

"I don't care who your husband knows. As far as I'm concerned, your Mr. Burns or Mr. Bennet, or whatever-his-name-is, can kiss his connections' arse." The constable returned to his desk. For his part, the conversation was over.

I turned and started to walk away. But I could not let this man defeat me. "I don't think the governor would approve of your language. Your suggestion that Mr. Burnet should kiss his connections' arse will not bode well for you."

The constable shuffled some papers on his desk, choosing one and then another, glancing at them but not reading. Slowly, he looked at me. His eyes piercing.

"I am sure our governor would be interested to know that one of his officers, the constable of City Hall, disparaged a close relative of our good Queen Anne."

"And how's that?"

"Mr. Burnet was related to Her Majesty's brother-in-law, the late King William. So, I guess you are suggesting that Mr. Burnet should kiss the king's, or maybe the queen's arse. Is that how it is?"

"I—" The Constable put down his papers.

"I don't think that would please our governor, do you?"

"What do you want, Madam?"

I held my breath and wiped my sweaty palms on my skirt. Thankfully, the constable did not question my story. William Burnet was not related to royalty. He was the godchild of King William, and William had been dead for eight years. "I want my husband to convalesce at home. When he has recovered, he will return to finish his sentence. I give you my word."

The officer scratched his head, sat again at his desk, and found his quill. "For a fortnight, Madam. Nothing more, nothing less."

"That won't do."

The man looked up as if I had just reawakened him.

I placed both hands on the rough surface of his desk and leaned in as close as I dared. "One month. Nothing less."

The Constable clenched his wounded fist and gritted his teeth. He grumbled a few choice words interspersed with 'damn woman.' Then, with a flip of his hand, he dismissed me like an annoying gnat.

❧

Alain came home to the Emmanuel's. A week later, his condition remained unchanged. But it was no worse.

Each day I asked, "Shouldn't we see some improvement?" The response was the same: "Healing takes time. Every man is different. We are still vithin the high mortality period." I felt comforted that Alain was surrounded by his loved ones. And he was eating more.

One late afternoon, Baruch stopped as he was leaving Alain's room. "There is something I'd like to discuss vith you. A private matter. Join me vhere ve von't be disturbed."

I hesitated for a moment, thinking I should stay, but changed my mind when Alain had fallen asleep. I followed Baruch down the hall when a breathless and distracted Deborah stopped us. Her hair was barely held in place by loose pins and smudges of flour whitened her chin. Her food-stained apron reminded me of the special dinner this evening. Many guests were expected to welcome the wealthy ship owner and his son.

"Do not forget. Our guests vill be arriving shortly." she said to Baruch. "I hope you vill not keep Anna too busy. I don't vant to keep our guests vaiting. Rachel vill never forgive me."

"Of course. Ve vill not be long." Then Baruch turned to me. "Anna, please vait in the surgery. There is something I must do. I vill be vith you shortly."

I entered the room alone. It reminded me of my father's library. On one end, floor-to-ceiling shelves were lined with books of every size, color, and age. Their pages, made from wood pulp, had a pleasing scent of vanilla.

Other shelves held bottles of different colors and sizes. Each was topped with a flat or teardrop stopper. The placement of the containers to my inexperienced eye, appeared haphazard. Various hued contents filled some to the brim while others barely registered. On the floor, several earthenware jars were stacked. An empty one was on its side.

On a narrow table against the third wall, just under a window, were wooden and stone bowls with their pestles. A grinder had recently been used; a green sticky residue stuck to its rounded head. Ginger root stumps filled a bowl, waiting to be crushed to remedy an upset stomach. My movements unleashed scents from above. Lemon balm, lavender, and mint were tied in bunches and hung like tiny constellations.

On another table, set under a window, were stalks of a fern-like plant with small white flowers shaped like saucers. Hemlock was found in the nearby forests and was widely used to cure everything. I remember when Father's doctor administered an ointment made with hemlock. It was to relieve his sore right eye. Curiously, the doctor applied the medicine to Father's left arm. I did not understand the logic, and Father did not question it either. A week later the eye was restored. Perhaps it needed time; or maybe it was the magic of the hemlock. But the musty odor was unforgettable.

As I returned to the book-lined shelves, I wondered what was keeping Baruch. Shadows were lengthening and the sun was losing its intensity. Shortly, guests would arrive and that would not leave much time for whatever Baruch needed to discuss.

My fingertips brushed along the worn bindings. Not all were medical. Some were the same that lined my father's shelves. One caught my eye. In another time and place, it had been a favorite: *Le Cid.*

There was another book on a chair; its place held by a fringed marker. I picked it up. *De Medicina*, by A. Cornelius Celsus.

"The author vas a Roman. He lived seventeen hundred years ago."

Startled, I returned the book to its place. "I'm sorry. I did not mean to touch your things. I am partial to old books and libraries such as this. My father had such a collection."

"It is fine, Anna. The book you vere holding is one of seven volumes of an encyclopedia of medical vorks. This one speaks to surgery and is the only volume that survives today. It vas a gift from Deborah."

"Did you read…it before—"

"Yes. Celsus wrote extensively about amputation."

"Would his advice still be acceptable?"

"Surprisingly, yes, although he vas not a doctor. But his vork is seminal to the practice of surgery." He picked up the book and placed it back on the shelf. "You are velcome to come in here and borrow a book any time."

"I noticed you have one of my favorites. *Le Cid.* I did not expect to find that here on a shelf surrounded by medical books."

"I have many books that have nothing to do vith medicine. A doctor needs diversion, too, from the daily pain and suffering that comes to my door."

I fidgeted with his last statement. It was a bleak reminder that not only had I come to his home, but I'd brought my sick husband to live under his roof. "You said you wanted to speak to me?"

"Yes. There's something...ve should...discuss." His voice wavered and then halted. "Please, have a seat. Now, vhere are my spectacles?" He turned and scanned the room. "Ah," he said as he plucked them from the table with the mortar and pestle. After placing them back on his nose, he sighed deeply. "Anna, there is something you must consider. I am hopeful that Alain vill improve, but ve...you, must be prepared for every eventuality. Even a grave one." Baruch leaned forward. "In the event of the vorst outcome, have you thought vhere you vant to bury your husband?" He took a deep breath before continuing. "He cannot be interred in the Jewish cemetery."

"He's my husband. I am Jewish. He's the father of my children."

"He's not of our faith. Only if he vent through a conversion. And even then, I could offer no assurances—"

"He saved my life many times. Doesn't that count for anything?"

"Alain is a vonderful husband. A good father. I am proud to call him friend and pleased that he is safe in my home. But others in the community vill not see it that vay. They will insist that the cemetery is only for the Jewish community. In their eyes, Jews have never been velcome in Christian burial grounds unless they converted, and I know from vhat you have told me about your family history, that conversion vas often forced. And even that didn't save them."

"Then, what am I to do?"

"He could be buried in a church graveyard."

"Then Alain and I could not be buried together."

"That is an unfortunate reality. Vith your permission, I vould like to discuss this vith Abraham and see vhat can be done. Although, I'm not sure he vill have an answer."

Nothing would change. Neither the minister nor the Jewish community would relent. I knew that from my father and his similar unwavering stubbornness. It was why I fled his home, when he tried to force me into a marriage based solely on religion. When it came to the laws of my faith, there was no compromise. I stood up to leave. "Baruch, I know you are well intentioned, and I thank you and Deborah for all you have done for my family. But if my husband and I cannot spend eternity together, then I will find my way elsewhere. I will do what is necessary. Even if it means renouncing my faith."

Tears stung my eyes as I rushed toward the stairs, hoping to escape to the garret to change my dress and wash my face.

"Anna, our guest, the ship owner's son, vill be here any minute." It was Deborah's voice calling me from the hall. "Please, come and meet the young man." Her voice sounded hopeful.

"Yes. Of course." I flicked away the tears with my fingertips and turned to face my friend, to tell her I would be down quickly. But all that was left was the sound of her footsteps growing fainter as she hurried back to her guests.

The room was filled with the hum of friendly conversation. The tall minister and his short wife flanked a young man, the guest of honor, as they guided him around, stopping only for introductions.

From across the room, I spotted Alexandra standing alone by the fireplace. Her favorite cream-colored dress with the tiny embroidered pink roses showed off her blossoming curves. Her braided hair intertwined with pink ribbon was pinned, allowing curly tendrils to frame her face. A pink shawl, draped off her shoulders, extended low in the back, showed off her best features.

I was about to join my daughter when the guest of honor approached her. Dressed in the latest fashion, a long waist coat, a linen shirt with many lace frills, and white silk stockings, the dashing young man offered a pleasant silhouette and an air of confidence that came naturally to the wealthy.

While Abraham made the introductions, I could not help but notice Alexandra's furtive glances. They alternated between the handsome guest and the expected behavior of a maiden. When she lowered her eyes, her lashes brushed reddened cheeks.

A part of the introduction included the ritual of hand-kissing, a sign of courtesy and respect. Polite society dictated that the acceptance of the kiss and its initiation was entirely in the woman's domain. I watched Alexandra hesitate for a moment before offering her hand. A maid did not want to appear too eager. Now the game shifted to the young man. Once names were shared, he held Alexandra's hand as if it were a delicate flower and gazed into her eyes. Then, he raised her hand, ever so slowly, to meet his lips which barely brushed her skin. Once the kiss was accomplished, he released her hand after a slight reluctance. Not too long to create awkwardness, but enough to show he relished the experience. I have received many hand kisses. Most without incident. Others more memorable. Especially those that left traces of saliva or a last meal. This young man played his part perfectly

"Mademoiselle MacArthur," I overheard the guest announce. "I am delighted to make your acquaintance. Please forgive. My English is not good."

"Monsieur, your English is perfect."

The two continued conversing in French until Alexandra saw me. "Mama! There you are. Join us."

Like an actor who received her cue, I greeted Rachel and Abraham and smiled toward the young man. "Welcome to New York. Have you been here long?" I asked.

"We arrive three month ago."

"Is your family with you?" I looked around expecting to see others I did not know.

"Father will be here shortly. A customer detains him. My father, he is consumed with business. I never seen him so intent."

"I understand you are from France. My father had connections with someone from Lyon. A long time ago."

"Ah, we are from Lyon. Perhaps we have friendship in common. Even more likely if they were of the Jewish faith. Our community in Lyon is much larger and grander than what you have here, but still, Father knows all. A merchant must have many contacts. Some are amiable, some less. But as Father says, that is life. To succeed, sometimes, one must do what is objectionable."

Toward the end of our talk, the young man appeared preoccupied. He kept looking at something or someone behind me. Then his eyes brightened. "Ah, *excusez-moi*, Madame. Mademoiselle." He ran off toward another. "*Père*. At last, you have come. *S'il vous plaît*. There is someone I like you to meet."

"*Oui. Oui.* Of course, *mon fils.*" The voice was high-pitched. Odd sounding, but familiar. And then, it jolted me awake like I was in the middle of a nightmare. I turned and searched the crowd. "*Excusez-moi,* Madame Emmanuel," the voice continued. "Forgive my delay. I hope I have not spoiled your *petite soirée.*" The last word was almost muffled behind a lace handkerchief pressed against his lips.

From deep within, something, some ancient calling, forced me to step in front of Alexandra to protect her.

The young man took hold of his father's arm. "*Père*, come. Meet my new friends. The madame has an acquaintance in Lyon." Before I could flee, the father was planted squarely in front of us. A gloved hand pressed a handkerchief to his mouth. It could not silence his gurgling stomach.

"Madame MacArthur. Mademoiselle. I am delighted to introduce my dear papa: Monsieur Maurice St. Martin."

PART THREE

CHAPTER TWENTY-SIX

SET IN STONE

NEW YORK CITY – OCTOBER 2009

AUTUMN HAD RETURNED. The air was chilly. It was time to retire lighter-weight clothing in exchange for turtlenecks, puffy vests, and sweaters. Autumn in Manhattan, my favorite season, had arrived.

My boots crunched dried leaves and fallen acorns on my morning walk through campus. Greetings and a short conversation with a colleague interrupted my thoughts of yesterday's call with Alec which included his teasing that Scotland was already on the edge of winter. I loved snuggling in front of a log fire, the woodsy smell, and the crackling and popping sounds of the burning wood. Maybe that was a sign of where I was meant to be: with Alec, in Scotland. Shrugging off such thoughts, I rewound the scarf around my neck. No need to tie back my hair. I needed all the warmth I could get.

I wondered if the students I passed on the College Walk heading toward Amsterdam Avenue could tell I was a professor, or did they see me as another student? I wasn't much older than most undergrads. Sometimes, I had to pinch myself that I was in this position. Just a few short months ago, I was like them, living in the library, doing endless hours of research, and prepping my dissertation. Now, I was an ocean away, spending my days standing in front of a lecture hall filled with wide-eyed and inquisitive freshmen. I chuckled. Who was I fooling? The required survey course, "The Rise of Civilization," was dry. Especially, for the pretty coed who flirted continuously with the jock behind her, or the nerd in the front row with the uncombed hair. He yawned so much I had to stifle the urge not to imitate him. I must remember to ask Alec for some advice.

Students quickened their pace so as not to be late to class. Most were dressed in jeans and hoodies. A few hardy souls, still in shorts and sandals, refused to accept the inevitable. One fellow, who weaved his way in front of me, topped his summer outfit with a knitted cap. I glanced around and found I was the only one in a skirt and blazer. I readjusted my heavy leather backpack to the other shoulder. It was a negotiated graduation gift from Alec.

"That's okay for you or Ira," I told Alec shortly after graduation, "but I'd rather not carry a briefcase. My students will think I'm stodgy and archaic."

"Archaic?" His usual eyebrow went up. "That is our line of work, Dr. Duncan. You need something more dignified than your satchel."

"Well, maybe when I'm older and I've been doing this for ten or twenty years."

"Okay, I'll get you something else: a compromise."

Another addition to my new look was glasses. They were a result of years of poring over texts and deciphering hard-to-read documents. At first, I wasn't sure, but eventually, I found I liked my new look: more studious, more professorial. Alec agreed. Although he enjoyed taking them off when we were seriously into lovemaking. I chuckled to myself. I usually wasn't that concerned about my appearance. That was Jess' realm. However, the weight of the backpack was a reminder that brought me back to Alec and my decision to take this position at Columbia. I wondered if I made the right choice.

I arrived in the States in mid-summer. Maggie, my supervisor, was able to secure an apartment for me. It was owned by a political science professor and his wife. They were traveling the world for his sabbatical. Our one-year arrangement worked for both parties. The owners were thrilled to find someone to rent their Morningside Heights flat, within walking distance of my office. They also needed someone to care for Meow, their calico. In New York terms, my new living quarters was beyond spacious with two bedrooms and two bathrooms. The quality and style of furnishings, with all the little extras, revealed that the owners took great pride in the place. There was a garden terrace off the living room that stretched to include the master bedroom. Distressed brick walls, a fireplace, and a galley kitchen with granite countertops and a hooded range added to the appeal. Compared to the apartments I shared with Alec or my place in Philadelphia, this was upscale living. The rent was doable, just under two thousand. However, I still had plenty left from the 9/11 fund to reinforce my paycheck.

A few weeks after moving in, I took New Jersey transit to visit Jess and her family. She no longer lived in center-city Philadelphia. Like so many young families, Jess and her husband fled to the suburbs and single-home living.

Jess met me at the train station in Hamilton, New Jersey and we talked the entire thirty-minute drive to her home.

"Dr. Duncan. Your new title fits you."

"Thanks. It takes a bit of getting used to. When a student calls my name, I look around to see who they are referring to."

"And when will you get another title?"

I looked at her, but with her focus on the road, she hadn't seen my eyeball roll. Jess didn't let up with the marriage bit.

"What's up with you and Alec anyway?" Jess continued relentlessly. "Are you going to tie the knot anytime soon? This century? I'm anxious to be your matron of honor."

"We decided to wait until the end of the year. I need time to get settled with my new living situation and classes. Prepping is a lot of work. I never realized." This was true. I had seen Alec spend hours getting ready for his classes. Especially if it was a new assignment. But I wondered if this was just another excuse. Other people, with busy schedules found time to get married.

"Well, just in case it doesn't work out, I have a back-up plan."

"Plan?"

"One of Sam's partners is single and looking. He's a really nice guy, great body and personality—"

"Thanks, but I'm not interested. Alec is still…we just have a few issues to iron out."

"Okay, if you say so. I won't push it, but don't forget the clock is ticking." Jess slammed on the brake, honked the horn, and gestured wildly toward the driver in front of her. When the light turned, she continued her conversation. "Josh comes to dinner every so often. Being a bachelor, he misses a home-cooked meal. So, if you want to meet him, just say the word."

"Have you added matchmaker to wife and mother? I'll let you know if I'm ready for a change, and I appreciate the offer not to push."

"It happens to the best of us. You meet a nice guy and before you know it, you buy a house with a backyard. What surprised me the most was that once kids come along, you become your mother." She stopped short. "Sorry."

"No apology needed. My mother's been gone a long time ago, now."

We turned into a tree-less development of mini-mansions, each set on a spacious lot; many with multi-tiered decks, pergolas, a pool, and a tennis court. I wondered if Jess noticed the wealth around her or if this was her new norm. She slowed down and made a right into a circular driveway. Sam was waiting to greet us and, after he carried my bag to an upstairs guest room, Jess pulled me away for the grand tour. "Before J.D. wakes up and all hell breaks loose."

Jess used to joke that J.D. stood for Junior Doctor. The baby's full name was Jeremiah Douglas Goldblatt. She said that was too much for a little kid, so she started using the initialized name, and it stuck.

Later, after a feeding and diaper change, I spent the afternoon crawling on the floor with the most adorable curly-headed toddler. We played peek-a-boo a thousand times and then I recited what nursery rhymes I could remember. Entertaining J.D. was easy. He giggled at my funny faces, and whenever I pretended to tickle his tummy and toes. Then came another bottle and burping. Feeding was simple except for the sour spit-up on my top and jeans. While Jess washed my clothes, J.D. stared at me in his mother's robe. He must have thought I transformed into Jess.

Watching my friend with her family, and especially interacting with her husband, made me yearn for the warmth of a home and family, even if it did smell a bit like curdled milk. It awakened an unfamiliar gnawing.

"Hey, good to see you." It was Jess. She was talking to someone outside the front door. "Come on in. Did you want to see Sam?"

Sitting on the floor with J.D., I tightened the slackness of the robe and covered my legs. Looking up through curls, I saw someone standing next to Jess.

"Yeah. He asked me over to discuss the practice. Our search for a new office manager."

"Sam's out back. Can I expect you to stay for dinner, Josh?"

I sat up, pushed my hair back and found I was staring at a near-perfect male specimen. Tall, slim, dark brown hair, blue eyes, and just the right amount of bicep bulging from his shirt. I stood immediately, not wanting him to mistake me for J.D.'s nanny. After tightening the bathrobe again, our eyes locked amidst a moment of awkwardness.

"Hanna...um...this is Joshua Stein. Sam's partner. Josh, this is Hanna. Hanna and I went to Penn together. We've been friends forever." While Josh and I shook hands, Jess added to my resume. "Hanna has just returned from Scotland and now she's living in New York. Teaching at Columbia. She's a doctor. Like you."

Josh stepped back. Eyes wide. A look of surprise? Or was it shock? What was he expecting from the woman on the floor dressed in a bathrobe in the middle of the day?

"Not an MD," I corrected Jess. "Outside of the university, I'm Hanna Duncan. Nice to meet you, Josh."

Josh immediately turned to Hanna. "Thanks for the invite. I'd love to stay for dinner."

⁂

Dinner was awkward. At least I thought so. I glanced at Jess and Sam sitting on opposite ends of the table. I tried not to be too obvious, but I couldn't help noticing they were giving each other looks as if they were desperate for a private moment. I wondered if this dinner was timed for Josh's 'accidental' arrival. If that was the case, it backfired. At least on my end. Sitting across from Josh, only made me think more of Alec. I missed his sense of humor and his raised eyebrow whenever I said something that didn't come out the way I intended. I also missed our easy conversations. Maybe there was some truth in my dad's old saying: *Absence makes the heart grow fonder.*

Josh was polite and thoughtful and tried his best to make the embarrassing situation bearable. "So, Hannah, why did you go to Scotland in the first place? I hear it's a beautiful country. Mountain climbing is sort of a hobby of mine and I'm anxious to tackle Ben Nevis. Have you ever done it?"

"I'm not into climbing, but I hear the Ben is not difficult. About four hours to get to the top and another three down." I was relieved when he added the second question so I could ignore the first. "Best time to climb is September. It's not so crowded and there's less chance for extreme weather. You don't want to wait much later. It may snow and it might—"

259

I stopped speaking. Remembering autumn in Scotland overwhelmed me. I longed for the crisp mornings, early nightfall, and the mountains blanketed in gold, bronze, orange, and crimson.

Unfortunately, Jess didn't let me off so easily. In a few minutes, she brought the good doctor up to speed on what transpired in my life from the time we graduated. I just sat and smiled and filled in a few gaps when Josh looked puzzled.

"That's quite a mystery. So, what's left to solve about your ancestor?" Josh asked.

His question was jolting although it made sense for him to ask. I usually tried not to dwell on Anna's story. It was a big riddle, and if I figured it out, I feared the grand adventure would come to an end. And I didn't want that. I knew there were still unknowns to unravel. What happened to Anna? Did she go back to Scotland? To Thistlestraith, Alain's home? Is she buried next to Sally and her mother-in-law? Or were her remains interred in some ancient burial ground in Manhattan which long ago had been bulldozed? And what about Alain? Where was he?

There were other riddles, too. The most intriguing was the journal. It had crossed the ocean at least three times. The first was with Anna and the final time was a couple of months ago. What happened in between? I had read the journal many times, but not since graduation. Did I miss a clue? Maybe, another read was necessary because Anna had all the answers, and she had been dead for three-hundred years.

When Jess drove me back to the train station, we talked about Josh and then, she dropped it due to my lack of enthusiasm. "What are your plans now? Beside teaching, I mean. Any more investigating your ancestor?"

"Yes, I plan to visit any burial grounds that existed during her time and search for her marker. Shouldn't be too hard. There was only one cemetery for Jews."

"What about her husband?"

"I don't know. He was not Jewish, and he could be in a church graveyard or common ground. I'm hoping there are records."

"That's so sad if they couldn't spend eternity together. Makes me think."

"About?"

"Sam and me. He's Jewish and I'm a hodgepodge. I don't want to be alone. I've been thinking of converting. Sam wants to raise J.D. Jewish. It would be easier if we were all the same. Don't you think?"

"I didn't realize you were considering such a drastic change. Does Sam care? Did he ask you?"

"No. He said it's up to me. But I care. I want a united front for J.D."

I giggled. It sounded like Jess and Sam were preparing to go to war. Up to this point, I always thought Jess and I traveled vastly different roads. I was on an expressway; Jess was on a one-track lane. But here we were considering the same life-altering decision. Hers was to bring harmony to her family, and I was hoping to bring the same to Alec's.

Too soon, Jess pulled into the drop-off lane at the Hamilton station and stopped in front of the ticket queue. She jumped out of her car and came around to give me a hug. We both held on for as long as we could until the driver behind blared his horn.

I laughed when I thought about the old Jess. She would not have hesitated to give the driver the finger. But now, she glared for a moment and then refocused her attention. "Don't be a stranger, Dr. Duncan. Come back and visit. You are welcome any time."

"Thank you." I started tearing up. "I don't know why I'm crying. I didn't shed a tear when I went off to Scotland, and now I'm only an hour train-ride away. Silly, don't you think? Thanks for the lovely weekend."

I turned to go. She reached out and touched my arm. "I'm sorry about Josh. He's a nice guy, but I won't put you on the spot again." She hesitated and then smiled. "Only if you ask me, too."

The train was almost empty. It was the middle of the day. The hustle and bustle to and from Manhattan occurred either early in the morning or during the rush of the evening. Unlike four years ago, when I first made this journey southbound to Philadelphia, after I emptied my dad's safe deposit box, there was no lemon-scented elderly lady urging me for small talk.

I often wondered if I had not found the mysterious key, would my life be any different? Would I have gone to grad school, earned a doctorate and ended up teaching at an Ivy League university? I doubted it. I would have known nothing about my ancestor and my religious past. Even Jess' life would have been different. She would never have met Sam in the ER at Jefferson. Most importantly, Alec and I would be strangers.

I know Jess would disagree with me. She believed that if something was meant to be, the circumstance didn't matter. It would happen. One had no control over Fate. She made her point many years ago when we were standing on a platform waiting for the Market Street train.

"Hey, see that guy over there? The one who can't walk in a straight line," said Jess.

"Yeah, I see him."

"If he's not careful, he's going to fall off the platform and get run over by the train. It's coming soon. I can see the headlight."

As the man continued to wobble, his hat fell off his head and landed alongside the iron rail. He walked up to the edge, peered down, and looked like he was about to jump.

"Oh my gosh. Is there a cop?" I spun my head around, looking, but there was no one. "Maybe I should grab his arm or something—"

Just then, a young guy, a marine, or maybe he was army, rushed over and held the man back just as the train rumbled into the station. The doors swished open and the man and the soldier entered, swallowed whole.

As we grabbed our seats in a different car, Jess said, "You know, if it's your time to go, then it's your time. Nothing you do will change it."

"Then the soldier couldn't have saved him."

"Yep. If that's what was meant to be."

"Does that mean everything that will ever happen to us is already set in stone?" I asked.

"Hmm. Don't know about that, but I guess so."

Back then, I didn't share that belief with Jess. I thought my meeting Alec was accidental. Plain and simple. But Jess' idea of Fate, that Alec and I were destined to be, had a certain charm to it. I chuckled to myself, thinking about my friend. Maybe her idea of destiny had diminished somewhat now that the reality of husband and child was central to her. Otherwise, why was she tempting Fate by throwing Josh in my face?

Ira had a similar belief. During one of our many discussions he told me about *bashert*, the Jewish concept of destiny, that there is someone out there meant to be my soulmate, and if we found each other, we would live in harmony. If not, if I married someone who was not my *bashert,* then it would be an unhappy union. I remember Alec grabbing my hand during that discussion, and saying that for sure, he was my *bashert.*

Leaving Secaucus, the last stop before Manhattan, I pressed my head against the window, waiting for the city to come into view before the train burrowed underground. The skyline was not much altered except for the new Freedom Tower, meant to replace the fallen twin towers. A museum was expected to be built on the site memorializing 9/11. I promised myself that when it was completed, I would visit the place where my father had perished. But for right now, I was going to be busy searching through ancient cemeteries.

Just then, my phone buzzed. It was Alec. I was sitting in the quiet car, so I silenced the phone deep in my pocket. I didn't need others glaring at me for breaking the rules. I quickly texted and explained where I was.

In a few minutes, Alec's message appeared. "Hey. Hope you had fun at Jess'. I miss you terribly. Just wanted to tell you I have some interesting news. I'm working on the family Bible to make sense of the great-greats and connect them to their offspring. I have a bit more to do, but something came up in my research. I don't want to tell you this in a text. Call me when you can. You won't believe what I found."

CHAPTER TWENTY-SEVEN
FOR DUST THOU ART

"WE'RE RELATED." THAT'S all Alec said. No, *what took so long, are you okay,* or *I love you*. Not even *hello*. Those two words bolted me upright in my chair.

"What are you talking about?"

"It's all there in the Grant family Bible. Or Bibles, I should say. Your ancestor…I mean my ancestor. There's a good chance we are cousins. First cousins, at least ten times removed."

I put the phone into the other hand, got up, and paced the room only to find myself back on the chair. "I've never understood all that 'removed' stuff and don't explain it now. It will just confuse me. Wait! This is crazy." I heard Alec's long-distance chuckle. "This is not funny." I pulled my fingers through my hair to get the curls out of my face. "Alec, I think you better start over. From the beginning."

Alec drove around to the back of his mother's house. He breathed a sigh of relief at the sight of no cars, and therefore, no confrontation with Iain. One of Alec's conditions for coming home and working on the family tree required his brother's absence. Mora had told him that Iain and Kate were living with her family. Kate was near her due date and wanted her family, especially her mother, for support.

No one came out to greet Alec. Maybe that meant his mother was away as well. That pleased him. He relished a few moments of solitude in his childhood home. A chance to walk the rooms and the gardens alone, to reminisce. He missed his father terribly.

As usual, the back door was unlocked. "Hello." No answer. "Anyone home? Mother?" Nothing. He thought it unusual that he was so formal with his remaining parent. Other people called their mother: mom or mum. Mora insisted on a certain decorum with her children. At times, Alec wondered if his mother would have preferred Mrs. Grant.

He returned to his car for his briefcase and duffle bag filled with his toiletries, underwear, jeans, T-shirts, and a sweatshirt; nothing formal which his mother would've preferred. After dumping the contents on his bed, he scanned the room for a place to stack his books. On the bureau was an aging program from the Military Tattoo he and his father attended ten years ago. And leaning against the only chair was his shinty stick. It looked like he had just come in from a game with the local lads.

Alec hurried downstairs to explore. First, he went to the library, which served as his father's office, and for a few weeks, as a makeshift infirmary. The rented hospital bed was long gone as well as the smell associated with the sick. If he closed his eyes, he could still see Hanna sitting with him, for hours, and then knowing when it was time to leave; to give Alec and his father their last private moments. Hanna knew what it was like to lose a loved one. Her father on 9/11. Her grandmother, no so long ago. Alec missed his parent, but what surprised him was that the memory of Hanna was even more vivid. He could feel the touch of her hand, her reassuring whispers as his father sank lower and lower into the depths of oblivion. Is this what it meant in Genesis? *Therefore, shall a man leave his father and his mother, and shall cleave unto his wife, and they shall be one flesh.*

Now the office was returned to its original use. His father's large wooden desk was placed before a floor-to-ceiling bookcase. Heavy drapes and an area rug, a purchase from a trip to Istanbul, lent some warmth to the room. Near the window was a worn-out upholstered chair, his father's favorite, and on a small table next to it was a rosewood box. Alec lifted the lid, releasing the aroma of tobacco. He picked up his father's wooden pipe and brought it to his nose. It smelled as if it had been lit yesterday. When he tapped it, a tiny residue of ash fell into his palm. Touching it with his fingers, he rubbed it into his skin until it disintegrated like dust, leaving a gray smudge. Alec clenched his fingers into a fist, grateful that someone had forgotten to clean out this last vestige of his father. He pressed his hand to his lips and tears came to his eyes. He was reminded of another saying from Genesis: *...for dust thou art, and unto dust shalt thou return.*

Alec's next stop was the dining room. He touched his father's chair at the head of the table and imagined his deep-throated laughter filling the room. It was usually timed with his hand slapping the table accentuating some off-color comment or joke. This always annoyed Alec's mother who showed her displeasure by excusing herself from the table.

But again, his memory diverted to Hanna's first dinner in this room. His mother and brother had connived to include Kate, his one-time girlfriend. Kate was placed strategically across from him, so he had no choice but to watch her childish antics and the flirtatious toss of her hair. That's when Alec realized that Kate was dull. Nothing like Hanna who was smart and funny and gorgeous. He couldn't understand what he ever saw in his old flame. Perhaps it was the folly of youth and uncontrolled hormones.

"Oh, you're here," said a voice. It was Mora.

Alec wiped his eyes before he turned.

"Any trouble with traffic?"

He cleared his throat to swallow the lump. "Traffic on Skye at this time of the year? No, it was easy."

"Well, I'm glad you made it. Let me show you where the family Bibles are." They walked back to the library and Mora went to the bookcase. Running her fingers along the bindings, she paused at six leather-bound books, pulled them off, one by one, and placed them on the desk. "You can do your work here. No one will disturb you. I have pruning to do in the garden. I'm far behind with the roses. Dinner is the usual time." Mora turned to leave, brushed past him, and stopped. "How is your girlfriend? Is she back in the States?"

"Yes. Hanna's in New York."

"Well, maybe that's for the best."

"What does that mean?"

"A long-distance affair rarely works out."

"I plan to marry Hanna. Even if that means moving away from Scotland."

"Your girlfriend wants you to give up your career? For hers? You've worked too hard."

"Her name is Hanna, Mother. Hanna will be my wife. You'd better get used to the idea."

Mora glared at her son and grumbled, "Mmph." She turned again, walked out of the library, and slammed the door.

❧

266

The next morning, Alec avoided his mother by waking up early. He troweled apricot preserves on a scone, poured a cup of black coffee, and locked himself in the library. He settled himself at his father's desk, ran his fingers over the thick black Bibles and considered how he would begin his task.

The first order of business was to put the books in age-order. That should be as simple as opening the covers and locating the dated entries. But he wasn't sure when the family recordings started and what they included. Was it just marriages or did they include birth and death dates? Many of the old clans went back hundreds or maybe a thousand years, and he knew from his research he could expect the entries to be reliable. In the days before the government kept such records, clans relied on family Bibles for an individual's lineage.

One of the books appeared newer than the others. Out of curiosity, he chose that one and turned pages until he found the last couple of entries. His father's death date and his brother's marriage written in his mother's disciplined script. Alec was pleased she was continuing the family tradition. He envisioned his marriage to Hanna would be added. Followed by their children.

Then, Alec turned his attention to the most worn and probably the oldest Bible. He wished Ira were here, guiding him like he had helped Hanna with Anna's journal. One rule he remembered. Never wear gloves. No problem. He didn't bring any.

Alec turned the book over and around, checking the page edges for tell-tale evidence of book worms. There were none. That didn't surprise him. These books were kept in his father's office not like Anna's journal hidden in a dark dank vault.

He opened the cover slowly and found a list of names and dates written horizontally. This continued for several pages and, every so often, the penmanship changed when a new author took over. Turning back to the first page, the edge was stained with a dark liquid. He glanced at his coffee and moved it to a safer distance.

The first name listed was *Angus James Grant. Born Sept the 10th, 1616 Saturday.* The second name was another Grant child born the following year and then after a two-year gap, a third birth followed. In between the second and third child, Angus appeared once more: *Angus*

James Grant. Died. Monday, Aug. the 8th, 1618. Shortly after, his brother followed him. Like so many at that time, new life was fragile.

Based on the dates, this Bible was the oldest. Alec reached for a stack of notecards he had brought for the purpose of creating the tree and wrote each family member's name along with statistical information and placed them in date-order. He noticed that different authors added additional notes. One wrote a sentence or two about a newborn offspring. *On Sunday, Feb the 16, my daughter Fionela was born in the morning at half past 6 o'clock 1620.* In other entries, Alec got a glimpse of family history: *Agnes, my daughter was borne to Agnes, my second wife.* Or: *My son's mother dyed three days after, and my son six weeks after his mother.* By piecing together these valuable tidbits, Alec was able to create a rough outline of a 17th century family tree and place descendants on the correct branches.

What was most interesting were the things he found between the covers. Bible number one had dried brown petals. They resembled the Scottish roses his mother's garden was famous for.

When he finished with the first Bible, Alec spread the notecards on the floor in front of the desk. Seventeenth century families were large, and the number of cards had become cumbersome. With five Bibles to go, at this rate, the cards would take up the entire room. Then, he got a better idea. One-inch Post-it notes would take up less space, and they came in various colors. Alec could color-code each Bible. This way, he'd know instantly where each entry belonged. Also, blue and red markers would denote sex, and poster-board would work for mounting.

Alec decided to call it a day and head into Portree, the largest town on Skye, to purchase supplies. Compared to Glasgow or Edinburgh, Portree was tiny, but the island boasted many artists. That might be to his favor. Hopefully, the Co-op or a craft store stocked what he needed. He figured the search would take all afternoon, and since the sun set early this time of the year, he needed to set out. His break from work would also give him a chance to talk to Hanna.

The next day, Alec arrived early to the library. He found this routine to his liking and allowed him to forego any conversation with his mother. Except for dinner, he barely saw her anyway.

Alec reached for Bible number two. This one had silver etched corners and beautiful etchings. The book was published in 1660. He quickly scanned the first few dated entries which continued where the other Bible left off. Besides birth and death dates, this one included wedding data. Alec pulled out the small Post-it notes from a bag. This one would be designated yellow.

Before Alec started, he decided to go through the Bible and see if there were any gifts from the past. Sure enough, toward the back he found a thin ribbon with a few strands of fine hair. He had no idea whom they belonged to but maybe the mystery would be solved if an author expanded on an entry. He turned some more pages and found a few more petals and then further in, a dog-eared page. That is where he found a note. The paper was tri-folded and sealed with a small wax circle. Alec considered opening the letter but decided against it. His impatience would crack the wax which had three intertwined initials. Additional scrutiny might lead to the owner of the letter. He placed the petals back in the book and put the note and the lock of hair in a separate box and made note of which Bible and what page they were found. Pleased with his new organization, he moved onto the listed family members.

The name, Gordania Grant, born in 1662, started a new family grouping. Maybe the child's father wanted his offspring to be the first in the new book. Gordania was the oldest of a dozen children because her father had three wives. Many of her siblings passed while they were young. Except for one little fellow, Colin Grant, born in 1680. Gordania would have been nineteen-years old by the time she welcomed her new sibling.

Further down the page, Gordania's wedding date was inscribed along with her spouse's name. A small note was added: *It rained all day.* There was no other mention about Gordania's children, if she had any, because with her marriage, her offspring would be listed in her husband's family Bible.

On the top of the next page, was the death date for Colin's mother and then his wedding. The date was June the 9th, 1712. Alec scanned the pages and noticed that none of the marriages were in May. His father once told him that the fifth month of the year was considered unlucky, an old Roman custom having something to do with celebrating the dead. He remembered the old superstition: *Marry in May and you'll rue the day.* Alec wondered if people still believed that. He didn't care. He'd marry Hanna the minute she said yes.

Colin's bride was listed next to his name. Alec glanced at it quickly and reached for a Post-it. He considered using another color marker to denote a wedding rather than a birth or death. Thankfully, he purchased a multi-colored pack.

After he wrote the information down, he stared at the Post-it. Something wasn't right. Or rather, something looked familiar. He checked the bride's name. Somewhere he'd seen or heard it before. Maybe his father had mentioned an ancestor. But that seemed unlikely. His father only talked about the ones he knew: his grandparents and one great-grandfather who lived to be one-hundred-and-two.

Then Alec remembered. The sealed note. The three initials. Alec pulled open the top drawer of the desk and found his father's magnifying glass. Hovering it over the seal, and turning on the desk lamp, he deciphered the letters: DMG. Then, he pulled the Bible closer and rechecked the bride's name, using the glass just to be sure.

There, written by a well-developed hand, was the name of Colin's wife: Davina MacArthur Grant.

CHAPTER TWENTY-EIGHT
GREAT GOOD FORTUNE
APRIL 6, 1712

ALEXANDRA'S SILK DRESS swirled and rustled as she hurried down the hallway. She stopped in front of the gilt-framed mirror, pinched her cheeks, and smoothed the curls that haloed around her head. Hands on her hips, she turned quickly to the right and then to the left; the light lavender skirt spiraled around her legs. While Alexandra nodded at her image, my heart swelled. I could never get enough. My daughter was here, living under my roof. I could embrace her any time I wished. But that did not quell the nightmare years we were apart. Every time I thought about the day when I left my infant daughter behind in Scotland, I shuddered.

"Father is home. I hear him," said Alexandra as she ran into the parlor and pulled back the heavy drape.

The rhythmic clip-clops of Alain's wooden leg, heard long before his arrival, was also part of my life.

"I hope he has the letter. Father promised he would check with the ship that arrived from Edinburgh."

The door swung open and Alain filled the open space. The site of him, healthy and strong, was a joy to behold. If hearts could smile, mine was grinning from ear to ear.

Alexandra stood in front of the door, barring her father's entrance or escape. "Did the letter come? Do you have it?" She encircled Alain, prying open his hands and searching the pockets in his jacket.

"Don't I get a hug or even a greeting? After a long weary day away from the most beautiful girls in Manhattan?"

"Father, Father. You're home." Sally dashed passed me toward Alain and threw her arms around his waist. It wasn't that long ago when she could only hug his legs.

"At least one of my daughters knows a proper welcome."

"Sorry, Father." Alexandra hugged the part of her father that was available.

Alain caught my eye and smiled. In a moment, we both flashed our mutual recognition of how far we had come, and how fortunate we were.

"Pardon me, Mistress." The voice belonged to Mary, our housekeeper. Almost as tall as Alain, she was wearing her gray work apron and the usual starched cap which framed her freckled face.

"Yes, Mary."

"The table is set with the rose patterned china you requested. I'm working on the silver, but I need to know the courses for tonight's dinner."

Not wanting to leave my family, I said, "Please check the menu. Cook has the latest version." Last minute changes for dinner parties were nothing new. Was it too warm to serve hot soup? Would a Gazpacho be more appealing? Does fish require another fork? Even as late as a few hours ago, some of the details were still being worked out.

"I have tried, mistress. But Cook says she's too busy, being that your guests will arrive in two hours."

"I'll see to Cook myself." Additional help had been hired to assist with baking and serving, but Cook was fussy about her work and would snarl at anyone, including me, who interfered with her concentration. Managing a large staff required time and patience. Occasionally, I longed for simpler days when we lived in the smaller house with no help. Before I headed toward the kitchen, new squeals of delight came from Alexandra. Like a magician, Alain revealed the hoped-for letter out of his hat.

"Father, I knew you had it. Not fair." Alexandra teased her father with a little scowl while sticking out her lower lip. But it didn't last. She broke into smiles and giggles and hugged her father again. "Thank you. Mother, may I be excused to read my letter?"

"Of course, but don't forget, we all want to hear what Auntie Davina has to say." As Alexandra scurried up the staircase, followed by her sister, I called out, "Our guests will be arriving soon. You need to be ready to greet them." That reminder was for Alexandra. Old enough to be a part of social events, she was approaching marriageable age. Several in the Jewish community were already eyeing her, including Maurice's son, Pierre. But that was something Alain and I would never consider, no matter how much Alexandra was enchanted by the young man's gentlemanly manners, pleasing looks, and French charm. I didn't care what I had to do, an alliance between Maurice's household and mine would never happen.

272

With our daughters gone, I rushed into Alain's arms and welcomed his embrace. The demanding concerns of menus and place settings melted away and it was only Alain and me. We had learned to treasure each day.

"I love you, Alain MacArthur."

"I love you more, Anna MacArthur. I am forever in your debt. For making me the happiest of men." He put his hand under my chin, directed my lips toward his, and pulled me closer. We embraced for as long as we could, until a loud thump from above disrupted our concentration.

Stepping back, I stared at the ceiling, and scoffed. "Sounds like a heavenly reminder. You'd better hurry and change your clothes."

Alec pulled me closer again. "Would you like to help? With my clothes. Removing them, that is?"

"Of course, but that would only delay your being ready. What would our guests think?"

"I don't care what anyone thinks. Besides, they would be consumed with jealousy."

"How is that?"

"Jealous that even after many years of marriage, I still find you a most intoxicating woman." Alain kissed me again and then motioned toward the stairs.

"I can't. There's still much to do. I must speak to Cook." I pulled back. "And you need to get ready. Your clothes smell of the docks."

Alec sniffed his sleeve. "You win." He pulled me close again. "But I won't be put off after our guests are gone. Promise?"

I nodded.

"Then I will do everything I can to encourage our guests' early departure." When Alain got halfway up the stairs, he turned. "Tell Cook, I order her to char the meat, so it tastes like leather, and salt the desserts."

I chuckled. As Alain disappeared, I headed toward the kitchen but stopped in the dining room to survey the table set with twenty chairs. At the ends of the table were silver cruet stands, and in the centerpiece was a polished engraved bowl that reflected the last rays of the afternoon sun and made the crystal goblets sparkle. Large mirrors on opposing walls played with the light and made the room appear larger. As soon as it was dusk, the wall sconces would be ignited, and then, just before the guests were seated, beeswax candles, placed in silver candlesticks at each place setting, would be lit.

Mary entered from the direction of the kitchen carrying a tray of fresh cut greens from our gardens and placed them prettily in the bowl. She stood back to inspect her work; once satisfied, she circled the table straightening a knife or positioning a napkin just so.

"It looks wonderful, Mary. The greens smell like the garden after a rainfall."

"Thank you, mistress. Your guests will be pleased, I think. The rose china looks lovely next to the tiny, embroidered flowers on the linen."

"Yes. That was a wonderful idea. I appreciate your advice."

"My pleasure, mistress. It is time this grand house was used as intended. For happy occasions."

Mary shot me a glance. I smiled to let her know I understood. Working for Catarina had not been easy, and when the woman became ill and moved with Innes to the farm, he had inherited from his first wife, further north along the river, Mary wasn't sure of her position. But Innes kept her on, to oversee the house in his absence, or at least, until he decided what to do with the property.

Not one to be idle, Mary asked, "Will that be all, mistress?"

"Was the stoop scrubbed?"

"Twice today. I scrubbed it myself after all the deliveries were made. We don't want your guests to think ill of the new mistress."

"Thank you, Mary. You think of everything. I'll stop by the kitchen before I change."

"No need, mistress. Cook relented, and as you can see, everything is where it should be." Mary turned and gestured toward the heavy buffet table under one mirror. Serving utensils, additional plates, and silverware were at the ready. And in the center, the place of honor, were my candlesticks. Although one was battered, it was polished so that it gleamed like the other.

"Perfect," I said. My table outdid anything I had experienced at Rachel's finest dinners and even what I remembered when my father entertained guests. In Mary, I had found my own Mrs. Gibbons.

As I walked around the room, admiring all the fine things that were mine, I absentmindedly traced the smooth wood of the armchair with my finger.

"The chairs have been wiped, too," Mary said. "All of the fireplaces on the first floor have been swept and the carpets were beaten this morning."

I nodded my approval. "You are a wonder."

When Mary returned her attention to the table, it was time for me to head toward the stairs, but I wanted one last peek at the front parlor where the guests would gather before the meal for greetings and conversation.

The room was filled with a clean lemony smell from a fresh layer of polish. The fireplace sputtered its greeting as a log fell, releasing a shower of sparks. Over the mantle hung a still-life of roses. It needed a minor straightening. The newly installed carpet, with its intricate green leaf pattern, continued the garden theme. It was the first of many changes Alain and I had planned for this house. In the years to come, we hoped to turn it into one of the finest in Manhattan.

Sometimes, I felt like Alain and I were living a dream. Not so long ago, we had no home. Alain was gaoled for a crime he did not commit, and we were reliant on community charity. Our future looked dim. And now, our lives were completely turned around. We were one of the wealthiest families in Manhattan. How did that happen? It could only be explained by the machinations of one man: Cook Davey Innes.

It was almost three years ago when Alain was released from gaol and returned to the Emmanuel's home for convalescence. He was given a one-month reprieve and as the deadline drew near, it was evident that he would need more time. Returning to his cell before he was healed, I was convinced, would be a death sentence. However, we had no influence nor the resources to hire any. The only other option was to pay the exorbitant fine to free Alain. Our situation made this impossible. The financial assistance we received from the Jews of Manhattan paid for our solicitor, Mr. Burnet. But his fees were steep, and funds were low. Dr. Emmanuel and Master Myers never said it in so many words, but their furrowed brows and the worried look in their eyes every time Mr. Burnet's name came up told the story. Then, just as all hope was lost, Fate knocked on our door.

Deborah walked softly into the front room. Alain was slouched in a chair, his stump propped up by a cushion. I was seated across from him, nearest the window, reading a book borrowed from Baruch's library.

"Anna, you have a guest," whispered Deborah. "I believe it's your friend. The one from the ship. The man who married the rich vidow."

Alain opened one eye. "Make that two rich women."

Deborah's lips grew into a smile. "He says his name is Mr. Innes. Vould you like me or Baruch to stay vith you?"

"No. Mr. Innes is harmless."

Alain straightened himself and scoffed. "I'd like to wring his harmless neck. He fled like a coward when you needed him."

"I understand your anger. I felt the same, at the time. But we are old friends. We owe him a chance to explain. If that is his purpose today."

"I'm not sure I want to hear his excuses." Alain winced and reached down to soothe the phantom limb. Baruch warned this would happen. "How can something that's missing give me so much pain?" He threw back his head against the chair. "Anna, go. See what your friend wants."

"Mr. Innes said he'd like to speak vith both of you. But if you're too tired, I can tell him another day."

"No, we will see him," said Alain as he continued to grimace. "Let's get this over with."

A moment later, Mr. Innes entered the room, his hat in his hand. I was always taken by surprise by how fine the old cook dressed these days. I still expected to see him in his stained shirt and pants held up by a rope around his waist. The only part of Mr. Innes that remained the same were the course graying whiskers that covered half of his face.

"Good afternoon, Mr. Innes. It is good to see you." I gestured toward another chair.

"Thank ye, Mrs. MacArthur. Mr. MacArthur." The former cook stared at the seat. "I prefer tae stand, if ye don't mind."

"Of course. Please. You know me as Anna, and that's what I prefer. We are old friends. Are we not?"

"Aye. I appreciate ye're still considerin' our friendship." He looked down at his hat, rolling the brim from nervousness. "I have fond memories."

"As do I."

"What is it you wish to say to us?" asked Alain. His tone was one of annoyance. His voice brusque.

"I came tae apologize for my behavior last time I was in this room."

"Seems that you've taken a long time to find your courage. Not for me. But for Anna. You left her, when—"

I placed my hand on Alain's arm. "Mr. Innes. Please explain."

"I shouldn't have left ye without even a good-bye."

"The way others told the story, you snuck out like a dog with its tail between its legs."

"Alain—"

"Mrs. MacArthur, ye're husband has a right tae be angry. I deserve it. There were reasons for my leavin'. I thought ye were in good hands. The Jews. They know how tae help their own." Mr. Innes grabbed the edges of his wool jacket. "I might wear expensive clothes and spend money freely at the local tavern where only the local drunks heed my words. Especially when another round o' ale is ordered. But I have no influence with government o'ficials. I've learned a sad truth, Mrs. MacArthur. Money means nothin' w'out the knowledge o' how tae use it. I'm full o' bluster sometimes. Ye might have noticed." He sighed deeply and took the seat that was offered. "Also, my wife—"

"The one who falsely accused me and put me in gaol? Lost my leg because of…her." Alain's voice was harsh and loud. His hands balled into a fist as if he were preparing to punch Mr. Innes in the nose.

Mr. Innes stood. "My wife was wrong. Her actions despicable." Mr. Innes hesitated for a moment. "But I can assure ye she will not be botherin' ye again."

"And how can you promise that?" asked Alain. "She has a mind of her own and does as she please."

"Catarina is dead."

An awkward silence filled the room.

"Mr. Innes. I'm sorry," I said.

"Thank ye. We weren't married verra long for me tae feel a loss. Our marriage was mostly a convenience and a wee bit o' companionship…someone tae converse with. O' tae argue with. But she's gone now and although there was a pretty little family graveyard on my farm, I've done right by her and had her buried at Trinity Church."

"To be near Joris?"

"Nah. She made me promise that she would lie as far away from him as possible. Maybe that was a last kindness she was offerin' the man." Mr. Innes stopped talking and pulled out a handkerchief to wipe the bead of sweat that collected in the furrows of his forehead. "Like I said, I came tae apologize. If you will accept it. There is another reason I came tae see ye taeday."

My husband glanced at me, and I nodded. "Go on," said Alain.

Mr. Innes wiped his forehead again. "I want tae make right for the pain my wife caused. I want tae pay off Mr. MacArthur's fine. Tis the least I can do."

I gasped. "It's…steep…very steep."

"Yes, I've heard. I also know there's another who's tryin' tae make it difficult for Mr. MacArthur tae gain his freedom. Let me assure ye, I'm a verra rich man. The price o' Mr. MacArthur's freedom is not out o' my reach. Even if it's doubled. O' tripled."

"That is generous of you, Mr. Innes," said Alain. His voice moderated.

"Mr. MacArthur, I came intae my fortune not by deceit. I came by it honestly. If you can call good luck, honest. Although luck did not spare my deceased wives." Mr. Innes looked up at the ceiling. "May God rest their souls. So, the least I can do is share my good fortune with others. I have no children, but Mrs. MacArthur has always been kind tae me. She may not realize it, but I've considered her the daughter I never had but always wanted." Mr. Innes reached for his handkerchief again, but this time to dab his eyes. "Which brings me tae the real reason I am here. I'd like tae hire Mr. Burnet tae write my will, and I want tae name you and Anna as my heirs. Tae inherit all that I own. And that might be sooner than ye think."

"Mr. Innes, are you thinking—"

"Nah! I'd never do anything so foolish. But I have made up my mind how I want tae spend the rest o' my days. The life o' a landsman is not for me. That I ken. I miss the salt air and the swell o' the waves under my feet. I mean tae go back tae sea."

"You're going to be a cook again?" I asked.

"Not a chance. I plan tae buy a merchant vessel, and I will be the captain. I can give the orders and have some other poor soul boilin' my porridge every mornin'." A smile crossed his face and his eyes looked wistful as if he was already standing on the deck, scanning the horizon. "I've decided that I'd much rather end my days at sea and let my bones rest at the bottom o' the ocean than in that pretty little graveyard on the farm." He closed his eyes and continued to dream. "I told ye, I'm a verra rich man."

This was too much to take in. I had to make sure I understood. "You're buying a ship and leaving Manhattan?"

"Aye."

"You want Alain and me to be your heirs?"

"Aye."

"What about Catarina's son? Mr. Krol?" I pictured the last time I saw the young man. I imagined his horror when he learned that his parent's fortune would be ours.

"Do not worry about Mr. Krol. I have nothin' personal against him. I'll be sure tae leave him a few pounds. But no more. The rest will go tae you: Catarina's house, the house at the farm, and all the land, orchards, and animals. I only ask that ye maintain the graveyard where my first wife and her father are buried." Mr. Innes stared at the ceiling. "It's the least I can do for them. God rest their souls."

I bit my lip. Mr. Innes was never a religious person. The only time I heard him use God's name was when he was in the middle of an irreverent moment.

Mr. Innes stood again. "And, if Mr. MacArthur agrees, I'm hopin' he will become my partner in the shippin' business. I plan tae sail north and then down tae the West Indies, transportin' cargo and passengers. In a few years, if we succeed, we will purchase another ship. And then another. I have no doubt that Innes-MacArthur Shippin' will be most profitable."

Now it was Alain's turn to gasp; and then he smiled. "I like the sound of that, Mr. Innes. Have you thought about the competition? It will be stiff. Many have been around for years."

"Aye. But some have grown a wee bit lazy and careless. Restin' on their laurels, so tis speak. With your knowledge o' the docks and your connections, we will have an advantage. Besides, the only real competition I want tae destroy is that little French weasel, St Martin. He gets on my nerves. Says one thin' and means another. He's been tryin' tae get me tae invest in his business, but I'd rather it went t'other way, and someday I buy him out. There's somethin' about the man I don't like. Maybe, he's tae French." Mr. Innes picked up his hat. "If ye're agreed, I will speak tae Mr. Burnet and have him draw the papers immediately. The sooner that's done, then the quicker I can get my sea legs back."

Alain and I looked at each other. "Mr. Innes," I said. "We will be proud to be your heirs."

"And business partners," added Alain.

Mr. Innes placed his hat on his head. A smile split his face. "Mr. Burnet will call on ye shortly." He nodded and tapped the top of his hat. "I wish ye both a pleasant evenin'."

In an instant, our lives had changed. From so much pain and suffering, we now had hope. For ourselves. For our children's future. As Mr. Innes promised, it didn't take long for the legal proceedings to commence. Within a few days, papers were signed, and at the end of the month, we moved into Catarina's grand house on Broadway.

What I didn't know then was that I was I about to experience an immense sadness. Mr. Innes had meticulously planned his escape to sea. And that late afternoon meeting at the Emmanuel's home was the last time I ever saw my friend.

CHAPTER TWENTY-NINE
CONSEQUENCES
APRIL 6, 1712

ALEXANDRA'S EYES WERE lowered and mournful looking; her chin almost rested on her chest. The only time she brightened was when there was a knock at the door announcing more guests. Then, her focus diverted, her eyes widened, hopeful, waiting for Mary to show the new arrivals into the parlor. But each time, my daughter sighed heavily with disappointment, glared in my direction, and resumed her unhappy stance. I knew there was only one reason why Alexandra blamed me for her wretched state. The St. Martins, Maurice and his dashing young son, Pierre, were not on our guest list. My neglect was purposeful.

Instead, another young man, who had just returned from school, entered the room, flanked by his parents, Elkanah and Myer Myers. Eyes turned to the tall lad with the broad shoulders. When he leaned over and whispered in his mother's ear, a shock of dark hair fell wistfully over one eye. His words might have been known only to Elkanah, but his eyes and her maneuverings revealed their joint intention.

"Pardon me." Elkanah interjected the moment there was the slightest bit of hesitation in conversation between Alexandra and two other young women. "Miss MacArthur, this is my son, Joseph Myers." Elkanah's voice was demanding and could be heard across the room.

Joseph took two steps forward, almost directly in front of his mother, bowed formally, and took my daughter's hand. "I'm honored, Miss MacArthur. You have a lovely home, tastefully appointed, and enhanced only by your great beauty." He said this while glancing at the other two young women. I could have sworn he winked as he addressed them. "Ladies."

Two fans snapped opened to conceal titters while Alexandra recoiled her hand. This was followed by a curt welcome tinged with annoyance as her friends excused themselves. As they retreated to other social circles, they looked back over their shoulders to Joseph's continual stares. When Elkanah's son returned his attention to Alexandra, she abruptly left him standing alone and joined her friends. I breathed a sigh of relief. My daughter was not blinded by a man's good looks.

After everyone had arrived, Mary invited the guests to take their seats in the dining room. Elkanah pulled me aside and asked if an accommodation could be made for her son. "Joseph is left-handed, you know. I wouldn't want whoever sits on his left to have their food knocked off their fork. My son is rather large. Could he sit here?" She pointed to a seat that would position him directly across from Alexandra.

Scanning the room, I tried to come up with an excuse, something to save my daughter more discomfort. But guests were quickly filing in and taking their places. "Of course." I motioned to Mary, and in a minute, seating assignments were switched. When Alexandra arrived, rather than confront her reaction, I took the coward's way out and tended to a guest nearby

Elkanah's request was not a surprise. She was a difficult woman and was not afraid to speak her mind. I knew from Deborah that Elkanah was anxious for a match between her family and mine. Although that was not always the case, especially when Alain was in gaol; but our new-found wealth had amazingly erased our sordid past. And Alexandra's beauty added to her desirability.

In some ways, I could find no objection to Joseph. He was of our faith, his parents were well thought of, and I admired Master Myers. But the young man had a reputation of playing with the hearts of young women. His behavior this evening was evidence, and in that way, he was a study of contrariness - pleasing to the eye of the ladies but socially reckless. Or as Alain described him, the sense of a boy existing in a man's body. I would have been shocked if my daughter accepted an offer from Joseph.

"Alexandra, you look lovely this evening," said Joseph who stood for the briefest of moments as she arrived at her chair. "The color of your dress compliments your green eyes."

Alexandra lifted and spread her lavender skirt as she prepared to sit. "Thank you," she said not to Joseph but to another male guest who pushed in her chair. When seated, she placed her closed fan on the table, and stared directly at Joseph. "My eyes are brown."

The boy squinted. "Pardon me. It must be the light. No matter. The color suits you."

Alexandra fidgeted in her seat, looked to her left and found help nearby. Deborah traded seats to sit next to my daughter and the two attempted a private conversation.

"Is that a new dress? It looks like silk," asked Joseph who was not to be put off. "That must have cost your father…well, he can afford it, but I daresay, your future husband might—"

Alexandra opened her mouth, about to say something. Deborah touched her arm.

"Mary," I called. "The wine. Now. Please." Deborah was not my daughter's only savior. Mary entered the room trailed by a server with bottles of various hues. "Please, everyone, choose your preferred wine."

Thankfully, Baruch Emmanuel launched into a variety of safe topics which focused the conversation to the other end of the table: the search for a synagogue, Governor Hunter's newest proposals, and Alain's appointment to the post of fire warden.

"Thank you, Baruch. I take the duties of warden seriously. We all know how devastating a conflagration can be. Even a small spark can bring down a city."

More toasts were made, and then the conversation turned, as it always did of late to slavery.

"Mr. MacArthur, how goes the shipping business?" asked one of the guests, a prosperous shopkeeper who sat in the middle of the table. He was well liked in the community but known for his candor. "Rumor has it that you are planning to add another ship. Trade must be good. Are you adding the slave trade to your business? I hear St. Martin has made a nice profit in Africans and is now adding a third ship."

All eyes turned to Alain. Slavery was a difficult topic, even more so, after the building of the new slave market along the dock. Some believed there were too many Africans in Manhattan, slave or free, which raised the fear of an insurrection. Others strongly opposed the institution. My husband took a sip of wine and cleared his throat. "The answer to the rumor is yes. And no, to the importation of slaves. I will not be a part of that filthy trade."

"Your decision, of course." The shopkeeper played with his silver fork, turning it over for inspection. "But you could give the Frenchman some honest competition."

"There is no profit large enough that could convince me to carry human flesh, sir. I saw for myself the inhumanity of it. The smell from a

283

slaver arrives before it is tied up. Men, women, and children chained below, hungry, thirsty, lying in their waste, crying out for an end to their torture." Alain hesitated. I remembered the haunting vision he shared with me the day he was invited to inspect the ship's hold. In a low gravelly voice, he continued, "I refuse to have anything to do with it."

"If you're so opposed to the practice, then why do you associate with those who count the enslaved as property? Surely, a man with your standards would choose other friends and businesses with similar attitudes."

The table went silent. Alain stiffened. It was true. Several of his associates and our friends owned Africans.

"Many say they have no choice," the shopkeeper continued. "To maintain a profit, they claim they must accept the ugly side of business. But I believe there's always a choice. Do you not agree, sir?"

The serving stopped. Mary stood against the wall.

It was Baruch who came to the rescue. "Let us set aside this important discussion until after ve dine. For now, let us raise our vine glasses to toast our gracious host and hostess. The food looks superb, the vine is excellent, and the conversation…titillating." A few scoffed. Others nodded and laughed.

Once the toast concluded, Alain stood. His chair scraped the oak floorboards. "Thank you, Baruch. Most kind of you. Anna and I are pleased to have so many dear friends join us this evening. You grace us with your presence." He stopped, leaned forward, and placed the knuckles of his hands on the end of the table. "But I will not dodge a response." He stared at his guests. "Like many here…no…I will only speak for myself. I have heard it said, that one in six souls living on this island are dark skinned and enslaved. They bake our bread, care for our children, tend our shops, learn the trades, and labor on our farms. Slaves are more numerous in Manhattan than in Boston, Philadelphia, and much of the south. And yet, I am ashamed to say, I paid little attention, or perhaps, I chose to look the other way," One hand balled into a fist. He raised it, ready to slam it on the table, but stopped mid-air. "I and my house will not take part in this ungodly trade." Alain pushed back his coattails and sat.

"Hear, hear, Mr. MacArthur. Well said, sir," said the shopkeeper who started the conversation. "I'm all for keeping slavery out. Tensions are rising, especially among those from the Indies. They have learned our ways and are quick to rebel. But I'm wondering how your partner, Mr. Innes, feels about this?"

"Mr. Innes is aware of my feelings on the matter. He knows I will end our connection if he insists on shipping slaves."

"Does Mr. Innes agree? Knowing the profit, he will forfeit?"

"Thankfully, my partner is happiest when spending his days at sea and wishes to remain so. He has little regard for the day-to-day financial matters and has left that to my discretion."

"You are indeed fortunate. To appease your conscience and your bottom line at the same time is something most men only dream about. I salute you, sir." The gentleman raised his glass. We all followed and made another toast.

I breathed a sigh a relief. Another storm weathered. The remainder of the dinner went surprisingly well. Alexandra avoided eye contact with her fickle suitor, and as soon as it was polite to do so, she excused herself from the table, complaining of a headache. The men rose in unison, and Joseph offered to escort her to the stairs. Alexandra declined and walked briskly out of the room.

My daughter's actions were a reminder of another dinner party, many years ago, when my father feted his old friend and my unwanted suitor, Maurice St. Martin. I remember feeling trapped and repulsed by his crude behavior. I escaped using the same excuse many women relied on. But unlike my situation, Alexandra had nothing to fear. Alain and I were opposed to any connection with Pierre St. Martin, even if he was the man she most desired.

A couple of hours later, the guests began to leave. That is, except for Deborah and Baruch. We had become especially close after our living together for many months. Their staying behind allowed us to enjoy each other's company.

Baruch was a great companion of Alain's. Even now, they escaped to our library, discussing whatever had been missed at dinner. The new stamp tax on paper or the rising friction between the French and the Fox Indians and its effect on trade would surely interest them. Any fluctuation in the balance of power, no matter the continent, had repercussions on the shipping business.

Deborah and I were just as close. We constantly sought each other's company. She offered valuable advice when we moved into this large home and I needed experienced help. We shared the same distaste for slavery. No African would cross my threshold unless they were free.

Rachel offered her assistance when we moved. She proposed that I hire one or two of her slaves: Lucy or Ruth's son, for short-term labor. This practice was quite common. It provided slaveowners with additional income. When Alain and I refused, I wondered if that was the reason Rachel and her husband turned down tonight's dinner invitation.

Alexandra was the other reason for our closeness. My daughter considered Deborah like an older sister or aunt. I often found the two whispering and giggling. I was not jealous of their relationship. It pleased me.

"Alexandra did not enjoy the evening," said Deborah as she returned her cup of tea to the saucer and dabbed her lips with a napkin. "Elkanah vas annoyingly persistent. Vhen it comes to her son the voman doesn't know vhen to stop. You may have to say something."

"Yes, I agree. I cannot allow Alexandra's agony to continue."

Deborah scoffed. "Motherhood has blinded Elkanah. Everyone can see that Alexandra and Joseph are not meant for each other."

"That does not matter. My daughter is too young. She has plenty of time. My father tried to force me to wed at an early age, and I won't let that happen to her."

"But your marriage vith Alain turned out vell. A union based on respect and affection. Your husband adores you." She hesitated and took another sip of her tea. "I know there's more to your story. You've hinted as much, but everyone is entitled to have a secret."

"Thank you." The unfortunate connection I had with Maurice would go with me to my grave. And I was sure that Maurice would stay silent as well. A confession would only ruin his reputation, his business, and his son's future.

"There are many daughters who marry young," Deborah continued. "Has Alexandra confided...I mean...has her heart set for someone else?"

"I know my daughter prefers Pierre, but Alain and I have agreed. She must look elsewhere. There are other young men in our community."

"Yes. Your daughter is beautiful and comes from good stock. She should only marry a man who is her equal. And one that she's mad about. But don't be surprised if you hear that some are betting on who she vill choose."

"Well, I can tell you it will not be Pierre. Nor Joseph." I replaced my empty cup on the saucer. "More tea?"

"No thank you, my dear. Baruch and I should be leaving. But I do have vone question. How are you going to keep Alexandra avay from the younger St. Martin? You can keep him off your guest list, but others vill not. The St. Martins are leading members of our community. Maurice just made a handsome donation toward a new synagogue. Alexandra and Pierre vill find each other. There vill be more dinner parties."

"She will be made aware of our wishes."

"I don't envy your talk, but Alexandra is a good daughter. I'm sure she vill do as you ask." Deborah placed her hand on my arm. "If I can help, in any vay, you know you can count on me."

I nodded. It saddened me that my daughter's heart would be broken, and I would be the cause.

Deborah rose to fetch her husband but was stopped by an urgent knocking at the door. "Who could that be? At this time of night?" asked Deborah. "Maybe someone left their hat or scarf behind."

I doubted that was the case. Mary would have notified me immediately.

The knocking brought the men from the library, but by the time Alain reached the hallway, it ceased. "Do you imagine someone is still hungry?" He chuckled while opening the door. The blackness of night filled the empty space. At first, it appeared no one was there, until a crumpled figure huddled by the threshold began to stir and moan. When the form looked up, the whites of two eyes stared from a dark face. At the same time, fingers wrapped around a swollen belly.

"Lucy!" cried Deborah. She knelt by the frightened girl and cradled her head.

"Mistress Deborah," mumbled the slave. "I knew you weh here. Please help us."

"Us? Who else is vith you?"

"He didn't listen. He refused to leave de others." Lucy began to sob.

"Who vouldn't come vith you?"

Lucy caught her breath. "Quaco. My baby's father." She clutched her belly tighter.

Although I was shocked by the news from Rachel's slave, my friend was not. Deborah spent much time with Baruch, tending the sick: slave or free. Known for her kindness, Deborah never arrived at a sick house without a basket of food and some cast-off clothes. The slaves considered her a savior; someone they could trust.

Deborah gently moved her hand, and noticed it was stained with blood. "Lucy? Who did this to you?"

"No one. When de fire started, I ran and fell. Hit my head."

"What fire?" asked Alain.

Instead of answering, Lucy sobbed until she gasped for air.

"Please bring her in," I said.

Baruch put his arm around the girl and helped her stand. The young slave wobbled. Her dirty head covering fell off, exposing her close-cropped hair.

"Put Lucy on a chair in the parlor, and I'll get Mary to—"

"Come take a look at this," shouted Alain.

I joined him by the door. The sky had a strange orange glow. It reminded me of the displays the city fire masters set off to celebrate important events. "What is it?"

"Fire. I must find out what's going on. In case, I'm needed," said Alain.

Just then, Lucy stood, clutched her belly, and screamed. I ran over to see if I could help. "Mistress Anna. Do not let Mr. MacArthur go. Make him stay."

"Why, Lucy? Why?"

Lucy continued her rant, while Deborah steered her back to the chair. She cupped the girl's face until she quieted. Deborah stared directly into her eyes. "Tell me Lucy. Vhy shouldn't Mr. MacArthur go?"

Lucy caught her breath. Her eyes went wide. "It's a trap...if he goes...he will be killed."

I turned toward the gaping doorway. I run outside, stumbled into the street and shouted Alain's name in all directions. A minute ago, he was here. Now, like a ghost, he had vanished. A frosty chill swirled off the North River and found its way up my spine. Alain was gone. And I was sure he had never heard Lucy's warning.

CHAPTER THIRTY
THE REVOLT
APRIL 6, 1712

I GRABBED LUCY'S shoulders. In response, she jerked back, her body trembled. I pitied her. A frightened girl, barely a woman, alone at night with no one to protect her or her baby. "Why is my husband in danger?" I asked. "Who will shoot him?"

Lucy's eyes grew into large saucers, her mouth opened and then went slack.

"Tell me. Damn it."

The slave girl continued to stare. The smell of fear was bitter and unpleasant.

"Listen to me." Deborah intervened by gently touching Lucy's face, turning it toward hers. Her voice calm, her words simple and purposeful. "I am your friend. You know that."

A tear slid down a dark cheek, settled on the edge of Lucy's chin, and disappeared when she nodded. Without her head covering, which added height and a sense of majesty, Lucy appeared small, fragile, and vulnerable.

"You came to get me," Deborah continued. "You knew I'd be here. Isn't that right?"

"Yes, Miss Deborah." Lucy breathed haltingly between sobs. "I heard Miss Rachel talkin'. About de dinner. Sayin' she not goin'. She tired of bein' talked down to. About her slaves."

Deborah and I looked at each other. Our suspicions confirmed.

"Miss Anna needs your help. Do you understand?" Lucy nodded and wiped her nose with the sleeve of her smock. "Tell me. Vhy is Mr. MacArthur in trouble?"

"De barn. It's on fire. Burnin'. Burnin' to de ground." Lucy swayed and stared at the ceiling. She seemed detached, like she was conversing with a spirit.

"Vhat barn? Vhere?"

"Out d'ere." Lucy pointed in an unknown direction. "It's a holy war. De you hear?" Her voice rose. "A war to kill all de Christians."

Baruch rushed to the door. "The sky's aglow, up north, beyond Vall Street."

"Maiden Lane," said Lucy.

"Are you sure?" asked Baruch.

"De barn. Vantilburgh's. Quaco must run. Run to de woods, I told him." Lucy stared directly at Deborah and grabbed her arms. "I came to warn you. Don't leave de house. De slaves are shootin'."

"Who are they shooting?" I asked.

"Any who comes a runnin'."

"You mean it's a trap?"

Lucy nodded, whimpered, and folded into herself again.

I grabbed my shawl. "I'm going after Alain. He was just appointed fire warden. That's why he ran off."

"You can't go," said Deborah. "Didn't you hear vhat Lucy said?"

"Alain has no idea the danger he's in. Please, stay with Lucy and the girls." My daughters were asleep, oblivious to the jeopardy.

"Deborah's right," said Baruch. "But Alain must be varned." He put on his coat and fitted his scarf snugly around his neck.

"What are you doing?" I asked.

"I'm coming vith you." His voice was firm, and I was grateful for his offer. If Lucy's story was half true, a fire and a few renegade slaves were a deadly combination.

I followed Baruch out the door and stepped into a world of eerie pre-dawn blackness. Without the moon to play with shadows and light our way, the surrounding homes, so familiar in daylight, looked like looming monsters of the deep. As we headed to the street, nature appeared discordant. Instead of sunrise from the east, a faint dawn-like glow spread over northern rooftops.

As we hurried along, the sounds of the night interrupted the silence. The snarl of a cat in heat and the quickened footsteps of a vagrant who wished to remain hidden caused me to fear every step. I pulled my shawl tighter to ward against this strange world and walked closer to Baruch.

The houses remained dark until we reached Wall Street, and then alarm bells, like a call to arms, awakened the townsfolk. Windows flew open, candles flickered, sleepy residents still in nightcaps, rubbed their eyes in disbelief. The eerie glow became a beacon of impending disaster.

In moments, the streets swelled with armed city-dwellers ready to battle the fire. Most grasped wooden buckets that made a racket as they clunked against their fast-moving legs. Others carried axes, flung dangerously over shoulders. Ladders of various lengths were heaved onto shoulders as teams of men snaked their way through what was quickly becoming a river of humanity. The streets themselves seemed to disappear. Mothers and small children, leaning out second-story windows, watched the growing spectacle, I clung to Baruch's arm so I would not be swept away.

As we neared Maiden Lane, the heat intensified; the flames flared casting a radiant glow on Baruch's hair and face as if he were Moses standing before the burning bush. The fearful voices of those around us were accompanied by the bleating and clucking of frightened animals, and what sounded absurd to my ears: a horn.

All at once, the crowd in front refused to surge further. Peering over heads, I saw a large fearsome-looking man with a beard that covered his chest. One hand rested on the hilt of his sword, a warning to any who dared to provoke his anger. Around his neck, like a pendulum, was a horn. This was a fire warden; his horn had just been used to get the crowd's attention.

The warden was joined by officials. They shouted and gestured directions to form bucket brigades to feed the coffin-shaped fire engine. Six stout men, three on each side of the engine, pumped the water. One warden clambered on top and shouted encouragement to the pumpers while directing the aim of the hose. Those who brought ladders were ordered where to place them in case anyone needed rescue. Young boys rounded up small, frightened animals from nearby coops and sheds. Axmen stood ready to battle wooden structures that were beyond saving and threatened a flare-up. The greatest fear of any city-dweller was fire. Their homes and shops were dry kindling.

Baruch and I ducked and skirted those who took their positions, running blindly through thick clouds of smoke. I covered my mouth and nose to ease my burning throat that worsened every time I gasped for air. When Baruch succumbed to a fit of coughing, we were forced to stop. Bent forward, he found some relief when a wad of darkened phlegm landed near his foot.

"Baruch, there's a stoop over there. You can sit." I directed him toward a temporary refuge.

"I'll be…better…in—" He spoke as he continued to spit until his coughing eased.

"Stay here. I'm going—"

"You there," called out a gruff voice.

I froze. It was the bearded warden. His hair was caked with ash and his face was streaked with grime. I turned the other way, pretending he was calling out to others.

"You there, I'm talking to you." With a few large steps he reached us, grabbed Baruch, and pointed to me. "You, join the bucket line." Then to Baruch. "Relieve one of the pumpers when he tires. Quick now."

"Sir," I shouted above the roar of the fire. "I'm looking for my husband. He's a warden. Do you know where I can find Alain MacArthur?"

"Don't know the man He's probably closer to the fire."

I picked up my skirts, but the warden blocked my path.

"No, you don't. Your husband, or whomever you're looking for, doesn't need you getting in the way. Now, grab a bucket—"

"I must find him. Please."

"Not until the fire's out. Or would you rather the constable throws you in gaol for disobeying a direct order?"

With no alternative, Baruch and I walked toward the heap of wooden and leather buckets but were startled by several short explosions.

I turned in the direction of the blaze. The shed was almost engulfed. Its bony frame was a contrast to the flames of orange and yellow. Then, I heard more pops followed by the scream of a woman in front of me. "Gunfire!"

Another turned toward her. "It's the wood exploding."

The first woman pointed toward a young man staunching blood flowing down his leg. "Fire doesn't do that. Someone's shooting." She tossed her filled bucket, lifted her skirts, and fled in the opposite direction.

"Lucy vas right. It's an ambush. Run," said Baruch.

"Hey! You! Stop!" shouted the warden as he came after us. "Get back in—" The man stopped and stared. When he tried to speak, a mouthful of blood strangled him. He stood for a moment, his eyes not understanding. And then he crumbled. A dark red splotch soaked his beard red.

Baruch bent over the man and ripped open his shirt. But I didn't see the warden. I saw Alain hurt, bleeding to death. "We have to go," I pleaded, but I knew if the warden had a chance, the doctor would not leave him. Desperate, I shouted, "I'm going. I'll be back." I don't know if Baruch heard me, and at that moment, I didn't care. Like the woman a few minutes ago, I picked up my skirts and ran. But I fled in the direction of the fire.

If one were to describe what hell looked like, this was surely it. Men and women, black and white, ran in all directions. Faces were smeared and blackened. Clothes were bloodied and torn. I watched in horror as one woman ripped off her smoldering skirt and ran away in her shift. Another carried a baby while dragging two small children, a boy and a girl, who clutched her legs as she walked. They wore only a dirty shift and an over-sized nightshirt. Their wailing was pitiful. The mother pleaded for help from all who passed her and held out her baby as if it were an offering to the god of fire.

I stopped and looked toward the fire while wiping my grimy hands on my skirt. The wind was ferocious, forcing the flames higher. My skirts whipped into a frenzy and my hair lashed around my face making it difficult to see. Capturing the ends in one hand, I looked back at the mother. She had collapsed. Her older children tugged on her skirts, begging her to move on.

"Get up. Follow me." I plucked the baby from her arms and took the hand of the little girl. "Stay close," I said to the mother. "I'll get you to where it's safe." We walked quickly, stepping carefully through a graveyard of the newly dead and against the tide of those moving forward to fight the fire. A new warden directed the bucket brigade and the team of pumpers.

When we arrived where I left Baruch, he was gone. The warden's body remained. "Here." I pointed after I handed the baby back to the mother. "Just follow this path. Keep the fire behind you." I waited and watched them disappear. Then, I headed back into the inferno.

The fire that engulfed the barn had done its work. The walls folded in on itself, and along with the roof, came crashing down, creating a roar that sounded like the end of the world. Just then, I saw someone I knew: the shopkeeper. The same man, who just a few hours ago, sat at my table and discussed shipping and slavery with Alain. I grabbed his arm. He turned and looked puzzled, like he was seeing a ghost.

"Mrs. MacArthur. What in God's name are you doing here?"

"Did you see my husband? He's a warden."

"Yes, he's—" A bullet whizzed by the man's head, but he seemed to barely notice. He looked up and down Maiden Lane. "Come with me." The man grabbed my hand, and we passed more bodies. Some were moaning, others begging for their mother or divine intervention. One older man was bleeding copiously from his arm, another screamed for a hand that no longer existed. "Hurry, please," the shopkeeper begged. We ran down a small alley where another line of men and women stood with buckets waiting for direction. "There's Mr. MacArthur." The shopkeeper pointed. "Over there."

"Alain!" I screamed.

"What are you doing here? Get down." He grabbed my arm and pulled me next to him. "We've been tricked. Someone is shooting at us."

"Yes, I know. I came to warn you. Are you hurt?" I felt his arms and put my hands on his chest. Then, I noticed a young boy, about Alexandra's age, sprawled before him.

"You'll be okay, lad. Just a minor graze," said Alain. The boy's blackened face was streaked with tears. His body shuddered so that he barely uttered a whimper before passing out.

I swallowed hard as the smell of urine mixed with the smoke-filled air.

"Seems like fear got the best of him. Better that than a bullet to the head." Alain motioned toward a knee-high wall enclosing an orchard about fifty yards behind us. "You'll be safer there. I'll come back for the boy. Are you ready? When I count to three, we'll make a run for it?"

"I'm going nowhere. I didn't come all this way to lose you again."

Alain looked as if he was about to say something. Maybe he knew it was futile to argue when I had made up my mind. Instead, he moved around to the boy's head. "Anna, grab his legs."

"Here, Mr. MacArthur. Let me help you." It was the shopkeeper. Without being asked, he picked up the boys' legs. Together, they ducked and carried the unconscious boy while I followed. Once safely behind the wall, the shopkeeper ran off.

The gunfire became sporadic at the same time the young boy regained consciousness. Our world went unusually quiet except for the barn that crackled and smoldered. A horn sounded. I began to stand, but Alain pulled me down.

"Not so fast, Anna."

Two more bursts of gunfire were followed by a woman's scream.

The young boy began to ask questions, and when he realized he suffered nothing more than a scratch that bled a bit, he tried to salvage his courage, and begged to rejoin the pumpers. When a second horn blared, others poked their heads from hiding places. The lad pointed to his father and limped off into anxious arms.

Slowly, the crowd grew as Alain and I emerged from our sanctuary. The smoke hung like a low-lying cloud, stinging and acrid. I wiped my eyes and nose with my sleeve that was blackened with streaks. I reached for a handkerchief tucked in my waistband and coughed up blackened sputum. We backtracked along the same path, I had taken in my search for Alain, the one I had shown the young mother. Now it was littered with the dead.

Alain stopped moving. He put his arm around me and pulled me inward. "Anna. Don't look."

"I'm not afraid." I stepped away from Alain and stared into the glassy eyes of the shopkeeper. He was sprawled on his back, legs spread, and his face twisted in pain. His stiff hands covered a gaping hole, a knife wound to his chest, as if he was trying to keep what was inside from escaping.

"He saved my life," I said.

Alain took my hand and whispered a short prayer. When he finished, he said, "Come, let's go home. There's nothing we can do for him. His family will be notified."

As we walked away, I kept turning back for one last look. To bid my friend adieu, to thank him, to thank God. We were the lucky ones. The fortunate few who staggered through the gates of hell and back, unharmed. Others, who left the safety of their homes this night, to help a neighbor, to save a city, to heed a call to arms, never returned.

❀

Deborah must have fallen asleep. She looked puzzled when the creaking door and footsteps awakened her. Her eyes fell on us and then went wide. "Vhere's Baruch?"

"He's not here?" asked Alain.

"No, Vhy isn't he vith you?" Deborah looked at me and then at Alain.

"We parted a while ago. A man was shot. Baruch went to help."

"You didn't stay vith him?"

"No, I went to find Alain. There was so much confusion. People were running everywhere. Trying to put out the fire. Someone started shooting. It was a trap. Mr.—" The gruesome memory of the shopkeeper was too vivid. I covered my eyes and began to tremble like the young boy.

Deborah ran toward the door.

"You can't go. The streets are not safe. I'll go look for Baruch. Stay here. Both of you."

I wanted to scream, but I knew he had to. Baruch would have done the same.

With Alain gone, I approached my friend and we held onto each other. That's when I noticed. "Where's Lucy?" I asked.

"She's gone. To find Quaco. I tried to stop her. I begged, for the sake of her baby, but she vas determined. She said something about a gun and taking revenge."

A shiver went down my spine. I wondered if it was Quaco who shot at us. Deborah knew, as we all did, that it was against the law for any slave to possess a weapon or to instigate a revolt. Either was a capital offense, and the same punishment would be meted out for any who knew or helped.

Then, with a whoosh and a clatter, the door swung wide. Deborah gasped. She covered her mouth, and let out a muffled scream, There, stood Alain, and from behind him, stepped out Baruch, His coat was gone, his stockings torn and blackened, and his face streaked. Dark singed holes pocked his white shirt. "Thank God you're here," she said while kissing his face over and over.

"I'm safe, Deborah. Nothing terrible has happened to me that a bath and a new shirt von't fix."

Deborah pulled back and studied her husband. "Are you sure. You look like you've gone to var."

"Ah. In a vay, I have." Baruch hugged his wife again and sighed. He turned to us. "I have something to tell you. I have seen Lucy. She vas taken into custody by the constable. She and many others. I saw it vith my own eyes."

"Vere you able to speak to her?" Deborah asked.

"No. The constable threatened to arrest me as an accessory."

"Ve must go to City Hall." said Deborah. "And tell the constable that Lucy vas vith us this evening. She's not responsible."

"I'm not sure how much that vill help. Others saw her vith Quaco a few hours before the fire. After vhat happened, vith so many dead, and so much property damaged, some vill seek revenge. The trial and execution vill be swift." Baruch turned to his wife. "Let's go home, Deborah. It has been a long night."

"Please, stay," said Alain. "The streets may still be dangerous. I would feel better if you slept under my roof."

"Many thanks, my friend. I think that might be a sound idea." Deborah laid her head on Baruch's shoulder. He smiled at her. "*Miene liebe* is exhausted. As am I."

The Emmanuels followed us toward the stairs and before we took one step, Alain turned. "We will talk about this in the morning. When heads are clearer. Baruch and I will venture out and discover what occurred last night, and what is the best way to proceed. Then, we will make a plan."

I didn't say a word. I was too tired to argue. But whatever plan Alain had in mind, I was going to be a part of it.

CHAPTER THIRTY-ONE
A GREAT OPPORTUNITY
NEW YORK

WHEN ALEC FINISHED his story, I was speechless. How does one react to mind-blowing news?

"Hanna? Are you there?" asked Alec.

"Yes. I'm…trying to take this in. Give…me a minute." Not in a million years, would I have guessed Alec and I had a familial connection.

"Are you still there?"

"Yes. So, your many-times great-grandmother is also my many-times great aunt. Plus, all those 'removes' you mentioned."

"Correct, and Alain MacArthur was my great uncle as well as your grandfather."

"Wow!" I sat down on the bed, grabbed a pillow, and hugged it as if it were a little kid needing a teddy bear. "When did Davina get married, again?"

"June 9, 1711."

"That's about two years after Alexandra arrived in New York. Anna never mentioned Davina's marriage, because the last journal entry was around the time of Alexandra's arrival." I rubbed my arms but couldn't erase the goosebumps. "Alec, do you realize it's only because of a sequence of events that you came to learn about this. If your mother hadn't asked you to work on the family tree; if Kate wasn't expecting; if your father hadn't…died." I bit my lip. I hoped he didn't think I was insensitive. "If these events hadn't occurred, we wouldn't have known about our connection."

"I'd like to be connected…I miss our coupling." Alec laughed.

"I'm serious. Ira told me about *bashert*; two people, soulmates, are brought together by an unexplained force."

"Nothing or no one is forcing me. I want you. All on my own."

I didn't respond. The silence between us grew uncomfortable. Why couldn't I say, *I want you, too. Let's get married. Now!* I knew Alec would be on the next flight. But there were other considerations, and right now, my thoughts were too jumbled to think clearly. It was easier to ignore this difficulty between us and return to the family tree. "How many generations did you say that was?"

"I'm not sure yet. I'm not finished with the second Bible and there are four more to go. Discovering Davina waylaid my progress. But I estimate at least ten generations, or the number of years it takes for a child to mature, marry, and have children. That varies in time of war, famine, or prosperity. I'll have a better idea after I catalogue all the names. But you should know that tenth cousins are so distant, that, genetically there will be little common DNA between us. However, we are genealogically related."

"Do you think…you should get your DNA tested? To be sure?"

"It's not necessary. These old family Bibles are reliable. There's no doubt that Davina married into the Grant family." He paused. I could hear a woman's voice. Mora's. "Sorry, Hanna. My mother just wanted to tell me she was going out." Another pause. "There's one more thing. I found something. A sealed note tucked away in the Bible. I'm sure it was written by Davina. Her initials are in the wax seal."

"Read it to me."

"The only way I can do that is to break the wax. I'd rather not since it protects the authenticity of the primary document."

This was a recurring problem, and it was because we valued research and were trained to be super careful when dealing with artifacts. Sometimes, it would be easier if Alec stocked shelves at a supermarket, and I was a cashier.

"There's something else to consider," said Alec. "I'm not the rightful owner of the letter."

"Davina was your relative, too. Being that you're a Grant, it belongs to you more than me."

"I know, but if it's anyone's property, it's my mother's. She's the owner of the Bible. And its contents. I must let her know what I've found and that I'd like to investigate further. I don't think she'll object. She could care less about some eighteenth-century bride. Also, I'm going to call Ira and see if he has any ideas about removing the seal without cracking it or destroying the paper and the ink."

"Okay. But promise you'll call me the minute you open the note."

"Better yet, I'll bring the letter," continued Alec, "when I come to the States over the winter break. We'll read it together."

I was so excited with Alec's news that I had to call Jess.

"You're related? I told you. Fate is bringing you and Alec together. This is not some accidental coincidence."

"Jess, accidental and coincidence mean almost the same thing."

"I know. I know. It's my baby brain. It doesn't allow me to think straight. Can you marry Alec? I mean, now that you are cousins, will your children have two heads? There are laws against marrying cousins, you know?"

"We are hardly related. Alec said there's little common DNA. But I'd like to find out more."

"Hey, I think Josh is an amateur genealogist. He's always talking about his family tree and searching for lost relatives in the Old Country. I'm sure he'd love to help. You made quite an impression on him."

"Jess, stop pushing. Besides, I thought this was something you said that the Fates controlled."

"Okay, but maybe they need some help."

It was a week since I heard the news. Alec called every day and kept me updated on his research. Davina and Colin Grant had five children: three girls and two boys. Two survived to adulthood. Colin predeceased his wife by many years. Davina died on October 4, 1766 at the age of eighty-six, a ripe old age for those days. There was no information about where she was buried, but Alec hoped to search for the location of Thistlestraith, Alain's seventeenth century home in the Highlands. If it still existed, there might be a family graveyard.

"Maybe I'll get lucky and find Davina's headstone. And Anna's or Alain's, as well."

"That would mean one or both returned to Scotland." I chuckled. "Duh." But Alec's words shocked me, nonetheless. Anna felt so alive to me. Like I could reach out and talk to her. Sometimes, I had to remind myself she was long gone, and perhaps, her bones rested on some hillside in the Highlands.

Early the next day, I got a voice mail from Maggie. *If you have time this afternoon, stop by for a chat. I have something to talk to you about.*

Being the newest hire in the department, I immediately wondered if there was a problem. Did someone complain about a lecture? Was a student unhappy with a test grade? Students forgot that they earned their grade, I didn't deal them out willy-nilly like a deck of cards. I decided to listen to the message again, and the word 'chat' made me feel better. No one asked an employee to come in for a 'chat' if they were about to get the boot.

As soon as my last class ended, I picked up my backpack and headed for Maggie's office. On my way, a student asked if we could meet. I couldn't say no, especially if the 'chat' was about my performance. I flipped my wrist for the time and told the student we could meet in five minutes.

A half hour later, I rushed to Maggie's office, hoping she hadn't taken off. Luckily, her office door was open. She welcomed me warmly and offered a seat. The smile on her face made me feel better. But her closing her office door did not.

"How's it going?" asked Maggie.

I wondered if she wanted an answer regarding my work or my personal life. Or maybe she just wanted to find out if my apartment was suitable. I decided to play it safe. "Everything's good. No complaints."

"Great. I take it the apartment is working out?" she asked as she poured a cup of coffee. The nutty aroma was comforting. "Want some?"

"Sure. Thanks." Another good sign. Someone about to get fired is never offered a cup of coffee.

Maggie handed over the warm mug and piled a couple of creamers and sugar packets on the edge of her desk. "How's the cat?"

"The apartment is perfect and the cat's adorable. I enjoy the company."

"It's got to be tough uprooting yourself and moving to where you don't know anyone."

"I'm so busy with classes that I hardly have much time to socialize, but I have met some of the faculty. They've all been nice."

"Good to hear." Maggie sipped her coffee and then ruffled through some papers. "I have something I want to propose to you. A great opportunity."

For the first time since I walked into Maggie's office, my shoulders relaxed, and the beginnings of a tension headache subsided. Now, I had to refocus on Maggie's conversation, midstream.

"…Easter Island. There's room for another professor to join the dig. It will start in January and right now I can't say how long it will go on. There's enough funding for at least six months, and hopefully more will come through, so you could be down there for twelve."

I must have looked puzzled because she quickly added, "I know you were supposed to teach two semesters. I'm sure I'll find something for you when you return. This is a great opportunity. A chance for you to get real recognition and your name in some important journals."

"Easter Island. You mean off South America? Isn't that in the middle of nowhere?"

"Yes, it is, but then you and the rest of the staff can concentrate on your research and findings. There will be a dozen students and three profs, one of which could be you."

"Why me?"

"Mercedes had to pull out. The dig didn't fit into her wedding plans. Well, to each his own, but I doubt she'll ever get a tenured-track position. Universities won't invest in a prof unless they are going to publish or take the university name around the world. You don't have to give me an answer right away. But this is a great opportunity. Think about it."

"Sure. Thanks. I will." I started to pick up my backpack when Maggie continued with her normal bluntness.

"How's the boyfriend? History, right? St. Andrews, I think you said?"

"Yes…he's fine. He just gave me some incredible news. We might be related. I mean ten generations ago kind-of-related."

Maggie raised her eyebrows. "That's fascinating. How did he come to learn about that?"

I told her the story, the abridged version.

"Well, I've dabbled a bit in my family tree, too. My DNA is from everywhere, some Native American, a bit from the Mediterranean area, and the Middle East."

"That's quite a combination."

"I'll say. It makes the search exciting. Wait a minute." She scooted to a file cabinet, second drawer down, and pulled out a folder. "I have something that you might find interesting." She pulled out a sheet of paper. "I found this on the internet. It's how your DNA is broken down over many generations." She leaned over her desk and shoved the remaining sugar packets to the side. In their place, she positioned a paper so I could see it properly. "This is a list of Queen Elizabeth II's ancestors." She pointed to the top of the list. "Elizabeth can trace her ancestry back to James VI of Scotland, who was also James I of England. His daughter, Elizabeth Stuart, inherited 50% of his genes. Her daughter Sophia had 25%. If you continue through the Georges, the Edwards and Victoria, Elizabeth has less than one percent of her ten-times great-grandfather's DNA. Genetically, they are hardly related."

I picked up the paper and scanned the queen's pedigree.

"Here. Let me make you a copy. You can tell your boyfriend about it."

"Thanks. I think he'll find it fascinating."

Maggie had a small printer behind her desk. In a minute, she handed me the warm paper.

"I appreciate the offer. The dig. I'll get back to you on it."

"Sure. It's a great opportunity."

As I turned to go, I could feel Maggie's eyes. I wondered if there was something else.

"Hanna. Easter Island is remote, and the location of the dig is even more so. It's primitive and there's no allowance for visitors."

As Maggie barreled out the facts of her offer, I fingered my engagement ring and envisioned Alec's disappointment. This could be a breaking point, the end of our relationship. Was this Fate playing with my life?

"Is this going to be an issue for your boyfriend?"

I mumbled something. I don't remember what. All I recall is my mouth went dry as if it was filled with cotton balls. I grabbed my bag and hurried out of her office, grateful to hear the door click shut.

CHAPTER THIRTY-TWO
TRINITY

MAGGIE FLOODED MY computer and faculty mailbox with information about Easter Island. Her description of the volcanic island as remote was an understatement. Discovered by the Dutch, it was twenty-five-hundred miles west of South America and eleven-hundred miles from the nearest land mass. Its real name was Rapa Nui, and it was one of those locales from which you couldn't get home at a moment's notice. Travel took time and planning.

To get to Hanga Roa, the capital city, meant flying into Santiago, Chile first. A flight from New York, with one layover in Miami, would take about thirteen hours. Multiple stops could save on airfare, but it would take almost twenty-four hours. Then, another five-and-a-half hours to get to what one brochure described as *the most remote airport in the world*. Maybe for some, who wanted to get away from their frenetic lives, this was a plus. I could deal with the isolation for a week or two, but six months to a year was crazy. I didn't come to New York City just to be shuttled away, six months later, to some island that most people have never heard of. At least that's how I rationalized it.

I practiced my refusal to Maggie: *Thank you for the opportunity, but I like...no, I love teaching and I want to work on my classes for another semester. Maybe take on a heavier load.* Or, *I have a dying aunt in New Jersey who is dependent on me. I'm her only family.* My made-up excuses sounded convincing, until I started to think about my career; then Maggie's words played with my brain. *This is a great opportunity, one that isn't offered to everyone. If you want to make a name for yourself, you must be willing to sacrifice.* I was betting Alec wouldn't see it her way.

After the arrival of the first brochure, messages popped-up on my computer. *Let me know your decision ASAP. The departure date had been moved up two weeks, to just after the NEW YEAR.* And: *The director is excited about your possible participation. Can I tell him – YES?!!!*

That was followed by another tantalizing brochure. The trifold was filled with photos of white sand beaches, tropical bungalows, spas, and the famous Mo'ai, the large carved granite statues with oversized heads. The dig was timed perfectly. Who wouldn't crave the warmth of Polynesia in January? But the pamphlet was meant as a tease to lure vacationers. I didn't fit that description. There would be little time to lay on a beach. The only tan I would get was while digging in an even more remote area along the north shore, near another archaeological site: Papa Vaka. The only diversion would be the faculty and staff from two other universities, one from New Zealand and the other from France. If this dig was anything like Darien National Park, leisure time would be spent sleeping or catching up on paperwork. Hopefully, that wouldn't include kidnapping by some paramilitary group.

I was not surprised that Easter Island was a chosen destination. It was a Mecca for archaeological expeditions. The major question that scientists were still searching for was what caused the decline of the civilization that built the statues? And how was that related to the ebb and flow of the island's rat population? Apparently, the two were connected. I had a lot more research to do, and while I found the prospect intriguing, I was not looking forward to uprooting myself again.

All thoughts of an exotic locale disappeared when my phone rang out. It was Alec. In the split second before answering, I wondered about connectivity on Easter Island. Would I even be able to talk to him? Or would I have to survive on letters? I'd have to ask Maggie about this.

"Hey," I said.

"Hi, Hanna. I love and miss you." He paused.

"I love you, too."

"Hey, I've been continuing the family research, but I'm afraid I don't have much more to show for it."

"Well, it's crazy busy here. I can hardly keep my head above water. I'll be glad when I have a few semesters under my belt and can rely on all the work I've done." On the other end, I could hear Alec groan, or maybe it was a moan. That was the last thing he wanted to hear – my future in the States rather than in Scotland.

"I checked out information about Thistlestraith. Alain's ancestral home. I'm coming up empty. None of the historical registries have any information."

"Did you look into clan registries, too?" I asked.

"Yes. Nothing. There was a MacArthur clan. But by the time Alain and Anna meet, it was on the down slide. The MacArthurs were historically important much earlier. I also checked the death registry and the only Anna MacArthur I found is someone from Cornwall. But the dates don't match up. For Alain MacArthur, there's nothing. It's as if they never existed."

"Then my guess is they didn't return to Scotland."

"I'm assuming that as well."

"That pushes me in another direction. I'm planning a visit to the colonial burial grounds in lower Manhattan. There's the oldest graveyard at Trinity Church, and surprisingly, the second oldest is a Jewish cemetery. It was in use during Anna's time. I talked to someone at the synagogue that owns the cemetery to get information. I was told I could get a tour."

"Is there a registry?"

"I asked and didn't get a firm answer one way or the other. The guy I spoke to said that once I'm on the tour, all questions would be answered." I waited for Alec's response, but for a moment there was nothing. It felt like he was waiting for me to finish. "Are you there, Alec?"

"Yes. Sorry. There's one other bit of news. Totally unrelated. I heard that Dr. Jones' case came before the court. He was found guilty of harassment and stalking."

"How did you find out? Was it in the news? Did he get jail time?"

"I bumped into your friend, Susannah. Every so often, I see her at St. Andrews. I think she's dating a faculty member, a prof down the hall. And yes, Max got some jail time but not as much as he should have. One month and a huge fine. Aberdeen has released him for good. He'll never find work at another university."

I mumbled, "He should be exiled to an island—"

"What was that? An island? I didn't hear you. Our connection isn't great."

"Nothing. It's not important."

"No, tell me. You want to go to an island? Over the winter break?"

"I'm not sure. I don't know—"

"The semester break starts a couple of days before Christmas and classes don't resume until the end of January. We could have four full weeks together."

I swallowed hard. Didn't Maggie say that the dig was starting shortly after New Year's?

"I could come to New York for the first two weeks." Alec sounded like a little boy opening birthday presents. "We could spend the first seven days in bed and only go out when we're hungry. The second week, you

306

could give me a tour of Columbia, the New York sites, and whatever else you think I might be interested in. I want to see the Christmas tree at Rockefeller Center. Maybe a show or two. Then, you could introduce me to some of your friends. I'd like to meet Maggie and we could visit Jess."

"Jess would like that." As if my comment never registered, Alec rambled on.

"Then we could take a flight to some island in the Caribbean, something remote, and soak in the sun and drown ourselves in one of those hot-tubs large enough for two. And Hanna…maybe…we could get married – destination wedding – barefoot on the beach, tropical breezes playing with your veil and your white dress whipping around your knees—"

"Alec. That sounds good…but I don't know." Normally, I would have loved Alec's suggestion. But I was unnerved by his mentioning an island and how close he came to the truth. At that moment, I made two important decisions. I was never going to introduce Alec to Maggie, nor would I tell him about her offer until the last minute.

The tour planned for the Jewish cemetery the following Sunday never happened. It rained the entire weekend. We rescheduled, but because of the bar mitzvah of the tour guide's youngest son, we had to postpone until November, a week before Thanksgiving. Therefore, I decided to make use of my time and prowl other colonial church graveyards in lower Manhattan.

That turned out easier said than done. Few still existed. And those that did, did not fit the time, location, or Anna's and Alain's religion. The First Old Dutch Reformed Church did not match the timeline. It was destroyed in 1690, almost ten years before Anna and Alain arrived. The next two churches, the second Dutch church, which turned Episcopal with the British conquest, and the Garden Street Church, would not have worked either. Alain's Catholicism and Anna's Judaism were unacceptable, and even if that was not the case, the New York Stock Exchange building obliterated any trace of the Garden Street Church and its adjacent graveyard.

Notwithstanding its name, another church, St. Andrew's, had possibilities. It was built between 1708 and 1712. It had a graveyard, and although it was an Episcopal Church, the ancestor of the first American Catholic saint, Elizabeth Ann Seton, was buried there. Maybe their liberality would make the church elders more accepting. But one condition the church didn't meet was its Staten Island location. I crossed it off my list.

A search for public cemeteries was also a dead end. The oldest, the New York City Marble Cemetery, was not started until 1831.

Trinity Church on Wall Street held the most promise. Construction was completed in 1698, so the timing worked. There was a large graveyard adjacent to the building, and occasionally non-members were interred. As a result, I focused on the most famous church in Manhattan. Unfortunately, no tours were offered, but the security personnel near the entrance appeared to answer tourists' questions. I watched them point out directions with a finger and a swish of their hand.

When I entered the gated graveyard, about mid-day, the air was chilled, and the wind whipped around the edges of the ancient building. The few leaves that clung to the trees for dear life were tossed about until they had no choice but to surrender and join their brethren swirling in tiny cyclones in and around the headstones. I pulled my scarf, a handmade gift from Grams, over my mouth and ears. Halloween was next week, and an ancient graveyard was the perfect place to visit.

Strolling along the path that separated the living from the dead, I felt an imaginary pull to this hallowed place. Piercing sirens, screeching tires, and blaring horns melted away. Like a time traveler, each step away from the hustle and bustle of the modern world brought me closer to Anna.

I must not have been the only one to feel that way. Visitors who roamed around the gravestones talked in whispers. In one corner, the leader of a tour group lowered the volume of his voice. I slowed my pace while he titillated his customers with the secrets of Trinity Church.

"You've heard about the treasure beneath Trinity Church?" His voice was enticing, like a circus barker, luring onlookers to pay to see the two-headed dog.

None of those standing around said a word except one teenage boy. "You mean like the movie, 'American Treasure?' Is it real?"

"'National Treasure,' young man. Sorry to disappoint you. There's nothing valuable beneath Trinity except the famous buried here." To prove his point, he stomped on the grass as if to wake the dead. "But there are a lot of other interesting secrets."

"Like what?" the teenager asked.

"Did you know that a pirate helped to build Trinity Church?" The guide closed one eye as if covered by an eyepatch. I half expected him to growl, *Aye Matey*. The audience shook their heads. I was tempted to join in because this was news to me.

"Well, it's true. Captain William Kidd was a Scotsman and a pirate, and if you ask me, I don't know which is worse." When the guide was the only one to laugh, he cleared his throat and went on. "Kidd lent the church builders the tools from his ship to lift and place the stones. And the only thanks he got was to be arrested and shipped off to England where he was executed twice for piracy."

"How can someone be executed twice?" asked a young girl next to the teen. This must have been his sister. They both had freckled faces and red hair, except most of her hair was covered with a knitted pumpkin hat.

"The first rope placed around the old pirate's neck broke as his body was tossed twelve feet from the gallows. The poor executioner had no choice but to try again. The second time was the charm. After the outlaw was pronounced dead, his body was left to rot for all to see, so they would learn the lesson of breaking the law."

Some in the audience giggled. The guide was a good storyteller.

Reluctantly, I left the group and continued down the winding path. The sun had reappeared, warming the air. I lowered my scarf and reached for my sunglasses in my satchel. I was able to read some of the markers, those nearest the path, but there were many more I couldn't access. That would have required walking on the graves. Since I didn't see anyone else doing that, I thought it best to stay on the solid path.

Some headstones were barely readable, the sharp edges smoothed by time. Many were chiseled to resemble bedposts. The thought that the ancients compared death to sleep gave me the creeps, but their explanation was not unusual. Every ancient culture, whether Egyptian, Mayan, or Mesopotamian, developed a religion around the myths of death. Dying was a scary prospect, and religion attempted to make it acceptable.

In the south churchyard, I passed by the impressive monument that held the bones of Alexander Hamilton. His wife, Elizabeth Schuyler, was nearby. To the left of Hamilton stood a memorial to inventor, Robert Fulton. I had read that John Peter Zenger was buried here somewhere. Zenger, a little-known printer and journalist, was a champion of the free press. He was one of Alec's favorite historical figures. Zenger lived during

Anna's time, so I felt a kinship toward the man. But his headstone was nowhere.

There was so much history buried here. I could have spent all day taking pictures or rubbings, if allowed. There was another grave I was anxious to see, the oldest in Manhattan. Located in the north churchyard, the rounded two-sided marker was for five-year-old, Richard Churcher. Although he died in 1681, the headstone's etchings were in remarkable condition. As I stared at the words inscribed, I couldn't help but feel a familiarity. I tried to remember if Anna had mentioned visiting this churchyard, or maybe it was just because the surname Churcher sounded like Churchill. I wondered if there was a family connection. Maybe Alec would know.

I spent much of the day searching the old churchyard for Alain's or Anna's headstone. At times, I pretended that if this was a scary movie, somehow the dead would get my attention: an exposed root causing me to trip and accidentally find what I was looking for, or my glove or hat would be tossed in the wind, only to land on my ancestors' tombstones. Of course, none of that happened, and I came away with nothing to show for my long day of searching. I was disappointed, but I reasoned it would have been too easy to find Alain's remains on the first try. I still held out hope. A church that was enlightened enough to allow a Jew, New York City's Mayor Ed Koch, to be buried in one of its newer cemeteries, might have accepted Anna Isaac MacArthur three centuries earlier.

The moment I turned the key in the door to my apartment, my phone rang. Alec always called about this time, and I wondered what additional information he had. Without looking, I said, "Hey, Alec. Hold on a sec. Let me put my stuff down. I have so much to tell you." I heard a voice, hoarse, like Alec had a bad cold. I threw down my coat, picked up the sleepy cat, and together we plopped on the sofa. "I hope you aren't sick. You don't sound good."

"That's because it's not Alec," the voice laughed. "It's Maggie. I hope this isn't a bad time."

"Why no." I hesitated. "Just a…long day." A lump wedged in my throat. "I'm good now," I lied.

310

"Have you given any more thought to Easter Island? The lead on the dig has been bugging the heck out of me for an answer. Because if your answer is no, he needs time to offer this great opportunity to someone else."

"Oh, he has to know so soon?"

"Well, it's almost November. The advance team leaves in six weeks, and the rest follow two weeks later. If you need more time, I can request you be listed on the later departure date. I'm sure that would be agreeable. Everyone is anxious for you to come. Especially after I told them about your success in Panama."

"That's nice. But I haven't had a chance—"

"Hanna this is a once-in-a-lifetime opportunity. I wouldn't be pushing it so much if I didn't think so."

"I appreciate your offering my name."

"My pleasure. You deserve it. I called Susannah with the news. This has her blessing, you know. She was impressed and is hoping you'll take it."

"Well, then…um…I…." My throat tightened. I felt like I was trapped in a box, strangled in a straitjacket. I knew if I said yes, the angst of that decision would weigh heavily on me. But when faced with a life-altering decision, I did what I always did; I thought about the future. I tried to see myself ten, twenty-five or even fifty years from now. If I declined the invitation, would I be sorry? Would I regret that I let Maggie's great opportunity slip through my fingers? I shut my eyes, as if that would help. But I knew that would be as useless as tossing a coin.

"I think I hear some doubt creeping into your decision. It's okay. I know I'm pushing. You don't have to—"

"No. That's not it…um." And then I heard a voice that was not my own. "I'll do it. Tell the team I'll join them."

"Great. I'm so thrilled for you. You won't be sorry. Did I ever tell you I've been to Easter Island? Long story. Another time." Her voice faltered, as if she was checking her watch. "We'll talk later. Gotta go. Have a good—"

If Maggie said another word, I never heard it. I clicked off the phone and shoved it between the velvety sofa cushions. The cat, not appreciative of sudden movements, scurried off my lap while I buried my head in a pillow and sobbed.

My tears were not because of my failure of finding Alain's or Anna's grave. I wasn't angry with Maggie's phone call and her constant

311

pressure. I wasn't even mad at myself for accepting the position. What did me in was my thoughtlessness. Not once during my conversation with Maggie, did I stop to think how Alec would feel. How my going away would impact him. Impact us. I could have said, *I need more time, another day, to talk it over with Alec.* Or *I promised to marry Alec after the fall semester.* I could have been more careful, looked at my phone, and seeing it was Maggie, not answered. I could have put Alec first and said, *No.* For once, I could have done this for him. After he had done so much for me.

I don't know how long I lay there, but when I awakened an hour later, the pillow was still damp, and I was reminded immediately of my terrible decision, which by now was also unalterable. Because, if I knew Maggie, she had already shared her victory with Susannah and the director of the dig.

I dragged myself into the bathroom, filled a cup with water and gasped when I saw my eyes. Sleep had not diminished the redness. It almost made me want to cry again, but just then the buzz of my phone made the situation even worse. This time it had to be Alec. As I picked up the phone and saw his name on the screen, I realized the only truth I knew. I loved Alec more than ever. And I didn't deserve him.

CHAPTER THIRTY-THREE
THE SINS OF THE FATHER
APRIL 7, 1712

"WHY WON'T YOU tell me?" asked Alexandra. "What is it about Pierre that you find objectionable? He comes from a good family. The St. Martins are prosperous and well thought of in the Jewish community. Pierre has been a gentleman to me...and polite to you, and Papa."

It was the next morning. Alain and Baruch were at City Hall investigating Lucy's whereabouts, and Deborah had returned home. I was at my desk where I faced a difficult conversation with my daughter. One that didn't have an easy resolution. For the truth would unearth the past and I preferred it dead and buried. Exasperated with my silence, Alexandra threw herself into the chair next to my bed and pushed out her lower lip. The longer I took to respond, the more insincere I sounded. Left with the only excuse I could think of, I justified our objection to the son because the father transported slaves. Having lived through the insurrection only hours ago, it seemed the logical conclusion.

That led to more argument, including the one proposed by the shopkeeper last night. Apparently, Alexandra was listening. "Many of your acquaintances own Negroes. You have invited these people to your home. They sit at your table. How is that different?"

I put down my pen, closed the inkwell, and turned to my interrogator. "If you are referring to Rachel, she knows my feelings. She defends her actions by saying she provides Ruth, Jenny, and Lucy a better life than what they would have had in Africa or at the sugar plantations in the Caribbean. She feeds and clothes them; when they are sick, she calls for Dr. Emmanuel."

"That is a paltry excuse. If slavery is loathsome to you, then none will do. Minister de Lucena and his wife's theft of labor appears more humane because their slaves are not chained in the hold of a ship."

Alexandra stood and stepped closer to offer her final summation. "And when is it fair to blame the son for the sins of the father?"

I looked at my child like I had never seen her before. When did she formulate opinions on such weighty matters? Would she have felt the same about slavery if it didn't involve Pierre? Or would she be like most of Manhattan who went about their daily business ignoring the number of dark-skinned workers around us. I wondered about her sincerity. And mine. And would our talk have been different if her father had been home?

When Alain returned from the gaol, he said nothing and fell exhausted into a chair. The loss of his leg made walking long distances tiring. Especially after being up most of the night saving the city from destruction.

He leaned forward and covered his face. I spread my skirts, sat on the floor by his chair, and unbuckled his peg-leg. There were times when the stump ached and burned, and it helped if I massaged it. He pressed his head to the back of the chair and closed his eyes.

Alain was still a handsome man. His body fit and vigorous. When we walked down the street, it was not unusual for heads to turn, and the more brazen ladies winked and nodded. Although the years had increased the number of lines in the corner of his eyes and the gray hairs at his temple, I still found Alain desirable. I wondered if he felt the same. Did he notice what my mirror reminded me every day?

After a few minutes, he roused, smiled faintly, and took my hand. After all these years, his touch still excited me. It was also reassuring. It had always been that way, the comfort we found in each other. I pressed his fingers to my lips and waited. The time for explanations about what had transpired at City Hall would come. When he was ready. Then, he would tell me everything.

"I'm looking for the whereabouts of the female slave, known as Lucy," said Alain to a city goaler with fat jowls that jiggled as he descended the City Hall steps. Alain remembered the man from his days as a convict, and the memories were not pleasant. The last time the two were in the same room together, the goaler had to restrain Alain so Baruch could saw off Alain's leg.

The man stopped, shielded his eyes from the sun's glare and glanced at Alain's wooden leg. "Eh. What's that you say?" The goaler continued to bobble his head from peg-leg to Alain's face, and back again. The official scratched his head and blamed his uncertainty on the empty whisky flask hidden in his jacket pocket. However, his confusion might have stemmed from another source. Alain's silver-tipped cane and his rich suit of clothes embellished with many silver buttons were not the usual adornments of a former prisoner.

"The voman vas arrested last night," added Baruch. "After the insurrection. She's vith child."

The official smirked. "You mean the bitch who almost bit off my finger?" He held up his right hand. One digit was wrapped in a dirty rag. "She's a wild one. Tried to be nice and this is the thanks I got."

"Can you tell us where she is?" asked Alain.

The officer hesitated while an open palm emerged. Alain tossed a coin at the goaler which he buried in his pocket. "She's in the cellar with the other murderers. But if I were you, I'd stayed away from that one. No telling what part of you she'll bite off."

Before the goaler was out of earshot, Baruch yelled, "Come to my surgery. Human bites can be lethal."

The man scoffed, tipped his hat, and disappeared down an alley.

Alain looked curiously at his friend with a half-smile.

"You never know vhen you vill need the services of a man in his position, Let's call it an investment."

When Alain stopped relating the events at City Hall, I asked, "Did you ever see Lucy?"

"No. No inducement could get us in. After the events of last night, no visitors were allowed in the building."

"The first goaler could have told you that. Surely, he knew."

"But then he wouldn't have fattened his purse. We'll try again tomorrow."

I stood, straightened my skirts, and checked the embroidered scarf tucked into my bodice. "Alexandra and I talked this morning about Pierre. It didn't go well. We need to talk again."

Alain followed me toward the stairs. "Aye. Maybe I should be the one who does the talking this time. Our daughter needs to know that we are united in our decision."

A heavy knock at the door jolted me. I was a bit on edge, even though the city appeared to be returning to its usual gusto. To my surprise, standing on our stoop was Pierre St. Martin. Simultaneously relieved and a bit surprised, Alain welcomed him in, but the young man's presence felt awkward. Especially since he and his father were not part of our dinner party last evening. I wonder if he knew. He must have.

"Monsieur. Madam. Forgive me for disturbing you without an invitation." Pierre removed his hat and fingered the gold braided edging.

While the men talked and exchanged pleasantries, I studied Pierre's silhouette. I was not surprised he caught my daughter's eye. Expensive lace frills cascaded from the sleeves of his brown waistcoat. White silk stockings and stacked leathered heels showed off a well-turned leg. His hair, powdered perfectly, was brushed back, and tied with a black ribbon. Pierre was quite the gallant.

After inquiring about our health, Pierre stated the reason for his visit. "With the troubles last night, I felt compelled to inquire about your family's welfare." He hesitated and played with the lace at his sleeves.

Alain looked at me. His lips showed the barest hint of a smile. "As you can see, my wife and I are in fine fettle."

"Yes. And I'm grateful the Almighty has spared you. Um…and your daughters? Are they…" Pierre's voice trailed off as he glanced at the staircase.

"My daughters slept through the disturbance, but then much of it was on Maiden Lane. Except for the smoke, they were in no danger."

"I'm relieved to hear that." Pierre passed his hat from hand to hand as if he was about to put it back on his head. A hopeful sign that his visit was coming to an end. "If you are in need of my protection, sir, to serve as a shield for your family, you have just to say the word. I would be honored."

Alain reached up a sleeve for a handkerchief to cover his mouth. His throat clearing disguised muffled laughter. "I beg your pardon. I must have inhaled too much smoke last night. Thank you for your considerate offer." He coughed again. "But why would that be necessary?"

"My father mentioned that you have been appointed fire warden. An honor, to be sure, sir. Therefore, your presence is required on the front lines of the battle. Word has spread this morning that almost twenty brave citizens were killed or wounded by cowardly ruffians."

With no more need of the handkerchief, Alain returned it to his sleeve. "Cowards, sir? I think that a bit harsh. Men fighting for their freedom are hardly that. Other than protecting one's family, it is the bravest act a man can undertake."

"Don't you believe the slaves behaved cowardly? When they ambushed those who were doing their duty to save the town?"

"That is easy to say, especially coming from a man like yourself who, upon arising this morning, did exactly as he pleased and went wherever he wished to go. With no thought of seeking permission. No one ordered your day or forced your compliance with threats and lashes. Bondage compels the enslaved to do what is necessary to gain his freedom, even if it looks like cowardice to others."

"Pierre." Alexandra ended the discussion between the men, and both smiled when they saw her standing on the staircase. "I didn't know you were here. No one told me."

"Mr. St. Martin was checking on our good health," said Alain. He turned his attention back to Pierre. "Will that be all?"

The young man placed his hat on his head and kept his eyes on Alexandra. "I'm pleased you are well. I bid you and your family *adieu*." He bowed toward Alain and me and then turned to Alexandra. "Mademoiselle."

"Good day." Alain took a step closer to Pierre and opened the door.

Alexandra rushed down the final steps. "Please, let me walk you to the stoop." She looked at her father for permission which he offered haltingly. Alexandra ignored his reticence. In her mind, a yes was a yes.

"Mama! Do you want to hear what Auntie Davina has to say?"

After Pierre left, my daughter was in a wonderful temperament. She had put aside our terse conversation from earlier in the day, and I had almost forgot about the newly arrived letter. It was just the other day when Alain surprised Alexandra with it.

Alexandra returned to the chair by my bed and unfolded the letter. Her lips moved as she scanned the words. "Auntie says she thinks about me all the time." More silence followed by a chuckle. "Here she says she misses my chatter, our outings to market, and my reading to her in the evening." She pressed the pages to her chest. "Do I really talk too much?"

"I think your aunt means that she misses the sound of your voice. It's lovely to have young voices filling a house."

As Alexandra continued to read, her smile slowly dissipated, replaced by worry lines on her forehead. "She's scared. She wishes I were home, in Scotland, to be there for her lying-in. I'm sure Auntie is worried, this being her first child. Were you scared when you had me?"

"Yes, of course. All women worry, but Auntie Davina and my friend Sally, who was like a sister, were with me when you came along."

"Is that who my sister was named for?"

"You were named for your grandmother, and Sally was named for my friend. She had no children to remember her by."

My daughter sighed and looked pensively out the window. She refolded the letter and traced the edges with her fingers. "I miss Auntie, too. It's hard to rely on letters that are months old. Her baby might have already been born. Maybe he's ill. Maybe Auntie needs my help." Alexandra waved the letter in the air, like a flag in surrender. "Sometimes, I wish I was back home." She looked at me sideways. "I would miss you and Papa and Sally, of course." Then she mumbled something and sighed again. "You may read my letter, if you wish." She placed it on a table and walked out of my bedchamber.

My father used to say, *A mother understands what a child does not say*. How true that was with Alexandra. In her eyes, last night's dinner was a debacle. Another reminder that there were few eligible young men, especially now with our newly acquired wealth. But after our talk earlier this morning, Alexandra realized that a match with the French lad was not acceptable. Was her reading the letter the beginning of a suggestion? That Alexandra was contemplating a different future? One I couldn't bear to consider. Twice, she called Scotland home.

"I'm coming with you. And don't tell me no," I said.

The next morning, Alain rose early to meet Baruch at the gaol. Quickly, I poured ice cold water in the basin, washed my face, and brushed my hair. "Lucy might need a woman and Deborah is in bed with a terrible headache. Didn't Baruch say so?" I pulled on my stockings and tied them with ribbon just above the knee.

"It won't be pleasant," said Alain after tugging at his breeches and buttoning the fore-flap and the knee band.

"You forget. I am familiar with the gaol."

Mary entered without a word and laced my stays, tied on the pockets and hip pad, and helped with the first of three petticoats.

"I've learned it's useless to say no to my wife." Alain laughed while he buttoned a fresh linen stock and straightened his waistcoat.

I took another bite of a buttered roll while Mary buckled my shoes. "You are the most intelligent of husbands."

Alain scoffed while pulling on his coat and I grabbed my shawl and my hat. On the way out the door, Alain finished his dress with his tri-cornered hat and thrust his sword between the slits of his coat.

It wasn't long before we joined Baruch at City Hall and a different goaler pointed the way toward a steep staircase that led to the cellar. Our elongated shadows, created by the goaler's candle, danced as we descended into the miserable conditions below. The thump of Alain's peg-leg on the stone steps aroused the sequestered prisoners. Chains rattled and men grunted. Perhaps they thought their next meal had arrived. With no window and thus no daylight, all sense of time was lost.

The narrow width of the brick walkway and the suffocating fetid air added to the oppressive feel. I wondered if this was difficult for Alain, and he was suppressing the urge to turn around and head for daylight. I know I was. Baruch seemed less disturbed by the restrictive surroundings, but that didn't stop him from placing a reassuring hand on his friend's back.

The goaler stopped at the first cell. He scraped the keys on the metal bars. Any prisoners who were still asleep had no choice but to awaken. Lucy was easy to find. The only female, she was alone.

"Make it snappy," the goaler said as he stepped back and waited for us to speak to the prisoner.

"I need to examine my patient. Could you open the cell door?"

The goaler looked wide-eyed. "It's filthy in there. Not fit for human habitation." He spat on the ground and then pointed to the inside of the cell. "Look at them walls. Look closely." He held the candle at a different angle and let out a stream of curses when the hot wax dripped on his hand.

I squinted where he pointed and waited until my eyes adjusted to the dark. The glow from the candle made the walls, the hay strewn on the floor, and the huddled figure curled under a blanket appear in various shades of gray. And then I saw it. The walls appeared to be moving. In response to the candlelight, many large black insects, scurried up and down the cold stone. Some scampered in the opposite direction, trying to hide from the goaler's flame. He thought it a game and laughed as he watched the monsters flee. A few didn't make it. When their charred bodies smoked and curled into themselves, the goaler chortled his success.

"Now, are you sure you want to go inside? The stench alone will kill you, and the prisoner has already attacked one man." The goaler eyed Baruch. "He was a lot heftier than you."

"I must check the mother's condition. I have strict orders from her owner. I am to look after his investment."

"Well, if you say so. Makes no difference to me if she lives or dies, but I don't need anyone complaining that they've lost their property on my watch." The goaler huffed while struggling to get the key into the lock, twisting it until the door sprung open. "I have to lock up before I go, but I'll leave the candle. There's about ten minutes left to burn." Then he looked at me and doffed his woolen cap. "At least it will keep the bugs away but I daresay the rats will care." As he turned to go, he gestured toward Lucy. "Hope she doesn't rip your hearts out. If she does, not my fault. I warned you." The goaler's footsteps grew fainter until they disappeared behind the door at the top of the stairs.

Lucy sat up but kept the blanket tight around her shoulders. Her hair, covered with bits of straw, looked like a pin cushion. Her skirt was torn and stained.

From my pocket, I brought out a napkin that held some biscuits, a piece of cheese, and an apple tart. Lucy plucked the food from my hands and thrust it into her mouth. Crumbs fell into her lap and on the ground, but none escaped. Each morsel was devoured.

While she ate, I found the source of the stench. In a corner of the cell, a wooden bucket served as a latrine. In another, was a similar bucket with a ladle. Alain picked up the dipper and threw it back. "Dead rat," he said.

"Lucy, ve have little time," said Baruch. "Ve vant to help you. Ve vill tell the constable that you vere novhere near the fire vhen it started. You had nothing to do vith it."

The slave began to rock and shake her head.

"Please," I said. "It will save you and your baby."

Lucy looked up. The candle reflected her wet face. "It don't matter. Quaco is dead. I told him to run. He wouldn't listen."

"We don't know for sure. Many were taken prisoner."

She hugged her belly and continued swaying. "All de same. Gonna die anyway. Better to be in de ground, your spirit free to be wid God, den to live on dis earth chained like an animal."

"You must live for your baby," I pleaded. "Quaco's child."

"So, de baby can grow up as a slave. I hope he dies along wid me."

"That won't happen. They will not execute you while the baby grows inside."

"Then I hope de baby is born dead." She raised her hand, clenched it, and meant to strike her belly, but Baruch stopped her.

"Times up." The goaler returned. His key plunged into the lock, and the door sprung open again.

"I must stay vith the prisoner. She's about to have the baby."

"She don't look like she's—"

"Some vomen have a respite between pains. But I can assure you, the child is coming, and it may come quickly. You von't have time to get me."

"And I need to stay as well. She'll need a woman."

Alain looked at me. His eyes were a combination of surprise and concern.

"Hmm. Well, if you want to stay here in this filth, be my guest." He pointed to Alain. "You must leave."

What surprised Baruch and I the most, and maybe even Lucy, was that the infant, a girl, came a few hours later. She was tiny and thin and wailed pitifully. Lucy held her to her breast but there was nothing.

The baby's cries brought the goaler, and he demanded that we leave. I wrapped the child in my shawl and offered her to Lucy, to hold one last time. But the new mother waved us away. She knew she was doomed.

"Give my daughter to Ruth. She will care for de baby as her own."

As I turned to leave, with the child in my arms, I said, "Lucy, we will do everything we can."

She nodded and then hid her tears behind the blood-stained blanket. As Baruch and I walked up the stone steps, our shoes echoed our ascent, but it couldn't block out the cries from the woman we were leaving behind.

When I reached Rachel's home, Ruth took the baby. "Did she give you a name for de child?" Ruth asked.

"No. We forgot to ask."

"Then I will call her Rose. A rose is beautiful just like dis baby. De rose is a sign of love, a mother's love. But don't be fooled by a rose's beauty for it is armed with thorns."

I stayed to help wash Rose and swaddle her in a clean cloth. She was a delicate child. Her fingers long and tapered like a stem with paper-thin nails. Her lips were soft like a petal. The baby's name suited her. Soon, another slave, a wet nurse, arrived. She went for the baby, unpinned her bodice. The woman and baby found relief.

When I left Rose in Ruth's care. the sky had turned grey as if the world was preparing for night, although it was still afternoon. I walked the streets that led to my home. How different the city felt since the revolt. Life had returned. The streets were full of matrons. Their market baskets filled with fresh bread, eggs, fish, or newly picked cabbage, peas, and kale. Street peddlers called out their wares. One carried many large lanterns fitted on a large metal ring. Over his shoulder, a haversack was filled with smaller lamps. The knife grinder pushed a wheeled sharpener, crying out the service he provided to housewives. He was a colorful fellow with a checkered scarf around his neck, a buttonless coat, and torn moccasins. The sweep and his son carried various sized brooms. One, carried over the father's shoulder, had many extensions to reach into the bowels of chimneys. His hat was secured with a scarf tied under his chin. The faces and clothes of both were soot covered.

Spring was still in its infancy, but the day was warmer than usual. Many of the doors of the shops were open, inviting customers to enter. An older man stood in the doorway of Master Myer's shop, talking to the apprentice who was now a foot taller. The man tipped his hat and rushed off. The butcher's stand was empty. His business was finished, and his assistant was left wiping off the knives and cleavers. The bookseller's open door revealed several shoppers perusing shelves. I decided to join them. Roaming this shop was one of my favorite pastimes and would serve as a diversion from Lucy and her baby.

The first thing I noticed was the familiar scent. That comforting mixture of paper, ink, and leather binding. Some of the older books had a different smell, as if their pages had captured former owners and far-away places. I wandered the shelves, letting my fingers run along the spines, stopping at beloved titles. Some, I recognized as part of Alain's collection. I looked for new books to add to his library. At the far end of the shop was an alcove where I decided to search. Perhaps a hidden treasure was buried there. As I turned the corner, I came upon a young man and woman. Their backs were to me, and they appeared to be in a private conversation. Their bodies close, heads inclined to each other. They were too involved to notice my presence.

I quickly backed out to the center of the shop, turned, and left. As I walked away, I glanced over my shoulder several times. Relieved the couple had not noticed, I rushed to get home. Alain and I had a bigger problem than we realized. We needed to save Alexandra from Pierre. The man she was with in the book shop.

CHAPTER THIRTY-FOUR

SOULLESS

APRIL 17, 1712

THE FIRST THREE prisoners to be sentenced were brought into the Court of Quarter Sessions of the Peace. Following the eyewitness accounts of seventy-six white citizens and a few slaves, these prisoners were accused of being the ringleaders of the revolt. To demonstrate the government's far-reaching power, and as a warning to others, the most severe punishments were about to be doled out.

Alain, Baruch, and I stood in the gallery of the largest courtroom in City Hall. We were surrounded by ordinary folk: shopkeepers, craftsmen, tavern owners, and a few brought their wives. Bertram White was there and so was his sister, Alexandra's one-time chaperone. When I met her gaze, she nodded. Her face seemed older, her shoulders sagged, and her eyes were dull and lifeless. Perhaps living with her brother was worse than she imagined.

I scanned the faces of those around me and wondered what brought them to court today. What would make them want to stand for hours through dry legal discourse? Some may have wished to see justice served. Others sought revenge or to satisfy their perverted curiosity. For them, this was a sport. They would mock the slaves' pathetic condition, snicker when sentences were handed down, and hiss or cheer depending on what they thought was fair.

A man and his wife stood nearby. Their gaunt faces and patched clothes suggested a difficult life. The husband was highly agitated, waiting for the sentencing to begin. "The judge better not set these scoundrels loose. Not-a-one. The last time a slave was tried for disorder, the judge came this close to lettin' that rascal walk our streets and prey on our families." At first, his remarks seemed intended for his wife, but when he raised his voice and shook his fist, it was clear he sought a wider audience.

"Roger, if the judge decides there's little evidence or the owner accounts for his slave's whereabouts, then the judge has tae free 'em."

I thought about her choice of words. Even if the prisoners were acquitted, they would never be free.

"Ha! The owner doesn't want tae lose his property. Puttin' money above the truth. Shame, I say. Anyone can see the Negros' guilt. It's in the eyes, I tell ya."

"What if you're wrong?" asked his wife. "An innocent will be killed."

"Mark my words, woman." He pointed toward the three accused slaves. "I know what I'm talkin' about." He turned and put his face close to hers. "And if you don't like it, get yourself home."

Another man in the crowd scoffed. "Why don't you go with her. There's not enough room for two judges in this court."

The husband raised a fist. "Yeah, and who's goin' tae make me? A pisser like you?"

Both men stepped closer. Like roosters battling for dominance in the coop, they butted chests, each staring directly into the eye of the other. Nearby spectators stepped back, and Alain pulled me away. The kerfuffle brought a goaler running. He grabbed the two men. They were quickly tossed out of the courtroom followed by the wife, mumbling apologies.

The judge, Mayor Caleb Heathcote, called for order, and silence spilled over the court. He motioned for two of the three prisoners to be pressed forward. Their feet and hands shackled in chains, created a great noise as the metal restraints dragged across the wood floorboards. Their bare feet and legs were raw with gashes, dried blood, and scabs. Clothes were torn and burned. What was left of one slave's breeches served as a loincloth.

"Which one is called Robin?" asked the Judge as he peered over his metal spectacles.

Neither answered, but when the taller man turned his back on the court, his identity was clear. A few gasps and a hum of disgruntled whispers erupted around me. The constable motioned to one of the goalers, and together, they grabbed Robin's arms, forcing his body around. The goaler shoved his club under Robin's chin pushing his head up. But he couldn't erase the contempt in the condemned man's eyes.

"Hmm, that's better," the judge said as he reordered some papers. "Says here you are to be sentenced for the crime of conspiring with others on the twenty-fifth of March to hatch a revolt. And then again on the seventh of April, at a local tavern to carry out your devious plan."

Robin remained stoic. His glare, unwavering.

"You don't have to respond. You've already been pronounced guilty and there are enough witnesses to support the facts. Um." The mayor placed his spectacles on his head and licked a finger to turn to the next page. "And you helped supply the others with hatchets, clubs, axes, daggers, swords, knives, staves, and firearms. Then, once the moon set and it was pitch dark, you encouraged the firing of a barn on Maiden Lane. Um. Nasty bit of business."

Robin continued to say nothing. His head turned to one side as he peered around the room.

The judge smacked the papers on his desk and removed his spectacles. "Is the owner of this slave here today?"

A young man, hat in hand, rushed forward. A bandage tied around his head covered one eye. "Yes, sir. Adrian Hoghland. My father, also Adrian Hoghland, was killed in the revolt. I guess you can say I'm the owner. The other one, Claire, is mine, too."

At the mention of the second prisoner, the judge gestured for him to be brought another step closer. Claire stared at the floor. His body shuddered and in between whimpers he begged for leniency. His face was wet, and he attempted to lift a restrained shoulder to wipe his nose and mouth.

"Hmm, your slaves, Mr. Hoghland, have caused a great deal of harm, leading a bloody conspiracy. This was a deliberate action to cause harm. Waiting until late at night, while the city slept. Causing the deaths of nine good citizens, men of property, hard-working men, and wounding many more. Are you aware of that, sir?"

"Yes, yes, I am. My father is dead. My eye was almost gouged trying to save him." The owner's face shifted away from the judge, looking for sympathy around the room.

"Your father did not control his property," the judge continued. "I hope you do a better job." His voice got louder. "Maybe if your father had, he wouldn't be filling a hole in a graveyard." The judge looked at the young man. "How many more do you own?"

"Three, sir. Two domestics and a small boy."

"Um. Take care. Follow the statute. Your Negroes must not congregate in a group larger than three. As you see, there's good reason for that law."

"Yes, sir." The new owner nodded in agreement and lowered his eyes.

The judge sighed, put on his spectacles, picked up his quill and scribbled. "Mr. Hoghland, you're going to lose two prime hands. Justice must be served. The citizens of this town demand a reckoning. But you will be compensated. Twenty-five pounds for each." After a moment of silence, he peered over his eyeglass again. "Um. That's all."

The owner took three steps back and slipped out the back door.

The judge shuffled some more papers and gestured toward Robin. "Bring the prisoner forward."

Robin continued to refuse to move. The constable and his helper pushed the slave, causing him to trip. The shackles on his ankles scraped against raw skin causing him to wince in pain. The constable grumbled, grabbed Robin by his arm, and hauled him to his feet.

The crowd in the room took advantage of the disturbance to mumble with neighbors and friends. The judge glared and the room went silent. "For your crimes, the slave known as Robin, owned by the younger Mr. Hoghland, is to be executed. The manner of death is as follows. He will be chained and left in the elements with no food or drink until he succumbs. No citizen is to offer him nourishment or comfort. The sentence is to be carried out as soon as these proceedings are concluded."

I wondered if the judge would add something about God protecting the doomed man's soul. But then, Africans were considered different, inferior to whites. Some said they lacked emotion and were soulless.

Robin was taken away but continued to glare at the judge as long as he was able. His lips moved silently. I wondered what curse he was putting on his enemy.

Mayor Heathcote turned his attention to Claire. "Your manner of death will also serve as a deterrent to those who think they can rebel and strike their master."

Claire whimpered and fell to his knees. "Please, suh, I beg you."

The judge ignored him. "You will be taken at the conclusion of this sentencing and you shall be broken by the wheel."

Alain leaned and whispered. "He should have taken his life when he had the chance."

It was hard to say which manner of execution was worse. But the wheel was horrific. Mr. Innes once offered a description in one of his colorful tales.

"Ye see, there was this fella who stole the governor's wife's jewels. She was fond o' her baubles. The thief claimed she gave them tae him in payment for his services. If ye know what I mean." The cook winked with an impish smile. "But the governor wasn't one tae take cuckoldin' lightly, so he ordered the poor fella tae be intimate with St. Catherine's Wheel. The man was tied flat on his back. A large, iron rimmed wheel, with spikes for an extra measure o' torture, was dropped many times on the fella. Until every bone was broken."

"That's ghastly. That's enough to kill anyone."

"You'd think so. But not until he was tortured some more. His arms and legs were weaved through the spokes o' the wheel. The broken bones made it an easier chore for the executioner. His body, left on the wheel, became fodder for the crows."

"What does a saint have to do with it?"

"St. Catherine was sentenced tae the wheel. But a miracle occurred. The moment she touched it, it broke intae pieces?"

"So, she was saved?"

"Not exactly."

"What happened?"

"They cut off her head instead."

The sound of heels clacking on the floorboards brought my attention back to the goings-on in the courtroom. A clerk walked quickly to the judge and whispered in his ear. The judge frowned, took off his eyeglass, and nodded curtly. Whatever the news, he didn't look pleased.

With great fanfare, the doors of the courtroom opened. Two soldiers entered and stood at attention. The judge rose and any who were seated did the same. A man dressed in rich attire, stood at the center of the doorway. Playing to the audience, he paused for a moment, and allowed all eyes to focus on him.

"The governor," whispered Alain. "And I might add, a Scotsman."

Governor Robert Hunter strutted into the courtroom as if it were a stage. He greeted onlookers, saluted those he knew, and nodded to well-wishers on one side of the room before he moved to the other. His manner was like one who was familiar with theater. In fact, it was rumored, he dabbled in playwriting.

"Why do you think he's here?" I whispered.

"Like any politician, he wants to take credit for repressing lawlessness and restoring order."

"I thought the governor was popular. At least that's what I've heard. And his wife, they say is quite pretty."

"And wealthy. With connections—"

"Ah, Mr. MacArthur. I'm surprised you're here, but always glad to see you." The governor put out his hand to shake Alain's. "Is this your lovely wife?"

"Yes, Governor. May I introduce Mrs. Anna MacArthur?"

The governor bowed and I returned with a curtsey. "Mrs. MacArthur. You are a compliment to your husband. I understand you are from Scotland?"

"Yes, Edinburgh, sir. That is where I was born."

"Ah. We have that in common. I should have known. The city can lay claim to the most beautiful and intelligent women. Isn't that right Mr. MacArthur?"

"I can't argue with you there, Governor."

The governor brushed back the long curls of his powdered wig and turned to go but added as an afterthought. "Please, Mr. MacArthur, call on me at the Governor's Mansion. And bring Mrs. MacArthur. I would love for her to meet Mrs. Hunter. I think they would get along splendidly." The governor walked toward the mayor. His stacked heels and cane clicked across the floor.

The judge appeared anxious to greet his surprise guest, but the governor ignored him. He called for a chair to be placed in the center of the room with his back to the court. With a flourish of spreading his pleated coat and tightening the sash around his waist, he took a seat. Speaking over his shoulder, he said, "Mayor Heathcote, I'd like the honor of addressing the people here today. This is a difficult matter, and they should hear the facts of this case. Have all the prisoners been sentenced today?"

"No, sir. We have one more, and then there is a delicate issue to adjudicate."

"No, matter. I will not be long. People have heard me say that if honesty is the best policy, then plainness must be the best oratory." He promptly stood, left his cane by the chair, and clasped his hands behind his back. Then, he walked the width of the courtroom twice before beginning.

A true Scotsman who knew how to build an audience's anticipation for a story.

"Fellow citizens of Manhattan. Shortly after midnight, on the seventh of April, thirty Cormentine Negroes and three Spanish Indians tried to kill and maim as many of your neighbors as possible. It has come out in testimony that the slaves were seeking retaliation for hard usage from their masters. But it is the owner's duty to keep their property in line, to teach an inferior the dangers of going astray. And if that means a heavy hand, so be it. God and the law are on our side. Others claim that the revolt was the result of our benevolence. The Negro has had the liberty to move about our fair city. They mingle with others of their kind, and in some cases, they are educated or taught a trade." He paused and faced the spectators.

"I can guarantee you this, ladies and gentlemen, a slave in Manhattan is treated much kinder than in the south. But instead of gratitude, a few renegades took up arms against us. And in a most heinous matter. They hatched a plan and formed a devilish brotherhood. They were bound to secrecy by sucking each other's blood. They stole and stockpiled weapons, set fire to a baker's barn, and waited. The brave men of Manhattan arose to fight the blaze. And what did they get in return? A bullet to the throat. A sword to the heart. And an ax to the head.

"What did these cowards do after their deadly work was finished?" He hesitated. Waiting for the audience to come to their own conclusion before he told them what to think. "They ran like animals and hid in the woods and the swamp."

The Governor returned to his seat. His ringed fingers played with the handle of his cane. "When I heard the cries for help and realized the mischief upon us, I ordered the firing of the huge gun at the fort, alerting the city. I immediately called out the militia from the fort and Westchester to drive the island. If it wasn't for my quick response, the city would have been reduced to ashes. By noon, the criminals were in custody. But six escaped." Again, he stopped to allow that last bit of information to sink in. "They didn't escape in the usual sense. So scared were they of our great English justice, that they laid violent hands upon themselves. Three took their lives with firearms, the other three slit their throats. I hear that one even killed his wife before taking his life. Indeed, they might have been the fortunate ones."

The governor tapped his cane on the floor and nodded. The room went quiet while everyone waited to see if there was more. But the governor remained silent. After a respectful period, the judge resumed control of the hearings.

"Governor Hunter. May I proceed?"

The governor said nothing but waved his hand in assent.

"Constable, bring the next prisoner known as Quaco before the bench."

Lucy's husband's face and head were covered with a thatch of thick black hair dirtied with burrs and straw. Nothing could conceal his anger and contempt. His lips were thin, and his eyes were slits. He looked at no one in particular but glared at all who came to witness.

The sound of chains filled the room again as Quaco was placed where the other two slaves had stood. Like everyone else, I waited anxiously to hear the judge pronounce sentence, but again the doors in the back opened. This time there was no high-ranking official representing the queen.

It was Lucy. Her hands were tied. Her skirts were bloodied.

Quaco glanced over his shoulder. His visceral reaction at the sight of his wife created a commotion of chains and cries of longing and helplessness. I closed my eyes and fought back tears. Bringing Lucy into the courtroom was a cruel prank. Quaco saw that his child had been born, and Lucy would learn her husband's fate.

The judge called for order and fidgeted in his seat. When the room quieted, he reached for his spectacles. He unfolded them and perched them on his nose and placed the side pieces over his ears. "Quaco, you have been charged with the ambush and murder of nine goodly citizens and wounding a dozen. You are accused of raising your hand to smite your betters, setting fire as a decoy, and destroying property. For that crime, I sentence you to death. You will be taken three days hence and suffocated by fire until you are dead."

The back of the courtroom erupted with Lucy's scream. Her pleas for mercy were directed toward the governor. He alone, as the Royal representative, had the power to pardon. Lucy's appeals were met with disdain.

Quaco was led by two goalers as he headed for the courtroom doors. As he passed near Lucy, he stopped. The goalers, not knowing what to do, looked at the judge for direction. He nodded and Quaco and Lucy were allowed their last moment. I thought of a thousand things they could have said, but there was only silence between them. And then, with a jerk of his chain, Quaco was gone.

Lucy was brought in front of the judge. She looked exhausted and overwhelmed. Her body quivered. Her eyes were red.

"You are the slave called Lucy?" asked the judge.

She said nothing.

"It is my understanding that you are with child, and therefore, the court will grant you a stay of execution until the infant is born."

"If you please, your honor." It was the goaler. The same one who led us to Lucy's cell. "The woman has given birth."

"Ah. So, there is no need to wait. The slave—"

"Judge, if you please. May I have a word?" Alain walked in front of the bench.

"And you are?"

"My name is Alain MacArthur. I came here today with my wife and Dr. Baruch Emmanuel, to say a few words." Alain gestured toward us. "We can attest that Lucy was in my home the night of the revolt. She was not at the fire."

"Are you a warden, sir?"

"Yes, I am."

"How would you know, then, that the Negress was at your home during the fire. If you were doing your duty, sir, and I have no doubt you were, wouldn't you have been engaged elsewhere? How would you know the slave's whereabouts?"

"I can vouch for Lucy being at my home." A man grumbled as I stepped forward. His eyes roving in a menacing manner. "Lucy came to warn my husband about the fire. She discovered the plot and came to get help. In the process, she fell and cut her scalp. She was bleeding when she arrived, but warned us, nonetheless. You are sentencing an innocent woman."

A rather stout man, whom I did not know, stepped forward. "Judge, I'm sure Mrs. MacArthur means well, and is obliged to support her husband's claim, but I saw with my own eyes the slave woman meeting with Quaco and the others in the tavern. I was there, finishing up my business."

"With Sadie the whore," whispered another, but loud enough to cause waves of chortles.

The judge called for order.

"They are married," I said. "It would be quite natural for them to be seen together."

"You mean common-law married," said the man. "She was in on the planning. I saw them whispering and conspiring to do harm. That slave is Quaco's woman, and she'd do anything he asked."

The judge stared, and then turned to the man who opposed me. "Sir, do you have proof?"

"Aye, I'm his proof." Another stepped forward. "I was there, too. I saw Quaco and Robin and the other one at the meeting And Lucy, too. I saw her begging him to flee. She was crying her eyes out. And then she ran off. But she was in on it, alright."

"Was there anyone else who saw Lucy at the tavern?"

Two other men stepped forward and pronounced their "ayes."

"Would you swear on a Bible to what you are telling me?"

All four men said aye.

"Then I have no choice." He turned his attention to Lucy. "You will be taken from this courtroom and held in chains for an appropriate time. Then you will be hanged by the neck until you breathe no more." He hesitated. "And may God—" The judge stopped. He took off his eyeglass and stared at the prisoner. He had almost forgotten. Lucy had no soul.

CHAPTER THIRTY-FIVE

REPRÉSAILLES

APRIL 28, 1712

ONLY ONCE HAVE I witnessed an execution. It was the hanging of Thomas Aikenhead near the town of Leith. He was eighteen years old. His crime was blasphemy. It was a gruesome event, and I had hoped to never see another. Now, I would be an onlooker again. This day and the one from the past had the same feel: cold and dreary. The early morning chill seeped through the layers of my clothes until it reached my bones. Or perhaps that's how one should feel on a day of a hanging.

North of the city, above Wall Street, was where eighteen Africans had already been executed for their part in the revolt. One more awaited. Lucy's death was set for noon.

A government-ordered hanging was not a rare event, but the killing of a woman was. It was expected, that even in the pre-dawn hours, the first spectators would appear, and by the time of the execution, their numbers would multiply until they stood shoulder to shoulder. When Alain and I arrived later in the morning. Baruch and Deborah were already standing near the scaffold. To the chagrin of many, we pushed our way through and were greeted with angry stares and a few mumbled curses.

I looked around at the sea of faces. Master Myers and his son were present, and Bertram White was off to the side, further back. Some of the onlookers were on crutches or had limbs and heads bandaged. These, I assumed, were the wounded who were attacked during the revolt. Rachel and her husband were conspicuously absent.

Maurice and his son, Pierre, were in the crowd. I found their attendance odd. Why would a man who was responsible for bringing slaves to the colony want to witness their execution? In a perverse way, was he contemplating how this would affect trade and if it would increase the size of his purse? Or would the citizens of Manhattan, fearful of another uprising, want to lessen the number of Negroes? Pierre looked strange as well. I had never seen him dressed in this manner. Usually, he wore suits made of rich fabrics, and lacy frills poured from his neck and sleeves. But today, his clothes were simple, more earthy. A red kerchief was tied around his neck and he wore a small tri-cornered hat that was angled over his eyes. His breeches were rough-spun and were topped off with a short jacket. The only sign of wealth was the watch he pulled from his pocket. He checked the time, not once, but again and again, before returning it. The father was dressed like he had an engagement at an elegant soirée; the son appeared to be heading on a journey.

"Do you see Maurice?" I asked Alain. "He keeps staring this way. I've tried avoiding his gaze, but I can feel his eyes on me. A few moments ago, he doffed his hat like we were old friends, but his smile was twisted and cruel like he knew something I didn't. Sometimes, I wish I were a man with a sword."

"I have a sword." Alain placed his hand on the hilt. "I won't have that bastard offending you. You have a right to despise the man."

"I try to ignore him. But I find it difficult. Especially when his son shows up at our door."

Alain put his arm around me. "I have spoken to Alexandra. I explained how we feel. Although, when she asked why, my response felt inadequate. But she's promised that she will have nothing more to do with the lad."

"Do you believe her? She has said the same to me, and then I find she's gone off to meet Pierre. I worry every time she goes to market or tells me she is visiting a friend."

Alain took my arm, hooked it in his, and patted my hand. "I'll talk to her again when we get home." He sighed deeply. "Maybe it's time to tell her the truth."

I glanced at Maurice. He was leaning toward his son, whispering in his ear. Before I could look away, our eyes locked, and his smile grew.

※

After the noon hour, the crowd fidgeted and grumbled. They tired of staring at the two upright posts and crossbeam that made up the scaffold. Some found it amusing when a gust of wind played with the heavy knotted rope, swaying it back and forth, mocking what was to come. Leaning

335

against the crossbeam were two ladders, one for the executioner and the other for the doomed. Tradition called for the gallows to be built high enough, requiring a thirteen-rung ladder.

Nearby, I heard the innocent voice of a young boy. "Papa, you said the prisoner had to take thirteen steps. The ladders have only twelve."

The father squinted; his lips counted silently. "That they do, lad. But the executioner knows what he's doing." The father pointed to the scaffold. "You see, the prisoner will take twelve steps to go up. And one more to come down." The man chuckled enjoying his sense of humor. His son looked back at the ladder. Wanting to understand, the boy offered a half-smile.

Baruch removed his hat and turned to speak to Alain while keeping one eye on the gallows. "That business vith the slave, Mars, gave the court a black eye. Even the governor vas not pleased."

"Aye. I only heard wee bits of the story," said Alain.

Baruch looked around as if sharing a secret. "He vas acquitted for shooting Mr. Beekman in the chest. Twenty-five vitnesses said he didn't do it, and the jury agreed. The Attorney General Bickley vasn't satisfied and charged Mars again for the same crime."

"And what happened?"

"The slave vas acquitted a second time. But Mr. Bickley vasn't done. He vas adamant Mars vould be found guilty."

"It's not up to him if the jury acquits."

"Mr. Bickley is a stubborn and prideful man. He charged Mars a third time, but this time vith the murder of Henry Brasier. And the third time vas the charm. The jury found Mars guilty. He vas hanged yesterday."

Baruch's story was an example of the inequities of the justice system and the hysteria of the townspeople after the revolt. The slaves faced prejudicial juries and judges who handed down hasty sentences. Rarely were they represented by defense counsel, and that was only if their owner happened to be a lawyer. Lucy never had a chance.

The last to arrive was a small group of Negroes. With hats in their hands, eyes staring straight ahead. Defiant. These were mostly freedmen who came to support one of their own. They walked in unison, surrounding Ruth like a shield, and in her arms, she carried Lucy's daughter. The crowd parted, and Ruth was escorted to the front row, closest to the gallows. Silence washed over the spectators as she took her place next to Deborah. But no amount of soothing could dispel the child's high-pitched wail. Not

336

the patting of her back, the gentle swaying of Ruth's hips, nor the rumble of wheels as they tumbled over uneven ground littered with pebbles and twigs.

Lucy sat in the bed of the wagon on a wooden box. She faced the rear of the open cart, so the crowds and scaffold were not in her sight. Once the horse was ordered to stop, clouds of dust and dirt swirled and covered her. The executioner approached the wagon and directed Lucy to get down, but she hesitated and instead, lifted her eyes. I wasn't sure what she was looking at: the sky, the sun, or the fluttering leaves on the nearby trees. Perhaps all of it. Lucy closed her eyes, spread her arms, and as if she commanded them, a flock of birds took flight, almost as one, from the trees. Their wings flapped uproariously as they soared and circled twice. The crowd followed Lucy's stare until the birds disappeared toward the horizon. But the executioner had a job to do, and he impatiently reminded her it was time. He offered a hand to help Lucy off the cart. Under normal circumstances, no white man would have done so. Lucy ignored him, lifted her skirt, and climbed down from the wagon on her own. She straightened her back and smoothed her skirt, the same bloodied one she wore when she gave birth.

The executioner walked first. Lucy followed. Their dirge-like cadence slowed while the spectators parted into a gauntlet. Townsfolk reacted differently. Some glared at the helpless woman. Their smug smiles and nods showed satisfaction that justice was being served. Others lowered their eyes, avoiding contact. Maybe they were ashamed of the unfairness of the court or afraid of the fragility of life. I tried to put myself in Lucy's situation, knowing that in moments she would never again see the sun rise, the moon set, and the stars light up the sky. She would never breathe in the fragrance of springtime or the smell of an afternoon shower. To never laugh or cry or to hold Rose in her arms. But I knew life's wonders as an unshackled woman. I was free to enjoy them without condition.

Whispers were silenced as Lucy stood at the scaffold, the bridge that would take her from this life to whatever comes after. The executioner brought one ladder closer to the noose and made sure its feet were well planted. Then he positioned the second ladder, clambered up, and checked the noose.

When all was ready, the executioner motioned for Lucy to begin her ascent. As she reached the twelfth rung, the noose was placed over her head and tightened around her neck.

At that moment, Ruth stepped forward. The executioner paused. Lucy looked down. Ruth turned the baby to face her mother and walked to the scaffold. She lifted the baby, tiny hands and feet flailing. "Dat's your mama, Rose. She's a good woman. She loves you wid all her heart. And all her soul." Ruth hesitated while she succumbed to sobs. The crowd said nothing. "Sear the face of your mama into your memory. Remember dis day. De day you lost your beloved mama." Ruth spoke no more. She turned Rose inward and pressed the baby against her bodice.

A few women sniffled. Others clutched handkerchiefs. Most were not moved. They grumbled to get on with it.

The executioner said something to Lucy, and then leaned away to give her space. She turned her head, found Rose, and took her thirteenth step.

Many in the crowd bowed their heads. Some whispered the Twenty-Third Psalm. I did not. I watched Lucy dangle, while I whispered other words.

For everything there is a season, a time for every experience under heaven:
A time to be born and a time to die,
A time to plant and a time to uproot what is planted,
A time to tear down and a time to build up
A time to weep….

The crowd did not move while Lucy's body was cut down and placed in the coffin in the bed of the wagon. After the lid was nailed shut, a gravedigger got on the wagon and loosened the reins. It took off with a jolt and disappeared down the road.

Men returned their hats to their heads. Women restored their handkerchiefs to hidden parts of their clothing. Ruth held the now-sleeping Rose while she resumed her lowly status and allowed her betters to pass.

Deborah turned to Ruth to offer what comfort she could. I was about to do the same, but a strange feeling came over me. Something was out of order. I tried to ignore it, but it nagged at me.

"Anna, are you feeling poorly? Maybe you shouldn't have come. I know how you felt about Lucy," said Alain.

"No, it's not that. Something's amiss. I don't know what it is." I looked at the crowd starting to disperse. Some were huddled in groups. The father, I saw earlier, was consoling his son who had buried his head in his father's coat.

And then Maurice walked by. A woman hung on his arm pressing her breasts into his side and giggling at something he said. Her perfume was strong. Its odor made me reach for my handkerchief again. He acknowledged her with a wink, but when he saw me, his demeanor changed. A gloved hand tipped his hat once more. His smile had not changed. I looked the other way but found it impossible not to look back. Before Maurice disappeared into the crowd, he turned to look at me. And that's when I realized what was wrong. I searched the diminishing crowd, all who remained. I looked back at Maurice. "Alain. He's gone."

"Yes, and good riddance."

"No, I mean Pierre."

"Good riddance to him, too."

"No, Pierre was with his father and now he's gone."

"Why should that matter? As long as he's not knocking on my door again."

"Something's wrong. Pierre kept looking at his watch. Looking for someone. Or waiting for…his father just gave me a look like he knew something that I didn't." I tugged on Alain's arm and pulled him away from Baruch. "We need to go home. Now."

"Alright. Let's go." He put his hat on his head and we hurried away, weaving our way through the last of the stragglers. It didn't take long to walk through the front door.

"Mary! Mary!"

"Yes, Mrs. MacArthur, what is it? Can I help you?"

"Where's Alexandra?"

"Why, she's with you." The woman looked around as if my daughter was hiding behind my skirts.

"She was never with us."

"Alexandra told me she was going to meet you. She wanted to talk to Deborah. She had something for…I assumed—" Mary placed a hand on her chest. "Oh my." Her hand covered her mouth. "I've been tricked."

"Tricked? Why do you say that?" asked Alain.

"Alexandra said you were expecting her. She took her satchel. Said it was filled with old clothes for the poor. She wanted to give it to her friend. I presumed that was Mistress Emmanuel. I suggested that she could take it another time, being that it was heavy, or I'd find someone to deliver it. When I reached to help her with it, she pulled back and told me she wanted to do this herself. I didn't think anything of it, at the time, but now looking back on it…I know she's close with the mistress, and after all that has happened, this seemed most natural." Mary sat down on the nearest chair. She shook her head and wrung her hands. "Right after she left…something didn't feel right…I pulled back the drape to watch her leave. I saw Alexandra do a most peculiar thing. She looked up and down the street, like she was searching for someone, and then walked off in the opposite direction of where she should have been heading. I ran out to find her, called her name several times, and that quickly she was gone. Disappeared like she never existed." Mary covered her face with both hands. "I'm so sorry. But I thought—"

"I know what was in the satchel." It was Sally. She was standing on the stairs and appeared excited, like she had a great secret to share.

"What was in it?" Alain asked.

"Stockings, two petticoats, a new skirt, her pretty blue shawl, and some food she asked me to get from the kitchen. When no one was looking."

"Did she tell you why she needed the clothes, darling?" I asked.

Sally came down the stairs and placed a comforting hand on Mary's arm. "She said that she was going to give them to the poor slaves. But I didn't believe her."

"Why not?" I asked.

"Because Alexandra loved the shawl. The one you knitted for her. She would never let anyone else touch it. She yelled once when I tried it on."

"Do you know where Alexandra is?" I asked.

"No." Sally hesitated while playing with the hairs at the end of her braid. "She won't be home any time soon."

"Why do you say that?"

"Before she left, she gave me a big hug and started to cry. Then she told me she would always love me, and I should not forget that. If she was coming back in a few hours, I wouldn't have had time to forget her."

Alain and I looked at each other. History was repeating itself. Many years ago, I had done the same. I had left my home and nothing my father could have done would have stopped me. Now, I was living the same nightmare, but as the parent.

340

"Mrs. MacArthur," said a revived Mary. "This might help." She cleared her throat and blew her nose. "Shortly after you and Mr. MacArthur left for the hanging, the French lad, Mr. St. Martin, came with a message for Alexandra. He asked me to deliver it. I didn't think anything untoward with the request. I did as I was told."

"Did Alexandra say anything? Or did she act in a peculiar way that now makes sense?"

"Yes." Mary eyes filled, and she grabbed her handkerchief again and held it to her nose. "Yes. Alexandra was delighted with the note. She hugged it to her chest, ran into her bedchamber and shut the door."

I turned to Alain. "I don't know how we will ever find her. She could go anywhere. North to Albany, to another colony. We may never see her again."

"One thing I forgot to mention," said Mary. "The lad also had a bag over his shoulder. And his clothes, not the usual expensive suits with all the lacy fussiness. He reminded me of my brother, Jack. He had on similar clothes and had that same look in his eyes the day he left. The day Jack went to sea."

Another piece of the puzzle now fit. Maurice's behavior at the hanging. His mocking smile, his constant eyeing me. He knew the treachery his son was about to commit. Maybe Pierre really cared for Alexandra, and she, him, but by aiding their elopement, stealing our daughter was Maurice's revenge.

While we hurried to the wharves along the East River, Alain and I devised a plan.

"We can't run on board his ships and search every cabin," Alain said. "Armed sailors will be standing guard. Even if there's a skeleton crew. Most likely, Maurice has already warned the captains of his ships to be on the lookout for two frantic parents who want their daughter returned to them."

"And paid handsomely for compliance, no doubt."

"I'll speak with the dockmaster. He'll know from his log which of Maurice's ships are in and when they are planning to leave. Hopefully, we are not too late."

"Unless Maurice has already bribed the man for his silence."

"I wouldn't put it past the wee bugger, but the dockmaster and I are old friends. He's an honorable man, and I'm sure he will help us." Alain clenched his fists. The scar on his warrior face reddened. "And if Maurice has paid enough to find the man's breaking point, we'll see how much I need to loosen his tongue."

The dockside along the East River was in a state of flux. Wharves were continually extended, thus narrowing the river by a series of retaining walls filled with all manner of refuse: dead animals, human waste, sunken ships, and sludge dredged from the bottom of the river. The air no longer had the fresh tang of saltwater but was filled with the smell of rotted fish and decaying flesh. The extensions were sold to the highest bidder, and Maurice, being one of the richest, was the owner of several new wharves for his ships and a warehouse.

We walked quickly to the dockmaster's office and found only his assistant. The young man explained that the master was seeing to an important matter that had just come to his attention. When we asked where the master went, the clerk shrugged and pointed in a manner that made me realize he had no idea.

By a bit of good luck, we didn't have to go far. The dockmaster was heading our way. "Mr. Jamison. Please. A word," Alain called out in a breathless voice. "Can you tell me…when…the St. Martin's ships…are sailing?"

"Good day, Mr. MacArthur. Well now, let me see. The *Pierre* and the *Représailles* are heading out tomorrow morning. The other, the *Lyonnaise*, isn't leaving until later in the week. I have to check the log to be certain about that...last…" The dockmaster spoke his last sentence in a very detached manner. His words trailed off. He looked at something over my shoulder, his face turned red, and then he pointed.

Alain and I turned. A three-masted ship pulled away from the wharf. Several sailors hauled in the mooring lines. Others scurried up the masts and around the deck to unfurl the sails that would eventually capture the breeze and hurry the ship out to sea.

"That's the *Pierre*. She's not supposed to go out now. What the hell…the tide's not right."

"The *Pierre*, you say?" Alain asked. "Do you know where's she's going?"

"Aye. Where a slaver always goes these days. Down to Jamaica to pick up more slaves. But she's not comin' back this way. Word's out she's headin' to Charleston to unload her cargo and then I hear – Africa. Probably won't be back for a year."

I thought I'd collapse. It made sense. Alexandra on a ship named for Pierre, leaving ahead of schedule.

We reached the West Dock just as the *Pierre* had cleared it. At the top of our lungs, we yelled for Alexandra. But we were too late. There was no way she could have heard us. The ship's officers were shouting orders, the opening sails whipped in the breeze, and the waves pounded the hull. I capped my hand over my eyes to search the deck, looking for someone who looked out of place. We continued yelling while the sails unfurled, taking the ship and our daughter toward the open sea.

"You missed saying *au revoir*," a voice called out. "Too bad. You won't be seeing the lovely Alexandra any time soon. I doubt her future husband will allow it."

I spun around. Maurice stood there, a gloved hand on his cane, a lacy handkerchief to his nose and the same sneer I saw earlier. "What a pity. What a pity." He dabbed his eyes to wipe away pretend tears.

"You monster. How could you? My daughter's only fourteen," I shouted. It took every effort I could muster to refrain myself from pommeling the man.

"Too bad. You were about the same age, if I remember, and now Alexandra has given her promise to my son. You saw it for yourself, *ma cherie*."

"What are you talking about?"

"In the book shop. Right under your pretty little nose. And now, your *fille* has accomplished what her *maman* failed to do. Keep a promise and honor a contract." Maurice sniggered and turned toward the *Représailles*. He put one foot on the gangway, hesitated, and looked back at us. "Do you know the English translation for the name of this ship? No? It's Retaliation. So appropriate, *ma cherie,* considering the circumstances. I have been waiting years to exact revenge. *Oui.* A fitting name, don't you think? And with that, I bid you *adieu*."

Alain pushed me aside and grabbed his dagger from its scabbard. He rushed over to Maurice, tossed his cane to the ground, grabbed the little man by the scruff of his neck, and dragged him off the plank. Alain's dirk pressed against the Frenchman's fat throat. "You bastard. You tried to rape my wife, and now you kidnap my daughter? I'll cut your—"

"And don't forget, monsieur," croaked Maurice. "It was I who paid to keep you in jail." Maurice eyes found Alain's pegleg before he looked up and smiled. "It was well worth the price."

Alain tightened his grip, until the stomping of feet caught his attention. Sailors from the *Représailles* descended the gangway with raised swords. Alain pulled Maurice further away. "Tell your men to stay back."

"I'll do no such thing." Maurice turned to his henchmen. "Gentlemen. Advance. Kill this ruffian." The sailors came forward, slowly. Maurice looked sideways at Alain. "Looks like you're out-manned. Pity that your dear wife will lose her husband on the same day as her child."

Alain continued to back away, but there was only so far he could go before he edged the wharf. The sailors kept coming, the gap between them and Alain diminishing. At that moment, I saw Maurice's cane. I scooped it up and with both hands, and as hard as I possibly could, I swung it at Maurice. When it hit his stomach, a whoosh escaped from his mouth and he doubled over in pain. He grabbed his chest, gasped for air, and looked at me. His smile had vanished.

"Stop. Stop what you're doing." A new voice entered the fray. It was the local constable. "Lower your weapons."

Alain returned the dirk to its home and I rushed into his arms. The sailors lowered their swords.

Still bent over, Maurice managed a breathy, "Thank you...Constable. Arrest...this man."

"My husband did nothing wrong. He was defending our family. This man, Maurice St. Martin, has kidnapped my daughter. She's on the *Pierre*."

"Ah, the...cries of a...*maman*. Hysteria," sputtered Maurice.

"I'm not hysterical."

Maurice straightened. "Officer, this woman...and her husband have accused me...of a heinous crime. You know who I am...the owner of several...ships. A leading citizen. I have no weapon on me." He opened his arms and held up his gloved hands, one of which was held in an awkward position. "And yet, they have attacked me viciously." He turned to the sailors still standing near the top of the gangway. "Ask any of them. They will vouch for what has happened here today."

Maurice's sailors nodded in agreement.

"Well, Mr. MacArthur, I'm going to have to take you in. I'll let the judge straighten this out."

"Constable, did you not hear my wife?"

"I never laid a hand on your daughter." Maurice turned to the constable and, in a much calmer tone said, "Thank you, sir, for doing your job. Mr. MacArthur should be thrown in gaol so decent people can walk the streets unharmed."

"Come on," said the constable as he began to drag Alain away.

"No," I screamed. I rushed over and began to pull on the constable's arm.

The officer pushed me away and just then, the dockmaster appeared. "Mr. MacArthur, what's going on here?"

"I'm being arrested. This man and his son have conspired to kidnap my daughter."

"That's not true," yelled Maurice. "Check the Port Log. You'll see there is no woman on the *Pierre*."

"Maybe that's because passengers aren't usually listed," said the dockmaster. "Just their possessions, so the Crown can collect its share of taxes. You should know that Mr. St. Martin." The dockmaster looked at the ship and then at Alain. "What about this one, the *Représailles*? Could she be on board?"

"No. Of course not. My sailors wouldn't allow that. Women are bad luck, you know."

"Well, let's just check and see." He turned to us. "I can't do anything about the *Pierre*, but I can put your mind at ease about this one. Would that help?"

"Yes, sir. Thank you."

"Well, Mr. St. Martin," said the dockmaster. "Lead the way. Constable, wait here until the inspection is over."

Maurice turned toward the gangway and for a moment remembered his manners. "Ladies first. Madam."

I lifted my skirts and began to walk the narrow plank. When we were midway, I was startled when a strong arm wrapped around my neck and pulled me so hard, I almost lost my footing. Maurice forced me to turn and together we faced Alain. A cold edge of a small knife pressed against my throat.

Alain froze and went for his dirk.

"I have waited many years for this day, Mr. MacArthur. I hope seeing your wife in my arms, is causing you terrible pain." With the weapon still at my throat, he slid his free hand down the front of my bodice, cupping my breast. "Very nice and still so sweet." Alain snarled and took a step forward. Maurice responded by pulling me further up the gangway. His hand continued to travel along my hip and thigh, raising my skirt like a curtain for an anxious audience. "You deserve this for all the pain I have endured. Being jilted by you caused me great embarrassment, and I became the laughingstock of Lyon." Maurice rubbed the inside of my thigh. "Enjoying this, my dear?" He chuckled and then his voice turned to a hiss. "Thanks to your husband, decent women won't come near me."

"What are you talking about? Alain did nothing to you."

"Have you forgotten?" Maurice held out an oddly shaped gloved hand. "Many years ago, your husband crushed my hand, breaking the bones." His hand went in front of his face. "Now, *ma cherie,* take off the glove."

Slowly, I pulled on the leather, one digit at a time, and when his hand was uncovered, he splayed his fingers in the air. "Do you think any woman would want me to caress her with this claw?" The three middle fingers were menacingly twisted and bent at the joints.

Maurice's momentary distraction offered me the advantage. I turned quickly and pushed the man with all my might. Maurice's startled eyes went wide. One foot stepped back to regain his balance, but he teetered on the edge of the plank. A further step met nothing but air before he splashed into the gray-green waters of the East River. His head cracked like a walnut on the hull. Slowly, crimson waves circled the body, swirling in the dirty water among rotting fish heads.

At the same time, I heard a cry. I looked up at the sky for its source. Startled seagulls responded with their cawing. As they soared and circled, they swooped close to the water's surface and ascended once more. And then I heard the sound again. High-pitched, not from the heavens, but from the direction of the ship. It was human. It was words. Their meaning wrapped around my heart, squeezing, and tightening, until I could feel every beat pounding through my veins, the blood thundering in my ears.

When my senses cleared, I considered every possibility until the meaning of the words came crashing down. "Mama! Papa!"

CHAPTER THIRTY-SIX

HANNA, ARE YOU THERE?

2008

FORTY-FOUR PAIRS OF eyes stared at me. Some inquisitive. Others playful. But all my students were waiting for an answer to the questions posed by the socially awkward young man who sat alone in the front row.

"Dr. Duncan, what made you choose archaeology? And, as a follow-up, if you don't mind, if you had to do it all over again, would you opt for the same major?"

I chuckled inwardly at the young man's word choices. He sounded more like an investigative journalist for the *New York Times*. But his inquiries suggested something more than a casual interest in my personal story. Something I had longed for. A tiny spark, enlivening the dull lectures that were part of the university's survey course. Even the jocks in the back row, along with the two pretty coeds, put their pens down and showed some interest. They shushed those around them.

Perhaps this was my chance to connect with these freshmen and be like other instructors. I watched their offices overflow with students; friendly laughter and chatty voices could be heard from one end of the hall to the other. Even Mercedes, who started a few months before me, had a large following. I wasn't going to let this opportunity get away. Today's lecture could wait two more days.

I closed my binder, and a few students responded by shoving their spirals into backpacks. Their smiles crossed the room at lightning speed, suggesting this detour down a rabbit hole was planned. Like little kids, restless to replace fractions with recess, my students were desperate for a break. I bit my lip to keep from laughing. My classmates and I had tried the same not so long ago? But I also welcomed a break. It took all the willpower I could muster to pretend today's lecture was interesting: compare and contrast the architecture of the Thutmosid Dynasty with the

Greek Empire. Maybe Alec could do it, but I didn't have his Scottish gift for gab.

"I've always been interested in history," I told them. "From the time I was little. And archaeology is just another branch of the same subject, sort of a kissing cousin."

Chortles erupted. *Kissing cousins*. My brain was playing tricks with my word choice. Ignoring the disruption, I went on.

"When I was eight-years old, 1 stumbled upon a book about the discovery of King Tut's tomb. It had a picture of Howard Carter and Lord Carnarvon peering into the young Pharaoh's darkened crypt. I couldn't get over the fact that the air in the tomb had not been consumed by another human being for three millennia. And the light from Carter's candle, illuminated treasures that had not been seen or touched by anyone since the door of the tomb was sealed. Those facts mesmerized me. I decided, right then and there, I wanted to be like Howard Carter."

Sensing my students' interest, I grabbed a piece of chalk and drew a rough outline of Tut's underground vault. I explained how the discovery was accidentally found, just days before the dig was to run out of funds.

"In the innermost room, concealed in the burial chamber was a huge granite sarcophagus. Once opened, three coffins, one inside the other, like Russian nesting dolls, were found. The first two were wood, covered with gold plate. The third was solid gold. One of the most poignant finds was a small wreath of flowers placed on the outermost coffin. The flowers were dried but still had color. Some have speculated Tut's sister-wife placed them there."

"Is there such a thing as King Tut's curse?" asked another student. A few heckles greeted the question.

I smiled. Discussion about King Tut always brought up the curse. But if that's what interested my students today, so be it. "You mean the one that says that anyone who disturbs the Pharaoh's tomb will die?" Some nodded their heads, and another whispered loudly to his friend, "The Mummy Returns."

"Well, let's see what you think. Here's an example. Lord Carnarvon financed the dig and was there when it was opened. Four months later, he cut open a mosquito bite on his cheek while shaving. The cut became infected, blood poisoning set in, and he died. When he passed, lights in Cairo went out." I paused and looked around. "So...curse or no curse?"

"Curse," said some in unison.

"Carnarvon's death started all the curse theories. But do you know what scared people? When King Tut's body was examined, it was found that he had a bruise on his cheek, about the same place where Carnarvon cut himself."

"Curse," more called out.

The students were transfixed. I had them in the palm of my hand. "Okay. Here are more examples. A visitor to the tomb died of natural causes a few weeks after. Others went to their graves mysteriously. One by arsenic poisoning, one by suicide, and another was smothered in his bed. Well?"

"Curse," yelled more students.

"And here's the last example. Carter, the archaeologist, who found Tut and opened his sarcophagus to inspect the body…lived another sixteen years. His death was cancer related. What do think?"

Silence.

"In fact, those who attended the opening, Egyptian dignitaries, royalty, Carnarvon's daughter, security guards, etcetera, lived, on average, another twenty-three years. Curse? Or not?"

Silence was replaced by smirks and then laughter. I glanced at the clock on the side wall.

"Do we have to stop?" asked one of the jocks.

The request was music to my ears. "Yes, I'm afraid so, but I have time for one more question. A short one, please."

One of the pretty coeds raised her hand. "The second question, that he asked." She pointed to the kid in the first row. "Would you do it again?"

"Are you asking me if archaeology's a lonely job? Maybe stuck in the desert, like in Egypt or some other place in the world no one wants to go? No friends? No shopping? And no bars?" At this, two boys in the class slapped each other on the back, as if reliving last night.

"And no girls," shouted one of the jocks.

"What do you think Dr. Duncan is?" the coed snapped.

"Yes, it can be lonely. No friends, no boyfriend or family, and sometimes, no communication." I looked at the clock again. "Well, I better get you out of here. See you in two days." As I began to pack up, I felt good about today.

"Dr. Duncan." It was the coed. She fidgeted while waiting for my attention. "Does the loneliness ever get to you? On a dig, I mean?"

I stopped what I was doing. "It can." Flashbacks of lonely nights in Darien National Park and missing Alec still unnerved me. "It helps if archaeology is a calling, and you love what you're doing."

The girl's voice lowered. She leaned closer. "I'd really like to major in archaeology, but I worry." She paused, as if trying to find the right words. "I don't mean to be disrespectful or sound stupid, but I wonder if I'd ever get married. Would a guy wait for me while I disappeared in some remote area of the world and buried my head in the sand?"

The room had emptied. It was just the two of us. How to answer the girl's question? The same one I grappled with. Thankfully, I didn't have the chance.

"Oh my god." The girl glanced at her watch. "I'm going to be late for my next class. Can I come to your office? Maybe tomorrow? We can talk some more."

"Sure. My hours are posted online or just email me."

"Great. See ya later." She headed for the door but stopped cold and turned. "That was a great lecture, Dr. D. This is one of my favorite classes."

Before I could say thanks, she disappeared. Dr. D? I liked the sound of that. This girl could be my first connection. Maybe soon, the sound of laughter would be heard coming from my office. I glanced at the seating chart: Grace. I had to chuckle at all the associations going on in my life lately. Hanna meant favored by grace.

My classes and office hours were over. I walked down the hall and felt my phone vibrating in my blazer pocket. I took it out and stared at the screen. *What the hell. Why is he calling? Again!* I shoved the phone back where it came from. This was ridiculous. I had to call Jess and ask, no demand, that she make it clear to Josh, once and for all, that I wasn't interested. This was the second time in two days. The first was while I was caving into Maggie. I couldn't put my boss on hold just to talk to a horny doctor. Or could I? Maybe this was how one's destiny could turn on a dime. If I had taken Josh's call, even if it were to tell him off, Maggie might not have had the chance to beg me to sign on for the dig. That would have changed things for the better. And I wouldn't be in such a pickle.

351

The old Jewish cemetery, located in Lower Manhattan, an area called Two Bridges, was surrounded by bleak multi-story tenement buildings. These were a reminder of the changing face of New York and the millions of immigrants who called the city home centuries after the cemetery was consecrated by its founders.

The section of the graveyard that was visible from St. James Street was protected by an iron gate and a waist-high stone wall topped with more metal fencing. Next to the entrance were a couple of stores, decorated with Christmas lights, enticing customers to get into the holiday spirit and shop.

Leaning against the wall, I shifted my coffee to my right hand and checked the time. Josh would be here in fifteen minutes. I couldn't believe how he had wormed his way into getting me to meet him. Even more incredulous was that I agreed. At first, I wasn't amused. Perhaps it was residual fear, like PTSD, from my experience with Max. His behavior still haunted me. After reading several articles about stalking, I learned the best way to deal with it was to confront the issue early on, even if that meant calling the police. That's why I called Jess after Josh's second call.

"He's been trying to reach you," said Jess. Her voice sounded excited like she had great news: *You just won the lottery.*

"Would you ask him to stop?"

"No, he's not trying—"

"I'm not interested. If he calls again, I will tell him off and if that doesn't stop him, I'll report him to the police."

"Hanna. Listen. It's not what you think. Josh wants to help."

"He can help by leaving me alone."

"Will you stop being a dumb ass. Josh can help you find Anna."

I paused and pulled the phone away from my ear. Was this his new pitch?

"Hanna, are you there?"

It took a lot of deep breaths to control my anger and return the phone to my ear. "Yeah."

"Now, can I go on?"

"I'm listening."

"Josh's father is on the Board of Directors at Shearith Israel. It's the oldest—"

"I know. "

"His father used to give tours at the old cemetery, so Josh asked his father if he could help. Long story short, Josh and his father can meet this Sunday. If that works. A private tour. That's all. No commitment. Is that okay?"

I stared at my shoes.

"Hanna, are you still there?"

I wanted to crawl into a hole and disappear. "I feel like such an idiot."

"At least you recognize your problem." Jess hesitated. "But I still love ya."

"I'm sorry...I didn't mean...I love you, too. Tell Josh, thanks."

"Tell him yourself. He said he'd meet you at Chatham Square at one o'clock on Sunday."

Five more minutes. I turned toward the headstones. Even though it was the end of November, and the air was cold and biting, my hands were sweaty, and a tiny bead trickled down my back disappearing into my jeans. I rehearsed my apology. *Sorry for not taking your call. But I—* That sounded lame. *Please forgive me for not picking up the phone. You see....* No. No excuses. Maybe I should just forget the apology and tell him how grateful I was. But not too heavy on the gratitude.

"Hanna. Hey. There you are."

"Oh, hi." I extended my hand and purposely widened my smile. I wanted Josh to know that Dumb-Ass Hanna was gone, replaced by a much friendlier version. Josh turned and introduced me to the elderly man beside him, his father. Another doctor and his look-alike. If the elder Dr. Stein was a window into Josh's future, he would age well.

"Nice to meet you, Hanna. Josh told me about your search for your ancestor. Interesting story. I hear you're looking for her grave." He held the squeaky gate open, allowing me to enter first.

"Yes. She lived in Manhattan in the first half of the eighteenth century. I imagine she would have been buried here. Where else for a Jew?"

"True. At that time, Manhattan Jews were members of the only synagogue in town and this is where they went. So, unless her demise occurred in another town or at sea, this is it."

For the first time since I arrived, I scanned the monuments poking through the brown grass. There were about ten raised vaults, a handful of flat slabs; the rest were upright or leaning markers. They were different sizes and their various colors depended on the type of stone. The oldest ones were headboard-shaped, like I'd seen at Trinity. Many were sinking beneath the waves of grass.

"Is there a list of who's buried here?"

"We know there are twenty-two veterans of the Revolutionary War." Dr. Stein walked to a flat white marker; the dried leaves crunched under his shoes. "Like this one here." He pointed at the dark etched letters.

SOLOMON MYERS COHEN
PVT. 3 BN. PA. TROOPS
REV. WAR
FEBRUARY 15, 1796

"Every year, the Sunday before Memorial Day, the synagogue has a nice little ceremony. Descendants of the veterans come and recite a memorial prayer after placing American flags by the graves. If you're around next May, join us. I think you'll find it worth your while."

"Thanks, but I'm not sure I'll be here." I pulled the scarf tighter around my neck.

We continued walking through the cemetery. Dr. Stein went ahead, leaving Josh by my side.

"Departing New York so soon?" Josh stopped which forced me to face him. "Didn't you just get here?" His brow furrowed. I thought I saw a momentary look of disappointment as his eyes searched mine.

I looked away, at the older Dr. Stein, wishing he would not leave me alone with his son. "Yes, I have been offered a position. A dig on Easter Island. I'll be leaving right after New Year's."

"Wow! Nice time of year to get away. Some place warm. Does Jess know?"

"I haven't told her yet. In fact, I haven't told anyone."

"How long?"

"At least six months."

"Jess will be disappointed. She was so happy you returned. You'll be back. Right?"

"Yes. I'll be back. But it's a great opportunity, you know."

Finally, Josh's father came to my rescue. "Hanna, join me. I'd like to show you something."

I did as he asked, but my conversation with Josh troubled me. I told someone I barely knew, a stranger really, my plans. Before I told Alec. How could I have done that? By the time I joined Dr. Stein, it took my brain a minute to focus on the mishmash of information he offered, dates and names like Generals Washington and Lee, the Revolutionary War, and the East River. But it was the mention of Anna's name that caught my attention.

"If we can't find Anna's headstone, that doesn't mean she wasn't buried here."

"Really? Some of the headstones are hard to read."

"Yes, but there are other reasons. Her body could have been exhumed."

"Why would that have happened?"

"Because New York City happened. You must use your imagination to envision this part above Wall Street. In Anna's time, it was rural, the cemetery was on a ridge, and nearby was a swamp. But as the area grew, roads were installed, eventually widened, or straightened, meaning some of the burial ground was encroached on. Even a few years ago, a proposed subway station for Chatham Square required an intensive study by a team of archaeologists. There's a good possibility that there are bodies interred under St. James Street and over there on Oliver. At one point, toward the end of the 18th century, some of the remains had to be moved because of erosion and retaining walls had to be installed. We don't know the original placement of the burial ground. The city lost the deed. But what we do know for sure is that the size was diminished by eminent domain and the young synagogue sold off unused land to pay some bills." Dr. Stein hesitated and then scoffed as he seemed to remember another detail. "Our cemetery history still haunts the members of the synagogue today. Anyone wishing to purchase a burial plot is reminded that it is conditional."

We continued to walk around the graveyard, but it didn't take much time. It wasn't large. I checked out the legible stones. None were Anna's.

"As I said, I still think your ancestor could be here," Dr. Stein continued. "Do you see where we are standing?" He pointed at my boots and the almost-dead grass. "Every inch of this cemetery has a body lying beneath. While we only see a hundred or so memorials, there are many more bodies beneath the surface. When the exhumation occurred, as many

355

as possible were reinterred. The rest were taken to a new burial ground uptown."

"So, she could be here," I whispered to myself. I could be standing inches from Anna's final resting place. Maybe she was near the tree or closer to the wall or alongside a Revolutionary War patriot. I spun around checking every corner of the cemetery. I fought back tears as I realized that this could be the end of my search. This was as close to the historical Anna as I would ever get.

"Hanna, would you like to say a prayer?" Josh touched my shoulder.

"What? Hm. Sure. But I'm not Jewish. I don't know any prayers."

"My father and I would be honored to say *kaddish*. It's the prayer for the dead. It's a mitzvah. The greatest mitzvah of all is to visit the deceased and to help ease the suffering of the mourner."

"Mourner?" I guess that was me. Anna was my grandmother, just like Grams, and I was mourning her loss. "That would be nice. Thank you."

Both doctors took out kippahs from their coat pockets and placed them on their heads. "Hanna," said Dr. Stein. "Repeat the words that Josh and I will say. We'll go slowly."

The wind whipped the dead leaves around my feet, but I never felt the cold. I was surrounded by warmth as the men stood on either side. As promised, they helped me recite the ancient prayer:

*Yitgadal v'yitkadash sh'mei raba b'alma di-v'ra
chirutei, v'yamlich malchutei b'chayeichon
uvyomeichon uvchayei d'chol beit yisrael, ba'agala
uvizman kariv, v'im'rua, amen.*

"Thank you. But I don't know what it means."

Josh pulled out a small prayer book from another pocket. He flipped to a page at the back and handed it to me. "Here," he pointed. "Start here."

*Glorified and sanctified be God's great name throughout the world
which He has created according to His will.
May He establish His kingdom in your lifetime and during your days,
and within the life of the entire House of Israel, speedily and soon,
and say, Amen.*

There was more to the prayer, but I barely heard another word. My mumbling made no sense. My vision blurred, my ears clogged, and I could hardly speak. Gasping for breath between sobs, I had blotted out the world. As Josh and his father completed the prayer, a comforting arm wrapped around my shoulder and offered strength. For a moment, I imagined it was Alec.

When I arrived home, I scrolled through my email. One from Susanna caught my attention. I forgot the others and opened hers first.

From: Susannah Oliver
Subject: Congrats
To: Hanna Duncan

Hi,

Got the great news from Maggie. Congrats on being chosen for Easter Island. I'd love to go. It's the ultimate dream for us diggers. What a coup for your career.

Did I tell you I'm seriously involved with a guy from St. Andrews? He's a prof there, and we've been seeing each other almost two months. His office is in the same building as Alec's.

That reminds me. I saw Alec earlier today. I had the day off and was visiting the boyfriend. Anyway, I congratulated your hunky fiancée on your big success. He looked like a deer in headlights. (What's up with that?) I'm sure he's thrilled for you.

By the way, Maggie adores you. As do I.

I promise a longer email later - on the weekend.
XOXO

S

CHAPTER THIRTY-SEVEN
MEANT TO BE
AUGUST 1712

DEAR DAVINA,

I hope this letter finds you & your family in excellent health & that you continue to renew your strength after the birth of your son.

In my last letter, I briefly mentioned the unfortunate circumstances concerning the scoundrel, Maurice St. Martin. Thankfully, my complicity was ruled an act of self-defense & his demise, an accident. Thus, I have been cleared of all charges. Although it pains me to have been the source of someone's death, I am not the least bit sorry. I hope you will not think me unkind. But when I relay the rest of the story, details almost too painful to write, I am sure you will agree that my feelings are warranted. Maurice was a cruel man who had haunted my family for years. The world is better without him.

First, it is about Alexandra that I wish to write.

After the tragedy at the wharf, we took turns supporting Alexandra as we walked along the narrow streets. Her sobbing, interspersed with apologies, begging our forgiveness, broke my heart. All this was added to the grief of losing the man she loved and once trusted. A broken heart is not easily fixed.

That's when I realized it was time. Time to reveal the truth. Perhaps, that would ease Alexandra's guilt and anguish. The next morning,

I knocked on the door of her bedchamber and entered a darkened room. The air was warm and musty. I restrained the urge to throw back the heavy drapes and open the windows, to allow the scented breeze from the orchard to fill the room with its sweetness. It took a few moments for my eyes to grow accustomed to the shadows. A satchel was tossed in the corner of the room, clothes spewing from a yawned opening. A shawl hung loosely from the back of a chair; its train partially concealing mules thrown haphazardly. In the middle of the bed, Alexandra was a mound of ruffled skirts and a roiled blanket. Huddled and curled like an infant, she faced the back of the room, the darkest corner. Her attempt to muffle sobs in her pillow could not disguise her condition.

I stroked her head lightly, afraid of upsetting her further. When she didn't pull back, I continued until the trembling subsided. "Alexandra, may I sit with you?"

She responded with a nod and didn't complain when I lit a candle. I continued by rubbing her back and silently shared her grief. Alexandra slowly raised her head and pulled the blanket to cover her shoulders. I wiped her eyes and nose, and when I held her hand, I was surprised with its fragility, as if it would shatter into pieces. Her lower lip curled. Her eyes brimmed. I wrapped my arm around her. She laid her head on my shoulder.

"I'm so sorry," she said. "Can you ever forgive me?"

"Your father and I understand. Truly, we do."

She pulled back. I dabbed her eyes again and wondered when they would cease to be on fire. Her hair still partly coiled on the back of her head was disheveled. Loose pins and long strands escaped and hung wildly down her shoulders. Her skirts, the same she wore on the ship, were rumpled from sleep or lack of it.

I don't know how long we sat like this, but when she straightened her legs and dangled her feet, I knew I could begin. I started off with an apology.

"Why are you sorry?" she mumbled. "I hurt you and Papa and disgraced our family. Sally must bear the shame I have brought on her."

I hugged her again and we rocked like Ruth had done with Rose. "Alexandra, I'm apologizing because I should have told you, when you were old enough to understand. I should not have kept my story from you."

"What should you have told me?"

"The reason why your father and I could not let you go off with Pierre. Why we could never allow you to be a part of his family; nor he be a part of ours."

She looked at me curiously as if trying to fit the last puzzle piece. "I'm still not sure I understand." She stopped, wiped her face with the back of her hand. "I've often wondered. Does your objection to Pierre have anything to do with the candlestick? The one you left with me in Scotland, when I was a baby?"

I took a deep breath. "My father gave the candlesticks to me as a wedding gift. But it was not for my marriage to your father." I hesitated to allow that startling fact to invade her consciousness. "I was betrothed to Maurice St. Martin. In a way, he was responsible for the battered candlestick. I used it to save your father's life."

Alexandra's brow furrowed. "Save from whom?"

"My marriage to Maurice was arranged by my brother, Nathan, and my father. I wanted no part of it. I detested Maurice. And I was falling in love with your father. We planned to run away."

"You ran away. Like me?"

"Yes."

Alexandra's lips curved slightly. Maybe she was grateful to learn she wasn't the only one who did such a thing.

"I knew I was breaking a wedding contract and my father's reputation would be ruined. But I didn't care." I swallowed hard and stared down at our intertwining fingers. "Maurice entered my bedchamber the night before our wedding and attempted to rape me. Your father stopped him and saved me. Later, I vowed to put the past behind me, begin my life anew with the man I loved, and never speak of this again." I put my finger under Alexandra's chin and raised her eyes to mine. "Do you understand? I was wrong. I should have told you. The minute I saw you were attracted to Pierre. My silence has caused you great sorrow."

"Tell me about the candlestick."

"When Nathan caught us leaving, he forced your father into a fight and almost killed him. I saved your father by hitting my brother with the candlestick. I lost my grip. It hit the icy ground and skidded away."

"Did Grandfather try to save you?"

"It was too late. By the time my father realized that Maurice was not the right man, your father and I were gone."

"Grandfather told me he missed you and he loved you. He also told me a secret. I promised not to tell, but I think you should know."

"Know what?"

"On the day your ship sailed, he came to say goodbye. He watched you sail away from Scotland. To Caledonia. He wanted to say goodbye."

As if it had happened yesterday, I could see the throngs of well-wishers cheering the fleet of five ships as we sailed down the River Forth out to sea. "I remember, there was an old man, with a long white beard, amidst the crowds, standing on a precipice, waving farewell. He looked like my father. I pretended it was him and he came to say goodbye. I wasn't sure." Now I knew for sure. A sob caught in my throat.

The inquiry into Maurice's death brought to light a frightening element. The captain of the ship revealed a private conversation, one in which Maurice suggested an evil plot against Pierre & Alexandra. To take our daughter for himself. It would serve as the ultimate revenge. The captain said he was never going to follow through on his orders to dispose of Pierre. Witnesses verified the captain's account. I cannot imagine how a parent could use his offspring so despicably.

I have not divulged this to Alexandra. Maurice is dead. It no longer matters. My daughter has chosen to have nothing more to do with Pierre. But in a small town that is difficult.

Often, I find Alexandra sitting by the window in the front parlor. A book in hand, but she's rarely lost in the words. Instead, the drape is pulled back so she can watch the comings-and-goings on the street. I suspect she is looking for a glimpse of Pierre.

I look for ways to engage her. We read together or have tea with Deborah. We visit the seamstress's shop and choose fabrics and patterns for new skirts. We order the latest shoes from the cobbler. I am sure to avoid the nearby lane where the book shop is located. I wonder if Alexandra notices.

A month ago, on a day when she seemed recovered, her eyes bright, and her hands no longer clutching a handkerchief, I asked if she wished to join me on an excursion to market. The walk and the cool morning air would do us good. We chatted about anything and everything, like our life had resumed where we left off. And then it all came undone. When we passed Master Myer's shop.

Alexandra stopped abruptly. I heard her gasp. She grabbed my arm. "Mama, can we go home?"

I followed her stare before she turned away. Standing on the stoop, talking to the craftsman, was a young man. I could not see his face, but except for his height, he bore a resemblance to Pierre. He wore similar fine clothes, with lace ruffles spilling out at his wrists and collar.

"Alexandra, that's not who you think it is. It's someone else."

"No, it's him. I know it is. Please, I have to go."

I looked up, and before I could say another word, the gentleman in question turned. It was not Pierre, but Alexandra never saw. She was already hurrying away.

That's when I knew, what I always knew. I had to do more to help my daughter.

I know you have missed Alexandra & wished she would come home to Scotland. I believe that is the only cure. If only for a year, & then when recovered, she can return. Alexandra adores you, & this would make you both happy. Although I will feel the greatest heartbreak, to be parted from my child again, I will be content knowing she is with someone who loves her as much as her parents.

Alain will search for a ship. He thinks there is one heading for Leith in two weeks. A friend has recommended a female companion, a woman from Danbury. Someone who will serve Alexandra well. We hope to accomplish this quickly.

The table was set, the china gleamed, the cut roses filled the room with their fragrance. From the flickering candles, soft shades of amber played against the walls. This was our last Sabbath meal together, the last time Alexandra and I lit candles, the last time the candlesticks would stand side by side. Our daughter was meant to leave in three days.

"I have something for you," I said as I got up, opened a drawer in the sideboard, and took out my journal. I placed it on the table in front of Alexandra. "This has always been yours."

"Mine? I don't understand. It's your journal. I've often seen you reading through the pages. It's never far from your side."

"Yes, I started the journal shortly after your father and I married. It was a gift from Grandfather MacArthur. It had once belonged to your father's mother. Much of what is written on these pages is about the years we were apart. It's meant to explain what happened."

Alexandra's fingers touched the smooth leather, tracing the embossed thistle with the curly leaves and the stitches around the outer edges. As she undid the thin leather straps, I noticed in one corner. the leather was beginning to separate. She turned the pages and felt the dried ink. Two tears slid down her face and dripped on the page. She didn't notice and closed the book.

"I will cherish it always, Mama."

I tried to offer her a reassuring smile. Our separation would feel like an eternity.

Sally reached for two rose petals that had just fallen from the crystal vase. "Here." She handed it to Alexandra. "Put the petals in mama's journal. Every time you see them, you'll remember me."

"Of course, I'll remember you," said Alexandra as she slipped in the petals and tied the leather strips into a bow."

Sally walked to my seat, put her arms around me, and buried her head.

"There's something else." I pointed to the battered candlestick. "It's yours."

"No, Mama. That's too much. They look lovely together. You should have two candlesticks for the Sabbath."

I patted Sally's hand. "When your sister and I are lighting ours on Friday evening, we will have a moment of silence."

"That's when mama, papa, and I will be thinking of you," said Sally.

"That will be our connection," Alain said. "Every seven days."

I smiled at Sally and pulled on her braid. I knew I would be thinking of Alexandra every minute she was gone.

"Thank you, Mama. I promise to return next year. It won't be long before the candlesticks…and we…are together again."

From the moment I placed Alexandra in Davina's arms, when Alain and I left Scotland forever, we were rushing toward the inevitable. I knew it with certainty during the long years of separation, when our only connection was letters - too few and far between. I tried to disallow the truth and hide it from plain sight when Alexandra, almost a stranger, arrived in Manhattan. I knew it the day I found her in the book shop, meeting secretly with the man she loved. And there was no denying it, when Alexandra escaped from the ship and ran into my arms, collapsing in tears of sadness and joy. I recognized it over and over, each time I placed my hand on my daughter's head and recited the parental blessing on Friday at sunset. As much as I tried to hide what was to be, by stowing the painful truth somewhere in the nether regions of my being, I always knew it would happen. Alexandra's return to Scotland was meant to be.

CHAPTER THIRTY-EIGHT
ONCE AND FOR ALL
2008

MY PHONE BUZZED. I held my breath, glanced at the screen, and breathed again. Barely. It was an overseas call.

"Dr. Hanna Duncan?" asked the caller. A man's voice. Older. Serious.

"Speaking."

"This is Brandon Harris from UA. University of Auckland…New Zealand."

"Oh yes, hello. I was told to expect your call." My heart sank. The voice belonged to the lead archaeologist for the Easter Island dig. The next thirty minutes included dry introductions and tedious information: flight times and dates, known research data, and hoped-for outcomes. Much of it didn't register. I mindlessly yessed him along until the call ended.

Click.

I plugged the almost-dead phone into the charger. I didn't want to miss Alec's call.

It had been three, no, four days. The last time we talked was when I met Josh and his father at the cemetery. The days in between were muddled: classes, final lectures, exams, and faculty meetings. During my off-hours, I pined away like a schoolgirl waiting for my boyfriend to call. The meeting with Josh was not the problem. The blasted email was. The one from Susannah.

❦

"Hanna, I heard Dr. Harris called," said an excited Maggie. "I'm glad he connected with you. You will love working with him."

"Yes. He seemed okay. A nice man."

366

"What? Okay?" Her voice sounded puzzled. Impatient, almost. But it was hard to tell for sure over the phone. "Dr. Harris was thrilled when I told him you said yes. You would have thought he had just proposed. I'm so excited for you."

Silence.

"Hanna, what's wrong?"

"I'm just not sure…I mean it's the end of the semester. I have finals to grade and a stack of papers waiting to be read."

"Yeah. Busy time," said Maggie. She didn't hear what I was really saying. "Oh, did Brandon say you won't need a visa, and your flight is the second of January? Two and a half weeks from today. I checked the weather. You'll need to bring…."

The conversation was a blur. I kept checking the screen, willing it to buzz in another call. Even someone trying to sell me insurance would be welcome. Anything to end this conversation.

Click.

It was now seven days since I had spoken to Alec. My mind began to play tricks. Lately, I wondered if he resented my meeting with Josh. I tried to recall our last conversation. What exactly was said and was there something troubling about Alec's tone? Was there a twinge of jealousy? No, there couldn't be. Not after I was sure to mention that Josh was Jess' friend, and his father, the older Dr. Stein was the tour guide. Alec knew my search at Chatham Square Cemetery required professional help.

I called Alec every day. More than once. I left so many messages that his voice mail was filled. I was almost desperate enough to call Mora. But each time I started pressing the numbers, I hesitated and turned off my phone. I wouldn't give Mora the satisfaction. I could just hear her mocking tone:

You mean Alec hasn't called you? I'm not surprised. You of all people should know how busy he is with school and friends. By the way, did you hear the news? Kate had her baby, a beautiful little boy. He has Alec's eyes. My son dotes on his new nephew and visits as often as he can. You didn't know? About the baby? You mean Alec didn't tell you? How odd. I was under the impression he called you every day. I'll be sure to give my son your message.

Click.
I could just see her lips twisting into a wicked smile. The victory was hers. She had won her son back.

I called Ira Mason. A couple of years back, I had to do the same when Alec didn't answer his phone all day. But he had been in a car crash and ended up in the hospital. Ira helped me navigate my way to see Alec. Maybe he could help me now. He didn't pick up. I left a message.

> *Hi Ira. Hope you are well. I'm trying to reach Alec. He doesn't pick up, and I can't leave a message. If you see him…talk to him…tell him I called. I hope he hasn't been in another accident. Maybe I need to get on a plane and come home. I don't know…that's it for now. Hope to hear from you soon.*

Click.
Ira never returned my message. Maybe Alec told him that it was over between us. That he was tired of waiting. Tired of excuses and delays. Easter Island was too much.

I searched for flights from Newark to Edinburgh. Empty seats were difficult to find. It was the holidays. Everyone was going home. Startled, my phone buzzed. I almost dropped it.

"Hanna. Sorry I didn't call you sooner," said Jess. "But the little devil just puked all over me. I had to take a shower to get the food chunks out of my hair. Motherhood is such a blast. Hey, what's up? School's over for you now. Aren't you excited?"

"Not really."

"I thought this is what you were waiting for. Time off from work. Alec coming to New York. When are you expecting your doctor? I hope he got a flight."

"I think he did, but I'm not sure. We didn't finalize our plans, and I haven't heard from Alec in almost ten days. We've both been so busy with it being the end of the semester."

"Is he okay?"

"As far as I know. The last time we spoke was the morning before I met with Josh."

"He's not thinking you and Josh—"

"No. He seemed cool about it. But I think I know what the problem is." I explained Susannah's email. "He must be furious. I can't blame him."

"Do you want me to call Alec? I'll tell him—"

"No. Don't you dare. I don't want him to think…I can't believe I was this stupid. I should have never accepted Maggie's offer. I should have never left Scotland."

"All couples have disagreements. You wouldn't believe what Sam and I argue about. Don't worry. Your love for each other will get you guys through this glitch. He'll forgive you. It was an honest mistake. You didn't do this on purpose."

"I should have told him. We should have discussed this first before I said yes."

Jess said nothing. Her silence told me that my summation was correct. "What are you going to do now?" she asked.

"I'll keep trying his phone, but I'm looking into a flight. I may have to wait until after Christmas."

"And in the meantime?"

"I'm going to visit Grams' grave. I haven't been there yet, and I've been wanting to do that since I came to New York."

"The cemetery is in New Jersey, right? I can help you with transportation. Do you want me to come with? Maybe you'd like some company."

"No. Thanks. I can manage. This is something I need to do on my own. I'll go tomorrow."

"Call me. I'm here for you, you know."

"Thanks, but I'll be fine. You know, it's funny."

"What?

"I've been going to a lot of cemeteries lately."

Click.

I stared at the screen, and with little hesitation, I knew what I had to do. I pulled up my contact list, scrolled through, and pressed a number.

"Hello, Maggie?"

<hr>

I didn't make it to Grams' for three days. Part of that was Jess' fault.

"I really want to help out. I can't pick you up at the train station. J.D. has a doctor's appointment. But I can come to the cemetery when you're finished. I promise. I won't bother you."

"Okay." I was grateful for the ride. One less thing to think about. "The cemetery closes at 4:30 so I'll need you by four. Will that work?"

"Perfect. Sam will be home to watch J.D." She paused. Her voice was muffled as if she was talking to someone. "I have an idea. Bring an overnight bag. You can have dinner with us, and I'll take you back to the train station the next day."

"Sure. Sounds good."

"Hanna, try to cheer up. Alec will call. I'm sure there's a good reason."

"I wish I had your confidence."

Click.

I sighed deeply. Thankfully, Jess couldn't see the pile of used tissues.

<hr>

The taxi let me off at the front gate of the large memorial park in Cherry Hill, New Jersey. The sky was overcast and gray, just like the headstones on the other side of the metal fence. I pulled my scarf tighter around my neck and tucked it inside the front of my coat. It was not enough to ward off the bone-chilling air that felt like it would start snowing at any moment. I had not been here since Grams' funeral. That day was such a blur. I barely remembered what this place looked like.

I stopped at the office and checked for the location and directions to the family plot. The woman who ran the office seemed pleased to have someone to talk to who wasn't overcome with grief.

"Let me see. You said the last name was Duncan," she said as she scrolled through her computer screen. "Ah. I have an Ann and Harold. Is that correct?"

"Yes, and—"

"And there's another nearby. Another Duncan."

"My...father. Philip. With one L. The Scottish spelling."

"Yes. I see now." She grabbed a piece of cemetery stationery and spoke while she wrote. "Section R. Third row. For your grandparents. Fourth row for your father. Same section."

The way the woman rattled off the locations, I was expecting her to hand me a copy of *Playbill*.

"It's not hard to find. Each section is clearly marked. Just follow the main path, past the reflecting pool and Doric columns. They're from the New York World's Fair, you know. 1939."

"No, I didn't." I shifted my backpack to my other shoulder, took the paper, and thanked her.

"It's an easy walk. Not too far. There are a few benches along the way if you need to stop and rest. Many like to sit by the pool and meditate." She leaned over the counter and looked out the window. "Looks like we might get some snow. Just in time for the holidays." As I turned to leave, she added, "Don't forget, we close at 4:30. Sharp. But you might want to leave sooner. At this time of year, it's almost dark by then."

"Yes, I will be mindful of the time. Thank you," I said again as I walked out the door.

The woman was right. The path I took was a narrow road that passed by the aforementioned landmarks. The air was still and quiet, and if it weren't for the fact that I was in the middle of a cemetery, I could have described it as lovely. Peaceful. Thankfully, it was a windless day and when the sun peeked out for just a moment, I stopped, lowered my scarf, and bent back my head. It felt good to be alive. I chuckled to myself. Quite a statement considering where I was.

The park was mostly empty except for a few stragglers from a recent interment. Two gravediggers scurried to finish the job now that the mourners' limousine pulled away. The older worker folded the fake grass cover revealing a mound of freshly turned soil. His much younger partner began filling in the hole. Each shovel of hard-packed earth thumped against the wooden casket. I hurried by to escape the awful sound.

After rounding a bend, I passed an empty car parked along the narrow lane reminiscent of the one-track roads I loved in the Scottish Highlands. The vehicle's right wheels were on the grass. I wondered where the owner was. I saw no one around.

Finding Section R was not difficult. On one side of the road the first section had a marker with an A on it. I could see the B and C signs in the distance, continuing up the right side, disappear behind the tall cypress trees in the center of a small roundabout, and then continue down the left. R was not far off.

As I passed rows and rows of headstones, the sun disappeared, and flurries twirled around my head. A harbinger of what was to come. Perhaps.

This cemetery was so different than the ones I had recently visited. The lawn, now a faded green to light brown, was manicured, the bushes pruned, and the graceful old oaks were bare. Markers were aligned perfectly like well-behaved children walking to class. None were toppled or sinking into the earth. The still-fresh carvings and family names suggested that all religions were accepted. In one area, crosses decorated the headstones and a delicate figure of Mary stood atop a memorial. In another section, off to my right, there was a cluster of markers with Jewish symbols: Stars of David, splayed fingers, and menorahs. How ironic. Here, the deceased would spend eternity with those they might have distrusted in their lifetime.

With only one more section to go, I looked around. Except for another car, a black one, I could see parked behind the tall cypress, I was alone. No surprise. It was a weekday, and the rest of the world was busy with last minute Christmas shopping.

A light snowfall began, crystals clung to the cold granite markers as I weaved my way among them. Careful not to step on the graves, as I'd been taught, I arrived at the double headstone shared by my grandparents. For the first time, I was seeing what Grams had chosen to have on her side of the marker.

ANNA DUNCAN
BORN MAY 29, 1919 – DIED JANUARY 1, 2006
LOVING DAUGHTER, WIFE, MOTHER & BELOVED GRANDMOTHER

The words were expected, and I was especially pleased to see that she added *beloved* to grandmother. But the single lit candle above her name was unusual. I looked around at other stones and none had anything like it.

Was that supposed to represent the candle my grandmother lit every Friday evening? Was this her way of setting the family tradition in stone? I quickly grabbed my phone from my pocket. How ironic. Today was Friday.

I walked over to the next row and found the flat stone inscribed with my father's name, birth and death dates. This was not where he was buried. After he fell to his death on 9/11, there were no remains. Not even a bone fragment. But my grandparents and I decided to put this marker here, close to their plot, so the world would know he existed. I bent down and brushed away snow encrusted leaves and brown grass clippings that clung to the cuts in the stone. I whispered, "I love you, Dad," and then returned to my grandparents. After I cleaned off the grass from their stone, my hands felt gritty and wet. I checked my watch. The hour was getting late, and I had much to say to my grandmother.

"I really screwed up, Grams. And I don't know if I can make it right. Because I don't deserve it." I leaned over. My fingers followed the sharp edges in the cut letters. "I should have followed your advice from the start. Married Alec as soon as I knew. When I realized that I loved him, and he loved me. Why didn't I listen?" I stood up and rested my hand on the top of the chiseled granite. "Dad used to tell me lots of silly sayings. Now, some make sense. There was one...something about *the folly of youth*. I looked it up. The author also mentioned *the idiocy of infancy* and *the remorse of old age*. I'm afraid I'm an idiot, and I will always be remorseful. Even when I am an old woman looking back." My fingers balled into a fist. I shouted, "I am such a god-damn idiot."

"No, I am."

I spun around. The voice came from behind.

"Alec?"

From a rather large memorial stepped out the most glorious sight. "Mistress Hanna, I am the idiot."

Alec spread his arms. We rushed toward each other, hugging, grasping; wishing to get closer. Defying the law of matter. If only that was possible. Then, my emotions let loose. I went weak and fell against him sobbing as if it was the end of the world.

I don't know how long we stood there, locked together; the snow coming down harder. At some point, I heard between sobs, "It's okay, Hanna. I'm here." Over and over, I heard the words while I burrowed into his chest, breathing him in like it was only way I could survive.

"Hanna, my love. I'm here."

When he lifted my face towards his, I sputtered, "I'm so sorry. Please forgive me."

"If anyone should be asking forgiveness, it's me. I didn't answer your calls. My stiff-necked pride caused you unbearable pain. I promise, I will never be that stupid again. I can't live without you." His lips met mine as I touched his face. We kissed as passionately as we had ever done. Lingering for as long as possible, clouds of warmth emanated from our embrace, melting the snowflakes when they touched our skin.

"I know you heard about Easter Island through Susannah. I meant to tell you, but Maggie beat me to it."

"Aye. I figured that out, but I can't lie. Another dig took me by surprise. I wasn't happy about it. Susannah must have guessed. She asked to meet, about a week ago. She explained what a break this was for your career. I thought, how could I stand in your way. Besides, it was only six months, and we have the rest of our lives."

"Twelve months. Could be twelve."

"Then, I'll wait a year. I'd wait longer if I have to."

I nestled back into his arms. "That won't be necessary. I told Maggie. I'm not going."

"Hanna," Alec pulled back. "Are you sure? I'm serious. I'll wait."

I kissed him again and then my fingers touched his scruffy beard and followed his strong jaw line. It was as if I was seeing him again, for the first time, on a flight to Scotland. "You're not the only one. I can't live without you either. But from now on, it's only local digs. No Easter Island. No Egypt. No more than one hundred miles from our bedroom."

Alec chuckled. His one eyebrow shot up.

I pulled back. "By the way, how did you know where to find me?"

"Jess."

"I told her not to call you."

"I'm glad she didn't listen. She called me three days ago, told me what had happened, and picked me up at the airport." Alec pointed to the cypress trees. "If you look carefully, you'll see her car."

"Jess is here. Now?"

"Aye. But don't worry. She told me to take all the time we needed. She's a wonderful friend."

I smiled and wiped new tears away.

"Oh, I have something else for you." He walked around the large monument and returned with his backpack. He reached in and pulled out a small stiff packet. "Open this."

I lifted the flap. Inside was a folded note.

"It's Davina's," he said.

"I'd completely forgot. Were you able to get the seal off?"

"Aye. Ira sent me to one of the curators at the library's special collections room. He knew how to remove the wax without cracking it. The guy's a wonder."

"How is Ira, by the way? I called him. He never called me back."

"Not well. He suffered a stroke a week ago. It's also one of the reasons I didn't get back to you. I was so involved with his care. With Esther gone. Until his daughter arrived, I was his only caregiver. I stayed with him round-the-clock at the hospital. He's going to survive, but he'll never teach again."

"I'm so sorry to hear that. I loved the man."

"I feel the same. He was like a father." He tapped the packet. "Now, look at what Davina has to say."

We huddled together to create a shelter from the falling snow. I gently took out the note and unfolded the paper. The penmanship resembled a woman's flare. The writing was small and cramped like she had much to say in a small space.

"It's addressed to Anna's daughter," said Alec.

"Alexandra?"

"No. Sally."

"Sally? Anna's other surviving child? I sometimes forget about the younger daughter. The journal was so much more about Alexandra. And look at the date. It's much later than anything in the journal. Maybe this tells the rest of the story. What happened?"

"Hanna, read. Read it aloud."

I brought Davina's letter close to see it better in the failing gray light. The paper had a musty smell, like old books in a library. My hands shook from excitement, dread, delight, apprehension, and a million other emotions.

March the first, 1730

Dearest Sally,

May this letter find you & your growing family in good health. I hope Baby Hannah is well & she has recovered. The winter months are so difficult for the weakest amongst us.

"Alec, the baby has my name. Maybe this is the beginning of naming all the daughters in the family with derivatives of Anna. Just like my father was named Philip for Filib."

Alec smiled. "Read on."

News of your dear father's passing has brought my spirits low. My tears join yours. I am proud to have called him Brother. He was a man among men.

I lowered the page, looked at Alec and stroked his cheek with the back of my hand. "There is no question. You are a descendant of the fine men of the MacArthur clan: Filib and Alain. You have inherited that same sense of duty and honor."

"How do you explain my brother, Iain?"

I laughed. "Don't you remember what Ira's friend, Charles, once told us? Genes can weaken or go rogue over time. Yours, my love, are strong."

Alec joined in my laughter and then reminded me. "Read on."

Anna's apoplexy was not a surprise. I always knew that once she lost her love, it would not go well for her. Your parents were bound to each other & their love will continue for all eternity.

I cherished the brief time I spent with Anna, before she & my brother went off to Caledonia. I wish circumstances would have been different & we would not have been separated by time & an ocean. I cherish the years she gave me with your loving sister. After all this time, I am still saddened by losing Alexandra so soon after she returned to Scotland.

"Alexandra. Dead! How?" A chill traveled down my spine and it wasn't from the cold.

"She doesn't say. We just know it was in 1712. I did a bit of research. There was no plague in Scotland at that time, but there was illness in Danbury, Connecticut, the same year. It was called a putrid pleurisy. It was quite deadly and lasted for almost a year. I know I'm guessing, but maybe someone brought the plague on board. That could be the reason Alexandra died so quickly and explains the rest of the letter. Read on."

> *In the end, the vagaries of time ravage us all. I hope your next letter brings joyous news of your mother's recovery.*

"Anna's still alive?"
Alec nodded. A gesture that also meant to read on.

> *I am an old widow now & I have little time left. The pull of my ancestors is growing stronger. Therefore, I must consider what to do with the journal, the candlestick, the lock of hair & the ring that was once my mother's. They belonged to Anna & then Alexandra. Now they are your legacy. A new bank has opened in Edinburgh - The Royal Bank of Scotland. For a fee, precious items can be held in perpetuity in a box & I will be given a key. I will send the key in my next letter. If you come to Scotland, even after I'm gone, your inheritance will be waiting for you.*

"So that's how the items ended up in a box in Scotland. Davina must have gotten the key to Sally, like she said, and Sally passed it down to her descendants. To Grams. And me. But why didn't she just send the things to Sally?"

"Maybe she was afraid they would be stolen. The silver candlestick and the ring especially."

"I guess that makes sense. But there's something I still don't get. She only mentions one key. There were two. The damaged candlestick was placed in the second box. And why was there a need for a second?"

"We can surmise different scenarios. Maybe Davina put everything but the candlestick in the first box. For some reason she kept the candlestick out. But later, realizing she needed to save that, too, she had to open a second box. Or maybe, she instructed her son to do it for her. I'm not sure we will ever know."

"It's a mystery, all right. I'm grateful we know so much more, thanks to you and Davina's letter." I turned and hugged Alec again. Careful not to crumple the letter.

When Alec stepped back, the space between us filled with large flakes that fell with greater intensity. I looked at him curiously. What was he doing? What other surprises did he have in store? And then, I understood when Alec went down on one knee and wrapped my hands in his warmth. Staring into my eyes, he said, "Hanna, will you, once and for all, make me the happiest of men. Will you marry me?"

"Yes, Alec. Once and for all. No more putting it off. As soon as we—"

"No, I mean right now."

"We don't have a license. It's Friday afternoon. We can't—"

"Handfasting. Like Anna and Alain."

"Really? Why yes. Of course."

"You have up to a year to change your mind," said Alec.

"No chance of that happening."

We walked over to a nearby tree. Its branches were leaf-bare just like Anna had described during her handfasting with Alain.

"Wait!" I pulled on the scarf, shook the snow off my hair, and placed the 'veil' over my head. "Just like Anna's."

"You look beautiful," Alec said while he took my hand and pressed them with his lips. "But there's one more thing we need. A ring. Something to seal the deal." Alec reached into his pocket.

I couldn't believe he came prepared. But what he presented me with, blew me away. "Anna's ring. How did you—"

"Kate gave the ring back when she learned the whole story. She asks for your forgiveness."

I reached for the thistle ring with the amethyst stone and the curly leaves.

"Allow me." He took my left hand and pushed the too-small ring up to the first knuckle on my ring finger. "Hanna Duncan, in front of your relatives, I take you to be my wife. Forever and ever." Alec removed the ring and placed in on my left pinky where it fit perfectly.

I then took Alec's hand. "Alec Grant. I take you to be my husband. For as long as time allows us. I will love you for the rest of my days."

We hugged and kissed while snowflakes continued to dance over our heads, covering our shoulders and clinging to Alec's eyelashes. What a strange place for a handfasting, but I wouldn't have wanted it any other way.

"We're closing. Fifteen more minutes." shouted the older gravedigger. The woman in the office was right. The sky was on the edge of nightfall. The snow thickened; gravestones were covered with a frosty stillness.

Alec waved to the worker.

"Hey. Look at the headstone. My grandmother's side. I didn't notice this before."

"What?"

"My grandmother's first name was Ann. Everyone called her Ann. My grandfather, her friend, Mrs. Shasta, the doctors. Everyone. But here, on the stone, it's Anna."

"Maybe that was her real name and Ann was like a nickname."

"I guess you're right. She pre-planned the funeral and the wording on the headstone. Between the name and the candle, she is reminding me of our bond with the ancient Anna. I think she knew all along." I stood there, staring, still in Alec's arms.

"Hanna, we better go. The worker is waiting. And Jess." Alec raised his hands and waved to the black car. The headlights turned on.

"Wait. I have one more thing to do. Something Ira told me about." I reached into my other pocket and pulled out three small stones. I placed one on my father's snow-covered marker, Gramps' side of the headstone, and the last one on Grams'. "This way they'll know."

Alec put his arm around my shoulder and pulled me close. "Know what?"

"I was here. And someday, I'll come back."

Alec put his other arm around me. "I love you, Hanna Duncan Grant. I love you very much."

As the stones disappeared under a blanket of white, I took a deep breath, and willed myself to say the words without succumbing to tears. "I love you, Alec Grant. More than ever. Now, take me home. Take me home to Scotland."

Notes:

Mannahatta is historical fiction. Like scales on a balance, the facts and the story must find equilibrium. But it is my hope that due to my extensive research, the scales tip a bit heavier on the side of historical integrity.

My three-year journey into early 18th century Manhattan was fascinating, because prior to this, I knew nothing much of the city's history. I was delighted to unearth historical gems that added richness and depth to the story. Such was the case with the gravely ill Edward Parkman, cured by his wife's breast milk. It fit perfectly into the scene when Anna hoped to save her newborn, Rebecca. Parkman's odd 'prescription' added levity to a dire moment.

Other finds gave dimension to characters like Lord Cornbury. He would have been rather dull except for the fact that he was a cross-dresser. If it weren't for his family connection to Queen Anne, his behavior in the 18th century would have been a career-ender. The same goes for fictional Máyli. When I learned about the high rate of albinism among the Kuna, (and other native populations in the American Southwest, Mexico, Panama, and Brazil) it made her character so much more appealing.

The description of birds freezing in mid-flight during the extreme winter in the German Palatine was hard to fathom. But this was witnessed by refugees, and even if it was an exaggeration, it didn't matter. People believed it, and it explained the desperate conditions that led to German flight; thus, delaying Alexandria's sailing to New York.

At other times, my search revealed events that allowed me to move the story in the direction I intended. The plague in Danbury, Connecticut in 1712 played right into my hands and helped explain the untimely, but necessary death of young Alexandra. And finally, Richard Churcher's headboard-shaped gravestone, the oldest marker in New York City, located at Trinity Church, was the perfect setting for Anna to grieve the loss of her child.

Like the first book, Caledonia, Mannahatta is based on historical events: Yellow Fever epidemic in 1702; the German Palatine exodus in 1709; and the slave revolt, trial, and executions in 1712. The last had a huge impact on Manhattan. Based on Minister Abraham de Lucena last will and testament, signed by William Burnet, his worldly goods included slaves named Ruth, Lucy, and Jenny. Ruth had a child, but the will does not specify gender. The slaves who were executed after the revolt were named Claire, Robin and Quaco. There were others as well. The manner of their death as described in *Mannahatta* was true to the history. One of the condemned female slaves was pregnant, and she was not executed until her baby was born. I brought that story to life in the character of Lucy.

While there were many taverns and inns in 18th century Manhattan, as far as I know, there was none named The Pearl. But there was and is a Pearl Street, named for the oyster shells that once littered the road.

Myer Myers was a well-known Jewish silversmith and a leader of his synagogue, Shearith Israel. However, he was not born until 1723, more than twenty years after Anna entered his little shop to sell her candlestick. Today, many of his silver pieces are displayed at the New York Historical Society. A good source of his life and work can be found in the book, *Myer Myers: Jewish Silversmith in Colonial New York*, by David L. Barquist.

While it is true that songs were sung in the taverns, "Sweet Mary McBride" was a creation of mine. The nursery rhyme, sung by Sally in the first Anna chapter, came from the era, but I changed some of the wording to fit the story.

There were laws that governed the cartmen. These statutes were in effect long before the arrival of Anna and Alain and were a carry-over from Europe. The probability that someone like Joris Krol could have operated an illegal carting business was doubtful. A good source for the history of the cartmen, the first labor group in early America and the forerunner of the Teamsters' Union, is *New York City Cartmen, 1667-1850* by Graham Russell Hodges.

The events at the trial for the convicted leaders of the slave revolt was how I envisioned it. I have no idea if Governor Hunter attended, but some of his dialogue is what he said about the event.

My research has taken me to many locales: five trips to Scotland including the Inner and Outer Hebrides, the Historic Dockyard in Portsmouth, England, the Caribbean islands and Panama, and Manhattan. Philadelphia was easy since that is where I'm from. But one place I could not visit was Darien National Park. As stated by the flight attendant while Hanna was flying over the isthmus, it is a dangerous place. There is a reason why fifty-five miles of the Pan-American highway is unpaved. Information about the park can be found in *Darien: A Journey in Search of Empire* by John McKendrick.

I started to write *Mannahatta* in 2018. I was about halfway through when COVID-19 hit the United States in early 2020. Once lockdowns became the norm, writing turned into a calming diversion. Not going anywhere, created huge blocks of time, allowing me to finish six months sooner than planned. The only downside was I couldn't tour Shearith Israel in New York City and see for myself the synagogue's collection of ancient artifacts. I also had to forgo visiting the oldest Jewish cemetery (the second oldest in Manhattan) at Chatham Square. Someday, I hope to rectify this.

It is said that authors write what they know. There is quite a bit about me in this book and *Caledonia*. For example, I have always wanted to be an archaeologist and the discovery of King Tutankhamen's tomb fascinated me from an early age. Like Hanna and Alec, my husband and I were engaged for almost three years. We also had excuses for delaying our marriage. And finally, after I finished my first book, *The Lucky One,* which is based on my mother's handwritten memoir about her escape from Eastern Europe, like Hanna, I carried the manuscript to New York City and donated it to the Yivo Institute for Jewish Research.

Other books used in my research that the reader may find of interest are the following:

Darien, John Prebble
Dust to Dust: A History of Jewish Burial Practices in New York, Alan M. Amanik
Gotham: A History of New York City to 1898, Edwin G. Burrows and Mike Wallace
A History of Scotland, Neil Oliver
How the Scots Invented the Modern World, Arthur Herman
In the Shadow of Slavery: African Americans in New York City, 1626-1863, Leslie M. Harris
The Island at the Center of the Word, Russell Shorto
Manhattan: Mapping the Story of an Island, Jennifer Thermes
Mannahatta: A Natural History of New York City, Eric W. Sanderson
New York: The Novel, Edward Rutherford

Thank you for reading my work. Rest assured, I am hard at work researching my next historical novel.

Acknowledgements:

Mannahatta took three years to write and that meant working almost every day, including when I was away from home. My laptop accompanied me wherever I went. When there was down time, a free evening in a hotel or a rainy day at the beach, I was pounding away at the keys, ready for Hanna's or Anna's next direction of the story. My characters, do indeed, talk to me.

The creation of a novel doesn't happen by itself. A super-patient family is required. A husband and kids who are willing to put up with a distracted wife and mother, easy leftovers or take-out for dinner, and the willingness to wait another fifteen minutes so I could jot down an errant thought before it disappeared.

There are many people to thank, but foremost are my two dedicated fellow writers and wonderful friends - my readers: John Matthews and Kyra Robinov. John has been reading my work since *The Lucky One* and Kyra came on board with *Caledonia*. Each has read my ramblings many times over and have offered valuable insight to make the story better. Their advice has always made for a better story. I value their honesty, their friendship, and our online chats about writing, the weather, and life.

Writing and researching during the Pandemic was challenging. No longer could I travel to the places mentioned in *Mannahatta*. Luckily, I discovered the New York Historical Society. Their online research was vital. I always got the answers to my questions with supporting evidence in a timely fashion. I'm looking forward to visiting the NYHS and thank them in person.

The Scottish rose appears *in* scene and part breaks in *Mannahatta*. I discovered the flower while touring Dunnottar Castle and then noticed it was all over Scotland. I knew I wanted it in my book, so as the case with the thistle in *Caledonia,* Ellen Gewen offered her artistic talents.

The New York Colony Manhattan map of 1700 was designed and created by BMR Williams. A map for Manhattan that fit the story's time frame, 1700-1712, is impossible to find. But with his perseverance he was able to create what was needed to describe Anna's world.

The cover design was created by the extraordinarily talented Judy Bullard. I had a different cover and title in mind, but she steered me (gently) in the right direction and came up with a masterpiece.

My husband, Arne, is my technical guru and chief encouragement officer. Without him, I wouldn't last ten minutes on the computer. He also accompanies me on all my book talks and has heard my presentations a hundred times over. He has read the series.

To all my readers and fans of *The Lucky One* and *Caledonia*, thank you for putting your trust in my work. I am forever grateful.

Happy Reading!
Sherry V. Ostroff

Sherry V. Ostroff is available to speak/zoom with your organization or book club.
She has three PowerPoint presentations: one for each book.
Contact the author at svostroff528@gmail.com.
Website: sherryvostroff.com

The author, Sherry V. Ostroff at Dunnottar Castle in Stonehaven, Scotland, United Kingdom. August 2019.